DARK ENCHANTMENT

First Book in the

CELTIC MAGIC TRILOGY

BY

KATHY MORGAN

Happy Reading!
Kathy Morgan

Published in the United States by Dreamweaver Publishing, Atlanta, Georgia

ISBN 13: 978-0692288634 (Dreamweaver Publishing)
ISBN 10: 0692288635

Cover design by Diana Buidoso
Cover Model by Boko Great
Interior layout by Thomas White
Author photo by Paige Sweany

Memoriam

I dedicate this book to you, Mom.
The One who taught me a love for words from my earliest childhood, The One who told me to Follow My Dreams, and The One upon whose unconditional love I could always depend.

I love you.

Acknowledgements

First, I would like to thank my sister, Judy Giovannetti, who read, edited, RE-read and RE-edited each draft of the manuscript for this book with the never-ending patience that only a sister can possess. Thank you, Sis, for believing in me all the way. You're the greatest!

Second, I offer my sincere appreciation to my brilliant son, Eli Price, who used his sharp eye and detail-oriented line-edit skills to discover typos, question sentence structure and syntax, and spot places on the page where even a simple space was missing. Thanks, honey.

Many thanks goes out also to Amy, Carol, Kim, Laurie, Praty, and all the girls at the Diagnostic Clinic who passed around the first draft of this book, offering this new author much needed encouragement for the journey ahead.

Chapter One

Samhain Eve...
21st Century Ireland

The night was sick with evil. The dark man could almost taste its wickedness on his tongue. He considered the mere mortal woman from his place in the vision. She was staring blindly over the windswept cliff, the encroaching thunderstorm tearing at her clothes and hair like a violent lover. A man, of sorts, he could feel his body stirring as the rising winds molded her gown to each soft, feminine curve. Her head tipped slightly downward. Her gaze fixed upon rioting waves reminiscent of a watery leviathan, spewing froth and foam over the rocky outcroppings far below. Though the pallid moonlight draped her in a gray silhouette, it could not conceal her identity. Nor did it hide the fact that her reappearance in his troubling dreams could mean only one thing.

The Waking Madness had begun.

A tremor of unease skated down his spine as a profane shadow rolled across the vault of heaven. The scudding thunderclouds painted a dismal portrait over a sky that had been bright and star-studded only a short while before.

The night grew cold and darker still. Veins of fire lit the heavens. The wind's screaming exhales threatened to lift the woman from her feet and toss her into the sea below. A stab of light slashed a paltry break in the thunderclouds, and the vision before the man shuddered and changed. Now his eyes were fixed upon an ancient gravesite, the 5,000-year-old dolmen that had stood, grim and forbidding, upon the gradient hillside of his property from prehistoric times. But now, stealing from its mist-enshrouded depths, he could make out sinister shadows.

From beneath the mantle of darkness covering the land a profound and somber silence fell. The total absence of sound brought an unnatural vigilance to the woodland's night creatures, quieting their squabbles even as it quelled their instinctive hunt for prey.

As if even the wild things knew.

It was nigh on the stroke of midnight on the Eve of Samhain...the Night of the Waking Dream, boundary of the Imaginal. On this one night each year the veil separating the spirit and natural worlds grew thinnest; and the portal to the realm of the underworld opened wide.

He heard it then: the distant tolling. The clock of the ages was sounding the alarm—a dire warning to all of humankind. The Abomination of Desolation, the Ancient Evil that had first been measured in millennia, and then in centuries and decades, would now be restrained but by a single year.

The countdown to the Day of the Awakening was at hand.

A groaning arose deep within the man's spirit, for he knew well the signs and the times. And that the slumbering Beast imprisoned deep within the bowels of the earth, in a netherworld beneath the void of eternal separation, had at last begun to Dream. Anathema, the creature was called, a being so damnable that throughout the ages his proper name had been spoken guardedly...and then only in the most solemn of whispers.

And as the Prince of Demons dreamt of the Awakening, a suffocating wave of despair rolled across the earth, flooding the hearts of man. Tempers flared. Docile husbands snapped and struck their wives. Children woke from night terrors, screaming of monsters in the night. Untold violence erupted across the globe with reports of murder and mayhem increasing a thousand fold. And through it all the desperate ones, those without hope, the lonely and the desolate, fought increasingly oppressive battles with the darkness invading their minds. And with the hypnotic voice that whispered, as if in benediction. "Take your life. Find rest for your soul. Death is peace, peace. Peace."

As if powered by the tidal wave of wickedness, the robed spirits drifting from the passage tomb began to take shape and form in the ether. These descendents of the Beast, progeny of the giants spoken of in Genesis, moved en masse to a nearby faerie grove. There in a clearing that had stood bare for thousands of years, where no blade of grass, no tree or shrub, had been able to grow, the specters' voices rose on the icy wind. Chanting blasphemies so profane they fouled the air, tainted the very heavens with heresy, the group encircled a rectangular slab of stone.

And there, the sacrificial altar in their midst, its pitted surface forever stained with the blood of innocents, began to well up and drip anew.

∾∾

October 31st...
Maine, USA

Arianna Sullivan awoke with a start, her heart hammering against her ribcage, every sense on alert. Adrenaline coursed through her veins like liquid fire.

Someone was in the room.

She forced her body to relax, her breathing slow and rhythmic, feigning sleep. From beneath her eyelashes, she searched the room's shifting shadows, until she spotted the intruder in front of the window, a dark silhouette backlit by the light of a full moon. As he edged around the foot of her bed, moving stealthily in her direction, she called upon her many years of training in the martial arts. Centering herself, she measured his progress. One step, two. But just as she prepared to strike, he passed through a shaft of moonlight spilling through a crack in the curtains.

Blowing out a loud breath, she pushed up onto her elbow. A groggy glance at the glowing blue dial on her alarm clock revealed it was three-ten a.m.

"Daddy? What's wrong? What are you doing here at this hour?" Her voice raspy from sleep, she cleared her throat. "Geez, Da, you shouldn't sneak up on me like that. I was just about to jump up and beat the living daylights out of you."

Arianna punched her pillow into a ball and stuffed it behind her back. Scooting her legs over, she made room for her father to sit down. The mattress on the full-size sleigh bed sagged beneath his weight.

With a forlorn sigh, he reached over and swept the sleep-tangled hair away from her brow. It was something he had done often when she was a child. Why, she wondered, did that sweet, simple gesture leave her feeling so sad?

Her father didn't say a word. He just kept sitting there in that brooding silence, a beseeching look in his smoky gray eyes. Unease descended over her now like a dark veil, a smothering, queasy sense of loss.

She squeezed her eyes shut, trying to shake the feeling off. But then—like scenes from an old silent movie—jerky, fragmented images began to project against the back of her eyelids.

There was a mad rush to the hospital, the cloying scents of alcohol and antiseptic. And then a doctor's grim face filled the surreal movie screen. Although Arianna could see his lips moving, the incessant buzzing in her ears drowned out his words.

Finally, a word here, a phrase there, began to filter through the white noise. "Your father...cerebral aneurysm...brain hemorrhage... Did all we could."

All we could? Her body numb, mind gone blank, Arianna began to shiver. As if the planet had suddenly tilted on its axis, the room seemed to dip and swirl. It took one slow revolution, and then another, faster and faster. Like a nightmarish merry-go-round, the waiting room revolved around her, the off-white walls spinning until everything faded into a dizzying blur.

She bent over, gagged up bile.

Willing herself to back out of the terrifying vision, Arianna was shaken to the core. She searched her father's face for answers, but found herself blinking, unable to focus on his eyes. Here, in the moonspun darkness, his features seemed insubstantial somehow, his profile all wavy and flickering like a defective hologram.

Arianna scrubbed at her arms, only now aware of just how icy cold the room had become. Anchoring her duvet beneath her chin, she had to lock her jaws together to keep her teeth from chattering.

"What's wrong, Daddy? Tell me you're okay." Her whispered plea frosted the air between them. His response was a sad look of regret. And more silence. "Please, Da. You're starting to *scare* me."

Now, Sean Sullivan was an Irishman, born and bred, and his many years in the States had done nothing to mellow his hearty Irish brogue. Which was why, as he finally began to speak, the difference in his speech pattern seemed so glaring. His tone was far too soft, his voice almost whispery. The sound of a cold winter wind soughing through the branches of a naked tree, Arianna reasoned, the thought further chilling her to the bone.

Leaning forward, she strained to hear what he was saying, but could make out only two words. "The truth? Is that what you said, Da? But the truth about *what*?"

For a brief moment, what looked like frustration tightened his lips. But then his solemn gaze seemed to intensify. It was crazy. Arianna would have sworn his lips weren't moving. Strangely, though, she could hear him clearly now.

"Forgive me, pet, for the things I was after keeping from you. Things I should have made known to you long ago. Wasn't I only trying to protect you, love, but now, sure... God knows, I didn't expect—I thought we still had plenty of time..."

"What are you talking about? Da, you know, you really are starting to freak me out."

"Listen to me carefully now, child, for I've been granted only a moment to spend with you, to instruct you in what you must do," he continued, the urgency in his eyes sealing her lips. *"You've to go home to Ireland, Arianna, go back where you belong. For it's there your future will intersect with your past, and light the way to your destiny."*

This sounded too much like "goodbye," she thought, grief like a serrated blade carving her heart from her chest. Arianna fell into her father's arms. *"No-o-o-o, Daddy.* Don't go. Don't leave me!"

He held her for a moment and then gently set her away, pity darkening his gaze. *"Follow your heart, me love, and open your eyes of faith. Though there'll be much you don't understand, remember, always remember, what our dear Lord said. That He has other sheep not of our fold."*

With one long last lingering look, he leaned over and kissed her on the forehead. *Goodbye,* she told herself as his large, warm hand encompassed hers. She felt him press something small and hard into her palm and curl her fingers around it. *"Know that I'll always love you, pet. And since I'll be with God, I'm ever only a prayer away."*

With his final words a whisper of breath in the air between them, her father rose from the bed and began to cross the room, moving in a kind of gliding motion, his feet levitating several inches above the floor.

A nightmare, that's what this is, Arianna told herself, locked in full denial, even as the bedroom walls became transparent, revealing an ethereal glow emanating from the other side. Drawn toward this light, as a piece of steel to a magnet, her father passed through what should have been stucco and wood. Even with the otherworldly beauty of the world drawing him away from her, however, her precious father looked back longingly, as if mapping her face with his eyes one last time.

He looks so young. Unspeakable joy lit up his countenance. Of course, Arianna thought, his one true love. The mother she had never known must have come to help him cross over to the other side. But then, before her eyes, her father moved into the embrace of a shining being of pure white Light. Melding, joining, his very essence became one with that glorious Presence, who pulsed like the beating of a human heart.

As the walls became three-dimensional once more, Arianna sank back heavily into her pillow. Still in denial. "A nightmare," she kept repeating. "Just another lucid dream." Although admittedly, this waking dream was substantially different from the many others that had plagued her since childhood.

Exhausted, she scrubbed at her gritty eyes with the back of a balled-up fist. *Wait, what's this?* she wondered, referring to a small object clutched tightly in her hand. Sharp-edged and metallic, it brought her back to the moment Da had kissed her goodbye.

Turning her hand palm upward, she uncurled her fingers and stared in bemusement.

Cradled in her outstretched hand, all scratched and tarnished, was an old skeleton key.

A key Arianna had never seen before in her life.

Chapter Two

"You're getting on a flight this morning and leaving the country? Just like that. Seriously?" Standing at the stove in the kitchen of the condo that Arianna shared with her two best friends, Tara Price waved a spatula around for emphasis. "The memorial service was only yesterday. You need your friends right now. It's too soon to go running off alone."

The early morning sunlight taunted Arianna as it streamed through the kitchen window, its cheery reflection bouncing off the stainless steel appliances and glass-faced wooden cabinetry. "My darkest hour drenched in sunshine," she murmured in a bitter monotone. "Such a mockery."

From her seat at the granite breakfast bar in the center of the kitchen, she turned her gaze to the mirror on the wall behind her. Staring back at her through dazed blue eyes was a stranger, expression drawn, cheeks pale and sunken, her long blonde hair lackluster.

Tara set a plate of bacon and eggs in front of her grieving friend. She exchanged a pained glance with their other roommate, Michaela Daniels, perched at the bar beside her. Michaela set her bagel on the saucer in front of her and covered Arianna's hand with her own. "Ah, babe, I'm so sorry."

"I know. Thanks." Arianna forced a smile at her little friend. A pint-sized pixie with super-sized Attitude, the two of them had been tight since childhood.

Arianna looked at her plate and grimaced. The glistening layer of grease on the two eggs staring plaintively back at her made her stomach roll. "Tara, you know I can't eat this early in the morning."

"Well, try. It's been five days since your dad...since.... You've hardly eaten a thing," she finished uncomfortably, then paused. "At least it was quick, sweetie. A blessing he didn't suffer."

Official diagnosis, a brain aneurysm. One mind-blowing explosion of pain and the lights went out. Permanently. He never saw it coming. "Yeah, a real blessing. My father dead at the grand old age of forty-nine. Happy days."

Tara sighed, the sound like a deflating balloon as she sank onto a wood and chrome stool beside Arianna. "Sorry. Dumb thing to say." Looking down, she went quiet for a moment. "Don't go, honey, please. It's too soon. You're still in shock. I mean, I haven't even seen you cry."

"Now that's not likely to happen, is it?" At that moment, the urge to lash out was paramount; the need to shake a fist in the Face of God uncontrolled. *How could Da just go and die like that? How could he leave me here all alone?* "You know I can't cry, Tara." *Never had. Not once in twenty-eight years.*

The flash of temper seemed to provide at least a modicum of relief. As if it had incinerated some of the grief, cut it off from the source like a smaller blaze seeded into the path of an approaching wildfire.

Tara's face fell. "I'm so sorry," she apologized again. "I just thought... I mean, with it being your dad and all...."

Remorse hit Arianna hard. Snapping and snarling did help transform her sadness into something that was, for her, far more manageable—a fit of temper. Still, dumping all that toxic waste on her oldest friend just wasn't fair. "No, Tara. I'm the one who should be apologizing. I'm being a bitch. And you deserve better than that."

Tara's lips pressed together; her brow furrowed in worry. "Cut yourself some slack, would you, babe? You just lost your dad, for heaven's sake." The nervous energy that kept Tara's tall, willowy frame model slim propelled her to her feet. The chunky blonde layers of hair framing her face fell forward as she gave another swipe of the dishcloth over the already immaculate island bar. "That's why I'm so worried about you leaving today. It's just way too soon for you to go gallivanting off to some foreign country on your own."

Nag, nag, nag. Arianna bit her tongue until she would have sworn she tasted blood. Still, the exercise helped her manage to keep the words a thought, even as she prayed for patience. She loved Tara; she really did. But, from the moment Arianna had mentioned leaving immediately for Ireland—purportedly, to scatter her father's ashes—the girl had just refused to let it go.

Tara muttered under her breath as she turned back to the sink. Something about locking Arianna in her room until she came to her senses.

And she'd do it, too, Arianna thought. "For the umpteenth time, Tara, Ireland is *not* a foreign country. Not to me. I was born there."

"Yeah, and left when you were only three. Which makes you about as Irish as...as the Pope. No, wait a minute, he's *more* Irish. At least *he's* a practicing Catholic."

"Yeah, very funny," Arianna muttered, chasing a strip of bacon around her plate with the tines of her fork.

"Stop playing with your food!" Tara ordered, hands on hips in that exasperated mother pose she had long ago perfected. "Lord knows, if you're bent and determined to fly out of here this morning, you need to eat something."

At the thought of food, Arianna swallowed, again tasting bile. The low-grade nausea she had been experiencing since her father's death had been only exacerbated by the smells of condolences pouring into the condo in the form of food. There were soups and salads, hot casseroles and desserts of every variety. The freezer was packed, the fridge and cupboards groaning, and still the stuff kept pouring in. So much so, she reasoned that they could have fed a small third world country on the surplus alone.

Catching Tara's insistent gaze, Arianna sighed. "Yes, Mother dearest." Dutifully, she shoveled a forkful of egg into her mouth and began to chew. Her empty stomach gurgled in appreciation, surprising her with how hungry she really was.

Until now, Michaela had sat quietly, managing to avoid getting caught in the crossfire between her two friends. But Arianna's snide remark brought about a forfeited snicker and an eye-roll.

"I saw that." Tara shot her a glare as she took another swipe of the spotless sink.

"Don't mind her, Mick," Arianna teased in a half-hearted attempt to lighten the mood. "You gotta know it's hopeless."

Tara had been seven, Arianna three when she and her da had arrived in Maine from Ireland. As soon as Tara discovered that the new kid on the block, the one with the funny accent, didn't have a mother, she had made Arianna her very own living doll.

"You didn't even buy a round-trip ticket." While Tara nattered on, Arianna amused herself with visions of her fair and slender friend. Hands wrapped around a baseball bat, she was pummeling a horse already sprawled lifeless on the ground. "What's up with that? You can't just uproot your whole life and run away on a whim. What about your business?"

"I have a manager? Karen's done a great job whenever I've been away at antique auctions and on buying trips. She'll keep things on track just fine until I get back."

"Okay, then, what about Damien? You don't honestly think the guy's going to hang around indefinitely, waiting for you to come to your senses."

Arianna hissed a tired sigh. "Let's not go there right now, okay?" Tara opened her mouth to say something else, but Arianna cut her off. "I mean it, Tara. It's not like that with us. We've only been dating for a few weeks. *Casually* dating."

"Casual? Is that what you call it? You've spent every night in his bed since..." Tara's voice trailed off, as if she couldn't bear to say the words.

"Since my father died," Arianna finished for her, *needing* to say the words. Maybe it would help her begin to accept the finality of his being gone. "I told you, Damien lost his own dad when he was a kid. Which means he gets what I'm going through. I can't explain it, but just having him hold me through all the sleepless hours...."

"He's not going to wait forever."

Michaela brushed crumbs off the counter onto her plate as she stood up. "Don't listen to her, babe. He'll wait. Dude's crazy about you. And he's smokin'! So, why the heck have you been dragging your feet?" The question was a tongue poking at a sore tooth. "Why not just jump his bones and give up the V card, already?"

Arianna frowned at the idiom. So what if she was still a virgin? With all the talk about women's 'choices' today, why did she get such flack over her decision to remain abstinent? It was true that her father had raised her with a healthy dose of Christian values—spiked with a liberal shot of Catholic guilt. But that wasn't what had kept her chaste all these years. Aside from the fact that she was overly picky about men—Damien being the first guy she had dated in several years—something else had stopped her from going further.

She felt like she would be cheating on another man.

Fact of the matter was, she was already in love—with a man she couldn't have.

And no, the guy wasn't married. Her luck, it couldn't be anything as *simple* as that. Nope, bat-crap crazy as it sounded, the man she loved was an illusion, a veritable puff of smoke. A late-night figment of her all-too-fertile imagination.

And every bit as real to her as the two women standing in the kitchen with her now. *Torn Between Two Lovers,* she thought, her lips in a wry twist. But, of the two vying for a place in Arianna's heart, only one was a mortal man conceived of flesh and blood. The other was the fulfillment of every woman's erotic fantasy, a dark angel born of her secret dreams.

"You already know why I can't be with Damien that way." Arianna watched her closest friends exchange troubled glances.

"You mean the magic man," Michaela confirmed.

"I thought you'd stopped having the dreams," Tara said.

"Just stopped talking about them," Arianna replied.

Yes, the waking dreams had haunted her for as long as she could remember. Of course, in the beginning, she had been too young to question the web of enchantment, the spell that spirited her through a mystical portal to another dimension. To some other place in time.

And, it had been there, on the far side of nowhere, that she had first encountered him.

The boy with eyes of green and hair as black as the darkest night.

Arianna had grown up like that, waking in a storybook castle stretched high above a wild and rocky shore. She had been in high school before recognizing the significance of the dream-carved setting: it was the rugged coast of the west of Ireland where she had been born. As the years fled by, she had watched manhood sculpt the boy's lanky body, carving ripped lean muscle into his lengthening torso.

The pattern of the dream had never altered, at least not until the night of her eighteenth birthday. It was then, for the first time, that he jerked to a halt in the sand. His head angled, chin tipped upward, his gaze appeared to sweep across the hulking fortress atop the rocky cliff. He seemed to be searching for something.... Or some*one*.

Now, she knew there was no way the young man could have seen her standing at that window. Not from that distance. Certainly not cloaked in midnight's shadows as she had been. And yet, like a laser in the night, his glittering gaze sliced through the distance and the darkness, until he had found her.

Over a decade had passed since that fateful night. And yet, Arianna recalled the incident as clearly as if it had happened yesterday. Tiny hairs rose now on her arms and legs, as she relived the stunning impact of that incandescent gaze. And the punch of supernatural power that had sent her reeling, her heart fluttering like a baby bird trapped in a nest of human hands.

The image had been burned indelibly into her memory. His hand raised, his index finger pointed at her, then crooked in a beckoning motion. It was an invitation to come and walk with him. Needles of ice danced over her skin as she had reached out to him, her hand slipping through the narrow castle window. A scream lodged deep in her throat as she felt herself being swept up, up into a dizzying whirlwind, into a blinding flash of crystal light. And then, somehow, within the space of a single heartbeat, she was there beside him, the two of them walking hand-in-hand in the cloud-dappled moonlight.

With their very first encounter on that windswept shore, Arianna's heart had become the possession of that dark and brooding stranger, her illusive phantom of the night.

Forcing herself back to the present, Arianna noted her friends worried expressions. Tara's pronouncement was short, succinct, and to the point. "You need to see a psychiatrist. Try to figure out what happened in your early childhood to mess your head up. Now, come on. Enough daydreaming. Flight's leaving in less than three hours. You have everything? Tickets? Passport?"

"Tara, *breathe*!" Michaela ordered. "There's no rush. We have plenty of time." Then, in an aside to Arianna, "I know you don't want to hear this, kiddo, but she *is* right, you know. You really haven't thought this thing through—"

Arianna gave her a stricken look. "Not you, too."

"You're losing weight and you have dark circles under your eyes," Tara bit out. "Just for the record, you look like hell."

"Hey, don't hold back. Tell me what you really think."

Tara's green eyes shot quicksilver. "Go ahead, be flippant. But I want you to know I have a bad feeling about this trip you're taking. A *very* bad feeling."

Tara was an archaeologist, a scientist. A pragmatist to the very core. So admitting something airy-fairy like that had to have cost her dearly. "But you don't *get* 'feelings'," Arianna reminded her in a soft voice.

"That's right, I don't. Which is *exactly* why you should take this one to heart. Look, why don't you just postpone the trip—" As Arianna opened her mouth to protest, Tara raised a silencing hand. "For a *week*. Is that too much to ask? It'll give me a chance to tie up any loose ends from the Tundra dig and come with you."

Tara had arrived home from her most recent expedition on October 30th, the day before Arianna's father had died.

Michaela's dark chocolate eyes, inherited from a Native American great-great grandmother, brimmed with compassion. "Better yet, just reschedule to a later flight today. I'll get packed and come with you myself."

Damned if they weren't tag-teaming her. "Might I remind you that you're already packed—for the horse show in Canada. A show you've been champing at the bit for months to get to."

At Michaela's mock-horrified grimace, Arianna admitted, "Okay, pretty lame."

Michaela, a champion show jumper, had been looking forward to the Royal Horse Show in Toronto for months. Due to some business matter, her absentee-celebrity parents would be attending. Having always disparaged their daughter's equestrian skills, it was to be Michaela's first face-to-face—or as Michaela had so eloquently phrased it, "in your face"—opportunity to prove them wrong. "Look, Arianna, I've been thinking, I don't have a darn thing to prove to those two. I'm really not that hot on going anymore."

Arianna snorted. "Yeah, right."

"Save it, kid. I've been planning to register for the Dublin Horse Show next August anyway." Michaela calmly refilled their coffee cups from the carafe on the counter. "Now's as good a time as any to make an advance trip to Ireland to set things up. So. You can either postpone your flight until later today, or I'll just follow you on over tomorrow."

Arianna groaned inwardly. Once the girl latched on to something... Well, let's just say that a crocodile with its jaws locked around its prey had nothing on her. "Look guys, you know I love you, right?"

Tara leaned toward Michaela conspiratorially. "Uh-oh, better roll up your pants legs. I got a feeling it's gonna start getting deep in here."

"I'm *serious*." Arianna's voice went soft and low. "You two have always had my back. And I...well, I honestly don't know how I'd have made it through this past week without you."

Tara's eyes filled and she looked down, picking at some invisible spot on the kitchen counter with her fingernail. "I hear a 'but' coming."

"*But,*" Arianna conceded, "this is something I have to do alone. Have to do *now*. I can't explain it, except to say that knowing I'd be leaving today...going to fulfill Da's final wishes.... Well, it's the glue that's been holding me together."

As one might expect, Arianna had related to them only her father's "wishes" to have his ashes scattered from the cliffs in County Clare, as stated in his will. Smart girl that she was she had purposely left out any mention of his visit from beyond the grave, a thing she had yet to get even her own head wrapped around.

Not to mention that an I-see-dead-people confession would have gone over like a sack of cement. They would have probably considered it their collective duty to have her committed—for her own protection.

"You know, that's another thing I don't get." Tara rinsed out the dishcloth and draped it over the faucet to dry. Leaning a hip against the counter, she crossed her arms. "Remember when we booked the graduation trip to Ireland? Your dad got so freaked about it we had to cancel. And as much as you travel on business, you never went back there...to spare his feelings."

Of course, how could Arianna forget. Ireland was the land of her birth. And yet, contrary to her snappy comeback of earlier, it really was a foreign country to this Irishwoman-raised-American. To make matters worse, while growing up, there had been no old family photos, no cozy talks about the life she and her father had once shared there with her mother. Subjects, he had made abundantly clear, that were strictly off-limits.

Consequently, whatever had happened in Ireland all those years ago...whatever anguish had caused him to dissociate himself from everything and everyone he had ever known and loved...remained to this day shrouded in mystery.

Old family secrets, Arianna reflected sadly. Secrets her father had taken with him to the grave.

To spare his feelings, Arianna had stood firm, refusing to give in to what, at times, had amounted to a near compulsion to return to her birthplace. Because nothing on earth...*nothing*...had been worth the risk of putting that haunted look back in his eyes. Or of unlatching the yawning black jaws of grief she had watched swallow him whole, time and again, throughout her childhood.

Tara cleared Arianna's empty plate away, and Arianna propped her elbow in its place, chin in hand. "Twenty-five years...and he never got over losing my mother." She stared off into space and sighed, her tone low, wistful. "Well, at least they're together now."

"Blows my mind he held onto the family home in Ireland all these years," Tara said, rinsing the plate and stacking it in the dishwasher.

"Never even mentioned it to me," Arianna said. "Just had the place privately deeded into my name, the paperwork stored with his will in his safe deposit box."

And then, there was the key to the property, Arianna thought to herself.

The key he had transcended death itself to place personally into her hand.

Chapter Three

"To the left, to the left." As she turned onto the N18 out of Shannon Airport, Arianna hummed the words to an old Beyonce song like a mantra, a reminder to drive on the *wrong* side of the road. Not to mention that she was driving from the *wrong* side of the car while shifting with her *left* hand. Not realizing that manual transmissions were standard on rental cars here, she had neglected to request an automatic when making her reservation.

She checked her watch, added the requisite five hours. It was ten forty-eight P.M. Irish time. Great planning, she thought, arriving here at this hour of the night. Exhausted—she was absolutely *fried*—and still had to find her way to the old family home in Ennistymon.

A flicker of lightning caught her attention and she glanced up. No moon, no stars, suggested a heavy cloud cover, she concluded as moisture began to mist the windshield.

Arianna successfully circumnavigated her first Irish roundabout, exiting onto the N85 west toward Ennistymon. The route took her through a long, dark tunnel of interlocking leafy branches into the small village of Corofin. As she left the town center behind, a bold flash of lightning took a snapshot of lush green hills and wooded farmland. The pristine acres divided by crumbling stone walls and overgrown hedgerows made a perfect picture postcard.

With a deafening crash of thunder that had Arianna's heart leaping from her chest, the gently weeping sky flew suddenly into a foot-stomping tantrum. Visibility was reduced almost to zero, so she slowed to a crawl. Even with the wipers on high, she was straining to read the half-Gaelic, half-English street signs posted at the intersections.

Just as she was thinking she had missed her turn-off, Arianna was thrown forward with a bone-jarring *thunk* and the grinding sound of steel eating pavement. And as her right front end slammed violently into a moon crater-sized rut concealed by the racing floodwaters, her engine sputtered and died.

Fingers crossed, Arianna turned the key in the ignition. *Nada. Zilch. Terrific,* She powered on her cell phone. *Roaming...roaming... No Service.* "Aaagh!"

"What the hell do I do now?" she muttered, trying to decide whether to stay put and wait out the next Great Flood, or abandon the ark in search of civilization and the use of a telephone.

Split seconds later, cannonball-size chunks of hail began to plummet from the sky, making her decision for her.

"Welcome home to Ireland," she groused, her voice drowned out by the deadly barrage of frozen artillery bombarding the car.

Staring straight ahead, wrists draped over the steering wheel, she felt a shiver of unease slide between her shoulder blades. With a quick check to be sure the doors were locked, she did a mental inventory. What specific event could have triggered this disconcerting sense of *déjà vu*?

Finally her lips tightened in disgust. "Michaela and her damned vampire romance."

In the chapter Arianna had finished just prior to landing, the heroine's car had broken down on a deserted country road, while a ferocious electrical storm raged around her.

"Well, duh..."

Of course, in *Love's Midnight Passion,* a tragic vampire hero had come rushing to the fair lady's rescue. Arianna sniffed. The way her luck was going lately, she figured any encounter with the *undead* she experienced would have to be with Count-freaking-Dracula himself.

Then again, this was Ireland, she reminded herself, not Transylvania. Which meant that any close encounters of the supernatural kind would more than likely be of the faerie folk variety. Hordes of tiny winged creatures, flitting from bush to bush—

But no, her luck, she would run into a member of the Dark Fey, the evil fairies she had learned about in her Ancient Legends and Folklore class in college. There were tales of the changelings, known as child stealers. And then there were the messengers of death, the wailing banshee.

Then, of course, Irish literature was rife with stories of the *coshta-bower*. Though invisible to the naked eye, the coffin-laden death coach could be heard on many a cold and moonless night, the clip-clop of phantom horses' hooves and the clatter of buggy wheels echoing eerily over the cobbles. But then a sudden silence would fall. As the story went, this signified that the headless coachman had reined in at some poor soul's front door, there to impart death and destruction with two resounding knocks—

Two loud thumps on the driver's side window jerked Arianna upright in her seat. With a squeal, she scrambled over the gearshift, almost impaling herself in the process. Her body plastered against the passenger door, she stared at the windows, blinded by the dark and impenetrable curtain of rain. But then, even as the wind continued to shriek and rock the car, the rain suddenly stopped. Abruptly. As if someone had reached out and shut off a spigot.

Arianna had always prided herself on her keen sixth sense, which went instantly on red alert whenever she was in danger. And, right now, she felt like a porcupine, the hairs on her arms and legs bristling as that precognitive spidey sense wailed like a fire alarm.

At that moment, an eerie whistling sent her exhausted brain into overdrive. What was that? The haunting nicker of spectral horses? Or, maybe, the creak of phantom carriage wheels? With sweeping brushstrokes, her overblown imagination began to paint a hideous portrait on the canvas of her mind. It was of the hell-spawned coachman, with his severed head tucked beneath one arm, his other hand... *jiggling the door handle?*

A bit back scream held Arianna's throat in a chokehold.

Over the clamor of the storm, she heard a voice. It sounded male and very angry. *"Oscail an doras! Anois!"*

The strange utterance was foreign and compelling. It struck a chord of terror within her. "Oh, God. Oh, God." *Had the words been a black magic incantation?* she dared to question. *A diabolical spell conjured in a devil's tongue?*

Arianna grappled madly for strands of reason. As she did, she became aware of a strange glow reflecting off the dashboard. With visions of alien abduction invading her beleaguered brain, she stole a cringing peek into the rearview mirror.

Headlights. On low beam. You idiot!

"Open the door, I said. *Now!*" Same voice, but in English this time...English with an Irish accent.

Hello-o-o-o... Irish accent? Might the man have been speaking Gaelic? You think?

Cursing her own stupidity, Arianna lifted a leg over the gearshift and slid back into the driver's seat. She was reaching out to unlock the door, when...

"Open the bloody door!" the man bellowed. "Or I'm coming in after you!"

Poised just above the lock release, her hand jerked to a halt. Now, there was no way she had touched that button—knew damn well she had not. And yet, in horrified disbelief, she heard the tumblers disengage. She made a mad grab for the door handle, but, too late. She could feel it being wrenched from her grasp. "No!"

Rampaging winds surged into the car, tearing at her long, blonde hair, and effectively blinding her to the masculine arms that were reaching for her.

A third degree black belt in *Tang Soo Do* karate, Arianna believed she was well able to defend herself in any situation. Now, however, as this man's long fingers wrapped around her upper arms, she could feel a strange sort of paralysis coming over her. Muscles weak, energy sapped, she felt herself being hauled out of the small foreign car as if she weighed no more than a matchstick. Strangely, as soon as he released her to stand beside the back door, strength flowed back into her body.

Standing spread-legged against the buffeting wind, she caught only a glimpse of the dark-haired stranger as he ducked his head inside the car. After a cursory look around, he pulled back out of the vehicle...all six feet, several darkly masculine inches of him.

Too pissed off at being manhandled to properly appreciate the view, Arianna braced for battle as the guy turned to face her. Her jaw dropped, heart tripped, literally stumbled in her chest.

She stared at him. "You can't be real," she choked out in a whisper. And yet, there he was. Framed in a savage backdrop of wild and raging tempest was the erotic dark angel of her secret dreams.

In that ethereal world, he had been beautiful. But here, 'in the flesh', the man was striking beyond belief. And there was that mysterious allure that had nothing to do with the exotic setting. She studied him silently. The way the low beams of a black Land Rover cast his body all in shadow. The light reflected off his hair, all wind-tossed and damp from the moisture-laden air. A shade, so black it held hints of indigo, accentuated the unusual, almost colorless, green of his eyes.

And as the man returned her stare, fixed her with those mysterious eyes, the thought came to mind that there really was something of the vampire about him. An unnatural stillness. That unmistakable ripple of reigned-in power.

The strong angle of his jaw, darkened with late-night stubble, added a rough masculinity to what would have otherwise been almost too-perfect features. His was a fallen-angel face, she mused. A face sculpted for the singular purpose of stealing a woman's soul.

She let her eyes wander south. A black leather jacket, unzipped, revealed a strong body. Not gym-bulked, which she detested, but naturally sleek and tightly muscled from hard, physical work. Further down, low-slung black jeans fit his long, long legs to perfection.

Arianna raised her gaze to his face—and collided again with those fathomless eyes. The slam of preternatural power felt like a mule-kick to the chest. A sensation she had experienced before. On a dream spun Irish shore.

"This can't be happening," she murmured. But, while her mind rebelled, her stuttering heart knew no such perspicuity. "Is it really you?"

As the impulsive words spun past her lips, Arianna willed them back inside her mouth. Lucky for her, the question had been lost, swept away by a whirling gust of wind. Relief rocked her. It would have been mortifying, to say the least, if he had heard her, since not an inkling of recognition warmed the glacial green of those achingly familiar eyes.

Still, this man's likeness to her illusory lover was uncanny. Not only were his facial features and build a dead ringer, but he even wore his too-long black hair in an identical fashion.

He even dressed as she remembered, favoring black.

And the resemblance didn't stop at the identical-twin good looks. No, it went far deeper, into the underlying essence of the man. This one exuded the same dark elegance, the same vibration of otherworldly power. It was as if he were either the personification of her dream lover, or the other's double.

And yet, with all their similarities, Arianna sensed something intrinsically different about this man, as well. Something colder, harsher; something fraught with danger. Yes, there was a definite dark side to his nature, she concluded, as if he were the other's evil twin.

Vampire. Again, the word whispered tauntingly in her ear. *And really, wouldn't that explain everything? The hypnotic thrall transmitted over thousands of miles. His masterful seduction in her dreams—*

Suddenly, Arianna's whimsical musings crashed to a halt as the entire Western Hemisphere seemed to explode around them. Lightning hissed through black velvet, turning night into day. As the jagged bolt of fire plowed into a nearby tree with a deafening roar, a thunderclap to herald the apocalypse rocked the earth beneath her.

And, though the wind wailed like a banshee, there was not a single drop of rain. Her gut tied in a knot of terror, Arianna shouted above the tumult. "Something's just not right here. We've gotta find shelter, get out of this storm!"

But he just stood there, unfazed by the naked display of nature's rage. He was an avenging angel, her mind reasoned, in command of the dark forces erupting all around them. His lips moved then, as if to whisper a prayer. Instantly, the gusting winds ceased. Of the vicious storm, only sizzling forks of lightning in the distance remained.

"Who...*what* are you?" Arianna whispered, her voice cracking.

The man's eyes were hooded, dark and impenetrable. And then they lowered, began to rove her body. Arianna bit back a low moan as fingers of heat danced arousal over her flesh. The feeling was intimate, palpable, as if he were physically touching her.

She saw him frown, give his head a shake. With that, the erotic sensations ceased.

The strange interlude left Arianna juggling a confusing jumble of emotions. There was fear, of course, and anxiety. But underlying that was a raw sensual hunger, an aching sense of intimacy. Feelings all at odds with one another, as if each vied for supremacy.

And all the while, her survival instincts were screaming at her. *"Run from him! Run as far and fast as you can and don't look back."* Something told Arianna that if she ignored this internal warning, life as she knew it would never be the same again.

The enigmatic stranger had yet to speak. But, as if he had sensed her inner turmoil, his gaze sharpened on hers. Arianna could feel herself falling, tumbling into the deep, dark depths of those captivating eyes. Intriguing, she mused, the way his irises seemed to refract the lightning. Transformed into dizzying, multi-faceted prisms, his eyes became a nebulous shade of gold-flecked green she had never seen before.

Except in her dreams....

Arianna gave herself a mental shake. *You gotta get a grip.* Death coaches and vampires and dream lovers incarnate—Oh, my. *Seriously?*

She needed to snap out of it, get back on the road. Not that her silent companion seemed to be in any hurry to offer assistance. Lounging against the back door of her car, he stared at her, arms crossed over his chest, his broad shoulders straining the leather of the bomber jacket he was wearing. It was a relentless assessment bordering on impolite.

Irritation narrowed her eyes, making it increasingly obvious that she had imagined the whole dark angel thing. Crossing her own arms in mimicry, she raised her brows. "Take a picture, why don't you."

He frowned, blinked once. "Sorry?"

Just one word. And a shiver of recognition slid through her. Impossible, she knew. But even the hot Irish whiskey voice sounded the same, full-flavored and intoxicating, with a twist of danger.

She swallowed. "You *should* be." Her head motioned toward the car. "Mind telling me just what the devil that was all about?"

His mouth set in a thin line. "You tell me. Then we'll both know, won't we."

His arrogance fanned the flickering flames of her temper. "Well, I *will* tell you one thing, buddy boy. You've got some colossal nerve putting your hands on me like that." Bad-tempered, tired and reckless, Arianna leaned in closer. "You know, a stupid stunt like that could get a man hurt."

And a woman couldn't help but be intrigued by the flash of fire in those strange feline eyes, a burst of heat turning the golden flecks into molten metal.

Pushing off the car, he took a step toward her. "'Twould be yourself then, would it? The one inflicting this *pain* you're just after mentioning?" His voice pitched low, seductive. A beat of arousal pulsed into the deepest heart of her.

He moved to tower over her, an intentional invasion of her personal space. Intimidation, it was meant to make her feel small and insignificant. *Mastered.*

Silly man. A cynical grin lifted the corners of her mouth; obstinacy stiffened her spine. And yet, with all her bravado, she knew wisdom dictated she keep one important fact in mind. That, notwithstanding his insane resemblance to someone who, in reality, *didn't even exist,* the big man with the bad attitude was a complete and total stranger.

Problem. She just wasn't feeling very wise. So, instead of retreating, she stepped boldly into the man, leaving no more than a hairsbreadth of space between them. Big mistake. Because just one whiff of his wild and woodsy scent elicited more dream-clouded memories. A visceral reaction she attributed to simple chemistry. *Pheromones.*

Because there was nothing familiar about his masculine scent. Nothing at all.

Oh, Arianna, you are such a liar.

Ordering herself to focus, she tipped her head back. Like a cat playing with her meal, she licked her lips as her fingers began a leisurely stroll up the man's chest. The ploy, which brought confusion to his eyes, backfired, however, when an unexpected rush of take-me-now sizzled through her veins. Not that he remained unaffected by her touch, she noted, as something hot and smoky incinerated the perplexity in his eyes.

Trapped in that fiery gaze, Arianna was becoming entangled in her own web of deception. Her breath caught at the sensation of an ephemeral caress, the back of fingers skimming one cheek. It was a lover's touch. Slow and intimate. *And familiar.*

Yes, God help her, she recognized that touch.

Suddenly the cool night air began to warm and thicken, her body growing slow and fluid. The hungry look in his eyes effectively erased any thought of self-preservation.

She moistened her lips, then shuddered as his heated gaze lowered to follow the movement. Her eyes drifted shut and she breathed him in. Yes, blindfolded, she would have known him, would have recognized him anywhere by his scent alone. Mountain air and rainwater clean, his was the fragrance of a night creature. Wild and free, he was a man who wouldn't be ensnared by the rules of polite society.

Arianna let her head fall back. Her hands trailed upward, mapping incredibly broad shoulders. His too-long hair tickled her wrists as she overlapped them behind his neck. What was happening here, she didn't know, nor, frankly, did she care. She had longed for this encounter, for this impossible moment, for far too long. Forever it seemed. And now she had only to pull his mouth down to hers, to reacquaint herself with his minty flavor, with the heady taste of the one and only man she had ever loved.

But as she tugged, she felt resistance. Her eyes drifted open—and met the amused male triumph in his gaze. Confused for a moment, then mortification seeped in, painting her cheeks with a flush of embarrassment.

"Jerk," she whispered, trying to control the breathless quality of her voice.

She failed miserably. Either that or he had read the humiliation flaming her face. Either way, his head tipped to the side, his eyes softened.

Oh, man, now he was feeling *sorry* for her. Could this thing get any worse?

"Hey," he murmured.

Arianna pushed at his chest. "No, just let me go." She went to step backward and stumbled. His arms slid around her waist to steady her. Trapped against his chest, she dropped her head forward onto her hands. She would die, literally *die*, if he were ever to learn how much that small embrace had touched her.

Still locked against his body, she could feel herself melting into his embrace. She was losing it here, needed to put some space between them, get her head straight. Desperate to break free of the mesmeric hold he seemed to have on her, she tried to pull away, but again, he resisted the movement.

Being restrained set off an alarm that blew the cobwebs from her brain.

Her reaction was automatic, not thought out at all, as she gathered fistfuls of leather from either side of his jacket. And she watched his stormy gaze transform into one of stunned disbelief, as she brought up her knee....

Chapter Four

There was a harsh, guttural spit of something muttered in Gaelic. Crystalline eyes flashed hard and dark with the threat of murder as the Irishman evaded her assault with the grace of a dancer. In a single, fluid move, he spun her in a perfect pirouette and cuffed both of her hands behind her in one of his. His right arm banded across her chest and he hauled her against him. *Hard.* An apt description, she noted, for every blatantly male inch of the body now imprinted indelibly against her spine.

Holy crap. "Let go of me!" No slacker in the dance of defense herself, Arianna proceeded to move like the mythical Whirling Dervish, delivering a back-kick, a sweep, a chop and an elbow jab in quick succession. All close-range karate blows that her opponent managed to sidestep as lithely as if their movements had been choreographed.

But did she use good judgement now and throw in the towel? Oh, no, not with her endorphins spiking and the rush of battle firing her blood. Later...if she managed to live that long...she would undoubtedly plead temporary insanity. Because what other than a serious mental lapse would account for her continued provocation of a martial artist so decidedly superior?

Even now, caged in his steel-banded arms, she could feel claustrophobia closing in on her. Desperate to escape his suffocating grip, she feinted an overhead blow to his neck, while simultaneously stomping down on his foot. The satisfying crunch of the wooden heel glancing off his instep told her she hit the mark.

"Bitseach damanta!"

"Yeah, same to you, bud," Arianna muttered. She didn't need a dictionary to translate the sentiment.

He shifted his body. Suddenly her hands were held captive in front of her, arms crossed so that she was hugging herself. His own strong arms securing hers like a strait jacket, he moved into a partial squat, knees pushing into the back of hers and causing them to collapse. He straightened then, lifting her off the ground so that her feet dangled in front of her. He leaned slightly backward, enough to avoid her peddling feet, and began to inch toward her car. His butt made contact with the back door and he braced against it, one muscular leg levered over both of hers like a human crow bar.

Trapped like a rat, she thought, and the infuriating man wasn't even winded. Boy was he was pissed, though, the fury radiating off him in waves. Probably battling the urge to strangle the life out of her.

Okay, so they had reached an impasse. And now, with her all but lying on top of him, her backside molded indecently to the front of his jeans, he would be forced to make a decision. Whether to finish this, or let her go.

Squirming in his lap, Arianna was trying to regain her balance when she heard an animal-like rumble through the walls of his chest. *Did he just growl?* Before the implications of that scenario could send her imagination winging down a path of werewolves and other shape-shifting creatures, she felt his arms lock down even tighter. The vice-like pressure against her diaphragm now prevented it from expanding at all. She was in trouble.

Officially freaked out now, she was afraid to move—hell, she was terrified even to blink—lest the action be misconstrued as a further attack.

With her constricted lungs growing increasingly oxygen-starved, she could only suck in raw, tiny gasps of air. Panic clawed its way up her throat.

Asphyxiation was making her drowsy, disoriented. Suddenly, death was a very real and frightening possibility. With the gray dots swimming in front of her eyes beginning to connect, to create a dark and murky pool, Arianna expelled her last reserve of oxygen in a frantic bid for mercy. "Please, I-I can't breathe," she rasped. "You're suffocating me."

The rigidity of his hold slackened instantly. Although only

marginally, it was sufficient for her to fill her lungs with a greedy gulp of the cool, damp air. Head reeling from the sudden influx of oxygen, she collapsed back against his chest.

"Thank you," she breathed, sucking in huge gasps of air. But each longed-for breath stirred a torment of dream-misted memories brought on by the familiar scent of him, of rainwater and damp leather, of sandalwood soap and...something else.

Something raw and wild. Elemental.

Arianna swallowed hard and twisted uncomfortably in his lap.

She froze as the man grunted and dipped his head, his nose nudging her hair aside. At the warmth of his breath on her neck, goose bumps sprang up all over her body.

"You think you might stop wriggling your arse in my lap that kind o'way?" he murmured in her ear, his deep voice strained and testy. "Unless, o' course, you fancy the two of us becoming even better acquainted than we are at present."

Aware that he was referencing his growing arousal, Arianna winced in embarrassment. "Please, won't you just let me go now?" she asked in a small, quiet voice.

She heard him inhale, felt the slow rise and fall of his chest. Silence. A thousand one. A thousand two...

"Would you be finished then?"

"F-finished?"

"Done. With trying to unman me, cripple me like." This said with a hint of dry irony. And, was it possible? A reluctant measure of respect?

"Yes, of course. I mean...absolutely."

He hesitated again, no doubt suspicious of her prompt and unconditional surrender. "Sure of that, are you now?" His tone was level, conversational. "Because you to have understand, *cailín*, that should you try such a thing again, you'll be leaving me no choice but to deal with you like a man."

"Eeeyeah. Got that."

Their truce agreed, the imposing male settled her onto her feet and uncoiled himself from around her, like a giant anaconda that had just decided it wasn't hungry.

If Arianna thought he was through with her, she would have been wrong. No sooner than he had set her on her feet, he reversed their positions, spinning her around and pressing her back against the door of the car. And then his mouth was on hers. She gasped and his tongue invaded, stroking, suckling, teeth nibbling. Not a tentative first kiss, but one of the practiced lover in her dreams. A lover who knew how she wanted to be kissed, to be held. She strained against him, swallowing his groan as he devoured her. *Yes, devoured.* Because no other word could adequately describe the feral essence of that kiss.

And then, just like that, it was over. He tore his mouth from hers. Pupils so dilated they almost obscured his irises he stared down at her with a look she couldn't comprehend. She waited. Surely he would say something now, make some mention of recognizing her. Some reference to the dreams.

Disappointment tasted bitter in her mouth when, with a slight shake of his head, he pulled away.

"Wait here. I'll send help," he muttered hoarsely, then turned abruptly and stalked toward the SUV parked behind them.

Left panting and weak-kneed from their erotic encounter, Arianna watched incredulously as he walked away. Surely, he didn't intend to leave her here, stranded on a dark country road at this hour of the night. "Um, hey, wait a minute."

Glancing over his shoulder, he glared at her. Glared. With a narrow-eyed scrutiny that made her feel like a specimen squirming in a petri dish. "Would you please *stop* that?" she said, still breathless. "Didn't your mother ever teach you it's impolite to stare?" For a fleeting moment, a black shadow slid over his face and darkened his features. "And while we're on the subject of manners, I believe you owe me an apology."

"For what? Stealin' a kiss?"

Arianna's cheeks burst into flames. "I wasn't talking about the stupid kiss, okay? I was referring to the way you manhandled me, dragged me out of my car."

"*Me* manhandle *you*?" His low chuckle sent a ripple of awareness zinging along her nerve endings. "I did nothing but defend myself, sure." He paused then, eyes growing thoughtful. "Though, now that I think about it, I believe I am willing to admit to being sorry."

"You are?"

"I am, yes. For I can say, in all sincerity, that I've never been more sorry for anything in me life than I am for pulling *you* from that car tonight."

Great. A freaking wise guy.

"I'd not have stopped a'tall had your car not been the same make and model as one belonging to a mate of mine. Thinking he may be broken down and in need of a lift, I knocked on the window. But then you went to wailing like a bleedin' banshee. Like someone after being murdered or worse."

"Oh." Suddenly, Arianna felt like a slug. "I-I didn't realize—"

"But then aren't we men the great eejits?" he interrupted with a scornful snort. "Ourselves fancying the female weaker and in need of our protection. But haven't you proved you're quite *man* enough to fend for yourself? That being the case, I'll be off then, will I?"

As he turned to leave, Arianna's jaw unhinged. "Un-freaking-believable," she said under her breath. "Well, if that...that *creep* thinks for a single minute that I'm chasing after him, he's got another— What the heck is that?"

Arianna's attention had been diverted to the hillside, where a strange evanescent glow was fluttering through the glistening shrubs and wind-torn trees. As the light danced in and out of a circle of standing stones, she murmured, "A-will-o'-the-wisp," in awe of being a personal witness to the legendary faerie lights.

Spellbound, she watched the iridescent anomaly begin to stretch and rise, until it seemed to take on human form. As icy fingers of fear trailed along the back of her neck, a swirling gust of wind dispersed the eerie band of fog.

Arianna took off after the man in black. "Hey! Hold up a minute."

"Yes?" Grasping the door handle of his vehicle, he spoke the word with a sigh.

"I need a ride."

She watched as his talented mouth twisted into a cynical smirk, but no response was forthcoming.

"Look, I'm sorry for attacking you, okay?"

His dark head slanted. "So, *you're* apologizing now?"

Ignore the sarcasm, Arianna. "I overreacted, and you have every right to be upset—"

"*Go raibh mile maith agat.*"

"What?"

"Thanks a million," he interpreted in a dry tone.

"Oh, yeah, well...Listen, I just got in from the airport, my cell phone doesn't work here, and I have no other way to get help." Her voice was pitching higher and higher, in direct relation to the building hysteria. With a calming breath, she willed it down several octaves. "Look, you can't just go and leave me here like this."

Oops. Wrong thing to say. She saw it right away in his unyielding expression, in the resolute set of his jaw. And in the tight smile hovering over those oh-so-kissable lips, without ever quite alighting. "Oh? Can I not?"

"Well...of course you *can*," she smoothly acquiesced. "But what gentleman would leave a lady stranded, cold and alone, on the side of the road in the middle of the night?"

"True, true," he murmured, his agreement surprising her as he took a step backward and cast a searching glance, first over one shoulder, then the other.

Arianna followed the motion in both directions. "What...what are you looking for?"

Green eyes settled on her blandly. "Why, the *lady* you're just after mentioning, o' course."

Hmmph. Funny man.

Without another word, he yanked his door open and vaulted behind the steering wheel. The door slammed with an ominous note of finality and the engine roared to life.

As if that weren't disheartening enough, the rain chose that moment to begin to fall again in a cold, steady drizzle.

The driver-side window lowered with a mechanical hum. "Go on now. *Ta se ag cuir baisteach.*" At Arianna's blank stare, the man translated impatiently. "It's raining! Go get in the car, for feck's sake! I'll ring the gardai on my mobile, let them know where to find you."

The discussion apparently over as far as he was concerned, he shifted into gear. But before the SUV's big wheels could make a single revolution, Arianna's hand shot through the open window. Abandoning pride, she clutched at the sleeve of his jacket, her hand so numb from the cold that she could barely feel the supple leather beneath her fingers. "Just get me to the next town," she pleaded. "I'll get a cab from there." He frowned, looked down at the steering wheel. "*Please*. You know how the cops are. I could end up waiting here for hours."

Arianna detested the note of desperation in her voice. More, that she had been reduced to begging. But the fact remained that never in her life had she ever been so utterly exhausted, felt so unspeakably alone. "Or so hellishly cold," she muttered under her breath, her teeth clacking like castanets, lips quivering with the violent shivers wracking her body.

When she felt him dragging his arm out from beneath her icy fingertips, her heart dropped to her knees. Clearly, he was determined to leave her here.

And she was just too damned tired and miserable to fight him on it anymore.

Her head dropped in resignation. About to turn away, she felt a finger slip beneath her chattering chin. With the gentle pressure of his thumb, the Irishman tipped her face up and silently searched her eyes. His touch, coupled with that provocative gaze, sent rivers of warmth rippling through her frozen body.

A sign you're lapsing into the final stages of hypothermia, she told herself grimly.

Now, what miracle of God triggered the man's sudden change of heart would have been anybody's guess. Maybe it was her violent shivering, or the utter hopelessness he had to have seen in her eyes. Whatever it was, Arianna knew she had won the battle of wills the moment his hand dropped into his lap. His head fell back defeatedly against the headrest.

He turned to look at her. "Best mind who you raise that knee of yours against in future," he threatened, with a menacing glare. "Now, go on, go on, get in."

Resurrected by the unexpected reprieve, Arianna bounded around the back of the SUV. Head dipping animatedly from side to side, she mimicked him under her breath. Still, she was careful to cut short the tirade before clambering into the passenger seat. She would bet a million bucks to a penny that he was just looking for an excuse to change his mind.

She slammed the door shut. He held his hand out to her, palm up. *The image of a young man on a moonlit beach, hand outstretched toward a castle window, morphed itself over his form.* Then the impression faded away, leaving her dazed and staring.

"Your keys," he said.

"Wh-what?"

"To the boot."

Confused, she frowned. "Boot?"

A controlled exhale of exasperation. "Is that not where you've stowed your bags?"

Oh, yeah. The trunk. Arianna searched the floorboard for her purse. "Wait a minute. I left my purse on the front seat of the car. Keys in the ignition."

Another impatient sigh escaped his lips. *Insufferable jerk!* "Hey, don't blame me for that. Not with you dragging me bodily out of the car. I wasn't thinking..."

Her words trailed off as he frowned a warning, and raised his index finger to tap a shushing motion against his lips.

That was just so...so... *Ohhh...* Arianna gritted her teeth. "Evidently you are unable to admit when you are wrong—"

Her protest slid to an unbelieving halt as he transferred the silencing finger from *his* lips to her own. *Of all the unmitigated gall!* Just that quick, she wanted to sink her teeth into the offending digit, but somehow managed to restrain herself. Just barely. Because, as wonderfully liberating as that would have been, it would have served only to get her *liberated* right back out into the icy rain.

Instead, she huffed and turned to stare out her window. But could the disagreeable oaf just let it drop there? *No, of course not.* He had to heave yet another all-too-audible sigh of annoyance as he pushed his door open.

That did it! "You know what? That's it! You just sit right there. I may be stuck for a ride, but I'm not crippled. And I sure as heck don't need a man to carry my bags." As she was reaching for the door handle, a strong hand shackled her other wrist. "What?"

With a surprised glance over her shoulder, she ran headfirst into a long, mesmerizing gaze. Her emotions spiked like an elevator gone madly out of control. Soaring first to the heights of euphoria, she dropped then, plummeting into an incapacitating lethargy.

"*Stop*." Freaky. His lips hadn't moved, and yet she had heard him clearly. In her head. Just like the experience with her father on the night he had died.

An insane thought lodged in her chest like a rock-hard chunk of ice. Had she been consorting with a ghost all of these years? Had her nocturnal romps in the night with this man been some kind of haunting?

But no. Hadn't she melted into his embrace tonight? Felt the warmth of his lips on hers, the strong beating of his heart? Who or what he was, she had no clue. She knew only that, right now, he was holding her immobile, restraining her with his eyes alone....

She could feel herself sinking, drowning in those fathomless depths, in eyes as deep and endless green as the Irish Sea itself. She felt drugged, her body weightless, afloat in a water world devoid of gravity. Somehow he was controlling her with his mind. And she knew, beyond a doubt, that she could not have moved at that moment...could not have disobeyed this man's telepathic command...

Not if her very life had depended on it.

As the peaceful floating sensation took her under, her breathing adjusting to the slow and steady rhythm of his heartbeat, a disquieting insight settled over her. That her ability to resist the enigmatical man beside her might one day prove to be truly a matter of life or death.

Chapter Five

Arianna must have lost time after that. Because when she became conscious of her surroundings again, they were making their way down the road. Staring blindly out the rain-spattered window as they plowed through the darkness, she might have been in a rocket hurtling through space, whisking her away to worlds unknown.

A peripheral study of the man beside her confirmed that he was unaware that she had awakened. A man lost in his own thoughts, he appeared relaxed, his demeanor unguarded. The unruly wisps of coal black hair framing his face served to soften his chiseled features. She felt an inexplicable sense of loss, comparable perhaps to what one must feel when a spouse suffers from amnesia. When the slate inscribed with all of the intimate, personal history of a couple's life is wiped clean, but only for one of them.

She was fascinated by the way he drove, his right hand draped casually over the steering wheel, knees parted in a masculine sprawl. A placid façade. He was like a sleek, black cougar lying tranquil in the midday sun. A beast, wild and dark and beautiful.

And very, very deadly.

Not wanting to be caught staring at him unawares, Arianna stretched and gave a sleepy yawn. "Sorry I conked out on you. Guess I was more tired than I realized."

The man flicked a startled glance in her direction, as if he had forgotten she was there. He grunted something unintelligible in response.

"I...um...my name's Arianna Sullivan, by the way."

"MacNamara," he said in a voice devoid of inflection. "Caleb MacNamara."

Apparently disinclined to further conversation, he went silent, his stony gaze fixed on the road ahead.

With an inward shrug, Arianna was turning back to the window when she heard the low rumble of his voice. "Excuse me?"

"I asked where you fancied being dropped off. You're an American here on holiday, I presume. Have you reservations at a hotel?"

"Actually, I'm Irish," she corrected pleasantly. "I was born here. In County Clare."

"But you sound—"

"American, I know. I was raised in the States. This is my first trip back since..." Her voice wavered and she swallowed, tried again. "I lost my da a few days ago. We moved to the States when I was small, after the death of my mother. I had no idea he'd kept our old home in Ennistymon until...." Realizing she was babbling, she stopped and reached into her purse, retrieving a scrap of paper from her day planner. She held it out to him. "Anyway, this is where I'll be staying. Do you know the area?"

Caleb took the proffered note. It was odd, the way the brush of his fingers against hers sent a comforting warmth through her body. After a quick glance at the paper, he drove the next mile or so in silence, his jaw visibly clenching and unclenching.

"I...uh, if it's out of your way..."

His head gave a dismissive shake. "It's barely a stone's throw from my own place."

"We're neighbors then."

"So we are. Arianna—"

"Caleb—" She gave an embarrassed titter. "I cut you off. You go first."

The bluish glow emanating from the dashboard fell softly over his cherished face. Arianna realized that, with him, she felt strangely safe, cared for.

Caleb's eyes met hers. An expectant glance. Arianna held her breath. Had he finally sensed the extraordinary connection between them?

"You were about to say?" he prompted.

"What?"

"When I interrupted you..."

"Oh." Disappointment flooded her heart. "I was only going to tell you again how sorry I am for attacking you. It's... I guess...being stranded alone in a strange place, in a storm like that, well, I kind of let my imagination get away from me."

A faint smile touched his eyes; the effect was devastating. "Thought I was *The Highwayman,* did you?"

Charmed by his reference to the early twentieth century poem set to music a few years ago, Arianna's expression turned sheepish. "The truth?"

"Mmm."

"Well, at first—and only for a second, mind you—I kind of went back and forth, trying to decide whether you were a...." She winced. "Well, a vampire. Or the Coshta-bower."

An incredulous look, then a slow chuckle rumbled from his chest. "You've quite an imagination there. And it seems a bit of knowledge about our auld Irish legends as well."

She grinned. "Well, I do know about the wee people who live in the faerie raths beneath the green hills."

Caleb's gaze slid to hers, probing. "Do you now? And what would you be knowing about them?"

"Well, legend has it that they were a race of mortal kings and heroes with magical powers, known as the Tuatha de Danann. The fifth group to settle Ireland, like 3500 years ago, they were defeated a few hundred years later. Rather than leave their homeland, they chose to embrace their supernatural natures, becoming the faery people dwelling today in another dimension of time and space beneath Ireland's crystal lakes and green fields."

Gold-sparked green eyes glittered in the darkness as Caleb leaned closer, as if to share a secret. But with his deep voice velvet-edged and steeped in the lilting accent of his heritage, he posed a question instead. "And in your own homecoming, Arianna O'Sullivan, will you be discovering that the faeries are real?"

Was he serious or only teasing? From the look on his face, she couldn't tell. But as an image of the will-o'-the-wisp she had seen earlier danced through her mind, she recalled her father's final words: *"Remember our Lord said He has other sheep not of our fold."*

"Faeries?" she replied thoughtfully. 'You know, I rather hope they are real."

Apparently caught off guard by her response, his unsettled gaze bored into her. She sensed an intrusion, a strange fluttering in her mind, and the perpetual mask he had been wearing seemed to slip from his face. In that instant Arianna caught a glimpse of something alien. There was something ageless, something timeless about him. Something that terrified her to her very core.

She shivered and Caleb adjusted the heater to high. Reaching into the back seat, he snagged a woolen tartan blanket and dropped it into her lap. "Your clothes are damp," he said, his tone gruff. "Best wrap yourself in this rug so you don't catch your death."

Rug. The same word her father had used when referring to a blanket made her heart ache. Snuggling under the warmth of the wool, Arianna smiled her thanks for his thoughtfulness. But there was no answering curve of lips from the man beside her. *How does he do that?* she wondered in frustration. How can anyone go from warm and pleasant, to cold and brooding, within the space of a single breath?

Lord, she couldn't even imagine trying to live with a mercurial man like that.

"Just what is it you're doing here, Arianna?" The question came out of the blue, abrupt, all business. More interrogation than conversation.

"Wh-what do you mean?"

"What brought you back to Ireland? Here, now? Where you know no one? Where you've no family, no friends? And so soon after laying your father to rest?" He fired the questions like ammo from an assault weapon.

Her lips tightened. "For your information, I *didn't* lay my father to rest," Arianna coldly explained. "I've brought him home. Brought his ashes back to scatter them from the Cliffs of Moher. To honor his...final wishes." She choked on the last two words and hated herself for the display of weakness.

"*Bollocks,*" Caleb muttered darkly under his breath. "Sorry, I—"

Arianna put up a weary hand. "Forget it. Look, just get me to a taxi—"

"I said I'd take you home, so that's what I'll be doing."

"Fine."

He plucked a CD from the visor in front of her, then slid it into the stereo. "Music?" he inquired politely.

Arianna lifted a sulky shoulder and stared pointedly out the window, her body language a clear talk-to-the-hand. Delirious with exhaustion, she let herself melt into the buttery leather cradling her as the haunting notes of an old Celtic melody floated from the speakers. She felt her body relax, her soul set adrift on a sea of tranquility.

Caleb began to sing along softly in Gaelic, his rich, full baritone a quiet harmony. The overwhelming rush of love she felt for this stranger had her despairing of her sanity. God help her, she was totally messed up. Confused. Conflicted. While her heart insisted that Caleb and her dream lover were one and the same man, her common sense was standing there, hands on hips, with an "Are you kidding me?"

And the chiding voice didn't stop there. It went on to point out that even if he were that one, life with a man like Caleb MacNamara would be a perpetual emotional roller coaster. The man was clearly an enigma, a dichotomy. A lover capable of taking a woman from freeze to burn—and back again—with a single glance.

With the soft Irish music dancing in the air around her, Arianna began to succumb to the long hours of travel, to the days with too much grief and too little sleep.

ﻌﻌ

In spinning dreams of a tawny sunset, a fork of lightning split a cloudless sky, as moonlit seas splashed the heavens with a tempest's fury. High above the crying wind, faeries strummed tinkling harps of gold, their songs of enchantment kept pace by the drumbeat of a distant thunder. At the command of the Fae Dark Prince, Arianna was swept up, up through the silvery mists, into a haze of diamond starlight. And clad only in silk and moonbeams, she danced with Caleb, her magic lover, high above the rainbow, beyond the stormy waters...

ﻌﻌ

"Just what were you playing at, anyway?" Caleb cursed himself roundly for giving in to the urge to taste the woman's plump, sweet lips. Left aching and inflamed, his appetite had only been whetted for more. "For something you can't have," he admonished himself sternly.

Why the devil had he engaged her in a test of wills to begin with? he questioned. There were, after all, other, far more expedient ways with which to have brought the situation under control.

At the corner, Caleb spotted a street sign swathed in darkness. No worries, though. With his intrinsic night vision, he could see that the name inscribed there matched the one scribbled on the crumpled paper in his hand. Downshifting into second, he prepared for a tight right onto the narrow country road. The abrupt downshift caused the fair-haired woman sleeping beside him to slump forward, her head hanging at an awkward angle.

Caleb's hand shot out and caught her chin to support her neck. Eyes closed, he visualized the lever on the other side of her seat, and concentrated. The seatback jerked once, twice, and then began smoothly to recline.

Settling her back comfortably against the headrest, Caleb could hear her whispering in her sleep. "Found you. Finally...found you." The words were disturbing, to say the least.

With a sleepy snuffle, she drew her right knee up onto the seat beside her, resulting in the blanket sliding off her lap to bunch at her feet on the floor. Caleb glanced at a creamy length of muscle-toned thigh exposed by her restless twisting and turning.

He drew in a breath. Blew it out. "Woman's driving me bloody demented," he muttered in frustration. Averting his gaze, he swept the blanket off the floorboards and covered her, his gallantry rewarded by the stirring of her light floral fragrance in the heated air. Bringing his wrist to his nose, he inhaled tentatively. *Brilliant.* Their invigorating tussle on the side of the road had left him all but saturated in her womanly scent.

Playing with fire, he was, and didn't he know it well. Just as he knew there was too much at stake for him to allow this to go any further. Still, he couldn't find it in himself to regret a single moment of tonight. In truth, he'd found it invigorating. To be sure, the little hellion intrigued him with her fascinating mixture of soft feminine curves and well-toned muscle. Of submission and aggression. Fire and ice, she was. And with a shocking mouth on her as well, he allowed with a smirk. He gave his head a shake. Considering her mouth brought certain other things to mind, things Caleb knew he'd best not to be dwelling on.

Oh, Arianna O'Sullivan had gotten under his skin alright. 'Twas the very reason he'd reckoned to leave her waiting at her car for the gardai. 'Twas the only way to escape this burning temptation, so it was. To avoid the siren call in those eyes of angel blue. He was a man, sure, and he'd have been pleased to oblige her—and himself.

If not for one minor detail: *Spill your seed inside the woman and she dies.*

Caleb turned his head and cast the subject of his musings a cold, measured stare. He inhaled again, testing himself. Purposely breathing her in. There it was again. *Wildflowers and musk.* The same seductive fragrance the little mortal had been wearing all those years....

That she'd haunted his nights.

Chapter Six

"Wake up, *cailín*. We're here."

Arianna curled into the warmth of the gentle hand resting on her shoulder. She stretched and muffled a tired groan. "Mmm... Sorry I keep falling asleep on you." Reaching beside the seat, she felt for the mechanism to return it to its upright position. Funny, she didn't remember lowering it.

"No worries," Caleb murmured, reaching for the key to turn off the ignition.

Through the windshield, Arianna caught her first glimpse of the two-story thatched roof cottage that had been her childhood home. The whitewashed exterior showed bright and crisp against the candy apple red of the door and trim. It resembled a fairytale dwelling in the chimerical glow of the headlights. "Well, I have to admit I'm pleasantly surprised."

"Surprised, why?"

"The condition of the place," she explained absently, finding it difficult to tear her eyes away. This was her family home, the place she had shared with her father—and the mother she had never known. "Da hired a property manager to maintain the house and land. But you know how that is. After all these years, I half-expected to find it rundown and abandoned."

Love, curiosity, awe, sadness, trepidation—a thousand different emotions raced through her like a rushing river because, no matter how well maintained the property, she could sense the myriad secrets lurking behind the darkened windows of the lonely abode. Arianna's fingers tangled in her lap, her resolve to stay here beginning to crumble like a cookie in a toddler's fist. What utter madness had possessed her to schedule this life-altering encounter with her past in the dead of night?

A ground-hugging fog rolled over the short-shorn grasses of the front yard before billowing against a wall of stones bordering the property. Low-hanging clouds crept below a waning moon. Here and there, light filtered through the trees, their leaf-bare branches painting eerie shadows on the pristine stucco walls. The unearthly glow silvered tightly interwoven shrubs embracing the long-vacant structure. The occasional breath of wind made a rustling sound as it scattered dead dried leaves across the rain-soaked ground.

"Perfect setting for a graveyard scene in a horror flick." Arianna shuddered.

Male fingers gently brushed her arm. "I'll leave you at a hotel in town tonight, will I? Sure, the old place here will seem a lot less daunting come morning."

Very tempting. In the full light of day, the quaint little cottage behind the hedgerows would undoubtedly be charming. But now, with the spooky haze enshrouding the grounds and the wind whistling through the branches of barren trees, the vacated old homestead looked just plain haunted.

And not, Arianna finished the thought sadly, *with Da's comforting presence either.*

"Arianna?"

Just deal with it, she ordered herself. Putting on a brave face, she turned to Caleb. "No, it'll be fine once I get the house opened up, the lights on."

"Right, so. Let me grab a torch so we can find our way inside."

Forcing her aching limbs to move, Arianna climbed out of the SUV. Making her way along the uneven flagstone path leading to the front door, she felt around in her wallet for the key that Da had given her. At the door, she slid the key into the lock and turned it.

It wouldn't budge.

She bit her lip and frowned. She had been so sure the key would fit the door of the house her father had bequeathed her.

Her hand trembled and knocked the key from the lock. It landed with a ping on the cement stoop at her feet. Caleb scooped it up and fitted it back into the lock. With a minimum of jiggling, the tumblers turned and he pushed the door open. "Lock was banjaxed from disuse is all."

"Thanks." Her feet glued to the raised front step, Arianna stared into the yawning black maw of a life she couldn't remember.

With a gentle squeeze to her upper arm, Caleb slipped around her. His flashlight sliced a path through the inky darkness of a small sitting room. The eclectic scatter of furnishings felt familiar somehow. There were several dark wood tables and bookshelves, a walnut Canterbury, and a sofa with anthemion-carved legs and fluted arms. Two tufted easy chairs sat in front of a gray stone fireplace occupying the far wall. Bud vases, small ornaments and sundry knick-knacks were scattered here and there, making the house a home.

Arianna stepped into the living room. She reached out with her sixth sense, trying to pick up on the remnants of any energy that might have been left behind by the former inhabitants. She was seeking a feeling of recognition, of homecoming, some sense of the young family who had once lived here.

Feeling detached, as if she were standing outside herself, she watched Caleb cross the room toward a mahogany drum table in the far corner. He reached beneath the six-sided shade of an owl lamp and a soft, amber glow trickled across the room.

Ariana found her gaze fixed upon that golden orb as it began to pulsate. Growing brighter and brighter, it became a shimmering wave of evanescent light, reaching and expanding, moving toward her, caressing and encompassing her unmoving form, until it had blotted out everything around her.

Caleb, the furniture, the musty family room...the entire scene in front of her first began to tremble, then dissolved before her eyes. Head spinning, Arianna covered her face with her hands to try to regain her equilibrium.

When she opened them again...

ം

The golden glow began to diminish, to twitch and flicker, fold in upon itself layer by layer, until all the light extinguished except for that emanating from the fireplace. A burning chunk of wood falling through the metal grate startled Arianna. As she watched the tiny orange sparks scatter like fairie dust she shook her head in confusion. When they had entered the room only seconds before, the hearth had been cold and blackened with soot.

The vision expanded and Arianna felt her heart wrench at the unexpected sight: it was her father stretched out on his belly on a Blue Qum rug in front of the fire. Another ghostly apparition? she wondered, taking a step toward him. She tried to call out to him, but discovered she couldn't make a sound.

A clanging of pots and pans drew her attention to the adjacent kitchen. The sound awakened her olfactory senses, the smell of soda bread and scones wafting in the air.

A sudden movement on the staircase caught her eye. A tow-headed little girl in a flowered dress climbed off the bottom stair and toddled toward the fireplace, her right arm in a stranglehold around the neck of a doll nearly as big as she was.

Her cherub face lit up as she squatted beside Da. "Get up, Daddy." Rosebud lips pursed in consternation at his lack of response. The doll tossed aside and forgotten, she scrambled onto Da's broad back. Straddling him, she leaned over one shoulder, and tried to pry one of his eyelids open and peek inside.

A slight smile lighted on Arianna's mouth. Her father used to play the same game with her when she was small, and she knew exactly what would happen next.

Her eyes fixed on her father, she watched his lips twitch, then he began to snore. Loud racking snorts startled the wee tyke so much that she sat down hard, plop on her backside. Brows wrinkled, lips pushed into a perplexed pout, the child heaved a long-suffering sigh, before quickly settling on a different tact.

Tiny arms around his neck, she placed her mouth to his ear. "Play, Da." When that too failed to elicit a response, she placed her hands on his forehead. Grunting, she tugged with all her might, trying to lever his head off his arms.

A ferocious roar bellowed from her father's mouth and, although Arianna had known it was coming, her heart lurched in unison with the child's delighted shriek. Oh, no! She'd woken up the tickle monster! In one smooth move, Da reached over his shoulder and tumbled the little one onto the hearthrug in front of him. With snarls and various animal

48

noises, he rubbed her ticklish belly with a whiskery chin, inciting a riot of breathless giggles and squeals for Mam.

The kitchen door swung open and Arianna's breath caught in her throat. Standing in the doorway, with an aura of golden light spilling all around her, was undoubtedly the most enchanting vision Arianna had ever seen in her life. The woman's slender hands coated with white flour, she used her dainty wrist to push pale strands of silvery blonde hair away from her face. A face stolen from the angels, Arianna mused, as she gazed into piercing blue eyes that were a mirror image of the child's...

Of Arianna's.

෧ ෨

Then, like sand through an hourglass, the scene dissolved before her, leaving Arianna staring dully at the kitchen door. Weird. It had been like stepping through a time warp, the vision awakening her first conscious memory of her mother.

She met Caleb's gaze. Standing in front of the cold, dark hearth, he was watching her, eyes dark with concern. "What's the story, Arianna? You look as if you've seen a ghost."

She swallowed a hysterical giggle. "Nope, no ghosts." *Not this time.* "It's just the memories...memories I never knew I had. You know, I was so young when I left."

"Ah...."

"Yeah. Everything is exactly the way it was when we left...almost twenty-five years ago."

"We'll go then, will we?" Caleb suggested again. "'Twill seem a lot less off-putting in full daylight."

"No, I'm okay now." A skeptical brow shot up. "Really, I am. I'm fine. Would you do me a favor though, and get my luggage? I'd like to walk through the house."

After he had left the room, Arianna peeked through a door on the wall beneath the staircase. Discovering a tiny half-bath, she made quick use of the facility. Her tour of the house revealed that the downstairs comprised only two rooms: the living room and an eat-in kitchen with a gas-burning stove and a compact refrigerator. Checking the pantry, she found the shelves stocked with various food staples, as the property manager had promised.

Crammed into a tiny alcove behind a set of white folding doors was a small washer. Washer *and* dryer? The label on the front panel said the one machine did both. Missing were a dishwasher, a microwave—and half a fridge.

Caleb banged back through the front door and set the suitcases down on the knotty pine floor with a quiet thump. As Arianna headed toward the living room, she saw he was on his cell phone. As she was stepping back to give him some privacy, she overheard part of his conversation.

Reality struck like a punch to the gut.

"I was after finding her earlier tonight," he was saying, his voice in a low, guarded tone. "She's a wild one, so she is. Bloody-minded and high-spirited as hell." He stopped to listen. "Sure, we'll be having to trank her, at least in the beginning." Again, he paused. "I'll not be turning her over to you straight away, mate. After the challenge she presented tonight, I'll fancy gentling this one myself."

Steeling herself against the doorjamb, Arianna swore softly. "Girl, you are so screwed."

There was only one explanation for what she had heard. The man was a white-slave trader, a peddler of human flesh. A nocturnal predator scouring the highways and byways for hapless women to sell as sex slaves. A niggling question wriggled its way to the surface. Why had he been grilling her for personal information? Showing more than a casual interest in whether anyone here was expecting her tonight? The implication—that if no one was, there was no one to report her missing—had her stomach doing back-flips.

The offhanded remark about the highwayman made so much sense now. The low, throaty chuckle that had followed it took on new and sinister undertones.

Unaware of her presence, Caleb stood facing the fireplace, studying the family photographs set in antique frames along the mantle. Every now and then, he grunted something non-committal into the phone.

Before Arianna could map out an escape route, he was saying goodbye and turning toward her. "There you are, so." *Said the spider to the fly.*

He started toward her, all loose-limbed and predatory male. His hands lowered to his belt. *Reaching for his zipper?* Relief washed over her as he proceeded to slip his android into his front pocket. Her eyes lingered, fixed in morbid fascination on the telltale bulge, on the threat against her encased in black denim. Two full seconds passed before she registered the focal point of her gaze. Good God, she was *gawking* at the front of the man's jeans! Knowing he would have misinterpreted the stare as a blatant come-on, she prayed he hadn't noticed.

Face flaming like a niacin flush, she jerked her gaze back to his. *Busted.* She knew it by the flare of his nostrils. By the size of his pupils, so dilated she could barely see the exotic green of his eyes. The look he was giving her was overtly sexual. *Uncivilized.* The look of a jungle cat stalking its mate.

Against her will, she could feel herself responding to his heat, her heart regulating itself to beat in time with his. Her body was melting, softening, as if she were running on instinct, hearkening to the call of the wild.

"Are you needing something else from me tonight, *cailín*?" He posed the question, voice low and seductive.

She swallowed. "No, I'm... um..." Okay, so she had to have misunderstood his conversation. After all, if he were a violent rapist, he wouldn't be bothered with seduction, now would he? He would have already made his move. And besides, hadn't Da always warned her about her tendency to jump to conclusions?

Forcing a false lightness into her tone, she changed the subject. "I...I was just coming to ask if you'd like something to drink."

"First things first," he replied. "If you'll lead the way to your bedroom, I'll...."

Arianna made a strangled sound. "My-my bedroom?"

Caleb cut her a strange look. "Is that not where you'd have me carry your bags?"

"Oh... *Oh*. Yes, of course. Thanks. Bedrooms have to be upstairs, so go on up. And while you're doing that, I'll pop into the kitchen and make you a cup of tea. I'd offer you coffee, but Mr. Kavanagh...do you know Mr. Kavanagh from the estate agents office...? Well, he stocked some supplies in for me, but forgot a coffee maker. There's a box of little cakes, though...Java or Jaffa or something like that. They don't have them in the States, but they look quite nice so I'll— "

"You don't—"

"—put a few on a plate for us. If you really want coffee, I did find a jar of instant in the cupboard, which is disgusting, I know...."

Her nervous chatter trailed off as she noted Caleb looking at her as if she had grown a second head. "Tea would be grand." He gestured toward the pile of luggage. "I'll just take those on up now, will I?"

At her nod, he slung the strap of her carry-on over his right shoulder and grabbed the handles of the large and medium rolling suitcases, one in each hand.

Back in the kitchen, Arianna ran tap water into an electric kettle and pressed the red switch on the side. As it rumbled, she poked around in the pantry, coming out laden with a bag of sugar, a box of Barry's tea and two packages of cookies, Jaffa and McVities.

Dumping everything on a forest green-and-oak pedestal table in front of a large bay window, she stopped. Now that she had gotten past the strange vision that had greeted her on arrival, she was thinking more clearly. Although a bit of a pompous ass at times, the man carrying her luggage upstairs was in no way an evil man. Still, she thought, chewing on her lip, she should get to the bottom of what she had heard and put it to rest once and for all.

Prepared for a confrontation, she headed back to the living room to find Caleb hunkered down in front of the fireplace, piling the grate with what looked like molded chunks of rich, black earth. Peat, she realized, identifying the stuff the Irish had been hacking from bogs for centuries to use for heating fuel.

She watched him for a minute. Focused on his task, he did look innocent enough. Well, maybe *innocent* wasn't the right word exactly. No, with the flex of those corded biceps, the ripple of sinew in his muscular thighs as he stretched and moved, the guy looked anything but innocent.

"Still, forewarned is forearmed," she muttered, as she sidled around to the left of the hearth and armed herself with a fire poker from the stand. Just in case.

Caleb gave her a casual glance. "Central heat is on a timer. I warrant it won't be kicking in again 'til morning."

"We need to talk," Arianna said simply.

"About?" He went on laying kindling between the uneven bricks of peat.

"I overheard what you were saying on your cell phone."

He glanced up unconcernedly. "And?"

"And?' Is that all you have to say for yourself?"

Caleb frowned, gave his head a shake as if to clear it. Pensive for a moment, he seemed to replay the conversation in his mind, then his eyes glinted with amusement.

A fiery red haze descended over Arianna, clouding her vision. "What? You think it's funny?"

Basically blowing her off, the irksome Irishman shook his head in derision and turned back to his task. Finished, he stood to his feet and brushed his hands together. Then he stretched his right hand toward the hearth and snapped his fingers.

A blue plume of fire shot instantly up the flu.

Arianna squeaked. "What the...?"

No, she told herself sternly. He did *not* have Pyrokinetic powers. There had to be a logical—a *sane*—explanation. Like...he had to have been holding a match in his hand. Yeah, that was it. A match. And the snapping sound she had heard...well, that had been the flick of his thumbnail against the sulfurous head. Of course, that didn't explain the way the flames had exploded up the chimney, as if drenched with kerosene. "The peat," she mumbled. *Stuff must just be extraordinarily combustible.*

At the sound of her muttering, Caleb glanced at her over his shoulder. His green eyes were doing that otherworldly glittering thing that sent chills skating up the back of her neck. He gave a nod at the poker in her hands. "Give it over."

She lifted a defiant chin.

His mouth quirked as he grabbed a pair of tongs, using those instead to stoke the fire.

With an exaggerated insouciance that had Arianna ready to brain him, he brushed his hands together, then clasped them loosely behind his back. For the next couple of minutes, he stared into the smoky flames, the hiss of burning peat the only sound disturbing the silence.

Firelight limned his profile in shadow. Tall and perfectly proportioned, with that longish black hair curling wickedly over his collar, he made the perfect picture of a dark wizard. A master oracle painted in shades of black.

Who *are* you? Arianna mused. *What* is he? an intuitive voice echoed inside her. As if he had plucked the thought right out of her mind, Caleb's head swiveled on his shoulders. His inscrutable gaze held hers as he slipped off his jacket, and tossed it over the cabriolet chair in front of the hearth.

Then he was moving toward her.

Nerves taut as a bowstring, Arianna shrank from his approach. A sardonic glint touched his eyes as he sauntered past her. At the sofa he sat, long legs stretched out in front of him, one booted foot crossed casually over the other.

Arianna scowled. "What are you doing?"

"C'mere to me, *cailín*." He patted the seat cushion beside him. "Might as well be comfortable whilst we sort this out."

Arianna narrowed her eyes, pushed her lips into a pout. And remained exactly where she was.

Caleb gave a neglectful shrug. "Have it your way, luv. Though I must say it's a bold brat you are, eavesdropping on a personal conversation that kind o' way."

Arianna's mouth fell open. "Eavesdropping?"

"Mmm."

"I-I..." she sputtered. "I wasn't eavesdropping, I just... Oh, you're so...so...grrr!"

He gave his head a reproachful shake. "My, but it's a contentious wee thing, you are."

Her eyes flashed. "Contemptuous," she shot back.

"Contempt-*ible*," came the thin-lipped return. "And now, if we've done with these childish word games, perhaps you'd like clarification about what you *overheard*."

Arianna shifted the poker to her shoulder, baseball bat style. "I'm all ears."

She could have sworn she heard him mutter, "All mouth, more

like," as he leaned forward and rested his forearms on his knees. "Now, when you heard me speak of a tranquilizer—"

"I can't believe you're admitting—" she began to whisper in horror.

"Only a light dose," he assured her. "So there'll be no injuries. It's a violent mating, so it is, what with all the biting and screaming, sweating and straining."

As Caleb's gaze remained level on hers, Arianna could feel herself blanch.

"But then, isn't that the nature of the four-legged beast?" he finished.

Her mind went blank. "Four—"

"'Twas my stud manager you heard me speaking with. About an unbroken young mare I was after purchasing earlier this evening." He stopped, let that sink in. "For feck's sake, woman, I was speaking of a bloody *horse. Not* yourself."

"A-a horse?"

"Damned if there's not a bleedin' echo in the room." This comment followed by an annoying eye-roll and a pointed sigh.

Arianna ignored the display of ill temper. If he was telling the truth, the man had every right to be feeling pissy. Granted, she was no expert on horse breeding, but she had listened to Michaela talk enough about the process to recognize some of the terminology. And as she let the dialogue play again through her mind with this new slant it all fit.

Shamefaced, she scratched her nose and cast a sidelong glance at Caleb. If his expression was anything to go by, the guy was definitely *not* having happy thoughts.

Then suddenly he was unfolding himself off the sofa and moving determinedly in her direction. She sucked in a breath and started to take a step backward, but the blazing fire behind her left no path of retreat.

As he drew nearer, she picked up again on that slightly musky, feral scent she'd noticed on him earlier. "Horses, you idiot," she muttered.

"*Cad é sin?*" He stopped a foot or more away from her. Not nearly in her personal space, although it felt like he was towering over her. "What did you say?"

"Nothing." Her response was glum. "Just talking to myself." *At least I haven't started answering myself back yet.*

She forced herself to meet those unsettling eyes. Dead cold now. And diamond hard.

Caleb held his hand out. "Give it to me."

Arianna stared at him. "What...?"

His furious gaze turned scornful. Reaching out, he pried the poker from her senseless fingers and tossed the "weapon" back into the stand. Strung tighter than an Irish fiddle, she jumped at the loud clang of iron striking iron.

"Now, as to your assertion that I was planning to have my wicked way with you—"

Arianna's expression was sheepish. "Okay, so I was off the wall about—"

His hands skimmed from elbows to shoulders, then settled on her upper arms. Holding her lightly in place, he bent his head. His breath against her cheek stirred memories of midnight fantasies in a shadow world of salt-scented breezes and silvery moonlight. "I've a confession to make," he whispered into her ear.

"So find a priest," she breathed.

"When I kissed you tonight, I wanted you more than I've ever wanted any woman in my life." His words both shocked and seduced. Daring to meet his gaze, she watched as something hot and dark, something tortured, rolled through those crystal windows.

Abruptly ending the intimate exchange, Caleb released her and stepped away. She felt instantly cold, bereft. He swept his jacket off the back of the armchair. "I'd best be going now. Before this leads to something we'll both regret."

He was leaving. *For good.* Arianna could see it in his eyes. The thought of never seeing him again hit her with a feeling of loss not unlike the grief of her father's death. "Before you go, I have to say something."

Caleb turned to her, lips tight, a forbidding expression on his face, as if he were expecting another wild accusation.

"You don't understand...there's more to...." She drew in a deep breath. How could she explain something like this without sounding crazy? She couldn't. "I'm sorry. You went out of your way to help me tonight, and all I did was heap on the abuse. Guess the proverbial straw was accusing you of being a sexual predator."

"Indeed," he said. "Not to mention a vampire and a dark faerie."

"Yeah." She let out a defeated breath, caught her bottom lip between her teeth. "I'm really sorry about that."

Arianna saw him taking stock of her appearance, shivering like a puppy rescued from an icy lake at dawn. Probably looked like one too, she thought, combing her fingers through her straggly hair without effect.

"Look at the soggy wet state of you," he said in a gruff voice. A glance at the hearth revealed that the fire had almost burned out. Stretching out his arm, a flick of his wrist brought about a loud *whoosh*, and a brilliant plume of red and orange flame shot skyward. As the blinding flare dissipated, the fire again burned hungrily, snapping and crackling as it consumed the remaining turf.

Caleb turned his head slowly, deliberately, meeting Arianna's startled stare with the full force of his entrancing gaze. The look conveyed a heady sense of carnality, sprinkled with a hint of some dark, mystical power. She knew he was daring her to say something about what she had just seen him do. *Oh, boy. You are in soooo much trouble, girlfriend.*

Legs weak, she sank into the chair in front of the fireplace and motioned her head toward the flames. "Thanks." *I think.*

With a curt nod, he pulled on his jacket. His hand reached into the side pocket. "Your house key," he said, dropping it lightly onto the coffee table in front of the sofa.

The light tread of his boots marked his exit as he crossed the lightly polished floor. But in the foyer, he paused for a moment, then turned and retraced his steps.

Pulling his wallet from his back pocket, he slid out a business card. "My mobile number, should you need anything," he announced without preamble. She reached for it, and traced her thumb idly over his name embossed on the card. "You know not another living soul here in Ireland, Arianna. It's not safe. I still can't fathom why you've come all alone—"

"Caleb?"

He stopped speaking.

"Look, I get why you'd be ticked off at me, okay? But I want you to know that weirding out on somebody like that...well, it's just not like me." Arianna knew it was now or never. She closed her eyes and took a blind leap of faith. "There's something else going on here that I don't understand. From the moment I first saw you tonight I've been feeling like I've always known you...like there's some...some fortuitous connection between us."

Her explanation drifted off as her eyes searched his for understanding, for some hint of recognition. But he only stared back at her, his face inscrutable, entirely devoid of expression.

Disappointment welled up inside her, a malignant mass settling in her chest. "Anyway, I just wanted to say I'm sorry. I know you would never do anything to hurt me."

Caleb was silent and still as death, the flexing of jaw muscles the only sign that he found her words unsettling. But at her honest vow of trust, a pained look slid over his features. He reached out...started to stroke her hair, but then pulled his hand back as if he feared being burned.

Or burning her, perhaps.

"Don't," he ordered finally, his voice cracked and grim. "Don't rely on that, Arianna. No, *cailín,* you need to be afraid of me. Be very, *very* afraid."

And with those cryptic words hanging in the air between them, he turned and left her. The sound of the front door closing behind him rang like a death knell in Arianna's heart.

Chapter Seven

Arianna awoke the next morning to a typical Irish winter day: Rainy, cold and dismal. Every muscle in her body ached and her head felt stuffed with cotton from jetlag. Punching her pillow into shape, she turned over and pulled the goose down duvet up over her ice-cold nose. Vignettes of the night before played through her head as she lay listening to the rat-a-tat-tat of the rain against the windows. Suddenly she remembered her promise to check in with Tara and Michaela the minute she got here. A promise she had forgotten what with all the craziness going on.

Tossing back the bedclothes, she glanced at her travel clock. Still set on American time, it read five a.m. Swinging her feet onto the sumptuous piles of a Persian rug, Arianna grabbed her white terry bathrobe and rushed out the door. She hurried down to the kitchen where she had spotted an old rotary phone hanging on the wall the night before.

She picked up the receiver and checked for a dial tone, then placed her call before stretching the long cord across the kitchen table and sitting down. One ring, two. As the phone trilled for the third time, there was a loud clatter on the other end of the line.

"*Damn it...Hello?*" *Tara.*

"Well, 'damn it, hello' to you, too," Arianna said dryly.

"Arianna, thank God. We've been worried sick. I tried your cell at least a dozen times last night, but I couldn't get through."

"I know, but I forgot to set up roaming before I left."

"What?" Tara called out. "Yeah, it's her."

The extension picked up and Michaela's sleepy voice came on the line. "Hey, you. What's up?"

"Sorry for getting you guys up so early, but I woke up and realized I hadn't called and knew you'd be worried. I hit a bad storm last night, and the rental car broke down on the way here."

"That's why I told you to take a red-eye," Tara nagged. "Arrive in the morning."

"I know, I know. But a guy stopped and gave me a ride here.."

Tara swore. "You climbed into a car with some strange man? Good grief, Arianna."

"Ah, give it a break, Tara," Michaela chimed in. "Our girl's a *black* belt. Remember?"

"Yeah, so am I," Tara shot back. "But a gun trumps a karate chop."

"Who said anything about a gun?" *Michaela.*

"Guys, guys, it's okay. Turned out he was a neighbor," Arianna explained.

"Hmmm, so the plot thickens," Michaela said. "Must have been cute, since you were so busy entertaining him you forgot to call your two best friends."

Tara sighed. "Arianna, please tell me you didn't invite the guy into your house."

"Okay. I didn't invite the guy into my house," Arianna replied by rote.

"Ha, ha. Very funny." *Tara.*

Michaela snorted. "Okay, so spill. Age, height, weight, body mass index, if you please. And not necessarily in that order."

"Mid thirties, about six-three, black hair." Pregnant pause. "BMI? Really, Michaela?"

"Wait a minute. That sounds a lot like your fantasy lover. You know, Dream Dude." Silence. "Arianna?"

More silence.

"Arianna, you don't really think...." Tara sounded properly horrified.

"No, of course not." Her protest was feeble, though why had she felt the need to lie to her friends anyway? Was it because verbalizing such a thing made it seem even more real? Or more insane. Not that any of it mattered now. Because if something as bizarre as an existential bond had existed between them, Caleb would have recognized her as well.

Maybe Tara was right. She really did need to see a psychiatrist....

While Michaela made disappointed noises at Arianna's response, Tara remained ominously silent. She wasn't buying her denial for a single second.

"Just think about it," Michaela went on dreamily. "Being rescued in the dead of night, in the midst of a raging tempest, by a tall, dark and handsome stranger. A mysterious Irishman, who just happens to resemble your magic man."

Magic... The word provoked a disturbing flash of memory. *Caleb's dark head in an autocratic tilt, capricious green eyes blazing. A snap of his fingers. Then an explosion of fire.*

Arianna gave her head a quick shake. Clearly, she had been *way* too tired last night. Mistaking what she was hearing. And seeing things that weren't there.

"How utterly romantic," Michaela went on.

"Utterly stupid," Tara spat. "Good Lord, girl, the man could have been a serial killer...a rapist." *A white slave trader?* "When I think what could have happened—"

"Mmm, me, too," Michaela snickered. "You know what your problem is, T? You have no spirit of adventure, no *joie de vivre.*"

"No spirit...." Tara sputtered. "I'm an archaeologist, for God's sake."

"Oh, yeah. A regular Indiana Jones."

"Okay, children, please." Arianna laughed as she got up from the table.

Resigned to choking down a cup of instant coffee to stave off a caffeine withdrawal headache, she stretched the phone cord over to the sink and filled the electric teakettle. "I'd better go, get that car reported to the rental agency. I'll be heading into town later to buy a local cell phone, but I'll give you the landline number for now." Reciting the digits etched onto a yellow sticky note stuck to the telephone, she hung up.

After a quick sip of instant coffee, she grimaced and dumped the rest down the drain. She made a quick call to the car rental company, then checked in with the property manager, Mr. Kavanagh. When she mentioned her transportation woes, he kindly offered her the loan of his second car until she could rent something else.

She adjusted the temperature on the thermostat Caleb had pointed out on the wall in the living room, then headed upstairs for a steamy shower in an old claw-foot tub with one of those circular shower curtains. Pulling on a favorite pair of old faded jeans and a white Nike T-shirt that had seen better days, she donned a fleece-lined sweatshirt and hiking socks. Finally, she was warm.

Standing in the middle of her parents' bedroom, she took stock of the furnishings with the practiced eye of an antique dealer. Neither the room's design, nor the quality of the furniture came as a surprise. Although young when he had lived here, Da was an architect and the room reflected his personality: doors and trim made of some ornate dark hardwood, offset by lightly textured walls the color of aged ivory. The walls he had splashed with a colorful array of paintings, prints, and old lithographs.

Arianna's lips thinned as she took in the painting hanging over a burr-walnut chest of drawers opposite the bed. The oil rendering of a sleek, black stallion nuzzling its mate would be a daily reminder of the complete fool she had made of herself the night before.

Unaccustomed to being idle, she got stuck into unpacking to wile away the time until Mr. Kavanagh would arrive with the loaner car. With a dress draped over one arm, she opened a door to the wardrobe. And froze. After more than a quarter century, what had to have been her mother's clothes were still hanging there. As if the woman had run to the store for a loaf of bread and never returned.

Majorly creeped out by the discovery, Arianna shut the doors with a firm push. "No way am I dealing with this kind of emotional baggage right now," she muttered, tossing the dress across a chair in front of the fireplace.

Her attention drawn to a 17th century cedar chest residing at the foot of the bed, she dropped to her knees and raised the lid. The hinges creaked in protest as the musky scent of cedar began to mingle with the earthy redolence of burning peat lingering in the air.

She discovered a Japanese black lacquered box, about eighteen inches in diameter, and opened the pagoda-shaped lid. Inside was a tiny dress made of pearly white satin, its hem, sleeves, and neckline trimmed in snowy lace. Buried within its folds was a child's white leather Bible whose cover depicted a smiling Jesus surrounded by laughing children.

She riffled the pages and a photo tumbled out. Her beloved father, a young man, with his arm draped around a woman's—her mother's— shoulders, while an infant wearing the baptismal gown nuzzled at her breast.

After a few moments in silent deliberation, as if she might will the picture to reveal the secrets of her childhood, Arianna slid it reverently back within the Bible's fragile pages. As she was closing the Book, an inscription inside the front cover caught her eye. She recognized the slightly neater version of her father's familiar scrawl.

To: Arianna Binne O'Sullivan,
Beloved daughter, child of our hearts,
May your life be a shimmering light in the ever-pressing darkness;
Your tiny spirit a bridge across the divisive chasm
That has for far too long separated love…from the ways of magic.
Our love always,
Mother and Da

A knock on the front door dragged Arianna abruptly back to the present. Too early for the property manager, she couldn't help but hope it was Caleb coming to check on her. She tried to hide her disappointment as she greeted an older man, his thick eyebrows, mustache, and hair all the color of rust.

"Ms. Sullivan? Miles Kavanagh," he greeted her pleasantly. "Finished with my appointments early, so thought I'd call over and collect you now, if that suits."

"That's wonderful. And call me Arianna, please. I can't tell you how much I appreciate all your kindness, stocking in supplies and loaning me the car. You've really done a wonderful job keeping the old place up."

"I regret we're meeting under such sad circumstances," he replied.

"Me, too. Would you like to come in for a few minutes? Have a cup of coffee or tea?"

"Sorry, but I've to get back to the office straight away. Would you be ready to go now, or shall I come back to collect you later?"

"Oh, no. I'm ready now. Just let me grab my things." Scooping her purse off the coffee table, she grabbed a gray hoodie off the back of the sofa.

In the driveway, they both headed to the same side of a silver Corolla. "Thought I'd drive us back to town," Mr. Kavanagh offered. "Show you the shortest route."

"To be honest, I thought I was going to the passenger side." Arianna grinned. "I forgot you guys drive from the *wrong* side of the car over here."

The man chuckled.

Not five minutes later, they were driving through the sleepy little market town of Ennistymon where ageless, weather-beaten buildings lined both sides of the street in a chorus of sizes, styles and colors. They pulled into a parking lot behind a red brick office building.

"I was wondering if I could get directions to the Cliffs of Moher," Arianna said.

Mr. Kavanagh pushed his seat back and balanced his briefcase between his slight paunch and the steering wheel. Raising the lid, he plucked a booklet from one of the side pockets. "Brought you a Clare tourist guide," he said, offering it to her. "There's a map and historic details inside. Thought it might help you get better acquainted with the area."

"That's perfect, thanks. Oh, and one other thing.... I'm trying to locate my mother's midwife. Her name was on my birth certificate. It was...um—"

"Táillte O'Clery?" he finished for her. "Sure, most everyone in Clare knows yer wan. Must be in her seventies by now." Reaching for his cell phone, he began to type. "I've her details right here."

"Just give me her phone number. I'll call and set up an appointment to see her."

Mr. Kavanagh made a hissing dismissive sound. "Here in Ireland appointments are meant for trips to the dental surgery and other such unpleasantness as that, not for visiting a friend. Anyways, I haven't her number." Scribbling an address on a notepad he had in the case, he made a rough sketch of a map and shoved the paper at Arianna. "Her place is along the same route you'll be taking to the cliffs. Call over on the way, if you've a mind. Sure, she'll consider it a blessin' seeing one of her wee sprogs all grown up like."

He paused when handing her the car keys. "The brakes are after squealing a bit, so I've made an appointment to have them checked. So, if you could drop the car off to the garage tomorrow, across the street from McColgan's Pub—"

"No problem."

Leaving the car outside his office, Arianna hiked down the sloping incline leading to the village center. She turned right at an eighteenth century church at the corner and picked her way along the cracked and uneven sidewalk. A loud rumbling noise sounded from behind her and she spun around to see what it was. The sight of an old farm tractor lumbering up the middle of Main Street brought a smile. "Now there's something you don't see in Beddeford."

Her father's child, Arianna was fascinated by the hodge-podge of architectural styles in the village's old buildings. Constructed from a wide range of materials, from bald medieval stone to eighteenth century red brick, the structures edged the narrow sidewalk. Windows were small and dark; lintels hung low over doors painted in primary colors, leaving Arianna with the distinct impression of having stepped into the pages of a history book.

Popping in and out of the little shops, she purchased food and supplies and picked up a pay-as-you-go smart phone. It was already after two o'clock by the time she got back to the car. As she flipped through the tourist guide looking for a map to the Cliffs of Moher, the scrap of paper with the midwife's address fluttered out. Arianna regretted that she didn't have the woman's phone number. She really would have liked to see her on the way to the coast.

Oh well, in these beat-up old jeans and T-shirt, she wasn't exactly dressed for visiting anyone's home.

Chapter Eight

When in Rome....

A few minutes later Arianna was knocking on the royal blue door of a modern, two-story townhouse on a quiet side street. A black lab meandering up the sidewalk lifted his leg on a bush, then took a detour to sniff at her heels. She gave his head a scratch and he ambled off again. There was no sound or activity from inside the house and the windows were dark.

"Another reason people should *call* first," she grumbled under her breath. As she was turning to leave, however, the door began to creak slowly open. An elderly woman looked out, blinking owl-like in the afternoon sun. Silver hair fashioned in an upswept chignon, she wore a dress in a bright, floral print. On her feet were sensible beige tie-up shoes.

"Dia duit." Her smile was inquisitive. Her voice warbled slightly with age. *"Tá brón orm—"* At her visitor's perplexed expression, the woman switched to lilting English. "Em...Sorry to keep you waiting, pet, but I was having a bit of a lie-in."

"Oh, jeez, I'm sorry to have disturbed you." Arianna took a step back, shifted from foot to foot. "I didn't have your number, or I'd have called first. I'll come back another time."

Straggly gray brows raised over faded blue eyes. "And you are, child?"

"Oh...um...my name's Arianna Sullivan. I don't know if you remember—"

"Your parents. I do, o'course." Creases in the aged face deepened as her eyes sparked with pleased recognition. "Well, fancy this. Me own little Arianna, and yerself all grown up." Clucking, she reached for Arianna's hand and tugged her through the door. "C'mere to me now. Let me have a look at you." The woman held Arianna's hands away from her body. "So lovely you are. The very picture of yer Mam."

Pleasantly taken aback by the warm reception, Arianna found herself being pulled unabashedly into the frail arms of the woman smelling sweetly of lavender, freshly baked cookies. *And home.*

One bony hand encircled Arianna's wrist and, with a vigor that decried the need for the *shillelagh,* the bent wooden cane in her hand, Mrs. O'Clery began to tow Arianna along behind her. "I was about to prepare me tea, so you'll be joining me now."

"Thanks, but I'm really not very hungry."

Pooh-poohing her protests, the woman continued shuffling down a long corridor, passing an elegantly furnished sitting room on the left, a formal dining room with heavy baroque pieces on the right. In the cozy kitchen, the fruited wallpaper and ruffled yellow curtains with lacy tiebacks gave the room a strangely familiar feel.

"To be honest, I've no appetite today meself. So what d'ya reckon we just have something sweet." She motioned Arianna to a whitewashed pine table. "And whilst we do, you'll tell me how you've been keepin'."

Tying a flowery apron around her thickening waist, she bustled over to a cabinet left of the sink. Stretching to reach the second shelf, she took down two sets of bone china cups and saucers edged in silver and sprinkled with tiny blue flowers. She flipped a switch on an electric kettle, then began loading a matching serving plate with a delectable selection of tarts, cookies and cakes. After the kettle whistled, she filled a ceramic teapot with boiling water, then arranged everything on a dainty silver tray.

Arianna got to her feet. "Here, Mrs. O'Clery. Let me help you with that."

"Now, don't you be 'Mrs. O'Cleryin' me," the old woman scolded good-naturedly as Arianna carried the tray to the table. "It's Granny to you, pet, just as 'twas back then. And didn't I earn the title, too, what with mindin' you and changin' yer wee nappies more times than I can remember."

She settled across from Arianna. "Yer da and yerself have been gone donkey's years, yet it seems only yesterday." As she filled their cups with steaming tea, she nodded at the serving plate. "Try the Irish pear cake. Made it meself just this mornin'."

Arianna obediently helped herself to a slice and took a small bite. "Mmm, this is delicious. I can't believe you still do all your own baking."

"And why not?" Blue eyes twinkled with mischief. "'Tis auld I am, luveen, not dead."

Arianna anticipated a litany of health complaints, but the elderly woman abruptly changed the subject. "Now tell me, how's things with yer da?"

Just like that, it was back. The marauding grief, which had retreated beneath the warm glow of homecoming, returned now with a vengeance. "He...he passed away. Last week."

For a moment, Mrs. O'Clery appeared stunned, and then the kindly face crumpled. "Ah, God love 'im," she murmured, crossing herself. Her blue-veined hand trembled as it covered Arianna's, patting gently. "Now, now. Tell Granny all about it so."

The grandmotherly woman listened as Arianna spoke quietly of her father, of their lives together, and of his untimely passing. Afterwards, she plied her one-time charge with offerings of sugary comfort food, a thing she had no doubt done countless times in the past.

"Mrs....Granny? Can you tell me about my family? About the way we were together, I mean. Da could never bring himself to talk about...my mother. Or our lives here in Ireland."

The gray brows wrinkled in consternation. "Yer da told you nothin' then." A statement, not a question. Leaning back in her chair, the woman rubbed the bridge of her nose introspectively. Several seconds passed before she sighed and leaned forward again. "As I'm the only one left who knows.... Well, it's best if I be startin' from the beginning. You see, yer da was after growin' up in a home for boys in Milltown Malbay, not far from here."

"Daddy was orphaned?" *Or abandoned?*

"That I couldn't tell you, pet. Though the home might have some record of your grandparents in the archives. Volunteered there on a regular basis back then, so I did. As it happened, I was there the day social welfare brought your da in. And the moment I capped eyes on the wee fella, sure wasn't I after losing me heart to him." Her gaze turned inward, a reflection on years gone by. "Tried to adopt him meself, I did, but weren't the courts after turning me down flat. As I was caring for two children alone already, me with no husband—"

Arianna's brows shot up.

Granny interpreted the look and cackled. "Ach, 'twas nothing as illicit as all that, luveen. And in those days an out-of-wedlock child would have been a scandal sure." Mrs. O'Clery freshened her cup of tea and refilled Arianna's. "No, meself and Mr. O'Clery—*Ar dheis Dé go raibh a anam*...God rest the dear man—were married over a year before the Good Lord blessed us with our precious Aoife. After ten years passed without any more bundles from heaven, we adopted our boy Conor, when the lad was just shy of two years old. Only a short while later, wasn't the consumption after stealing me darlin' man away."

"I'm so sorry." Arianna spoke quietly. "And you never remarried."

"Now, isn't there but one true love appointed for each of us in a lifetime, child. And wasn't I the lucky one to've found me own." After what had to have been close to half a century, the old woman's eyes brimmed with tears. Blinking rapidly, she leaned closer and lowered her voice conspiratorially. "Now, didn't I find a way around all that adoption craic though. First by havin' yer da over for visits at the weekend. Then for spendin' holidays and such, 'til by the end of it he was here more than there. After coming of age, he lived with me for a while before going off to college."

Trying for a smile, Arianna could only conjure up a sad twist of lips. "So you were the only family he ever knew."

"A few minutes after comin' through that front door," she said, giving a nod toward the hallway. "And wouldn't it be gone, that fierce sadness in his eyes." She wagged her head, sympathy deepening the lines on her face. "'Tis a sin against the Almighty's what it is, for a young lad ever to be feelin' so abandoned. So all alone."

"Do you know how...where he met my mother?"

"I do, o'course. 'Twas over across down below at Bailey, after he'd taken himself off to Dublin to study art and design. I'm a Dub originally meself, though I've lived here in the west now for nigh on sixty years." She pushed her plate aside. Untouched.

Arianna felt guilty that the shock of her news had stolen what little appetite the poor woman had. But Granny went on with the story as if nothing were amiss.

"After finishing his schoolin', didn't he bring yer mam back home to Clare. Already wedded and bedded, so they were." Mrs. O'Clery smiled into her tea. "Never again did I see that empty look in his eyes. Leastwise, not until—"

Arianna interrupted. "And then they had me."

"They did, and weren't you the joy of their lives so." The aged eyes glazed over again as she reached back into time. "There was I, attending yer mam. And there's Himself holding her hand and crooning silly love songs to make her laugh when the pains got bad. Finally 'twas downstairs I sent the lad to boil water—just to get him out from underfoot."

With a reminiscent smile, she went on. "Not only did I help bring you into this world, but wasn't it yer auld granny here, the one mindin' you when yer parents slipped off to the local of a Saturday night." The smile melted off her face like butter off hot toast. "And whilst yer da was working...after yer mother was gone. Hard on him 'twas, 'specially the wicked rumors. One of the reasons he was after taking you away, I reckon. So you'd not be hearing the gossip." She stopped, her eyes squinting as if she were trying to make a decision. "Now he's gone, I'm thinking you've a need to know the truth of it."

There was that word again, the one Da had spoken at her bedside the night he died. "The truth?"

"About yer mam...and what happened on that last day. May Day, 'twas. There was *ceol agus craic*...em, music and fun. The women cooking and the men collecting fuels for the bonfire all the week before."

Setting her plate aside, Arianna crossed her arms on the tabletop and focused on Granny's face.

"'Twas right before sunset your family arrived. Yer da sat singin' and strummin' his fiddle, yer mam stretched out on a blanket beside him. But didn't I see something in her face that day...'twas like the soft flesh had turned to stone. Broodin' and lookin' lost, she sat, those gorgeous blue eyes of hers starin' endlessly out to sea."

Granny coughed into her napkin, took a sip of tea and continued. "Later on yer da went to chasin' you, barefoot and laughing, up and down the water's edge. Figured on gettin' you all knackered out, I reckon, so's he could have a bit of alone time with yer mam. Finally, he brought you to my blanket, where you curled up beside me and drifted off to sleep."

Granny hesitated, strain evident on her face. She drew in a ragged breath, as if forcing herself to go on. "'Twas then I saw yer Mam walking into the water. Having no doubt what she was about, I gave a shout to yer da, he, himself, the only one with hope of stoppin' her."

"No," Arianna whispered, sensing what was coming.

"He went running after her, the poor divil, divin' into the surf and gulpin' seawater, beggin' her not to do it, to come back to him." Granny's mouth set in a grim line. "Plain desperate's what it was, but hadn't yer mam her mind made up already. Before he could get to her, she was gone. Disappeared beneath the waves."

Arianna covered her mouth with both hands. "Oh, my God, she drowned herself," she whispered brokenly. "All these years...."

Her father's deep dark secret had been his wife's...Arianna's own mother's...suicide.

The truth.... That her mother had abandoned her in the worst possible way, by choosing death over a life with her husband and little girl.

Suddenly, a sucking, strangled sound grated from across the table. Arianna's startled glance in Granny's direction found her hunched over, one hand clutching the table's edge, the other plucking at her bodice. Her skin was mottled gray, as if lightly powdered with coal dust. She stared at Arianna, eyes wide with disbelief, stark with pain and fear.

"Granny? Granny!" Arianna pushed away from the table so violently her chair overturned and clattered to the floor. *God, no! Not when I've only just found her again.* "Granny, hang on now," she said aloud, then whispered, "Please, don't leave me."

❦

"Don't leave me!" Her father's words echoed from the past, waking her where she lay curled on a blanket on the sand. It was dusk. The acrid smell of smoke tickled her nostrils. She could hear the crash of waves, feel the cool sea breeze tousling her curls.

Granny gathered the tiny child protectively into her arms. Confused by the sudden tension in the air, she strained to see her da. Her eyes finally found him, slumped to his knees in the shallow water, dripping wet, surrounded by onlookers. His shoulders convulsing, heart-wrenching sobs ripped from his chest. Tears streaming down his face mingled with rivulets of seawater.

Tears that Arianna had never learned to shed....

❦

As if trapped in a lucid dream, she ordered herself to back out of the vision...a rift in the fabric of time. Granny needed her now. Her distress had been an emotional dam bursting inside of Arianna. Floodgates overflowed, drowning Arianna in memories of the past. And all the love she had once felt for this precious woman.

"It's gonna be okay, sweetie." Arianna murmured nonsensical words as she eased the slight, slumped figure down onto the clean, tiled floor. Pulling her jacket off the back of her chair, Arianna bunched it into a lumpy pillow beneath the precious silver head.

Trying to recall the finer points of a Red Cross first aid course she had taken a couple of summers earlier at the Y, she knelt at Granny's side and unfastened the first few buttons of her smock. She stretched across the semi-conscious woman and caught hold of the cord of the telephone on the wall. Giving it several short, hard tugs, she managed to dislodge the receiver from its cradle.

Hands shaking, she punched "911" into the keypad. And swore silently when the call failed to connect. "Dammit!" she muttered under her breath. *What's the emergency number for Ireland?* Quickly disconnecting, she dialed Operator.

A European double-ring and a woman answered. "Operator. May I help you?"

"Please, I need an ambulance." The controlled calm in Arianna's voice was a façade, strictly for Granny's benefit. "Hurry, please."

Okay, they'll want an address. Her eyes were scouring the room for a piece of mail...*anything*...when she remembered the slip of paper that had gotten her here. *Now, what did I do with the thing? Oh, yeah. Jeans back pocket.*

"Emergency services."

After a quick explanation of the circumstances, Arianna read the address off the crumpled paper she smoothed obsessively. Tucking the paper back into her pocket, she stroked Granny's pale brow while answering the dispatcher's questions. "Yes, but her respiration's labored.... Conscious, yes, but her color is ashen, a terrible shade of gray—bluish gray.... Her—her lips and nail beds, too. And she's in a lot of pain—Oh, for God's sake! Just get an ambulance over here," she finally snapped. "The woman's having a heart attack, and you're playing twenty questions."

After hanging up, she leaned over and kissed Granny's cold and clammy forehead. "Rest now, sweetheart. Help's on the way. Do you want me to call anyone for you? Your son or daughter?"

A rasp escaped lips the color of blue marble. "Conor. And me grandson, Caleb." *Caleb?* "Me bag."

"Okay, shhh now, I'll take care of it." Fingers trailing absently up and down the thin, age-spotted arm, Arianna searched the room for a purse. "Everything's going to be fine."

Spotting a leather patchwork handbag on the counter beside a bowl of fruit, she got up and found a small, blue address book in a zippered pocket inside.

She called the number listed for Conor, and a woman answered. "McColgan's."

"Hello, this is...um...may I speak to Conor O'Clery, please?"

Silence. And then, "Conor's not in at the moment." Her tone was stiff, proprietary. "He's expected back shortly. Who will I tell him phoned?"

"This is.... Just tell him his mother's taken ill at home. An ambulance should be here any minute." *Please, God!* "He can try calling here when he gets back, but—"

"I'll have him ring the hospital straight away," the girl interrupted and hung up.

Arianna stared in puzzlement at the receiver, while reaching up to massage her throbbing left temple with her other hand. Sparing Granny a worried glance, Arianna noted that she was lying deathly still, eyes closed, purple lips pinched with pain. Stretching the phone cord over her reclining form, Arianna knelt again beside her.

She dialed the number for Caleb. Surname: MacNamara. *Small world*. Whispering, "Pick up, pick up," she bit back a groan when the call went automatically into voice mail. She waited impatiently as the deep, all-too-familiar voice recited a perfunctory message. "Caleb, this is Arianna — um, from last night. I...uh...there's been an emergency. It's Mrs.—uh...your grandmother. An ambulance is already on the way here, so I guess you should go straight to the hospital." Her photographic memory coming in handy, she recited her new cell number and hung up.

On the off chance that Conor or Caleb might drop by here before checking their voice mail, Arianna dug a pen and notepad out of the purse in her lap. Scribbling a message, she added her address and phone number, and left the note propped conspicuously in the center of the table.

As she gently chafed Granny's chilled hand between her own, a longcase clock in the sitting room chimed the hour of three. The sound faded into the soulful wail of a siren. *Thank God*. Strange, how she had always dreaded that sound, because it meant someone was in trouble. Today, however, it conveyed something else entirely: That help was on the way.

Chapter Nine

*H*is *grandmother.* That explained everything, Arianna decided as she thumbed through a magazine in the emergency room at Ennis General. With a sigh, she tossed the out-of-date publication onto a plastic table molded to the chair on her left. Resting her head against the puke green wall behind her, she realized she was shell-shocked. Understandable, given the way the missing pieces of her life had come flying back together like an explosion in reverse.

Still reeling from the midwife's disclosure, Arianna took the time to consider her childhood superhero, Caleb. Her magical mystery man.

Yeah, right. This whole thing would almost be funny if it wasn't so darned pathetic. Tara had nailed it when she suggested Arianna seek counseling to resolve the emotional issues surrounding her dreams. The whole thing was rather anticlimactic really. The discovery that her nocturnal lover hadn't been planted in the garden of her dreams through some mystical connection after all. It was clear now that the seed germinating his appearance in her psyche had been grounded in reality. Planted in her mind in early childhood, when she had spent time with him at his grandmother's townhouse.

It was a seed then watered and fertilized by the imagination of a grieving child.

She glanced at her watch. "Where is Caleb, anyway?" Hopefully Conor was here, at least. Idiotic hospital policy forbade anyone but immediate family from going back to be with Granny. And no one should have to die alone. *Not like Da had done.*

Before that mournful notion could lead her further down the road to despair, she heard the sound of a deep, resonant voice with a sexy Irish accent. *Caleb.* He was standing at the reception desk, his expression tight and grim. Shoulders bunched, he was conversing animatedly with a slight, balding man sporting wire-rimmed spectacles, who was stubbornly shaking his head.

"Casualty's chockablock right now," he was saying, "so we're allowing only one family member back with each patient. As her son's with her now...." All at once, the man's eyes seemed to glaze over, become vacant. "Of course, sir," he said politely. "No worries. You can go on back to see her now."

As if Caleb had sensed Arianna's steady regard, his head pivoted on his shoulders. A dark, enigmatic gaze locked onto hers. His green eyes glittered with the remnant of something that trailed shivers over her flesh. Consciously resisting the urge to scrub at her arms, she dropped her eyes and experienced an actual physical release as she broke the unearthly connection.

All testosterone and raw masculinity, Caleb stalked toward her in a pair of worn blue jeans that creased strategically with every step. *Damn.*

"How did you know...to ring me?" he asked, looking down at her.

Arianna stood. "Granny was lucid after it happened. Asked me to call you and Conor."

His brows raised. "Granny?"

"She said it was what I used to call her when I was small." She gave her head a quick shake. "Not important right now. Is there any news? I followed the ambulance over in my car, but they wouldn't let me go into the examining room because I'm not family."

The double-doors leading back to the treatment rooms swung open, and an attractive man, mid-to-late forties, came walking through. He nodded at Caleb, his gaze sliding over to Arianna and back again, then he disappeared through a door marked *Admissions*.

"My uncle, Conor. Mother's brother," Caleb explained, then his brows furrowed. "You look drained. You should go on home. Nothing more you can do here. I'll give you a shout when there's word."

"I'm staying until I know she's out of danger."

His eyes widened at her fervency, then, with a *'have it your way'* shrug, he was gone.

The round, black clock on the wall ticked away the interminable minutes. *Fifteen*. She went to the restroom. Two doors, one marked *MNA,* one marked *FIR*. Thankful for the silhouettes etched on the doors, she picked *MNA*.

Thirty-five minutes. A trip to the Coke machine for a bottle of water.

Back in the waiting room, she checked in again with the desk. The nurse picked up the telephone, dialed and spoke with someone. "The crisis has passed and the patient's stable," she informed Arianna. "But she's being admitting to HDU due to her age."

"HDU?"

"High Dependency Unit," the nurse explained. "For patients who don't require ICU, but need more support than an ordinary hospital ward."

"And visiting?"

"Restricted to families only at this time."

Arianna's cell phone rang and she excused herself. "Hello."

"Caleb here. Just wanted you to know Granny's suffered a minor heart attack."

"That's what I thought. And the prognosis?"

"Very good."

Arianna suddenly felt as wrung out as a wet dishrag. "Thank God."

"And thank *you*," Caleb said softly, his tone low and intense. "Had you not been there when it happened, not responded so quickly...."

Right. And, if not for the strain of being forced to relive my mother's death....

"I remembered how much I loved her," Arianna murmured, more to herself than to Caleb. When he began to question the remark, she cut him off. "I'm sorry, but I have to go. I need to go for a run. I've got the mother of all migraines trying to kick in and physical activity always seems to head them off."

Not to mention that the fresh sea air would help rid her of the sickening medicinal odor coating her lungs and clinging like a film to her hair and clothes.

The silence on the other end of the line stretched on for so long she thought she had offended him—*again*. Or maybe they had been disconnected. "Caleb?"

"Feel better, luv," he murmured finally. Strange. The words had no sooner left his lips than the headache lifted. "Caleb, what—?"

The line disconnected before she could finish posing a ridiculous question. *Probably just as well.*

Less than half an hour later Arianna passed through the gates of the Cliffs of Moher visitors centre. Her shoulders hunched inside her fleece-lined jacket, her eyes were watering from the raw nose-numbing bite of the November wind. Since it was officially off-season, a string of gift shops built into the hillside to her right were closed and boarded up.

With the breathtaking view of the ocean in front of her, Arianna mounted the concrete steps to the right. Perched on a windswept headland at the top of the steps was a nineteenth century round tower. Now locked up and abandoned, according to the tourist guide, OBrien's Tower had recently served as a souvenir shop, where a two-euro coin granted visitors passage up a rusted winding staircase to a lookout point on the roof.

A stone barrier lined the seven-hundred-foot cliffs that plunged to the thundering North Atlantic below. Arianna stared out at the horizon. Sky and sea came together in a majestic panorama of deep and aching blue. Seagulls screeched and swooped, gliding on the wind currents, while an oystercatcher skimmed the briny deep in search of a late day snack.

"It's beautiful, Da," Arianna whispered into the damp sea air, as if in a prayer. "I understand now why you would have wanted your ashes scattered here."

From her unique vantagepoint, she could see clearly the coast below. Spotting no beach area suitable for jogging, she tore herself away from the mesmerizing view and headed back to the car. She would drive further up the coastal road toward Liscannor until she found somewhere to run.

As if the route was mapped out in her head, she turned right at a sign pointing the way to Hags Head. Bumping along through a rock quarry, she found the place she was looking for: a golden apron of incandescent sand embraced by towering bluffs.

After parking, she picked her way down a pebbly, bracken-covered path. Already, she could feel the sea's primordial magic at work, purging the tension coiled tightly in her neck and shoulders. White-capped waves beckoned her to the ocean side with graceful hands. The ebb and flow of the breaking tide beguiled her, promised a catharsis for her restless soul.

Had her mother experienced a similar allure on this lonely stretch of sand? Was this the place a young woman with everything to live for had waded into the sea? Where she had drowned herself while her husband played a fiddle, her child lay sleeping on a blanket in the sand?

All at once, a mournful wailing arose from the sea. A haunted moaning, it sounded like a woman mourning an inconsolable loss. The sound made Arianna's heart gallop, left her weak in the knees. Being visited by the spirit of her loving father was one thing, she thought. But by the ghost of her suicidal mother? *No, thank you very much.*

There was a sudden movement in the water about a hundred feet offshore, where a small herd of seals were sunning themselves on a large boulder. As she looked on, one of the seals opened its mouth and let out that same howling sound.

"Okay, enough with the doom and gloom already," Arianna scolded herself. She scrubbed at her arms, telling herself that the chill in her bones was solely the result of the plunge in temperature from the approach of dusk.

Desperate for a run, she sank into a series of stretches and deep-knee bends, pushing her recalcitrant muscles into a punishing warm-up. She took off in a sprint, the pounding of her feet against the hard-packed sand muffled by the wind in her ears. The gusts pushed her along with the impression of flying.

Only about five-thirty and already the sun was going down, Arianna thought. The fiery disk plunged into the ocean, splashing the horizon with transcendental hues of copper and vermilion. At the first ambivalent glimmer of the moon, she decided it was time to turn around. Slowing her pace, she turned in a long wide arc, heading back in the direction she had come from. Endorphins pumping, she was beginning to feel like her old self again. Strong, healthy. Complete.

With a *whoop*, she shoved two clenched fists in the air and spun around in a happy dance in celebration of her oneness with this moonstruck land of her birth.

Head thrown back, she caught sight of something high up on the cliffs. A mirage, she thought at first, a trick of the failing light pitted against the encroaching darkness. An illusion created by the shifting shadows of dusk as the last rays of the dying sun reflected off the incoming mists.

Pushing sweaty, tangled strands of hair out of eyes, Arianna blinked several times. But the medieval castle sprawled along the verge of the craggy cliffs remained steadfastly in place. "Wow," she murmured, grinning. "How incredibly cool is that?"

Towers and crenellated walls rose from a jagged jut of rock like an artist's rendition in a child's faerie tale. Almost mythical in its grandeur, the imposing stone fortress was guarded by the sea at its back, its perimeter secured by battlements built into an outer bawn.

Castles had always fascinated her. Not surprising, she supposed, given the content of her dreams. Tragic, she thought, that time and political unrest had left so many in ruins. Captivated by the parapets intact after so many centuries, she felt a deep sense of satisfaction that this one appeared to have remained in its original state.

"Probably a five-star hotel," she muttered cynically, saddened by the possibility of the commercialization of yet another vital piece of Irish history.

Heated from her run, she took off her jacket and looped the arms around her waist. Surveying the property, she spotted a fifth-storey window facing the edge of the sandstone escarpment. "*The* fifth-storey window," she added, knowing the thought was irrational.

Because there was no way she could know the precise dimensions of the room behind that darkened window. No way she could picture the height of its vaulted ceiling, the texture of its silk-lined walls. She couldn't describe how the room was furnished, the heavy mahogany pieces standing stoically on plush Turkish rugs.

Neither was there any way on earth she could have sketched, from memory, the Celtic knot pattern of the draperies overhanging the mile-wide platform bed facing that outer wall.

Arianna rolled her shoulders. The sense of déjà vu she dismissed as a knee-jerk reaction to seeing her first Irish castle. Undoubtedly, she would have experienced the same rush of recognition at any of the hundreds of such heritage sites strewn across this ancient land.

"But I wouldn't have seen *you*." She directed her remark to the distant form of a man, a dark silhouette etched in the gloaming. *Caleb.* He was leaning forward, arms crossed over his knee, foot lodged against a stone abutment. Lord of all he surveyed.

It occurred to her then that he was...what? Three...four hundred feet above her? Too far from her to be able to discern his features. And yet, she would have known him anywhere.

Just as he had recognized her.

His gaze potent, caressing it seemed, he was studying her. His hand raised and she expected a friendly wave, but the trajectory of his finger continued upward. He was pointing something out to her in the sky. Suddenly a sonic boom reverberated off the cliffs and peaks that closed the area off from the east.

Arianna sniffed the air. *Ozone....* As she identified the subtle odor, an electrical charge spiked the tiny hairs on her arms and legs like millions of ants scattering all over her body.

Her gaze flew back to Caleb and she stared in horrified fascination. On the very tip of his upraised finger, a bolt of sizzling blue fire danced *en pointe,* a macabre ballet that forged his body into a human lightning rod.

Knuckles crammed against her lips, Arianna strangled on a scream and staggered backwards. Their eyes locked, his electrified and sparking a galvanized green, as he flung his hand downward in what she assumed to be an attempt to dislodge the fireball.

"Jesus...*God*!" she cried out as the rolling, hissing mass of electricity came hurtling directly at her. Scrambling backward, she landed on her butt in the sand, a deafening, high-pitched whistle ringing in her ears. Arms thrown over her head, she rolled into a tight, tiny ball only seconds before an ungodly explosion shook the ground.

The air smelled like the wet ashes of a campfire coupled with the mild scent of gasoline. Locked in a fetal position, she lay trembling for hours, for days it seemed, before gathering the courage to open her eyes. She stared in disbelief at the smoking, blackened point of impact...

Only inches from where she had been standing.

"You're okay, you're okay," she assured herself breathlessly. "You weren't struck."

But Caleb *had* been. The thought hit with a brutal impact, followed by a debilitating sense of grief as she rolled to her knees. If he was still alive, and *please, please, God he is*, time was of the essence. If she didn't get to him right away, get CPR started, he didn't stand a chance. Arianna tried to get up, but her knees buckled and she collapsed to the ground.

Trying again, more slowly this time, she managed to get to her feet.

"It's so cold." She shivered as the night curled itself around her, the icy sea winds penetrating clothes still damp from her tumble onto the wet sand.

Fear held her heart in a tight fist as she searched for a way to scale the treacherous rock-faced wall. Or maybe there was another way. If the castle were a commercial establishment, she might be able to alert a hotel guest to the emergency on the grounds above.

And that was when she saw him. *The luckiest man on earth.* Not only had Caleb miraculously survived a direct lightning strike but, from the look of him, he had managed the feat with no injuries of any kind. Right now, he was leaning casually against a section of the castle's outer wall, his fingers tucked into the front pockets of his jeans.

How could any mortal human being have lived through that direct hit and, more, been left standing? *The operative word here being mortal,* an insidious voice challenged inside her. *Stop and think. What did you* really *see? Had Caleb been struck by the lightning at all?*

Chewed on her lip, Arianna focused on the image burned ineradicably into her retinas. Like a tattling child, her optic nerve kept whispering to her frontal lobe that the lightning bolt hadn't come zigzagging through the atmosphere at all. Rather, it had leaped onto the tip of his finger as if commanded to dance an Irish jig.

The same finger he had then pointed peremptorily in her direction.

And not, as she had first thought, to dislodge the deadly thunderbolt. No, she was almost certain now that he had hurled it at her intentionally.

Arianna shivered as she recalled her impression of him at that moment. Despotic. Formidable. Cold and unfeeling. An alien entity endowed with authority over the elements.

"And that you would even consider such a thing is proof that you need to have your head examined," she muttered aloud. What was up with her, anyway? Within the past couple of days, she had imagined the man to be...let's see...a vampire, a fallen angel, a demon, a ghost, and the embodiment of some fabled creature from the annals of Irish folklore.

So, what is he today? she asked herself sarcastically. *An archangel? Or maybe the devil himself? Oh, but no. Chucking lightning bolts from the sky that way, he had to be a descendent of Jove. A freaking Greek god.*

That was ridiculous, of course. There had to be a logical explanation. The rogue bolt was probably the product of a hair-trigger storm churning many miles offshore. Caleb was simply a fortunate man—very fortunate indeed—to have escaped unharmed.

Glancing up to gauge the immediacy of a torrential downpour, Arianna found the moon shining brightly. A sweep of stars glittered the night sky like polished diamonds in a jeweler's case. But just then, almost as an afterthought, a thunderclap cannoned across the heavens with a roar so deafening Arianna ducked and covered her ears. Heart pounding, her knees turned to rubber; she searched the mist-enshrouded cliffs for Caleb.

But he was gone. He had left her alone to stand against the magic and the madness.

A haunting melody of drums and pipes road on the wind and waves. Then the breath of a whisper, a man's voice. *"Run...."*

Cold, gray fingers of fog clawed through the waves, stretching, reaching for her, as abject fear spurred her into flight. Over reef and rock and moon-colored sand she raced through the deepening twilight, leaping over shallow dunes and sandy inlets. Her throat ached, lungs burned. The thick, cloying mists dragged at her pumping legs like thick mud. It was like being trapped in a nightmare, running in place with a monster in pursuit.

Her skin crawled, the hairs on the back of her neck stood up as she sensed that monster stalking her. Malevolent eyes staring down at her from a scattering of boulders lining the ledge about a hundred feet overhead. The night enfolded her in a velvet shroud of impenetrable darkness, as endlessly black as time before the creation of man.

Again, she heard the hypnotic rise and fall of a man's seductive voice urging her on. In minutes that seemed like hours, she was finally scrabbling her way back up the shingled path to where she had parked the car. As she went to unlock the door, the key slid through her nerveless fingers. "No! No!" she spit out as she swiped them off the ground and jammed them into the lock. The adrenaline rush muted the pain of a fingernail torn to the quick.

Flinging the door open, she threw herself behind the steering wheel. She slammed the door and hit the automatic locks. Stomping on the clutch, she ground the key in the ignition until it screamed in protest, then scraped into reverse. Her heart skipped a beat as the car shuddered once and died.

"Okay, okay. Do it again," she said breathlessly. "Careful." The engine turned over and she shifted into reverse. She punched the accelerator and the car shot backward at breakneck speed. Slamming into first gear, she spun out onto the narrow ribbon of highway, tires fishtailing and spitting a stream of sand and gravel in her wake.

Chapter Ten

Seamus O'Donnell's penthouse apartment looked out over Galway Bay. But as Caleb stood staring out the floor-to-ceiling window in his best friend's apartment, the dismal weather obliterated much of the magnificent view.

"What a bollocks I'm after making of things." Caleb groaned and turned to glare at Seamus as if he were somehow to blame. "What was I thinking? Tossing lightning bolts about as if I were some kind of bloody Greek god. And the fire," he muttered darkly. "Not once, but *twice*, mind you, I was after lighting the hearth at her house *our* kind o' way." He scrubbed his face with one hand. "You know yourself, this madness must have some connection to the lucid dreams I was after telling you about."

Caleb checked his wristwatch. Ten-forty. Turning, he stalked past the sofa where Seamus lay sprawled, and fell into a recliner adjacent to the crackling fire.

"I dreamt of her again last night." Caleb had awakened at dawn, a layer of sweat coating his body. "I should be visiting one of my lady friends tonight, instead of yourself." He pushed back in the recliner and slung his forearm over his eyes.

"Sorry, mate, but I can't help you there," Seamus commented in a dry tone. He got up and padded across the carpet-strewn hardwood floor, his movements graceful for a man his size. Almost six and a half feet of solid muscle, he had inherited his height and body mass from marauding Viking ancestors. Not their fair coloring, though. His hair was a red-tinged black, so dark the color seemed not to reflect any light at all.

Retrieving a bottle from a rosewood cabinet on the far wall, he splashed amber liquid into two glasses and shoved one at his friend.

"*Uisce Beatha,*" he said. Water of life.

Caleb tossed back the Irish whiskey and mentally traced its slow, fiery burn all the way to his belly. There it spread into a warm glow, alcohol's one and only effect on his kind.

"Thirty-eight years old," he grumbled. "And no woman's ever been able to wind me up the way this one's done. Can't help but believe it's something to do with the *Geis.* So I'll lose control and take her like a bloody madman. Or perform some other magical mischief revealing our existence."

Seamus shook his head in disagreement. "We've been mates since we were lads. Take it from me, you're far too tight-arsed to be worrying about losing your monumental self-control."

Caleb pushed the recliner back again, and lay staring at the rafters as if he might find the answers he sought written there. "It's driving me fecking demented. Every time I come close to exorcising the bleeding woman from my mind, the Fates bring us together again." Frustration weighed heavily in his voice. "After dropping her off at home that first night, I planned to stay away from her. But then that old connection between herself and my grandmother pops up. I could scarce believe it when I heard her message on my voicemail about Granny taking ill." His tone lost its sharp edge. "When I got to the hospital, she was there, a fair-haired sprite in a ragged shirt and faded jeans."

"Sounds like you fancy the girl, mate."

Caleb's only response to the remark was a thinning of his lips. "I was bloody gutted by Granny almost dying, o' course, so I slipped away to my secret place to sort things out." His tone quiet, introspective, he sighed. "Damned if she wasn't there as well, like a sea nymph dancing in the arms of the wind. Nearly had me questioning whether my musings hadn't conjured the woman up."

"'Twas then you sensed the evil?"

With a huff of self-derision, Caleb pushed out of the recliner. He strode back to the rain-streaked window and braced an arm on the frame. "I was so...*entranced,* I reckon is the word for it, that I wasn't after sensing the bloody bastard 'til he was nearly dead upon her."

"Then you did what you had to, to get her out of there."

"Liked to have given the wee thing a heart attack in the process—"

"But you got her away from there...away from the danger. You know, there may well be another explanation for the dreamin'." Seamus hedged, as if mindful of the foul state of his friend's temper. "Some of us meet...virtually grow up with our *anam cara* in the Imaginal—"

"My soul mate? Are you daft?" Turning from the window, Caleb gave his friend an incredulous stare. "You're joking me, right? The girl's a mere mortal, for feck's sake? Are you forgetting that sex is forbidden? And even if mating between our races wasn't lethal, our sexuality's far too violent for the likes of her kind. We're like beasts in the field, man. Raw, primitive. Sure, I'd ravage the little mortal, eat her alive."

"And are you, my friend, forgetting that before the *geis*-imposed prohibition against sexual contact between our races, intermarriage was rampant?" Seamus smiled. "Their women quite enjoy being 'eaten alive'."

"And you know this how? Firsthand experience, is it?" Caleb's mood was dark, this discussion of impossibilities making it blacker by the minute. "I still believe 'tis the *Geis* somehow responsible for stirring all this up. And wouldn't it explain what transpired earlier this evening as well?"

"You mean *The Knowledge*."

Caleb gave a thoughtful nod. "'Twas that which alerted me to the sinister presence lying in wait for the girl."

The Sense of Innate Knowledge enabled Caleb's people, the Túatha de Danann, to witness events in the past, the present and the future, not as a vision, but in a physical state.

The past revealed itself clearly, for it was cemented in time and unchangeable. The present unveiled other locations through a fine golden mist, which dissolved into clarity as it folded into the past. Whilst the future, its nature capricious owing to the fickle will of man, presented itself darkly, a flickering image perceived through a densely matted fog of gray.

But the presence of evil cloaked the infinite timeline in an impermeable shroud of darkness to conceal its face. Just as it had done at the seaside earlier this evening.

His responsibility as Chief Brehon weighing heavily on his shoulders, Caleb scooped up his jacket and headed for the door. "Call the next meeting a wee bit earlier," he instructed Seamus, who acted as the Council's scribe. "Say three weeks, Tuesday. I'll ask the girl to dinner, bring her by your restaurant Saturday night. Tell the lads we'll be at the pub afterward. Best if they get a sense of her prior to the meeting."

Seamus gave a brief nod. "Good plan."

His hand on the doorknob, Caleb turned to look at his friend. "Though I can't say for certain she's the Chosen One, Seamus, there is a thing I *do* know. The winds of evil are beginning to blow, my friend. And sure, it's the little mortal they're pursing their lips at."

The storm raged throughout the evening. Torrents of rain, driven horizontally by the wind, battered the cottage walls. Virtually brain-dead from the day's harrowing events, Arianna dragged herself up the stairs, planning to make an early night of it. The central heat had come on automatically—for like about a minute. Not nearly long enough to combat the cold, damp chill seeping through the stucco walls. Shivering, she donned her nightclothes and finally managed to get a puny fire going in the hearth. Nothing like the three-alarm blaze Caleb had conjured, but, hey, she was only human after all.

Arianna walked over to the window and reached up to draw the curtains. A flash of lightning chased away the black of night and, in that fleeting instant, revealed a man in a hooded jacket on the wooded lot across the street. At the sight of the man hunched against the storm, she relived the fear of being pursued on the coast earlier that evening. Had the stalker somehow followed her home?

A firm yank on the drapes overlapped the panels by a yard. She clearly remembered locking the doors, but a compulsive need to check them again sent her flying down the stairs.

Back in her room, she doused the lights and sneaked a peek out a corner of the curtains. Another flutter of lightning revealed nothing but trees. Of course, the man could still be out there, hiding in the woods. Or sneaking around outside the cottage, trying to find a way in....

"Stop it!" she ordered herself. The doors and windows were locked. And in the unlikely event of a break-in, she was well able to defend herself—against *most* people.

Arianna climbed into the cold bed and curled up as tight as a rosebud, which began slowly to unfurl as her body heat warmed the crisp Irish linen sheets. The ebb and flow of the tempest outside her window proved that the events of earlier had simply been the precursor of a storm front moving in. She wasn't a meteorologist, after all, so what did she know?

"That no human being can control the elements," she asserted aloud, snuggling into the now cozy bedclothes.

Because no man—no matter how darkly enigmatic, how seductively charismatic he might be—possessed the power to summon a lightning bolt and hurl it through the atmosphere.

Or command a blast of thunder to explode across the sky.

Or send a whispered warning on the wind.

"*No* man," she breathed into her pillow, as the storm lulled her gently to sleep.

♥

Arianna followed the entourage through the arched entryway and into the matchless splendor of the nave. From entrance to chancel, green marble columns supported the arches of the ground stone ceiling. A bluish light shone through acres of stained glass, and splashed colorful patterns on the golden wood of the pews and on the inlays carved delicately on the chapel walls. Plush velvet in royal blue cushioned the white stone kneelers behind the pews. Set in the south transept to her left, a stained glass tracery window depicted various Arcadian settings. There was one depicting small groups of men, women, and children beneath a luminous blue orb, which seemed more sun than moon.

Intrigued by the various paintings on the walls, Arianna was studying them when the echo of retreating footsteps alerted her that she was being left behind. There in spirit only, her wraith-like presence followed behind them, down the labyrinth of connecting hallways and into a granite mausoleum guarded by sculpted multiple-winged angels. A stone tablet carved into a Celtic cross bore the name "MacNamara" in large Ogham letters. Written in smaller script beneath were the words,

"Aoife. Beloved wife, mother, daughter, sister."

How she was able to decipher the ancient script, Arianna couldn't fathom, any more than she could comprehend why she should be dreaming of Caleb's mother's funeral.

Near the front of the group, a woman, strands of gray threaded through her once dark brown hair, cradled a newborn in her arms. Her eyes were empty sockets, red and swollen with the grief she strove to bear. Granny. Arianna recognized the younger version of the woman, drawn from the inkwell of her own childhood memories. As the funeral service ended, tears glistening in the woman's soft, blue eyes overflowed onto the tousled black curls of the infant in her arms. The baby raised his tiny head off her shoulder.

And stared unblinkingly into Arianna's eyes.

Her heart jolted at the intensity of his emerald gaze, the hopeless sadness in his eyes.

Before she could think what it might mean, the whispery collage began to fade into another image, and she was staring into the riveting gaze of a boy of five or six. His long, dark curls danced in the gusty wind as she stood on a rocky ledge in the brambles beside him. His loneliness swamped her, as bleak and chilling as the icy mists rising from the sea below. She longed to embrace the small boy, to enfold him in her arms, to promise him everything would be all right.

But as she reached for him, the misty vignette trembled and dissolved into yet another ethereal scene. Her breath caught as she recognized the gangly adolescent who had first come to her in the silent hours of the night. And with the next shimmering transfiguration, the figure of the boy transformed into that of a man.

The man she had always loved to distraction. Caleb.

A few miles away a man sat slumped in a kitchen chair in a drunken stupor. His crusty chin sagged against his chest; saliva ran in a sour stream down inside the collar of his shirt. Rainwater dripped from his trouser legs and pooled around his feet.

Thunder ricocheted off the walls and he bolted upright, his hand wrapped around the neck of a whiskey bottle. "To meself," he grunted, raising it in a sloppy toast.

Paying no heed to the doctor's warnings against mixing drink with his medication, he drained the bottle, liquor dribbling down his chin as he slammed it back onto the table. He fumbled with a package of tobacco and rolled himself a fag. Letting it dangle from his slack lips, he attempted several strikes of a match before finally sucking the acrid, biting smoke into his lungs with great relish. "Another pleasure the doctors are after denying me."

"Indeed." A cajoling voice, that of his one true friend, surrounded him. As always, it seemed to come from nowhere, yet everywhere, at one and the same time. "You cannot trust them...not any of them."

"No one but yershelf," the man slurred.

"Yesss. And if you follow my instruction, you will have all your heart desires. But timing is key." The Minion of the Beast took on an admonishing tone. "Your actions today might have cost us dearly, my friend. And bought only torment in return. For the ordained time is not yet. But soon, soon."

"Shoon," the man echoed. And he who had become one with the Minion, who had invited the Evil to dwell within his flesh, slumped forward again, the rolled cigarette held loosely between his thumb and index finger burning itself out on blistered flesh.

Chapter Eleven

As she and Mr. Kavanagh had agreed, Arianna dropped the car off the following afternoon to have the brakes serviced. While the work was being done, she decided to pop over to the pub across the street for a bite of lunch. Pushing against one of the heavy weather-beaten doors, she entered a dimly lit, wood-paneled room. Smoking had been banned in public establishments in County Clare in recent years. Still, the smell of stale tobacco mingled with the yeasty scent of hops, the odor of deep-fried food, and the mustiness of time.

Arianna approached the woman behind the bar. About Arianna's age, she was cute in a pierced-black-and-pink-highlighted-Goth kind of way. "I...uh... Are you serving lunch?"

"Bar food only 'til six."

"That's fine. Um, could I get a table?"

"Here or the snug?"

"Snug?"

The woman smiled. "A private lounge like. Ladies often prefer it to the open bar."

They passed through the arched entry into the small, adjoining room where a cleverly carved pair of leprechauns guarded the entrance. Brass plates affixed to their legendary pots of gold bore a Gaelic inscription. No doubt, some enchanting conundrum, Arianna reasoned, secretly charmed by the thought.

Sitting at a table along the far wall, she glanced at the menu. She ordered a Coke—listed under the heading, *Minerals*—and Fish and Chips, in honor of her first trip to an authentic Irish public house.

Arianna settled back in her chair, soaking up the atmosphere. From her unobstructed view of the bar, she could see that, even at this early hour on a Friday afternoon, cream-topped glasses of dark brew flowed without restraint. In no time at all, the waitress was back, bearing a platter piled high with food. There was a plank of cod, fried to golden perfection, and nearly buried beneath a glistening mound of thickly sliced fries. A plastic cup sitting haphazardly on the side of the plate contained a miserly scoop of coleslaw.

"Would you be needing anything else? Vinegar?"

"Just tartar sauce," Arianna replied. Unable to resist the temptation, she broke off a steaming bite of crusty fish and popped it into her mouth. "Mmm, delicious."

Reaching into her apron, the server pulled out a packet of tartar sauce, and set it on the table. "You're an American so," the woman said, in that way the Irish have of telling you something you already know. "I've a break coming up, if you'd not mind me joining you for a bit of a chin wag." Without waiting for an invitation, the woman plopped into the chair across the table. "Deirdre McMahon is my name."

Arianna dabbed her lips with her napkin. "Arianna Sullivan. Nice to meet you."

Deirdre cocked her head to one side. "Are you visiting family here? With most of the heritage sites closed, tourists are usually a bit thin on the ground this time of year."

Arianna squeezed catsup from a packet in a stand on the table and dipped a fry. "Actually I'm staying at a property I inherited here in Ennistymon. My old childhood home."

"You've lost someone dear to you then." Compassion took Deirdre's raucous tone down a notch.

"My da. It was...unexpected." Arianna devoted much more attention than was necessary to the piece of fish she was cutting.

"Sorry for your loss."

"Thanks. Haven't been back here since I left as a child, so I really would have liked to take in some of the sights. But, like you said, most of the tourist spots are closed."

"I've an acquaintance whose mate runs a tour company, if you're interested." She gave a very unladylike holler in the direction of the bar, then slumped back against the rounded oak slats of her chair. With a tired sigh, she lifted one scuffed black shoe off the floor and rotated her ankle. "Only four o'clock and already I'm knackered," she complained under her breath. "It's been bloody desperate in here today."

Face set in a frown, the attractive man making his way to their table looked strangely familiar. Tall and solidly built, Arianna guessed him to be in his forties, although the flecks of steel in his light brown hair was the solitary hint of his age. "For feck's sake, Deirdre. Must you be shrieking for me like a bleedin' fishwife?"

"Fishwife, is it? And all this time I thought you fancied me screaming for you." Pouting up at him, she fluttered her lashes suggestively. "Anyways, Arianna here's from the States and I told her about yer man who runs the ferry service to the Islands."

"Not during the off-season," he replied shortly.

Although the man's stone gray eyes moved over Arianna with studied indifference, she didn't miss the spark of interest in the clandestine perusal. And, if the quelling look Deirdre shot him was any indication, she hadn't missed it either.

In response to the woman's silent set down, he seemed to erect an invisible wall. "Conor O'Clery," he said, reaching out his hand. "You were with Mam when she took ill."

"Oh, you're Mrs. O'Clery's son. That's where I've seen you before—at the hospital."

At the comment, Conor sent a smug look in the other woman's direction. Apparently, Arianna had just been a witness for the defense. Her *testimony* had confirmed that he hadn't known the woman who had left a message at the pub for him the previous day.

"How is she, Conor?" Arianna asked. "I called the hospital today, but all they'll say is that she's stable."

"She's much better, thanks. Look, I've to get back to the bar now, but let Deirdre know when you've a mind to go to the Aran Islands and I'll get it sorted for you."

"Thanks."

His hand raised in a salute as he disappeared into the adjoining room.

"I've a word of caution for you so," Deirdre said. "It's soft weather we've been having here on the mainland. But at Dun Aengus, sure the wind's been known to blow a body right over the cliffs. So mind yourself if you go to Inishmore."

"Thanks for the heads up." Arianna scrunched up her napkin and dropped it on her plate. "Speaking of storms, that one last night was really strange."

"Strange? How so?"

Arianna explained about the lightning and thunder coming from a clear blue sky, but made no mention of Caleb's involvement. *Did they still have insane asylums here in Ireland?*

As it was, her comments had the woman's brows disappearing beneath a fringe of pink-tipped black bangs. "Can't say as I've ever heard of such a thing before. We've loads of wind and rain, but thunder's really quite rare. Lightning, rarer still."

"Hmm." So *not* what Arianna had wanted to hear. "Oh, yeah, about the heritage sites. I was taking a run along the coast yesterday, not far from the rock quarry on the way to Hags Head and I spotted a castle on top of the cliffs. I looked in the Clare tourist guide, but I can't seem to find the place listed."

"That's because the castle you're speaking of is privately owned." The woman got up and began stacking the dirty dishes. "Not open to the public a'tall."

"Owned by a private family you mean."

"By Caleb MacNamara. And himself not one to fancy folks trampling all over what's his, I hear. Don't fancy folks a'tall, if you ask me. Right bit of a strange yoke he is." Her voice lowered to a conspiratorial whisper. "Rumor has it, he had that moat of his stocked with man-eating crocodiles. *Crocodiles.* When there's not been even a snake in Ireland since St. Pat—"

Arianna had heard nothing after his name. "Caleb MacNamara *lives* there?"

"He does, yes. The MacNamara." There was a soft intake of breath between pursed lips. "A right dirty ride is that one," Deirdre said with a sly wink. "Not that any of us *commoners* has ever got a taste of that, mind." She sniffed disdainfully. "Probably fancies himself too good for the likes of us locals. But if you'd care for a wee gander at the gorgeous man, you'll be finding Himself over at a table in the bar right now."

Here? Now? Butterflies were suddenly using Arianna's stomach lining as a trampoline.

Deirdre dug into her apron pocket. "Just pay the bill over to the bar till on your way out. No hurry, now."

He's here. Nervous as a rabbit in a cave of slathering wolves, Arianna searched her purse for a hairbrush. Not finding one, she combed her fingers through her windblown hair. She checked her teeth in her compact mirror for errant pieces of her meal. After replacing the lipgloss she had eaten off with lunch, she popped a mint.

As she passed the legendary leprechauns on her way out of the room, she jerked a suspicious glance at the one nearest the entrance. For a minute there, she would have sworn the thing had winked at her. But of course, she found its features frozen in the sly smirk created by the artist.

"You really are losing it, girlfriend," she muttered under her breath.

Her gaze averted from the wooden tables scattered about the bar, she stumbled over the small step leading up from the snug. "Good job," she mumbled to herself.

At the bar she spotted Mr. Kavanagh and stepped up next to him. She paid for her meal with colorful Euro notes that reminded her of Monopoly money. Smelling strongly of alcohol, the property manager greeted her and slipped an over-familiar hand over hers on the bar. Put off by the inappropriate behavior, she pulled her hand away. Next thing she knew, Caleb had inserted himself neatly into the small space between her and the man.

"Arianna," Caleb murmured a greeting, then acknowledged his uncle behind the bar with a curt nod. "Conor, how's the craic? I'm off to call on Granny now." He handed Conor his check and a twenty euro note.

Conor deposited the money in the cash drawer, counted out the change. "Stopped by the hospital meself before coming in this morning."

"Is she needing anything so?"

"She is, o'course. To go home." Conor grabbed a glass and began to layer in a Guinness. "You know yourself, there's no good reason for them to be keeping her there. Not when they can't find a bloody thing wrong with her. First, they're after diagnosing a massive coronary. Now they're saying there's no damage to the heart muscle, no evidence of a heart attack a'tall." Still grumbling, he placed the pint of dark beer in front of a wrinkled old man wearing a wooly cap and a green flannel shirt.

While Caleb was conversing with Conor, Miles Kavanagh turned to Arianna. "The garage rang me a few minutes ago," he told her. "Brakes are more banjaxed than they suspected, and one of the parts isn't available 'til Friday next." His words were heavily slurred and his eyes had that bleary, red-rimmed look of someone who had had a few too many. "If you come back with me to the office, I've a number there you can ring to hire another car to drive whilst this one's being fixed."

With Caleb standing so close, she could feel his body heat, Arianna found herself playing nervously with the strap of her purse. "No, it's okay," she told Mr. Kavanagh. "I have some things I need to do at the house. I'll get a ride."

Caleb cringed. A man further down the bar smirked and nudged the guy beside him.

Kavanagh chuckled. "So it's a ride you fancy."

Before Arianna could respond, she felt Caleb's hand squeeze her shoulder. When she looked up at him, she saw that his eyes had gone flat, his features etched in stone. With a voice cold and hard as steel, he said to Kavanagh, "*I'll* be giving the lady a lift home."

The man blinked twice, then with an indifferent shrug turned back to nurse his lager.

Totally clueless about what had just transpired, Arianna could feel the air snapping with tension. Caleb's arm encircled her shoulders as he urged her away from the bar. The gesture was protective. Innocent. And yet it ignited a raging wildfire inside her. Jeez, she had it bad. One simple touch and her heart went to tripping like a jackhammer.

"Thanks for the ride, Caleb."

He frowned down at her. "Don't say that."

"Say what?"

"What you just said."

Perplexed, she looked up at him. "What? Thanks?"

Caleb's lips quirked, eyes danced with devilment, as he put his mouth to her ear. "Sure I can't say as I've ever been *thanked* before, Arianna." His voice went low and wicked. "Well, not in so many words." Playing with a strand of her hair, Caleb leaned close again. "Here in Ireland," he explained *sotto voce,* "'a ride' is a euphemism only for having sex."

Arianna tugged away from him, face flaming. "You can't be serious."

The mocking amusement in his eyes was answer enough.

"Ah, man, that is so wrong," she moaned. "You know, the tourist board ought to warn Americans about stuff like that in their travel guides." Arianna tipped her head back, raised her brows. "Any other expressions I should avoid while I'm here?"

Caleb considered for a minute. "Fanny," he declared.

"Fanny? What—?"

"Don't ask," he replied with a smirk. Eyes alight with mischief, he glanced at his watch. "I've time to give you that *ride* now if you'd like."

"Let me think about it—NO," she shot back. "But I would appreciate a *lift*." His warm chuckle stirred nerve endings she never knew she had.

Chapter Twelve

While driving her home the day before, Caleb had invited Arianna out for dinner. Now, after a forty-minute car ferry ride—a ferry Caleb had rented privately for their date—they were in County Galway, just north of Clare, on their way to a restaurant near Clifden. "The place is a renovated seventeenth century farmhouse owned by one of my friends," he informed her as they traveled up the Sky Road.

Gazing over the sheer drop-off to the sea below, Arianna decided that the roadway had been most aptly named.

"After dinner we'll drive to Galway City for a bit of craic."

"Crack...?"

"Not the drug, *cailín*. It's spelled c-r-a-i-c, Gaelic slang for a lot of things, but usually means fun."

Arianna huffed. "Another one of those tricky Irish words."

"Mmm." Caleb looked at her inquisitively. "I wonder that you're not familiar with any of these expressions, your Da being Irish and all."

Arianna lifted a shoulder. "I don't know, maybe it was easier for him that way. You know, leaving everything Irish behind. Except his accent," she added, her smile sadly reminiscent. "Guess you can take the boy out of Ireland..."

Caleb chuckled. "So, how've you been settling in?"

"Fine, thanks. Other than not having much luck with cars. But at least I have a cell phone now, in case of an emergency." Arianna took a breath, then blurted out, "Which reminds me: What the heck was with the lightning strike the other day. I—?"

"I'd really rather not discuss that, if you don't mind."

"Oh...." *Well that was rude.* Arianna darted a furtive glance in his direction. The stubborn set of his jaw, his shuttered gaze, told her it would be futile to push for more. Maybe he was still feeling traumatized by the incident and was just too macho to admit it.

Outside her window, the Irish countryside flashed by. The view was breathtaking. The moon, peeking poignantly from behind the clouds, cast a silvery haze over sea and valley. Basking in the rugged beauty, Arianna felt her heart fill with a feeling a lot like infatuation. "I think I'm in love," she murmured.

Caleb frowned at her questioningly, before realizing she was speaking of the scenery. "Lovely, isn't it? Sky Road's been named one of the most scenic spots in all of Ireland."

"It's all so different here, from where I live in the States."

"And where is that exactly?"

"Beddeford, Maine. I share a condo there with my two best friends. It's about a mile from the house where I grew up, where my da lives...." She paused, breathed in, braced herself to ride the wave of pain. "I mean *lived*."

Caleb reached over, covered her hand with his. "How long are you planning to stay?"

"I don't know, to be honest."

He raised a black brow. "Your ticket wasn't a return then?"

"Return? Oh, you mean round-trip. No, you see there's something I have to...."

Her words trailed off. But she had Caleb's full attention. "Go on, tell me," he encouraged gently. "I've sensed there's something more." The low rumble of his voice was hypnotic, his words a compulsion no woman could have resisted.

Suddenly Arianna wanted nothing more in the world than to open up to him, to share the incredible burden she had been bearing alone. She wanted to divulge all of her secrets. About her father. Her mother. *The waking dreams.* "For as long as I can remember, I've had these...dreams, where I wake up here in Ireland."

In your castle. In your wide platform bed. In your arms.

"Crazy as it sounds, you were there," she admitted softly. "First as a boy, and later a man. That's why I totally freaked out on you that first night. I thought there was some kind of strange kismet at work.

Some weird psychic connection."

"You thought I was a vampire," Caleb reminded her dryly.

"Yeah, well. There is that," she admitted sheepishly. "Anyway, I think I've finally got the whole thing figured out."

His eyes cut to hers. "Your conclusion?"

"Remember when I told you Granny had taken care of me as a baby?"

He gave a slight nod.

"Well, it's fairly obvious, if you think about it," she said, warming to her theory. "I was only three when I left. So the dreams must have sprung from a subconscious memory of you." *This still didn't explain how I knew exactly what he would look like now.*

Caleb stretched like a lazy tiger, then settled back in his seat. "I've been meaning to ask. How was it you reconnected with my grandmother?"

"Yeah, it must have seemed like I was stalking you. Turning up at your grandmother's the day after we met," she joked. "Actually, she was my mother's mid-wife. I found her name on my birth certificate. When I went to visit her, she told me she'd been like a mother to my da. And that she'd taken care of me after my mother died."

Caleb gave her a thoughtful glance. "I seem to remember a lad hanging about when I was very young. About Conor's age, he was. Patrick...." His voice rose at the end.

"O'Sullivan," Arianna finished. "He dropped the 'O' when we moved to the States."

"Right. I also remember when I was a bit older, eleven, twelve or so, I'd come to call on Granny and find her sitting in her rocker." Caleb reached out and tugged a strand of Arianna's hair. "With a wee yellow-haired tyke all curled up and sleeping on her lap."

"That would have been me," Arianna offered with an impish grin, before growing pensive again. "You know, Caleb, I've always felt like something was drawing me back here...calling me home. You see? I said 'home'. That's how this place feels to me, even though I was only a baby when I left."

"'Tis the Spirit of Hibernia," Caleb murmured. *"An ceangal.* A living bond, this connection between Eireann and her people. Take the burgeoning tourist trade, for example. That which was after turning a nation the likes of a downtrodden whipping boy into the fierce Celtic Tiger of recent years."

Arianna grinned. "It's gotta be faerie magic." She grinned. "I mean, what else can explain how people from all corners of the globe are drawn to a tiny island no more than a splash of green in the Atlantic."

"There seems to be a sense of homesickness amongst the Irish Diaspora, no matter how many generations removed they are from the land." Caleb's voice had deepened, his brogue thickened, as he settled into a rhythmic story-telling cadence. "Their holidays here become pilgrimages bordering almost on the spiritual."

Arianna scratched her nose. "I heard something on the news a while back. A Swedish geographer wrote a book claiming that Ireland could be the lost continent of Atlantis. He said it's the only place on earth matching Plato's description exactly. So, who's to say, but that there really is some kind of mystical allure here."

Caleb tensed slightly, an expression she couldn't decipher moving across his face. "You're speaking of a book by Dr. Ulf Erlingsson," he offered. "But the National Museum in Dublin denies there's any archaeological evidence to support his views."

"Yeah, and our government insists there's nothing alien about Roswell's Area 54," she said. "Be that as it may, I've personally experienced the inexplicable bond you're talking about. It's almost as if we who are born here, are somehow Ireland's betrothed. That wherever the winds of fate may blow us, we're destined always to hear her voice calling us home." Arianna bit her lip, suddenly self-conscious. "And I wax lyrical."

"'Tis the Irish in you," Caleb said softly.

"Must be," she murmured distractedly, then thinking aloud, "Maybe that's what Daddy meant when—" Catching herself just in the nick of time, Arianna slammed her lips shut. She was so *not* going to admit to seeing ghosts.

Count on Caleb, however, to hone in on the aborted statement like a heat-seeking missile. "What your father meant....?"

As she sat in silence, Arianna felt a warm rush flow over her, like waves breaking on a tropical shore. "Do you believe in God, Caleb? In the afterlife, I mean?"

Caleb slanted her a look. "Mmm. Seems I recall the Scriptures referring to the man who doesn't believe in God as a fool."

Arianna chewed on a thumbnail, collecting her thoughts.

Caleb pulled a tin of mints out of the console, pushed the lid open with his thumb and offered it.

"Thanks." She slipped one into her mouth, enjoying the cool, minty sensation on her tongue, as she weighed the pros and cons of sharing the experience of her father's visitation with a virtual stranger. Solidly in the *Pro* column was the fact that Caleb hadn't scoffed at her talk of the waking dreams. Had gone so far, in fact, as to put a Gaelic expression to the connection she had always felt to her homeland.

She took a deep, calming breath, then began to speak. "That first night you asked me why I came here so soon after Da passed away. And, while it's true that his final wishes *were* to have his ashes scattered from the Cliffs of Moher, there's more." She hesitated, then gave a long sigh. "The day he died...well, that night actually...he came to me." Her words, which had been measured at first, hesitant, now began to spill freely from her mouth "As he was leaving...to go into the light...he told me to come back here."

Caleb's head turned, his gaze intense. "You're saying your father appeared to you after his death and sent you here." A statement, not a question.

"He said something about my meeting my Fate here, or my destiny, or some such."

It was almost imperceptible, Arianna thought, the whitening of his knuckles on the steering wheel, the tensing of neck and shoulders. "Maybe the experience was only a dream," he suggested mildly. "A *normal* one."

Emphasis on 'normal'. As opposed to what? she thought irritably. Crazy? Demented? Deranged? She opened her purse and reached into the change pocket in her wallet.

"I might have thought the same thing. But when he kissed me goodbye, he gave me this." Arianna held out her hand, uncurled her fingers.

"Your house key."

"I'd never seen it before that night, didn't have any idea what it might open. It was only the next day, while going through his safe deposit box, that I came across the deed to the cottage. A property I hadn't even known existed. And all at once, I knew...I just *knew* the key would fit that door."

Caleb responded, the tenor of his voice melodic. "There are more things in heaven and earth, Horatio—"

"Than are dreamt of in your philosophy," she finished quietly. *Hamlet*. God, what kind of man was this? A despot one minute. The next, a poet quoting The Bard to validate her experiences. And managing to sum up the running theme of her life in that one, single line.

Arianna patted his knee, felt the ripple of lean muscle beneath the fabric. "Enough about me now. Tell me about yourself. Have you always lived in Clare?"

"Except for a few years when I traveled abroad," he answered absently. "Em...whilst I'm thinking about it, let me see your mobile for a minute."

Arianna pulled her cell phone out of a zippered pocket on her purse. "Why?"

"I want to program my number in for you, so you can reach me in case of trouble." He glanced at her, a teasing look in his eyes. "Sure, aren't you after attracting the stuff to yourself like a daffodil draws honeybees."

"I wasn't the only one almost struck by lightning," she countered, clearly baiting him.

Refusing to bite, Caleb kept his eyes on the road, his hand held out to her. Arianna smacked her cell into his palm. With his attention divided between the twisty road and the phone in his hand, he added his number to her contact list. "There now," he said, handing it back. "I've set it up on speed dial. If ever you need me, just press '9'. I've my mobile always with me—even in the bathroom while I shower."

That was all it took. One offhand remark. And—with the precision of an Olympic gold-medallist—her mind did a swan dive straight into the gutter. Her head filled with erotic images of that delectable male body draped in nothing but sandalwood-scented clouds. Of hot water sluicing in steamy rivulets over wide shoulders and sculpted pecs, trailing down....

"We're here." The SUV lurched as Caleb shifted into low gear and steered hard to the left—sending it up an embankment and into a nosedive onto a narrow, pebbly path not visible from the road.

"Crazy driver," Arianna teased.

Caleb chuckled as they wound down the rutted lane for several yards before pulling into a small, uneven parking lot, the Jaguars, BMWs and other luxury cars forced to park so haphazardly the scene resembled a train wreck.

Caleb helped her out of the vehicle. His large hand wrapped around hers, he led her along the uneven path with the grace and sure-footed agility of a mountain lion. Arianna inhaled the moist, salt-tinged air as they tramped through a lush thicket of greenery. The ground-hugging mists and shimmering moonlight gave the setting a smoky, dreamlike quality.

A slight rustling in a clump of bushes drew Arianna's attention. A tiny winged creature seemed to be spying on them through the foliage. "What the heck is that?"

Caleb glanced over his shoulder at her.

"Never mind," she mumbled. After playing true confession on the way here, there was no way in the world she was copping now to seeing faeries.

So intent was she on watching the bushes for further activity, however, that she tripped over a raised slab of rock on the path in front of her. Caleb's hand tightened around hers in a bruising grip, saving her from falling on her face.

"You okay?" he asked, steadying her.

"Yeah. Good save, thanks." But as she went to take another step, a stabbing pain shot fire through her ankle. She crumpled and, like some lame heroine in one of Michaela's novels, fell into Caleb's arms. He scooped her up and set her on a waist-high, crumbling stone wall bordering the path.

Definitely red-faced and humiliated here.

Caleb hunkered down in front of her and began to untie her bootlaces. "I'm fine," she protested, batting at his hands. "Seriously, it's nothing. A little twist is all."

Naturally, he ignored her, the stubborn man. As he eased the boot off her foot, she stiffened and jammed her knuckles against her mouth to stifle a moan.

He gave her a benign glance. "Fine, is it?" He gently rolled her sock down, and removed it from her foot. His tight-lipped expression had her peering at the angry, bluish-black lump. "C'mere to me." Handing her the boot and sock, he slid one arm under her thighs, the other around her back and picked her back up. He expended no more energy than if he were lifting a three-year-old. "We're going to the A&E."

"If you mean the *emergency room*, think again." He stopped walking, and looked down at her. "It's only a little sprain, Caleb. *For real*. I'd know if it was anything worse. And besides, I'm half-starved. I want to eat."

"Trust me in this, Arianna," he said, moving again toward the parking lot. "There's no way you'll be putting any weight on that foot tonight. Nor any time soon, I'd reckon, with the looks of it. I'll stop at a takeaway on the way to hospital and pick you up a burger and chips."

"I don't want to go to the hospital." Fine, so she sounded like a whiny brat. But first Da, and then Granny? Two trips to the E.R. in a under a month? She just couldn't deal with anymore.

Caleb's longsuffering sigh was like air rushing from a deflating beach ball. Arianna jumped on his hesitation and began to plead her case. "I've had bad sprains like this before while doing katas. Once, I even thought I'd broken my ankle."

"Katas, is it?" He muttered something under his breath that Arianna could not make out. Aloud, he said, "Lets give it another look."

Lowering her body onto another section of wall, he squatted in front of her and cradled her heel in his palm. He made communicative noises as Arianna tried to distract herself from the throbbing pain with chatter about karate classes with her two friends back home.

Caleb seemed oddly focused on the injury. Eyelids lowered, he was gently massaging the sore area beneath her ankle when waves of heat began to radiate from the pad of his thumb. Friction from the rubbing, she told herself, although she couldn't feel any pressure from his touch. As her flesh grew warmer, the intensifying heat seemed to absorb the dull ache beneath his artful hands.

After a minute or two, she felt the warmth of his touch drain away. He pulled the sock from her boot and slipped it over her foot. "Sorry? You were saying?"

"Oh, um...I...I was just asking what form of martial arts you study."

"It's...em...an ancient form." He proceeded to fit the boot back onto her foot. "A sort of mixed martial arts discipline. Our children... em...children in my family begin training almost before they're old enough to walk." Tying the boot, he helped her slide off the wall. "There now. Feel better?"

Arianna gingerly applied weight to the injured foot, her eyes wide with wonder. "Wow. It doesn't hurt at all." After a few hesitant steps, she raised her good foot off the ground and balanced all her weight on the other one. "To be honest, I really thought I'd done a number on it." Taking a little hop, she smiled up at him. "Good as new. I can't believe it. You really ought to have those healing hands of yours insured." Stretching onto her tiptoes, she brushed a grateful kiss across his cheek....

Completely missing, in the process, the way her teasing remark had made him flinch.

Chapter Thirteen

The maitre d' was a tall, cadaverous man. Lurch, Arianna dubbed him as he greeted them. "Mr. MacNamara, you're very welcome, sir, yourself and the lady. Sorry, but if you'll excuse me, Mr. O'Donnell wished to be informed of your arrival."

Arianna took in the reception area with an appreciative eye. Lighting subdued. Décor rich and plush. A shelf carved into the stone wall beside the front entrance displayed a selection of antique bric-a-brac, old copper kettles and crockery.

Caleb had told her to dress casual. But her black designer jeans and leather jacket made her feel more than a tad underdressed in these elegant surroundings. When she voiced her misgivings, her date inclined his head toward a sign posted behind the Maitre d' station. *CASUAL ATTIRE IS REQUIRED*, it read tongue-in-cheek.

A booming male voice had Arianna spinning around. "Caleb, how's things, mate?" A handsome mountain of a man, with hair the color of red-hot embers, pulled Caleb into a bear hug. They traded slaps on the back in that hetero-male greeting ritual. "Welcome, my friend."

With a mischievous glint in his eyes, he took Arianna's hand and raised it gallantly to his lips. "And yourself, pretty lady. Tell me, have we not met somewhere before?"

She felt Caleb tense beside her. Not much, just an overall tightening of joint and sinew. More obvious was the look of reproach he shot his friend before reclaiming her hand and tucking it possessively into the crook of his arm. *Jealous? Mmm...nice.*

"Sure, that chat-up line's older than the dolmens," he admonished his friend, referring to the megalithic burial chambers consisting of gigantic upright stone slabs supporting a horizontal capstone or table.

"Arianna O'Sullivan, meet Seamus O'Donnell," he continued. "Mind yourself around this one, *cailín*. He's always fancied himself a bit of a lady's man."

A hearty laugh resounded from the giant's mouth. "Ach, you're just jealous. Always have been." Blue eyes twinkling, his next words were for Arianna. "Sure, I'm not taking the mickey, luv. It's good with faces I am, and I know I've seen yours somewhere before."

After relieving them of their wraps, Seamus led them down a corridor, past what appeared to be a Da Vinci on the right wall, a Botticelli hanging directly opposite. Stopping at the first door to the left, he stepped aside and bid them to enter.

A private parlor, Arianna thought. It was a veritable paradise of fine antiques set in haphazard elegance on a room-size Oriental rug. Against the far wall a Tiffany bronze lamp sat delicately atop a George IV mahogany table. In a nook to the left a 17th century regency oak table held a matching pair of early Victorian brass oil lamps. And on the right side of the room, a George III giltwood mirror occupied pride of place over a gray slate fireplace.

It was then that she noticed it. The Fromanteel and Clarke Dutch longcase clock to the left of the hearth. *Nunh-unh.* Leaving Caleb's side to investigate her suspicions, she crossed the room. Yes, the identifying mark was there—a faint scratch on the glass covering the dial.

Turning to mention her discovery to Seamus, she caught the two men staring at her, while conversing earnestly in Gaelic. The way their eyes darted away guiltily left no doubt that *she* had been the topic of their conversation.

Caleb left his friend and joined her. "*Gabh mo leithscéal,*" he apologized, smooth as whipped cream. "Sorry, *mo chroí.* 'Twas unforgivably rude, ourselves slipping into a language you don't understand. I was just telling Seamus that you're a fellow antique connoisseur yourself."

Yeah, sure you were. Deciding to let it pass, she turned to Seamus. "The clock here. You got it at a Christie's auction, March, a year ago."

"I did, yes." He tipped his head, gave her a curious look. And then his eyes lit with recognition. "Ah, that's it, then. That's where I saw you. 'Twas yourself there in New York, the one bidding against me and driving up the final price."

"I was determined to have that piece for my shop in Maine."

"As was I myself." He spread his hands, gesturing widely. "Everything you see here, save a few pieces in my private collection, have been discreetly marked for sale."

Arianna's face lit up. "What a unique concept. A restaurant/ antique store combination."

Pleased by her exuberance, Seamus motioned the two of them to settle themselves onto a camel-colored leather loveseat facing a blazing hearth. With an undisguised wink of approval directed at his friend, he turned and left the room.

As if on cue, their waiter appeared, dressed in a period costume from the time the house was built. The 1600s, if Arianna remembered correctly. With great panache, the man flourished a single menu; a scroll made from tan parchment. Caleb untied the piece of twine and unrolled it. The menu offered items both in English and Gaelic with an archaic font.

"Dishes vary from week to week," Caleb informed her. "Therefore, each menu is drawn by hand, using calligraphy."

At the bottom of the scroll was written: *a pledge of cosmopolitan cookery exactingly prepared, using only the finest organically grown herbs and vegetables.* The flourish of Seamus's bold scrawl sealed the guarantee.

When the waiter requested their drink order, Caleb suggested the house specialty, the mead. "It's a medieval wine made from apple juice, clover, heather and fermented honey."

"Clover and heather, huh?" A grimace. "Oh, why not? Let's live dangerously."

Caleb nodded at the waiter, who turned and left. With his arm draped casually around her shoulders, the two of them studied the menu. A log and turf fire gave the room a cozy feel. Somewhere off in the distance, a woman's bewitching voice began to stroke a tragic melody.

Goosebumps popped up on Arianna's arms. "An angel," she whispered in awe.

"It's called *Sean-nos*," he explained. "Singing in the old style, without accompaniment. Except for the *bodhrán*."

Arianna heard it then, the poignant double-drumbeat of the traditional Irish drum. The one-two rhythm was so faint the microphone might have been amplifying the gentle pulsing of the singer's heart. The ancient cadence stirred misty, salt-scented memories....

"Have you decided what you'd like to eat?" Caleb asked.

"Everything looks so good, it's hard to decide. Suggestions?"

"Lobster brochette's absolutely gorgeous."

"Lobster, yuck."

He gave her a perplexed stare. "Yuck?"

"Well, being from Maine—you know, lobster country and all—I managed to get up close and personal with the pitiful creatures during cook-outs on the beach. I've refused to eat the poor things ever since. On principle."

A smile played around the corners of his lips. "The poor things."

"Think of the way they're cooked, Caleb. Now, there's gotta be something just plain cruel about dumping a living creature into hot, boiling water. And that awful sound they make...." She shuddered. "It's like they're screaming in agony."

Caleb winced. "Now there's a thing I've not considered before."

"And how about the way they look...claws and antennae. Cockroaches of the sea is what I call them." She pulled a face. "Why would anyone want to eat a thing like that?"

"Why indeed?" His lips twisted wryly. "Sure, haven't those astute observations of yours cured *me* of ever having a taste for the sadly mistreated creatures ever again."

Arianna elbowed him playfully in the ribs for his teasing, then sent the hovering waiter an apologetic glance. "I'm sorry for taking so long to decide."

"I'll order for the both of us, will I?" Caleb suggested.

Eyes like polished jade in the firelight, his voice caressed her senses. Now here was a man who could have her agreeing to almost anything.

"Arianna?"

"Um, yes, please. Some kind of seafood. Fresh."

Caleb acknowledged the waiter. "A warm salad of monkfish, salmon and pine kernels topped with an herbed balsamic vinaigrette for the lady, if you please. For the main course, em... how about giant fresh prawns pan-fried in garlic butter, served with champ."

"Champ?" Arianna asked.

"Potatoes. Mash with spring onions," he replied, before turning back to finish the order. "For myself, the fresh prawn cocktail with sauce Marie-Rose and passion-fruit mayo. And chateaubriand, rare." He finished the order with some exotic-sounding French wine.

The waiter cleared his throat, as if embarrassed. "Will I put the order in now, sir, or...?"

"Now would be grand, thanks."

Within minutes, they were snuggled together, sipping the sweet, fermented mead, their conversation as intimate as a kiss and punctuated by quiet laughter. Was the warm glow she was feeling the result of the cozy fire, the ancient libation, or being cuddled up beside the man she had longed for her entire adult life? All of the above, she finally decided.

"The parking lot was packed when we got here," she said. Her skin tingled under the caress of Caleb's long, tapered fingers trailing absently over the silky gray sleeve of her shirt. "And yet, we scored our own private parlor. Is that an advantage of being personal friends with the proprietor?"

"Actually, the place is known for offering its patrons a romantic... interlude." His voice dropped an octave, warm satin sliding over heated flesh. "A crackling fire, soft music, candlelight, and certain other...unique...features."

"Unique? How?"

"A latch on the parlor door, for one thing." His lips turned up at the corners, giving her a glimpse of the rare smile that made her heart sing. "So that couples can be quite as *private* as they'd like."

She wasn't slow, but the concept was so outrageous, it took her a second to catch on. "You can't mean people actually lock the door and...and...." She took another look at the room, noticing a plush set of drapes, like stage curtains, drawn across one wall. Did it conceal a small alcove? A bed?

An uncomfortable suspicion began to take shape in her mind. "Caleb, I hope I didn't give you the impression that I...that we—"

"You're safe, *cailín*," he assured her softly. "I've no plans to be seducing you this evening."

The word *seduce* coming from that sensual mouth did something twitchy to her stomach, enveloped her in a moist wave of heat. It was their first date. She was relieved that he wasn't planning to put the make on her, wasn't she? Why, then, did his assurance make her feel deflated, a helium balloon a week after a kid's birthday party?

Because he was broodingly handsome, sinfully sensual. And every time those wide, full lips parted, that deep, accented voice of his stroked every erogenous zone on her body. And she wouldn't be the only one. No doubt, the man had a string of tall, willowy, model-types all falling at his feet.

Kind of makes a girl wonder just how often he *has availed himself of this restaurant's* unique *features. How many times—?*

"How many times have I what?" Caleb asked.

Oh, Lord, please tell me I didn't blurt that out. "Um...eaten here," she sputtered.

He tipped his head, gave her a long, considering glance. "Now and then, but it is a bit of a journey from Clare." Then he leaned closer, and whispered in her ear. "To the other question, never."

He *had* been in her head! How did he *do* that? Plant thoughts, impressions. Read someone's mind. Well, she had best learn to keep her thoughts to her herself.

Quickly, she changed the subject. "You mentioned traveling abroad for a while. Did you actually live in other countries?"

"I did for a time. But even while away for extended periods, I kept my legal residence in Clare. Upon learning my father's death was imminent a couple of years ago, I returned from my travels. After he passed, I stayed on, assuming the heir's responsibility for the property as I'd promised him." His carved features seemed to evoke regret. Then the moment passed.

"So, the castle...where I saw you the other day? That's your ancestral home?"

"It is, yes." Caleb sipped his mead. "Generations of MacNamaras have lived—and died there. My parents are both interred on the grounds in a neo-gothic abbey my father had constructed in my mother's memory."

Arianna flashed back to the strange dream she had had the night before. Was it starting all over again? Had she entered an altered state, passed through some obscure gateway into the past, and actually witnessed his mother's funeral?

God, this was getting way too weird, even for her. Until now, apart from the after-death encounter with Da, the inexplicable dreams, and a touch of sixth sense, she had never experienced anything even remotely metaphysical. "I'm sorry, Caleb. I didn't realize both your parents were gone, too."

"'Twas long ago my mother died." His reply was short, dismissive. "I never knew her."

"My mother died when I was three," Arianna said softly. "I never knew her either." For the next few minutes, they shared a comfortable silence, staring blindly into the flames. Then Arianna shifted, and looked up at him. "Caleb, about that business with the lightning—"

"*No buc leis!*" He gave a short sigh of impatience. Whether at her insistence on bringing up a subject he didn't wish to discuss, or at having slipped again into his native tongue, she wasn't sure. "Pay it no mind. 'Twas nothing, *cailín*. Nothing a'tall."

"Nothing? I was darn near fried like a chicken nugget. And I keep picturing you—"

"*Leave it*, I said!"

Arianna jumped, startled by the harshness of his tone. How dare he snap at her like that! Whipping around, she gave him a fulminating glare. To no effect, however, as she got only his profile. He hunched forward, his demeanor dark and brooding, hands clasped loosely between his thighs, his jaw muscles working overtime.

"I will not 'leave it'," she shot back. "And don't you ever raise your voice to me."

He turned, slowly, deliberately. Not just his head, but his whole upper body. Arianna felt her insides begin to quake at the cold, naked fury in his eyes. "You would dare defy me in this?" His voice was low, caressing, all the more menacing for its softness.

She swallowed the irrational panic, squared her shoulders. *"Defy* you? Do you hear yourself, Caleb? What the heck do you think this is, the freaking seventeenth century?"

He didn't respond, just continued to fix her with that black, indicting stare.

"You want a laugh?" she plowed on, digging the hole even deeper. "I'd almost convinced myself there had to be a logical explanation for what happened there. But every time I broach the subject with you, you brush me off. Now, why is that? I have to ask myself. Why do I get the feeling that something *really* weird is going on?"

Where angels dare to tread... The words filtered through her mind.

"Belligerent to a fault, so you are," he murmured. "So bold as to beard a lion in his den, without a thought to the consequences. Leastwise, not until the bloody beast has your stubborn head in his mouth." He swore fluently under his breath in Gaelic.

"What-*ever.*" Arianna heard a scraping sound. Did people actually grind their teeth when they were angry? Hmmph, clearly the man was unaccustomed to dealing with a strong, independent woman. An equal. In the macho world of Caleb MacNamara, a female undoubtedly knew her place, respected the male's dominant position in society.

Wrong woman, wrong society, wrong freaking century. Arianna matched him glare for glare, outrage snapping from her eyes.

But then she saw his gaze slide down, and consider her quivering lower lip...as if he were contemplating catching the plump, juicy morsel between his teeth. And nipping. She felt a jolt of pleasure at the light sting of his punishment. And then she imagined his mouth covering hers. His hands tracing her curves, molding, possessing, stirring her hunger, as he redirected the fiery temper in her—in the both of them—into an explosive passion.

She shivered. Her defiance had not only fueled his fury, but seemed to have stoked up the boiler on his libido as well. Blinded by lust and rage, he was hot. Reckless.

Dangerous.

Caleb's head turned slowly toward the door. And his eyes narrowed in concentration. The unmistakable snick of a lock engaging reverberated through the strained silence. Arianna shot a puzzled glance at the door. Then returned her gaze to him, staring slack-jawed.

No, he didn't. He did *not* just lock that door. *With his mind.*

With what seemed a perverse sense of satisfaction, he held her astonished gaze for several beats, while her mind busily sifted, sorted, catalogued data. After first considering, then discarding various hypotheses, she came finally to a conclusion of sorts.

"*Parlor* tricks," she muttered, an ironic use of the word. "Smoke and mirrors, all of it." Her lips curved in a frigid smile. "So, you're an amateur magician. That's it, isn't it? Why you've kept putting me off? Not wanting to admit you let the juvenile games go way too far."

"Amateur *magician?*" Caleb repeated her words quietly, incredulously, stressing the second one with cold precision, as if she had dared to cast an aspersion on his family name. She could feel the anger radiating off him. A match set to an already volatile keg of emotion.

Well, if he was so darn sensitive, he shouldn't have been playing those games in the first place. Arianna tipped her head back, eyed him speculatively. "You're good, though. I'll have to give you that. A regular Irish Criss Angel," she went on grudgingly, ignoring the unmistakable sound of thin ice cracking beneath her feet. "So, how'd you pull off the lightning thing? Come on, 'fess up. After scaring me half to death, I think you owe me."

A vein throbbed prominently in Caleb's temple. Buried beneath the tons of mad she had going on, Arianna's spidey sense had failed to get through to her. She had no idea that his control had snapped, tipping the scales, offsetting the precarious balance between the two sides of his dichotomous nature.

One that was very human. The other...not of this world.

Caleb leaned forward again, elbows resting on his knees. He sat quietly, staring into the flames, lost in thought as if he were plotting the course of some future action.

Finally, he turned to her again, his expression cold, aloof. His knuckles skimmed the underside of her jaw, then his thumb tipped her chin up, forcing her uncertain gaze to his. "Such a bold brat, you are, *a mhuirnín*," he murmured, shaking his head in admonishment.

"So very, very brazen as to think you can win a battle of wills against the likes of me." His gaze dropped to her throat, where a rapidly beating pulse made a lie of his observation. "Or maybe not so bold.... But no matter. For I've a mind to grant your request. To, shall we say, *revisit* those things that seem to have snared your interest." A chilling smile touched the corners of his lips. "And that, *cailín*, we'll be doing my way."

Chapter Fourteen

Arianna shivered at the cruel twist of his mouth, a mouth with the skill to pleasure or punish at will. Now she didn't like being snapped at. Usually gave as good as she got. But there was just something about the way he was looking at her that had her beginning to regret the provocation.

Still leaning toward the belief that all of the weird goings on had been nothing but a mind game, an illusion, she couldn't get her head around why he would have staged such an elaborate hoax.

And her suspicions that he was a mentalist did nothing to lessen the spellbinding effect of that dark, hypnotic gaze. Though she fought it consciously, she could feel herself sliding under his power. Little by little, she succumbed to the serenity of a floating sensation that numbed her limbs, loosened her inhibitions. Joy, lust, fear, a plethora of jumbled emotions all jockeyed for first position inside her. She trembled. Amber-colored liquid sloshed over the rim of her glass, spraying tiny drops of honeyed mead across her wrist.

"Allow me." Caleb's husky voice trailed across heightened nerve endings, as he slid the crystal wineglass from her fingers. Setting it on a piecrust table beside his own, he raised her wrist to his mouth.

"What are you—?"

Eyes holding hers, he lapped up the sticky drops. The rough texture of his tongue poured accelerant on the passionate embers flickering low in her belly. "Mmm...sweet."

Finding it difficult to separate dream from reality, she caught her lip between her teeth and bit back a low moan. Somewhere in the part of her brain still functioning with conscious thought, she noted he had neither acknowledged—nor refuted—the charges of trickery she had leveled against him. And yet...something in his enigmatic gaze whispered a warning: *None of what you've experienced in my company has been the result of sleight-of-hand, but rather, the invocation of some ancient and esoteric power.*

His regard seemed to intensify. And for a single, hysterical moment, Arianna wondered again if he wasn't reading her mind. Before she could fully process that thought, however, he was holding his hands out to her, palms turned upward. At her frown of confusion, he tipped his head, arched an ebony brow in an imperious command.

The summons made her mouth go dry. Her muscles seemed to atrophy. The arousing power rippling off the man in hot, sensual waves had her so seduced by this point that she feared the simple touch of his flesh would send her flying over the edge. With a tongue like sandpaper, she attempted to moisten parchment-dry lips. Again, his shameless gaze followed the movement. When his eyes returned to hers, embers of dream-spun passion smoldered in them, searing her insides. The look was raw. Elemental. Blatantly carnal. *A shared memory? God, help me. What's going on?*

"Arianna."

She started at the low rumble of his voice. Forcing her heavy eyelids to open, she felt drowsy, disorientated. Had she dropped off to sleep? "Caleb, what...."

"Your hands," he ordered quietly. The voice, the face was familiar. But not the eyes. Those were cold and implacable...the eyes of a stranger. "Place your hands in mine. *Now.*"

She did as he commanded. Without hesitation, without question. Because, with this strong compulsion stirring her desire, stealing her very will, she could do nothing else. As her hands touched his, a jolt of static electricity arced between them. In reflex, she tried to jerk away. But those long, elegant fingers curled vice-like around her wrists held her shackled.

His touch enflamed her, a raw, aching desire within a floating, dreamy euphoria....

"What...?" It was the oddest sensation. An invasive, shivery feeling...as if he were seeking entrance into her mind. A seductive quest to be admitted into her most private heart.

Reaching deep within herself, she drew on her own strength of will to subvert whatever he was trying to do to her. If he were a mentalist, he was skilled in manipulation, in playing on parapsychological elements of the psyche.

Why then did she fear she would be laying herself bare to him? Risking him coming to know her every hope, every secret desire? Made privy to every resounding victory, every crushing defeat? Did she really believe that all the experiences of her lifetime would be open to his scrutiny?

Including her mad obsession with him, she thought, suddenly in panic mode, mortified that her secret yearning for him might be revealed, her untamed passion for him unveiled. She just couldn't bear to have this nonsensical, incomprehensible, hopeless love in her heart stripped naked before him.

The truth came like a beacon light. It was all real, everything she had witnessed in his presence. *Caleb* was who...*what* her da had been warning her about.

"No," she breathed, refusing to let him into her mind. She couldn't...wouldn't allow this...this...dream weaver...this creature, unclassified as man, angel, or demon from hell, to know her foolish infatuation with him. She sensed that the mental barrier she had thrown up against him had slammed a steel door shut in her mind.

Arianna could hear him...actually *hear* him...swearing darkly inside her head. She experienced the sullen ripple of his impatience as if it were her own.

"*Oscail, cailín,*" he demanded softly in Gaelic. "Open your mind to me. *Now.*"

All at once, Arianna was flooded with childhood memories of him, of all the times they had walked together on that dreamswept shore. And although she sensed an aloofness there, a dark-clouded peril she had never felt in him before, he reciprocated his request for entry by opening himself to her first, enough to reveal that his honor in this thing was inviolate. Whatever the purpose of his exploration, he vowed, in the most intimate way possible, that he would eschew the secret places she marked as private. Leave untouched, unsullied, the cherished memories residing within her heart.

Slowly, of her own free will, she brought down the mental wall she had erected against him. The drugging numbness she had been experiencing intensified. A kind of psychic paralysis crept up her body and turned her limbs to stone.

"Caleb," she moaned deep in her throat, as she felt him slide into her mind. It was a mating of souls somehow more seductive, more intimate, than a mere physical joining. So entangled in her thoughts was he—and she in his—that it was impossible to distinguish where one of them ended and the other began. *God, who...what are you?*

Although certain he could hear her thoughts, her question went unanswered. Then suddenly the world turned upside down. The room in which they sat began to dissolve; the sofa, the floor, the very earth beneath her feet melted away. Like Alice falling through the rabbit hole, she began to tumble, head over heels, through a thick, viscous void, through a darkness suffocatingly devoid of light.

Spinning.... She was circling dizzily through a vast expanse of time and space, through a kaleidoscope of jagged shapes and luminous color. Eidetic images spun and twirled, puzzle pieces coming together in disjointed memories not all her own. For some were as old as the ages, as timeless as time itself.

She was alone and terrified, an apparition in a netherworld where hyper-intuitive senses warned that a monster prowled the night. Her perception shifted then. She was standing on a cushion of sand, the sea at her back, eyes raised to the splendor of a medieval fortress crowning the mountainside.

She searched the cliff's edge. She sensed the presence of her dark lover, a man of hereditary magic cloaked in the Irish mists and dusky shadow.

A frightful memory began to emerge then, infiltrating the ethereal haze that surrounded her. To Arianna's great horror, she discovered that she had stumbled back in time, sentenced to relive the terror of that fateful night on the coast.

Her gaze jerked first to the cloudless sky, taunting in its clarity, then settled on Caleb in silent supplication. And, as if on a director's cue, he began to point.

No, no, God, please. Not again.

Her prayer must have been answered, because the vision no longer repeated history. Instead of conjuring a lightning bolt, Caleb's outstretched hand indicated a specific location along the precipice overhead.

Against her will Arianna found herself searching for the shadowy male figure she had sensed before. She found him, crouched on a ledge above her. It was a strange sensation, she thought, this feeling of sharing her focal point with another. With Caleb, who seemed to be looking through her eyes, straining to see the face of the man hidden in the cleft of the rocks.

Arianna squeezed her eyes shut against the sensory overload. Holy God in heaven, this couldn't be happening. She must be losing her mind....

ॐ

Sensing her distress, Caleb ended their travel through the mists of time. Before departing her consciousness, however, he planted a suggestion that she would have no recollection of the experience, no ill effect from the experience. She would be left with a feeling of peace, a belief that she had simply nodded off to sleep in his arms.

Frustrated at not being able to identify the stalker, he uttered a pithy Gaelic curse and withdrew abruptly from the past. His fit of temper returned him to the present with an unpleasant jolt. Aware of Arianna's fingernails digging painfully into the meaty flesh of his palm, he glanced down at her. Trembling like a frightened kitten, her normally sun-kissed complexion was pallid, her eyes scrunched tightly shut.

"Easy now," he murmured, in the soothing tone he used to gentle a skittish colt. "All's well, luv. The journey's over."

That her eyes remained closed, breathing shallow, he first attributed to an attempt to stave off nausea. A residual motion sickness often plagued the occasional time traveler.

A closer look at her, however, told a very different story. *"Dia's Muire*, she's hyperventilating." Swearing grimly, he searched her face for some sign that she was regaining consciousness.

She wasn't.

Planning to massage her neck and shoulders, to get the blood flowing toward her brain, he wrested one hand free of her determined grasp. A pitiful, mewling cry spilled from her lips. Eyes still clenched together, she swiped frantically at the air until he had slipped his hand back into hers. She had quieted, but there was nothing natural about her state of calm.

The Gaelic word for "catatonic" sprang to mind.

"Holy Mother of God, what have I done to you?" Bringing their intertwined hands to his lips, he blew on her fingers, his thumbs rubbing the tops of her hands. "Open your eyes, Arianna." He gave the command a subtle push. "Come back to me. Here. Now."

Still nothing. Eyelids glued shut; nails, curved into talons, bit into his palms.

Caleb closed his eyes and summoned Seamus.

Within seconds, his old friend was unlocking the door and letting himself into the parlor. Brows drawn together, he stared at the scene confronting him. "What's the story, mate? Has she taken ill? What seems to be her problem?"

"Myself," Caleb muttered darkly, shaking his head. "I lost it, man."

"How...what happened?"

"She was on about the lightning, so she was. Demanding answers I couldn't give, winding me up. Finally, she got the notion that she was the victim of some kind of hoax. Accused me of being an amateur magician...em, how did she put it? An 'Irish Criss Angel' were her words exactly. Next thing I knew my bloody temper got the best of me."

"An amateur magician." Seamus looked stunned, then angered by the blatant insult.

Caleb's response was defensive of Arianna. "She's no understanding of who and what we are, Seamus. No clue that such a remark was akin to a racial slur." The magic in a de Danann man's blood defined his race, an integral part of who he was, of his history and heritage, no less than the color of a man's skin. "The fact that she was innocent of any intentional affront didn't weigh into the equation at the time."

Seamus nodded his understanding as Caleb went on. "I asked myself then, did her faulty reasoning not serve the greater purpose? Did it not provide a reasonable explanation, not only for the feats of magic she's already witnessed, but any she might do in future?"

"Logical," Seamus murmured.

"But I was gone, my friend." He sucked in a deep breath. "As sure as if a switch had been flipped inside me, my mindset became totally *sidhe*, of the faery world."

Seamus winced at his confession of giving himself over to his alternate nature.

"Just like that," a finger snap, "the cold-hearted side of myself slid into place, assuming dominion. 'Twas in that state, I devised a strategy, a plan born of anger...excused by faulty reasoning."

Caleb paused, searched Arianna's face again. *No change.* "I thought it likely she'd caught a glimpse of the stalker. And was it not she herself, I argued, the one demanding we review the events of that day? And did I not—in my *magician's* bag of tricks—possess the very tool with which to grant her wish?"

"The Sense of Innate Knowledge," Seamus murmured, waving a hand absently at the hearth. The dying flames burst into brilliant plumes of orange, blue and gold.

"Exactly," Caleb replied. "I'd only to forge a mental link between us and transport ourselves back to the day in question. Once there, the mind merge would allow me to identify the bastard by looking through her eyes. Armed with the knowledge of his identity, the Council could sit in judgement, make a ruling as to whether the Minion was to live or die."

"Makes perfect sense. So, what did you discover?"

"Not a bleedin' thing. She didn't see his face."

Seamus perched his large frame on the arm of the sofa nearest Arianna. Towering over her, he leaned down to examine her more closely. "She's breathing normally, muscles functioning, holding her upright. Sometimes a full recovery takes a wee bit of time."

Caleb let out a long, tortured sigh.

"Don't be too hard on yourself, *a chara*. 'Twas a reasonable assumption, my friend, your thinking you might identify the culprit in that way. And I've heard of no previous instance where *double tripping* has left a mortal any the worse for wear. On the contrary, our scribes and bards have likened the experience to a pleasant daydream for the one experiencing it. Like being cast adrift on a balmy lake at the break of dawn."

"And so it might have been for herself," Caleb admitted darkly, "had I not lost my effin' temper. With our minds linked, ourselves drifting serenely through rainbow arcs of light, sure, the altered state would have been the likes of a child's sweet dream for herself—instead of a fecking nightmare."

Caleb continued to scrutinize Arianna's delicate features. But her eyes remained tightly sealed, almost as if to shut out the new reality he had thrust upon her.

Seamus reached down, his thumb gently lifting her eyelid to assess the reaction of her pupils to light. His touch was casual, unassuming. Completely innocent. And yet, Caleb's hands curved into fists, his jaw clenching, body going rigid in possessive rage.

"Pupils are reactive. Color's better, I'm thinking." Seamus glanced at his friend, a flicker of surprise touching his expression at Caleb's stiff posture. At the flinty steel girding the green eyes glaring murderously back at him.

Seamus cocked a brow in savage amusement. "Only trying to help, mate," he demurred, raising both hands in a defensive gesture.

Caleb blew out a heavy breath. "Sorry, man. I don't know what's gotten into me. And you're right. Already I can see a hint of rose warming the pallor of her cheeks."

"A bit of a spitfire, is she not?" Seamus asked.

"She is indeed. Our first night together she told me she knew I would never hurt her." He gave a disgusted huff. "And what did I do with that trust? Violently, single-mindedly, dragged her spinning through the annals of time...*on a bloody magic carpet ride.*"

Seamus squeezed his shoulder. "There's been no permanent harm done."

"I'm not so sure of that."

At the cryptic remark, Seamus tipped his head in question.

"Me, with the iron will." Caleb gave a half-laugh. "And where this one's concerned, it seems I've no bleedin' self control a'tall. You've notified the other members of the Council of my suspicions, that she may be the mere mortal woman we're awaiting, the 'Chosen One'?"

Seamus nodded and rose to his feet. "I have. And, as you requested, several of the lads will be at the pub later tonight for a look at her.

Caleb, as your friend, I have to reiterate that there could well be another explanation for the dreams, for your sudden lack of control." Seamus paused, shot his friend a pointed look. "'Twould account for the violence you felt toward your closest friend for daring to lay his hands on her."

Caleb looked sheepish.

"At the risk of repeating myself, it's not uncommon for a man of our race to have lucid dreams about his *anam cara*—"

"Soul mate, is it? A mere mortal? Seamus, would you ever just cop the frig on! We've been over this. You're suggesting I may be destined to spend my life with a woman who'll die if I take her to my bed?"

Closer than a brother, Seamus clearly took no umbrage at his friend's outburst. He responded in the quiet, patient tone one would use in explaining something complex to a young child. "Have you not considered the possibility that the girl may be both the Chosen One AND your Anam Cara?"

"And, in her encounter with the darkness as the Chosen One, she could very well end up *dead*," Caleb countered grimly, choosing to ignore the sick throb of loss the suggestion lodged in his belly. "An outcome, which seems the most likely after three thousand years—"

"Or she succeeds in her quest," Seamus interrupted. "Thus ending the curse that prevents our two races from coupling. Aside from that, our men have been known to marry a mere mortal." At the instant flash of pain, of outrage, in his friend's eyes, Seamus sighed. "I'm not speaking of your mother here, Caleb. I'm only suggesting that in these modern times, there are ways.... Though mortal contraceptives aren't effective, there's always surgery—

"You know very well, the snip doesn't work on a de Danann male," Caleb argued. "Our bodies heal—"

"'Twould be the woman having to undergo the procedure—*her* decision," Seamus asserted. "Is she consciously aware of the dreaming?"

"She is, yes."

"Hmm... So, you've admitted that much to her at least?" Seamus asked.

"I've admitted nothing as yet."

"But you will?"

"Once I determine a way to explain it to her, without revealing the existence of our people." Caleb was referring to the requirement in the *Geis* that the Woman of Promise be forbidden knowledge of his kind. "When I can tell her just that much, and no more."

Seamus grunted. "Either way...and I'll give you a free pass to eat the head off me for saying this again...I've a strong sense that this is the woman you're destined to wed."

"*Go raibh maith agat,* Seamus. Thanks, but I think not. Just remember the auld mortal saying: *Nil aon leigheas ar an ngra ach posadh.*" The only cure for love is marriage."

Seamus slanted him one of those knowing looks only a best mate could hope to get away with.

"Look, man, this is all naught but a classic case of lust," Caleb insisted. "A matter of wanting a thing all the more for it being something I can't have. For that reason alone, I should be staying away from herself." Continuing to massage her fingers, Caleb noted that her frantic death-grip had begun to relax. "The wee thing's likely more at risk from me and my raging libido, than from any satanic minion. Which is why I'm considering, at the next meeting, appointing another Council member to champion her."

Seamus laughed out loud and clapped him on the back. "*Tá brón orm, a chara.* Sorry, my friend, but you know it doesn't work that way. It's written in the ancient scrolls that the mortal woman will inadvertently choose her own protector, the one of us to whom she gives her heart. And that man is ordained to feel drawn to her, mindful of her safety. Your reaction when I touched her satisfies the one requirement. So, what d'ya reckon, lad? You've been in her mind. Is it yourself she loves?"

Caleb snorted. "*Love.* And what would I know of that mortal emotion? Anyways, you know how I feel about invading a person's privacy. I wasn't after delving into such areas."

Seamus chuckled. "You'd not have had to be digging very far beneath the surface to find the truth of it, my friend. Her feelings for you shine so brightly in her eyes, you'd have to wear sunglasses not to be blinded by the glare of it." Seamus rose from the arm of the loveseat and strode toward the door. "I've to be getting back to the kitchen now. Just give her a wee while, mate, and she'll be right as rain."

Thanks be to God, except for the occasional tremor, the shivers racking Arianna's body had all but stopped. "What the devil have I got you into, *a mhuirnín?*" he said softly.

When she finally allowed him to ease one hand free of her tortured grasp, Caleb drew her into a tender embrace, her head cradled against his shoulder. Lips against her ear, he whispered to her in an ancient tongue and slowly, gently, coaxed her back to the present.

Chapter Fifteen

It was almost midnight by the time they pulled into the Jury's Inn parking lot in Galway City, Ireland's Gaelic hinterland, according to Caleb. Something had changed between them at the restaurant, Arianna noted as they strolled along Quay Street, a pedestrianized walkway. After a fainting spell, which she attributed to drinking alcohol on an empty stomach, Caleb had been overly attentive, romantic even.

They passed smokers mobbing the streets outside the late-night pubs, the glow of streetlights through the swirling mist providing the setting a surrealistic quality. Brightly colored doors hung on two and three-storey limestone buildings standing flush beside each other. The hand-painted shop signs lettered in Gaelic, the window boxes, sculptures, and hanging flower baskets adorning the buildings alluded to another place in time.

"It's kind of like...a medieval outdoor shopping mall," Arianna said, the layers of cool, soft fog circling their feet.

On Mill Street, they crossed O'Brien's Bridge, aptly named for the Old Bridge Mill at the end of the block. Arianna looked over the concrete barrier into the turbulent River Corrib, so swollen from recent storms that the waters almost reached the street.

Turning left onto Dominick Street, Arianna pressed her nose against the darkened window of a boutique. "I'm coming back sometime when the stores are open. The shopping in Ennistymon leaves a lot to be desired."

Caleb reached for her hand as they crossed the street. He pulled her into a private alleyway, a narrow gravel footpath snaking beneath an archway between two buildings. In a courtyard on the other side of the arch, Caleb edged her backwards against a white stucco wall.

"Only a taste," he murmured, whether asking permission or making a solemn vow to himself, Arianna wasn't sure. Eyes searching her face, he tucked a lock of her windblown hair behind one ear.

Her hands clutched his forearms, felt the flex of his biceps as she leaned into him. Eyes fluttering closed, she followed the artful design his fingers drew across her lips.

His hands braced against the wall behind her and caged her between his strong arms. In the cool, murky darkness, her eyes found his. She reveled in his familiar features, the heavy-lidded eyes, aquiline nose, strong jaw, and the sensual lips she couldn't wait a moment longer to taste again.

"Just kiss me already," she breathed.

She inhaled him, that woodsy, all-male scent that was Caleb alone. His head dipped, lips tracing the sensitive flesh beneath her ear. Her bones went fluid, her body melting into the wall behind her.

"What ever am I to do with you?" His voice was low and smoky, the languorous timbre reacquainting her every secret place with his dark sensuality.

"I'm sure you'll think of something," she whispered.

His mouth descended, hovered just above hers. She could feel his warm, minty breath against her lips. His mouth teased hers, a brush of butterfly wings. And again. She trembled, sighed. Her stomach dipped into a slow, liquid swirl as finally he sank into the kiss, leisurely sampling, savoring every sensation.

He raised his head—just enough to change the angle of the kiss—and her mouth chased his. Demanding more. Insisting that the teasing be over.

Her lips parted on a gasp as he complied, taking her mouth now to raid. To plunder. With no apology, no restraint, his tongue invaded that inner sanctum. Passion exploded into white-hot heat, an unquenchable flame. He tasted of animal lust and recklessness, Arianna thought. Of magic and dreams. *Not a man to toy with*, a small voice inside her warned. *Be sure. A cautious woman would step away from him now, take time to think things through.*

When had she ever claimed to be prudent? she countered. And instead of drawing back, she stepped in closer still. She felt the earth tilt on its axis, begin to spin madly out of control. Arianna steadied herself with her arms around his neck, fingers tangled in his hair.

Not for a minute, as she whimpered in need, as she slid one leg along his outer thigh, did she stop to consider the risks of her total lack of restraint. Nor did she consider the indecency of urging a man she barely knew to take her against a cold, damp wall in a darkened alleyway.

He caught her bottom lip between his teeth, and nipped, the slight sting of his bite snapping her out of the fever possessing her. "We'd best be ending this before it's too late, *cailín*," he whispered, his warm breath tickling her ear. "I'm sure you'll agree that this is neither the time, nor the place."

She swallowed a moan of protest, stunned by what she had almost done—would have surely done—had he not had the wherewithal to bring things to a halt. Her body was trembling, whether from the damp and cold, or the unspent passion she couldn't be sure. Caleb unzipped his jacket and wrapped it around her, enfolding her in his warmth, his unique musky scent. He held her until she stopped shaking, then pulled away and slipped an arm around her. "Come, *a chailín mo chroí,* let's get you in out of the cold."

The fog parted around their feet as they dashed the last few yards to their destination. The pub had been erected in 1783 according to a plaque beside the entrance. "Trad sessions began at half-ten," Caleb told her, as they swam against the tide of people spilling out the thick, oaken doors.

Inside, the bar was all dark wood and crumbling stone walls. A varnished flagstone floor was strewn with sawdust. Glass globe lights hung from poles placed strategically around the room. To the left, built-in wooden drawers were stacked to the ceiling. "From the days pubs doubled as grocers." Caleb spoke into her ear to be heard above the festive din.

In an immense stone hearth in front of them, a hungry fire took gulping bites out of a massive stack of logs and peat. To the left was a lighted alcove, enclosed by a black wrought iron gate. Inside, water flowed freely from the rusty spout of an antique wooden pump.

On the small stage in front of the alcove, a female fiddler stood with her back to the rowdy crowd, reeling madly in 4/4 time. Arianna felt a hand clamp around her wrist, as Caleb dragged her out of the path of a couple spinning to the lively rhythm.

"So this is craic," Arianna called out to him.

Caleb gave her hand a squeeze as he guided her through the mayhem with the precision of a sergeant moving his troops across a minefield. They managed to snag a stone-topped table in a private corner, safely out of the melee. As soon as they were seated, a waitress with an hourglass figure, a slender waist and jutting breasts, made a beeline in their direction. Her flawless skin seemed translucent against her dark, wild beauty, the red of her lips—and the tiny scrap of black fabric she undoubtedly calls a dress. She slithered up to Caleb, blatantly ignoring Arianna—and another couple who had arrived ahead of them.

"*Dia duit*, Caleb," she purred through wide, full lips. Her inky curls were caught back by a black velvet band, the subject of the joyful singsong currently being performed on stage. "*Cé chaoi bhuil tú?*"

Caleb inclined his head, polite but distant. "I'm grand, thanks. But would you be speaking English so? My lady here's from the States. Doesn't have the Gaelic." *My lady?*

"A blow-in, is she?" Pouty red lips pursed in disdain, cat-green eyes appraising.

And finding her not worth the effort of a more elaborate put-down, Arianna thought as the woman turned those kohl-lined eyes back to Caleb. Hungry. Smoldering. Arianna was appalled as the woman's gaze took a long, slow journey down his body—before halting shamelessly in his lap. Her tongue moistened her lower lip, like a cat sizing up a mouse on the dinner menu.

"Will it be a pint for ye, then?" Her voice was soft and sultry.

Arianna cast a quick glance at Caleb who appeared not only deaf, dumb, and blind to the vixen's seductive charms, but totally unimpressed with the female arsenal pointing at him from beneath her shoulders. Just in case the woman had any misconceptions about that, however, he made his preference for Arianna clear by taking her hand, brushing her knuckles lightly with his lips. *Oh, yeah. Major brownie points there.*

As the lively trad music blasted from the front of the room, he leaned over to speak into Arianna's ear. A chill of delight danced up her spine. "Fancy a Guinness, luv?"

Love.... Okay, so the word was a casual endearment, like "honey". Still, she liked the way it had sounded on his lips. With a possessive hand on his arm marking her territory, Arianna shrugged. "Never had it, but, hey, I'm in Ireland. I ought to give it a try."

Caleb raised two fingers, then turned his attention back to Arianna. Summarily dismissed, the seductress glided away. Even so, the green-eyed monster lurking inside Arianna tried to convince her that the woman's bold advances had been indicative of something more between Caleb and her.

She felt Caleb's eyes on her. "Is something troubling you, *cailín?*"

"No." Her reply was short and succinct, its brevity a clear contradiction.

Caleb's eyebrows pulled together. "Our server, Gwen, is Seamus's new girlfriend. I was after meeting her for the first time only last week."

It was disconcerting. This talent he seemed to have for reading her mind.

Sitting on the same side of the table, they were both facing the stage. Caleb lounged in his seat, long body angled, arm draped over the back of her chair. His foot kept time with the pulsing rhythm of a ribald Irish ditty.

Gorgeous Gwen was back in short order. Serving the dark, frothy beer, she made a point of leaning over Caleb's shoulder, positioning breasts—which were struggling valiantly to remain inside her bodice—in such close proximity to his mouth, he could have taken a bite.

Exactly what the black-haired hussy no doubt had in mind.

As the waitress departed, Caleb clinked glasses with Arianna. "*Sláinte.*"

As he took a long drink, she hazarded a sip. *WD40 with a kick.*

She must have made a face, because Caleb chuckled and leaned toward her. "It's an acquired taste, *cailín.* Now you've tried it, will I order something more to your liking? A Bailey's or a Jameson perhaps?"

What? And have that Irish poster girl for the sensual Celtic woman flaunting herself back to their table again? "No, it's fine. I'll just sip on it, give it a chance."

The music too loud for conversation, Arianna focused on the stage. A kilt-clad man weighing easily over three hundred pounds played his heart out on a tin whistle like a child's toy in his thick and cumbersome hands.

As the group broke into a lively rendition of "The Galway Girl", the female fiddler climbed onto a chair, eliciting the boisterous appreciation of every male patron in the place. Encouraged by the clapping and foot stomping, the girl stepped from the chair up onto a barstool. Amidst whistles and wolf-calls, she swiveled her hips in time to the music, stroking not only her instrument, but also the well-oiled crowd into a frenzy.

Caught up in the spirit of things, a mother and daughter duo danced their way to the foot of the stage. Mom beamed with pride as the red-haired teenager moved her feet, arms stiff at her sides *a la* Michael Flatley's *Lord of the Dance*. Then the girl stopped, planted her hands on her hips and, with a saucy nod, challenged her mother to a dance off. And so it went, the two of them exchanging dances, back and forth, faster and faster, until their feet were pummeling the flagstones together to the roar of the crowd's delight.

"Brilliant!" Caleb clapped, his smile wide.

The musicians announced a break and chairs scraped away from the tables. The place emptied as customers stepped outside to indulge their habit.

As they stood up to stretch their legs, Arianna sent Caleb a warm smile. "This is amazing. Thanks so much for bringing me here."

"My favorite spot in Galway. A couple of the musicians are mates of mine. Hold on a bit and I'll introduce you."

Arianna spotted Seamus coming through the front door and pointed him out to Caleb, who motioned him to join them. As Seamus wove his way through the milling crowd, he stopped to speak with one person or another. By the time he arrived at their table, he was flanked by two of the musicians.

"How's things?" Caleb greeted 'the lads', his voice raised above the hubbub.

He moved slightly in front of Arianna, angling his body in an almost protective stance. Was she imagining things again, or had Caleb tensed as the three men joined them? "Arianna, meet the piper, Sean O'Casey," he began, referring to the uillean pipes. "And Paddy McClellan's yer man on the bodhrán." To the men, he said, "Arianna here's just after arriving from the States."

"Hiya," said Paddy, reaching out a hand. Sean gave a distant nod.

Arianna accepted Paddy's hand and acknowledged Sean with a smile. "Nice to meet you both. I was just telling Caleb how much I've been enjoying the set."

"*Go raibh mile maith agat,*" Sean replied, looking deep into her eyes. His penetrating gaze was disquieting, made her feel light-headed.

She broke eye contact. She was probably just being paranoid, but she couldn't seem to shake the feeling that she was somehow the focal point of their gathering. That they were there to size her up. *But for what?*

The two musicians exchanged a clandestine glance. Although nowhere near as beautiful as her Caleb, they both possessed an almost breathtaking sensuality. *Sheesh.* Irish men ought come with a warning label: Too Hot To Handle.

A few minutes of small talk and assessing glances later, Sean and Paddy returned to the stage for their next set. Seamus wandered off, arm around his new girlfriend, Gwen.

Two or three hours—and four or more Baileys Irish Creams—later, the lights began to flicker on and off, signaling closing time. After the Guinness, Arianna had switched to the liqueur. Not much of a drinker, she had never been drunk. Probably why the mead at the restaurant had hit her so hard. And after all the alcohol she had consumed at the pub, she was surprised to be feeling so clear-headed.

Raising a hand in farewell to Seamus, Caleb helped her on with her coat. "It's after two o'clock," Caleb said as they stepped out into the foggy night. "The trip to Clare takes about an hour and a half. What d'ya reckon we stay at Jury's and head back in the morning?"

"Works for me." The quiver in her voice gave away her nervousness.

Even though she had wanted this man, *or his twin,* for as long as she could remember, they had only recently met in the here and now. It just felt too soon for the two of them to become intimate. But the effect he had on her left her feeling panicked and unsure.

At the hotel reception desk, however, Caleb requested two rooms. *Long sigh of relief here.* As they rode up the elevator to the second floor, he gave her hair a playful tug. "Relax, *cailín,* I won't bite. Not tonight at any rate."

Arianna's heart squeezed at his sensitivity, while another part of her body sobbed with regret that she wouldn't be lying naked in his arms tonight.

She changed the subject. "I've been wondering.... Why do you call me Colleen?"

"It's the Gaelic for 'girl', spelled c-a-i-l-i fada-n,."

Girl? That's it? And all this time she had been thinking it was some romantic endearment.

They said goodnight at her door. "We've connecting rooms if you need anything," he said, then brushed her lips in a brief kiss that left her aching for more.

Arianna lay in bed, tossing and turning, imagining him undressing, his magnificent male body sliding naked beneath the sheets. Lying there now. Within reach. Totally accessible. All she had to do was knock on that connecting door.

But no. It was too soon. She had to be sure.

Imprisoned three thousand miles beneath the surface of the earth, deep within its molten core, Anathema has been slowly waking since Samhain Eve. His evil gaining strength, his sleep is spinning off into lucid dreaming, a kind of corporeal awareness. In this state of false awakening, the Beast sent forth telepathic directives to his Minion to go forth and locate a physical body suitable for habitation.

An evil emissary was chosen from amongst the descendents of the Nephilim, the giants fathered by fallen angels who mated with human women. They were those who dance to him in the faerie grove each year on All Hallows Eve, a celebration of the pact they made with his dark power nigh onto three millennia past.

Possessed by the spirit of the Minion, the Mortal Man burns with bitterness. Like the molten iron surrounding the chamber of the beast, his anger is destined to overflow and burn...burn...burn a diabolic path of destruction.

The music in the Mortal's head is mesmeric, brooding, the Lost Chord of the Ancients weaving through the tapestry of creation from a time before time, until time is no more. But as the Mortal tips his head to listen, a discordant key shatters the peace of the sacred melody. It becomes a funeral dirge...a fugue performed by monsters and madmen.

The hollow click of a metronome speeds the days exponentially as humanity races hell-bent toward the eve of destruction. The profane sound increases, echoes, coalesces with the ticking of the clock of the ages, each strike marking the moment until life will be no more.

Already the alarm is sounding, ringing out a dire warning. The desecration of all mankind grows close at hand. The prophecy of doom transcribed onto the pages of tomorrow, thousands of years before yesterday, fulfilled.

The Mortal paces first in circles, then in squares, each footstep counted aloud. He stops to listen, before arguing with the roar of voices in his head. The spirit messenger sent forth to buffet the Mortal on the Eve of Samhain has taken root within him. Tentacles of evil, like a visceral cancer, now gnaw at his entrails, devouring all sanity, all reason, until it has consumed every vestige of what was once a man's free will.

Stripped of the burdensome chains of conscience, the Mortal dissolves into dementia, until he becomes the very Evil that seduced him with promises of great wealth, great power...and immortality. In their ungodly mating, the Mortal and the Minion, the insane and the damned, become one...

The spawn of he whose name shall not be named: Anathema.

"The time is now!" The Minion's words are slurred, his voice a serpent's hiss cold as death itself.

A death rattle sounds in the throat of humankind as the unholy Minion shrieks a curse to the heavens. "NOW!" The echoing roar of his madness explodes off the planets and stars, races like a hind up the mountainside, and tears through the tall green grasses. And that which was once the Man throws his head back and howls like a beast at the moon.

❦

Arianna's screams woke Caleb from the lucid dream they both had shared. His feet hit the floor running. The power of his mind flung the door to the adjoining room open. He found her whimpering and thrashing about, but otherwise untouched by the malignant creature he'd heard roaring in the night.

Caleb sat beside her and shook her shoulder gently. "Arianna wake up. You're having a nightmare, love." Moving restlessly, she pushed the duvet down. The lacy black thing she was wearing barely covered her small, firm breasts. *Bloody hell!*

"No..." Her head rolled back and forth on the pillow, releasing the delicate fragrance of honeysuckle and wild meadow flowers.

"Wake up, love." He brushed one sun-kissed cheek with his knuckles. His fingers sifted through the golden strands of tangled silk floating over her pillow.

She settled. "Caleb, I need you..." she sighed in her sleep. Lips pouting, her face turned into his hand. Her pink tongue moistened her lips, grazing his palm.

Smothering a vile oath, he snatched his hand away as if he'd been burned.

The sudden motion woke her. "What...what's wrong?"

He turned on the bedside lamp to chase away the darkness. "You were having a bad dream," he murmured.

Arianna shuddered. "It was awful. Demons and a crazy man...."

"I know, love. It's all over now. Go back to sleep." He reached out to shut off the light, but her hand stopped him.

"Stay with me? Please?"

Her expressive features let him know the moment she realized he was sitting beside her completely nude. She caught her bottom lip between her teeth. "I heard you screaming. Didn't waste time getting dressed," he explained, stating the obvious.

Her cheeks pinkened. "Please, just hold me for a while? I don't want to be alone."

Caleb clicked off the lamp, then slid beneath the duvet. Careful to keep a sheet between them, he spooned her. "Sleep now," he whispered and felt her relax against him.

When her slow, even breathing indicated she was sleeping restfully, he uncurled himself from around her. Quenching the fires of temptation, he slipped from the bed, cursing himself for a fool.

The door between their rooms made a quiet click in the silence as he drew it shut behind him.

Chapter Sixteen

"Don't bother getting out, Caleb. You're running late for your meeting." House key in hand, Arianna released her seatbelt and leaned over to give him a peck on the lips. "I had a really amazing time last night," she said, then paused, her cheeks growing pink. "And thanks for staying with me until I went back to sleep. That dream really creeped me out."

He smiled, tapped her nose with his finger. "'Twas my pleasure."

She slid out of the SUV and, at the front door, turned to wave goodbye. Caleb knew that the suggestion he had left in her mind during the episode at the restaurant had wiped out any memory of their disagreement in the parlor.

Wanting to be sure she had no problem getting into the house, Caleb watched her slide the key into the lock before backing out of the driveway. He had traveled no more than a block, when his mobile rang. Not particularly in the mood to speak with anyone, he was about to let the call go into voicemail, when he felt it. A sharp jolt of precognition that told him something was wrong.

He tapped the phone. "MacNamara here."

A choked sob came from the other end of the line. "Caleb?"

At Arianna's ragged cry, Caleb spun the Land Rover around on the narrow road as if he were driving a Mini. "Somebody broke in." The tremor in her voice betrayed her shock. "My God, everything's destroyed! Why? Why would anybody do something like this to me?"

"Get out of there." The command was automatic. Absolute. "Do you hear me, Arianna?" When she didn't respond, he shouted, "Get out! *Now*!"

"I am, I *am* out." She seemed to be fighting to disguise the whimper in her voice. "I left as soon as I saw the damage. Whoever did this could still be inside."

"I'm almost there. Walk across the street, away from the house, and wait for me." He disconnected and called the gardai. He sounded calm, in control. 'Twas a bloody lie.

As he rounded the corner, Caleb found her standing in the middle of the road, arms crossed, hugging herself. He slammed on the brakes and bolted out the door. He took her into his arms and she melted against him. Like it was the most natural thing in the world for her to seek solace there.

Caleb held her and stroked her hair, murmuring words of comfort in Gaelic. After the trembling lessened, he led her to the passenger side of the Land Rover and opened the door. "Sit here, whilst I've a look around."

Arianna clutched at his jacket. "No, Caleb. You are *not* going in there. It's way too dangerous. Please, just stay with me while we call the police."

"I rang the gards and they'll be here straight away. I'll only peek in the door. Sure, whoever did this is undoubtedly long gone by now."

"That's not what you said two minutes ago." At the implacable look on his face, she huffed a breath. "Okay, fine. But if you're going in there, I'm going with you." As he opened his mouth to dictate otherwise, she held up her hand. "*Not* negotiable."

Pure, unadulterated rage rose within Caleb at the destruction greeting him. The tiny cottage lay in ruins, resembling the aftermath of a terrorist attack. Pictures and knickknacks made a heap of rubble, of broken glass and twisted metal strewn across the bare wooden floor. The thick-piled hearthrug in front of the hearth had been thrown on top of the over-turned sofa. Ash from the fireplace scattered about the living room left everything coated with gray and greasy soot.

The fire iron with which Arianna had armed herself on that first night now hung lopsided from a hole in the wall. Vases and figurines were smashed in a million pieces beneath a cracked front window clearly their target.

Caleb closed his eyes. Attempting to trace the vile energy patterns left by the intruder, he sensed a whirlwind of disappointment, hatred, greed and blood lust, all leaving a penetrating chill.

"Came for her, did you, you twisted bastard?" he muttered under his breath. A vein throbbed in his temple as he tried to contain his temper at what had been done.

Too late. Already full-blown, his fury reverberated off the walls. The floorboards began to sway and vibrate beneath their feet. Broken bits and bobs of what had once belonged to Arianna's parents shimmied off the end of tables and shelves. As the wee mortal's startled gasp penetrated his meditative state, Caleb fought to regain control. Within seconds he had brought the quake-like tremors to a halt.

At the sound of gravel crunching beneath the wheels of a motor vehicle, Caleb and Arianna returned to the front door. Two uniformed officers climbed out of the patrol car. One, a wiry, efficient-looking fellow, identified himself as Tommy Varden. Stepping past them into the cottage, he let out a long, low whistle at the extent of the damage.

"Looks personal to me," he concluded, flipping open a notepad. "Act of rage. Revenge. Have you any enemies, Miss...em?"

"Sullivan. And yes, from the looks of the place, I would imagine I do."

Caleb's lips quirked at the sarcasm, which sailed right over the other man's head.

"Miss...Sullivan, is it? Would there be an ex-husband in the picture? Or a former boyfriend not taking a break-up very well?"

"Nope. No exes. Husbands or otherwise."

"So you're an American?" the younger garda commented. "Anyone back in the States with a grudge? Business deal gone badly? Family member cut out of an inheritance?"

"I'm Irish, not American. And no, I haven't had any such problems."

While Arianna's statement was being taken, Caleb slipped away upstairs. On his way back down a few minutes later, he passed the younger garda, pad in hand.

Garda Varden looked up. "Like this upstairs, is it?"

"I haven't been up—" Arianna began.

"'Tis," Caleb interrupted.

The younger officer joined them. "No sign of forced entry. Has anyone else a key to your home?"

"No one ex—"

"Except the property manager, Miles Kavanagh," Caleb interrupted again.

Arianna shot him a wide-eyed "let me speak for myself" look.

"Right, so. We'll look into it. Course the locks are virtually worthless. Anyone can get past them with a credit card. I'd advise you have some proper locks installed on your doors—front and back. Steel pins for the windows as well." He paused. "Have you anywhere else to stay, Miss? Until you get the place sorted?"

"Umm—"

"Yes, she does." Caleb met Arianna's exasperated stare head-on.

"Would you mind not stepping on my tongue?" she hissed.

He ignored her. "I've guest quarters the lady's welcome to use."

"I'd take him up on that, Miss. Least, 'til you've things set to right around here. No harm in installing an alarm system either."

A mournful sigh escaped Arianna's lips as she took in the mayhem. Gazing longingly at the bare mantle, she glanced down at the collection of family photographs smashed and strewn about the floor like so much garbage. All the years her father had held this place in trust for her, and in only a matter of minutes...

"Miss? Miss Sullivan?"

'Wh-what? Sorry, my mind was wandering."

"They're asking for a phone number," Caleb said.

The wee thing looked so forlorn that he slipped a comforting arm around her, while she recited her cell phone number.

"C'mere to me, fellas. Take my card as well," Caleb suggested. "You'll be able to reach the lady at my place with any news."

Promising to stay in touch with progress on the investigation, the officers left.

"Go on up now and collect your things."

"Look, Caleb, I appreciate the invitation to stay with you, but it's still early in the day. I should be able to get somebody in to fix the windows and locks, and get most of this mess cleared away before nightfall."

"Bollocks! You're thinking to get a repairman out here today, just like that?" He snapped his fingers. "'Twill take days, maybe a couple of weeks, to put things to right around here. Now do as I say and go collect your things." He bit off a Gaelic curse as she angled a stubborn chin in his direction. A flame of warning kindled in his eyes. "Don't fight me on this, Arianna. Because I'll win, I assure you. It's simply too bloody dangerous for you to be staying here all alone."

She scalded him with a glare. "How *dare* you presume to order me around," she ground out through clenched teeth. "It's something my own father wouldn't have done."

Jaw set, Caleb widened his stance. "And therein lies the problem, so."

Arianna's mouth moved soundlessly.

"Accept it, *cailín*. I'm not leaving here without you. Not with that smarmy devil after you. So you'll either come with me now—" The pitch of his voice went dangerously quiet— "Or it's a flight back home, you'll be booking today."

Caleb could tell she was about to scoff at his threat, and so he sent her mental images to let her know that he meant what he was saying. He watched her eyes narrow suspiciously, as she pictured the lightning. And the fire. And the way she had lost consciousness on the ride home that first night. Something that felt like victory sang through his veins when he sensed her resignation.

This, after she saw herself boarding an Aer Lingus flight back to the States. Like an automaton. Unaware of what she was doing until after the plane had taken off.

"Okay, Caleb, you win this round. And let's even say you're right about the safety thing. But you just don't get it, do you? That you should have *invited* me to stay with you, not *commanded* me to stay with you."

Cutting short an exasperated eye-roll, he bowed his head with mock cordiality. "You're absolutely right. What was I thinking? Let me remedy that now, will I? Ms. Sullivan, would you do me the honor of accepting the hospitality of my home?" Still, he couldn't help but end the polite façade by growling, "So you'll not be getting yourself bloody murdered in your sleep."

The postscript must have tickled Arianna's funny bone, because he could tell she was biting her lip to hold back a grin. "Why, thank you, Caleb. And I expect it should only be for a day or two at most."

He followed her upstairs, watched her grow pale as she witnessed the extent of the vandalism. Everything was in shambles. The cedar chest at the foot of the bed was upended, clothes spilling out of closets, chests and drawers. Most disturbing of all, however, was the shredded state of the mattress. It had been stabbed repeatedly with a long, sharp implement. Exactly where she'd have been sleeping had they not decided to stay overnight in Galway.

Caleb slipped his arm around her. "Most of the furnishings survived intact. Those that didn't, well, they're replaceable, aren't they? Unlike yourself." She trembled and he massaged the back of her neck. "Come. Let's get you out of here now, will we?"

Chapter Seventeen

"I don't like this." Arianna spoke somberly, forehead pressed against the window. The view was breathtaking...literally, the altitude so high the lack of oxygen made getting air into her lungs laborious. The incline was so steep they seemed to be driving perpendicular to the high and winding road bordered on one side by a sheer rise of rock, on the other by an endless drop to the sea.

"Don't like what?" Caleb asked, glancing in her direction. "Being up in the clouds?"

Clouds? With a shuddering glance, Arianna looked *down* at what she had believed to be scattered patches of fog. And below—much, much farther below—at the waves splashing against the jagged rocks. "Now that you mention it," she muttered. "But no, that wasn't what I was talking about. I just hate letting some sick jerk get the best of me, run me out of my own house. I've never run away from anything before."

"Ever had someone fancy hacking you into a million wee pieces before?" he inquired blandly. She figured she must have turned a lighter shade of pale at his remark, because he gruffly apologized.

"No, I'm the one who's sorry." She looked at his hands. Long fingers, lightly dusted with hair. Neat, square-cut fingernails. God, she loved his hands. *Focus, Arianna.*

His head turned. He fixed her with those bewitching green eyes. "Sorry, for what?"

"Take a woman out to dinner," she quipped. "Next thing you know she's moving in."

"You're very welcome in my home, Arianna." His voice was girded with steel. "Were that not the case, sure I'd not have insisted you come here. I don't do polite."

No, he wasn't exactly the type for the grand sacrificial gesture, the obligatory kindness. Still, she hated the thought of invading his privacy, intruding on his reclusive lifestyle.

Resting her head back, Arianna stared at the cumulus clouds etching the sky in shades of charcoal and gunmetal gray. "Looks positively ominous," she said to the window.

A scatter of whitewashed villages dotted the valley below, so far away that the white-fleeced sheep looked like tiny cotton balls grazing the scraggly farmland. Thatched-roof cottages resembled toy houses set on a velvet backdrop of faded green.

At that moment, the road snaked sharply to the right leaving nothing in front of them but an endless expanse of sea and sky. "Oh, God!" Arianna shrieked. She grabbed for the armrest just as the front wheels found purchase on a slice of roadway even narrower than the one before.

"Breathe," Caleb ordered dryly, slanting her an indulgent look.

She obeyed, sucking in a deep breath. Blowing it out. "Bet that can be tricky at night."

"Deadly." Like the suppressed violence in his voice, that murderous glint in his eyes. "'Tis a private road," was all he said. Though the rest was left unspoken, his meaning was clear. That anyone fool-hearty enough to ignore the *Private Property* notices posted prominently at the foot of this treacherous drive did so entirely at his own peril.

A seething anger was emanating from Caleb; she had felt it building in him, like steam in a pressure cooker, since the moment he had discovered the desecration of her home. Silent and sullen, he had spoken barely a dozen words the whole way here. And when he did speak, it had been in monosyllables. All that coiled violence inside him served only to increase Arianna's sense of foreboding. What was she thinking, moving into some desolate, gothic castle with a man she didn't know?

The road took another sharp right onto a cobblestone drive, a road much wider than the bumpy single lane they had been traveling. As they rounded a long, winding curve, Arianna spotted the hulking fortress looming off in the distance. Constructed of cut medieval stone and wrapped in flowing skirts of cool, gray mist, the castle resembled something out of a Tolkien fantasy. Barely visible now through a densely wooded thicket, Arianna knew that in the spring and summer, when leaves dressed the naked branches of the trees and shrubs, it would be all but hidden from view.

There was a lingering sense of menace in the air, as if some otherworldly presence warned potential trespassers off the estate. Two round towers rose in the distance, their pointed slate roofs set equidistant along the outer wall. In front of the ancient fort flowed a stream of water that was dark as the river Styx.

A moat? No way. *Yes* way.

As he approached the water's edge, Caleb reached up and touched a remote control device attached to the visor. A clanging rang out as the huge iron gate, a portcullis, began to ascend with the screech of metal on metal. When the gate had disappeared into the gabled roof of the gatehouse, a wooden partition began to lower across the water, like the opening of a giant jaw.

A drawbridge. Un-*freaking*-believable.

Arianna glanced at Caleb. Staring straight ahead, fingers tapping the steering wheel, he looked like an impatient commuter in rush-hour traffic.

Should she say something? Make some polite remark about his lovely home? Arianna opened her mouth, closed it, and then opened it again.

For the first time in her life, she was totally, utterly speechless.

She must have made some sound, though, because Caleb turned to look at her. A twinkle lit those intriguing eyes as he slid a finger beneath her chin—and gently lifted her gaping jaw.

His large hand covered hers in her lap, where her fingers were still intertwined from the frightening ride up the mountainside. That was all it took. One simple touch and a sense of wellbeing flooded over her. The feeling that she was entering the enchanted domain of some supernatural entity ebbed away on a tide of peace. After crossing the drawbridge, they passed through a short, dark tunnel beneath the gatehouse.

Caleb pointed upward. "Machicolations," he told her. "Murder holes built into the turreted outer bawn, as well as the entrance of the keep."

"The keep?" she asked, eyes alight with a childlike excitement she didn't care to mask.

"The main residence, command post, the last line of defense in times of battle. Many refer to the building as 'the castle', when in actuality all that you see inside the bawn," he made an expansive gesture with his hand, "is part and parcel of the *castle*. The curtain wall is constructed of granite...em...measured in feet, about eight thick, twenty high. The ramparts along the wall-walk above us have crenellations, or gaps, for the shooting of arrows or guns."

"My God, all the history here... This is just so...so amazing...." Arianna rolled her window down. A spray of soft, cool mist dampened her face as she strained for a better look.

She closed her eyes and inhaled a deep breath of the salty sea air. But then a rumble of thunder in the distance set her heart to pounding. After the abject terror of that day on the coast, was she forever doomed to be frightened by the sound of thunder? As she wondered at this, she realized the sound she was hearing wasn't thunder at all, but a kind of reverberation that was getting louder, drawing closer. Stunned, she identified the sound.

A stampede of horses. Dozens, possibly hundreds of them, were galloping straight in her direction. So close now that she could feel the impact of their hooves shaking the ground beneath her feet. The *ground* beneath her feet? But she was sitting in the Land Rover.

Her eyes popped open. She scrubbed at them, but it didn't alter the vision, this...delusion that had wrapped itself around her. *Oh, no. Not again.* Icy fingers of fear gripped her heart in a fist as Caleb, the SUV, all that was real in the world was suddenly, irrevocably, swallowed up by the thick alien fog swirling around her feet.

Standing beside the gatehouse, she was caught up in an appalling scene of pandemonium. Women with small children clutched to their breasts ran screaming from the small wooden outbuildings enclosed within the castle walls.

A garrison of foot soldiers milled truculently behind the portcullis. The sun struck a sharp gleam on the battleaxes and broadswords clutched in their powerful hands. Fierce knights, their muscular bodies clad in rough-hewn leather, sat astride giant war-horses. The destriers nickered and pranced about, impatient for their master's battle cry.

Attempting to retreat from the melee, Arianna began to ease backward until she felt the rough coolness of the curtain wall against her back. In disbelieving silence, she watched a volley of flame-tipped arrows zip over the outer bawn.

There were screams, shouted commands. Death burned in the eyes of the battle-worn warriors positioned strategically along the narrow wall walk. Clearly, there would be no mercy, no quarter given those who had dared lay siege against this mighty fortification.

Targeting the invaders, rocks and other missiles began hurtling from the parapet above Arianna's head. Huge cauldrons of boiling oil were tipped, dumped ruthlessly upon the heads of those attempting to breach the sanctity of the outer bawn.

Blood-curdling screams rent the air, and Arianna gagged at the sickening smell of petroleum mixed with burning flesh, and the metallic smell of blood. Knees too weak to hold her, she slid down the rough stone at her back. Arms locked around her legs, face buried against her knees, she tried to block out the revolting violence.

"This is the bailey." Caleb's voice echoed in her ears, as if he were in a tunnel. Penetrating the miasma clouding her mind, the sound of his voice drew her slowly away from the edge of a precipice, inch by nail-bitingly-slow inch, until she was finally seated again in the vehicle beside him. "Gardens and orchards are over there. A fishpond..." His recitation began to trail off. He tapped the brakes and brought the vehicle to a sudden halt. "What is it, Arianna? What's happened?"

Foggy-headed, she tried to look at him, but found it hard to focus. "I saw...." *What? Ghosts re-enacting an ancient battle?* "I don't know. I just got dizzy for a minute."

He slid a hand around the back of her neck and began a gentle massage. Then, with his thumb applying a light pressure on her chin, he turned her head, forcing her to meet his gaze. "Tell me."

"It was weird. A...a vision, I guess it was. I found myself caught up in the midst of some ancient battle. There were war horses and men in armor."

Caleb's face became a thundercloud.

"Look, it was nothing," she said. "Strain from this morning, from the last couple of weeks catching up with me is all." She bared her teeth in the effigy of a smile. "Now, you were saying something about a fish pond?"

Caleb tipped his head, and eyed her askance for a few seconds. "Right," he finally muttered, shifting into gear and traveling on. "It's stocked with trout and pike."

"And the river flowing around the entrance...the...moat? Is that stocked, too?"

"'Tis. With crocodiles."

Arianna cut him a sharp look. Was he serious? Or had that been some glib reference to the gossip being circulated by local rumormongers?

As they drove around a bend in the road, she saw several wooden structures. Replicas of the cabin-like huts she had seen in her vision. "Caleb, h...how long have those buildings been here?"

He glanced over his shoulder. "I'm not sure exactly. Let's see...The round tower was after being built in the ninth century. After that, some time in the late 1200s, the northern-most end of the square tower was added. I reckon the outbuildings...the mill, a chapel and an alehouse...were erected during that latter period. Why do you ask?"

Arianna licked her lips. "I saw them in the vision. Witnessed women running from them." She turned beseeching eyes on him. "What's going on, Caleb? Do you know? Ever since the night I arrived here, I've been experiencing strange, inexplicable things. My father warned me...you know, the night he died...he warned me that I would encounter things here that I wouldn't understand."

Caleb pierced her with a look. "You're father said that to you?"

"Yes, he did." She lowered her voice almost to a whisper. "Why is it I get the feeling you know exactly what he was talking about?"

There was no response to her question—not that she really expected one. But his jaw muscles did that clenching thing as they continued along the winding cobblestone drive in a discordant silence. Leafless trees towered over them like mighty sentinels, interlocking branches moving as one in the bracing sea wind.

As the Land Rover drew ever closer to its final destination, the sense of doom Arianna had been experiencing returned. Her hand touched her mouth, eyes riveted on the imposing structure in front of them. Five levels of wild and sibylline charm struck a haughty pose atop the rocky promontory she had first seen in her childhood dreams.

"God, Caleb," she whispered in awe. "It's breathtaking."

"The keep." Spoken softly, the two words conveyed a wealth of family pride. "In the mid eighteen-hundreds, my great-great-grandfather had the original medieval trussed roof removed, windows enlarged, the exterior otherwise modified. Around the time of the potato famine, it was. Our family had plenty, so wasn't he after opening the gates to the starving hordes living on our land. And to some who lived beyond the thousand acres, as well."

"Sounds like a wonderful man," Arianna murmured. "And this place...it looks almost mythical...like something out of an Irish faerie tale."

She watched Caleb's lips curve in a secret smile as he parked in front of the massive edifice, where a dozen thick, broad slabs of white stone led to a towering entryway.

"Look, I know dealing with all that mess at my place this morning has made you really late for your meeting. So, feel free to just dump my suitcases out here on the driveway. I can knock on the door and find my way in from here."

His reply came with the lofty nonchalance one might expect from someone born into this level of affluence. "Sure, the servants will be out to collect your things straight away and deliver them to your quarters. I warrant you'll be finding your stay here amenable."

Ouch. Wounded by the formality of his tone, Arianna stiffened. "Thank you," she said softly. "I'm sure I'll be quite comfortable."

As Caleb was getting out of the Land Rover, an older man with a slight, wiry build, opened Arianna's door. Caleb rounded the rear of the vehicle and the man stepped aside, his head inclined in respect. Caleb's wide boyish grin evidenced his fondness for the little man, doing away with any misconception that he required such deference.

"Arianna Sullivan meet Flanagan, steward of the demesne," Caleb introduced them. "If you're in need of anything when I'm not around, he'd be the one to sort it for you."

"Miss Sullivan." The small man inclined his head again. Attired in stately black with a crisp white shirt peeking out from beneath his jacket's lapel, his demeanor was so utterly reserved Arianna half-expected him to click his heels.

The mental image that presented was so absurd, especially after the absolute insanity she had experienced so far that day, that it instantly triggered Arianna's giggle nerve. You know, that uncontrollable urge to laugh, to dissolve into a fit of hilarity, and always at the most inappropriate of moments. Like during a church service. Or a funeral. Or like right now, when laughing in someone's face would be unforgivably rude.

To stifle the frantic urge, she bit down hard on her lower lip. The self-inflicted pain seemed to do the trick. "Please. Call me Arianna."

"Of course, Miss...Arianna." Her request that he breach proper etiquette with so gauche a display of familiarity was clearly beyond the little man. But it was the way he had strung the words together—like one of the old Gullah servants in *Gone with the Wind*—that finally did her in. *Oh, God...he's killing me!*

As laughter bubbled up her throat, Arianna knew she was finished. So, she did the first thing that came to mind—which was to move hastily into Caleb's arms and bury her face against his broad shoulder. Then, body shaking, eyes spilling over with tears, she dissolved into a silent fit of giggles. Her only salvation at this point would be if the two men were to believe that the poor girl had burst into sobs, finally overwhelmed by the emotional upheavals of the day.

For a moment, Caleb held her stiffly, as though shocked by the unforeseen outburst. But then she felt his arms tighten around her. Stroking her hair, he murmured words of encouragement.

Sniffling, she lifted her head off his shoulder and began to ease away from him. *Awkward.* "Sorry," she mumbled, cheeks on fire at the awful spectacle she had made of herself.

"Not a'tall. Sure haven't you had a trying day altogether." Though Caleb spoke the words soothingly, the glint of amusement in his eyes revealed the truth. *He knew!*

"Flanagan, I've a meeting in town. Arianna's feeling a bit stressed. Will you show her to her rooms, please?" He turned to her. "I hate leaving you here on the doorstep like this—"

"It's okay, go." He seemed undecided. "*Seriously*, I mean it. I'd like to freshen up a bit, maybe lie down for awhile. I'm sure Mr. Flanagan will help me get settled in just fine."

At that, the man coughed. Color splotched his sallow cheeks as he drew himself up to every inch of his five-foot stature. "The chamber maid will assist you directly, miss."

Caleb quirked an eyebrow at his manservant's discomfiture and sent Arianna a tiny wink. "'Tis Flanagan's own granddaughter, sweet Molly, who'll be looking after you, *cailín*."

Out of the corner of her eye, Arianna saw a heavy-set man with a shock of strawberry-blonde curls struggle past them loaded down with her luggage. Huffing and wheezing, he climbed the stone steps and disappeared through the castle entrance. Why had she packed so much? Just how long did she plan to stay here in Camelot, anyway?

Giving her arm a squeeze, Caleb brushed a kiss across her cheek. The steward's gray eyebrows rose in disapproval. "I'll be off. Let Flanagan know if you require anything."

As Arianna followed Flanagan up the wide stone steps of the gothic fortress, angry clouds crept across the meager sun, like a shade drawn to shut out the light. A jittery sense of foreboding came with an unsettling question.

Just what had she gotten herself into?

Chapter Eighteen

Arianna preceded Flanagan through the grand entrance into a towering foyer. A crystal chandelier spilled shards of light over dark wood furnishings and floors inlaid with gray marble. Heavy antique pieces, velvets, silks and brocades comprised the décor. Verdant with living greenery, the foyer resembled a forest garden. Plants of every variety overflowed solid brass planters and urns, and spilled over exquisite pieces of blown glass and hand-made pottery. The heady perfume of fresh cut flowers mingled with the homey scents of aged wood, burning peat and lemony furniture oils.

Following the steward down a hall to the right of the entrance, she passed an elegant selection of paintings and other works of art. In this setting of quietly stated opulence, she would have bet there wasn't a print or a copy amongst them.

Flanagan led her upstairs, around and around a narrow, winding staircase carved from stone. "Guest rooms are on the fourth floor," he informed her as they stepped off onto a small landing and traversed a corridor the length of a city block. About halfway down the hall, he opened a door and stepped back. "Molly's been up to unpack your things. I'll send her back in a bit with your tea."

"Thank you, Flanagan."

Still stiff with disapproval over the PDA he had observed between her and his employer, he gave an abrupt nod and turned to leave. Arianna reached out to latch the door behind him, only to discover there was no lock. Although she felt somewhat uncomfortable with the lack of privacy, she certainly couldn't fault the accommodations. The spacious suite consisted of a private sitting area, a gargantuan bedroom, and a walk-in powder room that opened onto a private bath. Furnishings were heavy and masculine, like the main areas of the house...uh, er...*castle*, she corrected and grinned. "Awesome. I'm staying in a real Irish castle."

The flakes of ash floating in the air at the cottage had left a sooty film on Arianna's skin. Intent on scrubbing it off, she expected a drafty, unpleasant dip in an ancient tub. But upon opening the bathroom door, she found a marble-floored convenience, replete with tiled walls and gleaming full-length mirrors. Bending over the over-sized sunken tub, she rotated a brass fixture at its center. Hot, steamy water poured from the faucet, as a heating unit overhead automatically began to hum and glow.

Her bath oil decanter, razor, shaving cream, shampoo and conditioner—items from her cosmetic case—had been set within easy reach on a shelf above the tub. Ferns and leafy green plants that thrive in the forest and other moist, dark places spilled over the ledge of the shelf above it.

She sighed audibly as she immersed herself in the hot, fragrant bath, and rested her head on a bath cushion attached to one end. *Sheer decadence.* She fiddled with a dial on the side of the tub and soothing jets began to rumble and whir. The water flowing from them whipped the bath oil into mountainous clouds of white foam. She could feel the stress draining from her body like golden wisps of honey dripping off a spoon. "Ah, pure heaven," she purred. "A girl could really get used to this."

On the verge of dozing off, she dragged her slumberous body out of the water. God forbid young Molly should have to report to the stone-faced Flanagan that their ignominious houseguest had been found floating in the guestroom tub.

Most inappropriately naked—and even more inappropriately dead.

Arianna stepped under a multi-headed shower on a stone wall on the other side of the room to wash her hair. Then she toweled off, sloughed lotion all over still-moist skin, and bundled up in her big fluffy bathrobe, laid out on a padded bench beside the tub.

Back in the bedroom, she searched through an antique tallboy in the corner for the clothes missing from her suitcases. She pulled on a pair of jogging pants and a tee.

Same as at the cottage, she could find no electrical outlets in the bathroom. Figuring it was an Irish statutory thing, she plugged her blowdryer in beside the bed. She climbed up the bedsteps onto an elevated, pillow-top mattress and sat cross-legged while she dried her long, thick hair. When it was done, she flopped backward onto the gold brocade duvet with a tired sigh. "Rest my eyes for just a minute," she yawned. "Then I'll go exploring."

A light tapping on the door woke her out of a sound and dreamless sleep. Feeling disoriented in a room that was pitch dark, it took a couple of seconds for her to remember where she was. Then it all came rushing back to her. *Caleb...the castle...*

Groping blindly for a lamp beside the bed, she flicked it on. A glance at the drop-dial clock on the wall had her groaning. Almost six o'clock. Darned if she hadn't slept the entire afternoon away.

Another hesitant knock and a muffled voice called to her through the heavy wood door leading to the hall. "Miss...Arianna? Dinner's served in the great hall in half an hour."

Great Hall? Sweet. "Oh, thanks, Mr. Flanagan," she called out loudly enough to be heard through the sitting room.

"I'll return in twenty-five minutes, miss, to escort you down below."

"Perfect. I'll be ready."

With a huge yawn and a feline stretch, Arianna clambered out of bed. At the tallboy, she pulled out a pair of black silk panties and matching bra. Catching a subtle whiff of her signature fragrance, she sniffed at the air. Jasmine and geranium, essentials oils of lavender and rose. Yep, it was the unique scents she had combined when creating her own personal fragrance at an herb shop back home. Apparently, Molly had made a perfumed sachet to tuck inside the drawers.

"Hmm... Casual? Formal? Just what does one wear for dinner at a medieval castle?" she wondered aloud. Opening the double doors to a dark worm-holed wardrobe, she selected a long, flowing peasant style dress. The deep mauve cotton-blend boasted cream-colored embroidery at the neck and wrists. Simple, yet stylish.

She finished a light application of makeup and was dragging a brush through her hair when she heard the anticipated knock on the door.

"Be right there, Flanagan." Dashing back to the wardrobe for a black lace shawl in case it got chilly, she opened the door. Her heart did a little flip. "Caleb."

"Arianna." His voice was deep and smoky; his appreciative gaze whispered over her flesh like spun sugar. "Lovely," he said softly.

Accepting the arm he so gallantly offered, she smiled up at him. "Why thank you, Sir. You know, I've been meaning to ask you about Granny. I called the hospital yesterday, but they wouldn't give me any information. Said I'd have to speak to the family."

"We restricted inquiries so she'll have a bit of a rest. They're doing a battery of tests, but she's on the mend, thanks be to God. I'll let her know you've been asking after her."

"At her age I'm kind of surprised that she doesn't live here with you."

"*Ach*, yer wan is much too set in her ways to agree to such an arrangement. I suggested she come here for a wee while to get her strength back after she's released from hospital." Caleb gave a sheepish grin. "And the auld woman just about ate the head off me."

Arianna chuckled. At the narrow stairwell, Caleb stepped aside for her to move in front of him. Passing the third floor landing, he pointed out, "This level houses the servants quarters, though most of the staff choose to live in their own homes on the demesne."

In the enclosed space, his subtle scent teased her senses. Fresh air and green forests, leather and a hint of sandalwood soap. Very masculine. Uniquely Caleb.

There was one good thing about staying here. It would grant her the opportunity to explore yet another facet of his fascinating personality. The private side. The one he revealed to those with whom he shared his home.

Arianna had experienced his reserve, his reticence. The discreet air of arrogance of which he seemed unaware. But here, where the man's home really *was* his castle, she noticed the changes in him. Her date of the previous evening—the casually clad owner of a stud farm—had been replaced by the tall, dark, and dangerous lord of the manor. A refined man of the world, the epitome of sophistication and charm, and an inherently lethal grace.

Now how freaking sexy was that?

On the second floor, they turned right onto a corridor bisected further down by another hallway. They turned again and passed through a gigantic set of double doors that were open wide.

The Great Hall was milling with activity. Built into either end of the palatial room were fireplaces large enough to roast a whole cow. At the far end of the room, a massive head table constructed of intricately carved dark wood sat on a raised dais. Nearby, a small group of men huddled in a circle conversing. Trestle tables scattered about the room were filling up quickly. Arianna estimated about eighty people in all. "What's going on?" she asked. "A banquet?"

"The evening meal." Caleb took her arm to escort her up the three leather-inlaid stairs to the dais.

The evening meal?

As they took their seats, the men in a huddle began to gravitate toward the head table. While Caleb welcomed his guests, Arianna poured herself a goblet of water from a silver pitcher within easy reach. It was surreal, she thought. Rather like waking up and finding yourself in the sixteenth century. The quaint setting included an extravagance of plush, colorful tapestries. A scatter of expensive Aubusson carpets stretched across the bare stone of the floor. The thick, rich fabrics served a dual purpose, she supposed, there not only for their beauty, but to retain the warmth generated by the dueling infernos in the matching hearths.

Caleb joined her again and introduced her to his guests as they took their seats. Brian Rafferty, an attractive man with white-silver hair, looked to be about fifty. His eyes, a strange hue of silver-gray, reminded Arianna of a wolf. As she shook his hand, she noted something so unpleasant—so completely unnerving—about the contact that she pulled away. The eerie sensation of having had one's soul invaded remained with her.

After that, she kept her hand purposefully in her lap, offering only a smile and a brief nod as she met the rest of the group. There was MacDara Darmody, tall and lean, with chestnut brown hair and eyes like sweet dark chocolate. Tomas O'Dhea had a swarthy complexion, likely of Spanish origin. Both men she estimated to be about Caleb's age. Fair-haired Padraig Murphy appeared slightly older than the others; however, age had done nothing to diminish his lazy sensuality and striking good looks.

Arianna realized she was the only woman at the table. She couldn't quite put her finger on it, but the way Caleb's friends kept glancing her way while conversing was unsettling She felt as if she were on display, an insect under a microscope.

Flanagan seated himself unobtrusively at the end of the table closest to the kitchen. When a priest joined them the older man started to push to his feet, but the man of God squeezed Flanagan's shoulder. "Sit now, sir. No need to go troubling yourself."

At Caleb's direction, the priest took the vacant seat beside Arianna. "James, I'd like you to meet Arianna Sullivan," he said. "She'll be staying with us for a while. Arianna, Father James Conneely, a childhood friend and our castle chaplain."

Good heavens. The man had his own private priest?

"Miss Sullivan, it's a pleasure to meet you." Father Conneely's blue eyes were kind as he offered his hand. Feeling distinctly put on the spot, Arianna accepted the contact warily. But his touch was warm and comforting, allaying any lingering anxiety.

"And I you, Father. But please, call me Arianna."

He leaned closer, his tone confidential. "Wasn't Caleb after mentioning you'd a bit of scare at your own place earlier today. So distressing, that sort of thing. I trust you're feeling better now." His hazel eyes warmed with concern.

Arianna smiled at him. "It was a shock, I admit. But I think I'm over the worst of it."

He nodded sagely and gave her hand a gentle pat before releasing it.

Caleb stood to his feet and raised both hands in a gesture for silence. Conversations and titters of laughter quickly tapered off. "We'll all bow our heads now," he directed, "while Father Conneely offers the blessing."

After a short prayer, the happy rumble of voices again filled the air, and a flurry of activity began on the part of the kitchen staff. Bottles of red wine were uncorked and left to breathe. Bottles of white, iced down in silver buckets, were placed on the tables. Carts laden with steaming platters were rolled into the Great Hall in a steady stream. "Mmm, everything smells wonderful. And I'm starved, haven't eaten a thing since breakfast."

Caleb smiled. "Molly went up with a tray for your tea, but found you sleeping."

"Yeah, I just died." Surveying the scene around her, she said, "So, this is evening meal, huh? You put on a major production like this every night?"

"An old family custom, the gathering of all who work at the castle for dinner." He held a bottle of red wine poised over her stemmed crystal glass and raised his brows.

She gave her head a shake. "Better not. Red gives me a wicked headache. But I'd love a glass of white."

Retrieving a bottle of Sauvignon Blanc from a silver bucket, he filled her glass.

"I have to admit, I wasn't expecting all the modern conveniences here," Arianna told him as he poured. "The Jacuzzi was an especially nice surprise."

"A surprise. Why's that?"

"Well, I've read books about how bleak and miserable castle-living was—"

"Not *this* castle," Caleb offered dryly.

"Apparently not." She smiled and sipped her wine. The cool, crisp taste burst pleasantly on her tongue.

Kitchen workers lined up in front of the head table, each laden with a heaping platter. "Good heavens. I've never seen so much food at one time," Arianna remarked.

"Spoilt for choice," her host agreed.

Aside from main courses of beef, chicken and pork, there were several Irish dishes she had never tried. In a large tureen was nettle soup. "*Stinging* nettles?" she asked incredulously.

Caleb's eyes lit with good humor. "Try it, *cailín*. It's quite tasty. Healthy as well."

She said yes to the soup, and to the colcannon and the boxty, potato dishes. She also accepted a serving from a steaming kettle of beef and Guinness stew.

Then there were crubeens. "Pig's feet?" she asked and declined.

By the time the servers left the head table and began to circulate around the room, Arianna's plate was piled high. A short, plump woman bustled into the hall, her light brown hair highlighted with threads of gray. Hands perched on her generous hips, she surveyed the state of the service.

Caleb motioned her over. "Arianna Sullivan, meet Cook. Maeve McGee would be her given name, but doesn't she prefer being addressed by her title."

"And why wouldn't I so?" she replied jovially. "It's pleased I am to meet you, Miss—"

"You may call her Arianna," Caleb interjected, a teasing light in his eyes as he stole the words right out of her mouth.

"Arianna, then. And I'm hoping you've a more discriminating palette than Himself here," she goaded her employer good-naturedly. "Prefers plain old meat and spuds, he does."

"Cook is Flanagan's daughter," Caleb explained, clearly in his element. "Born and raised right here on the demesne. She was after leaving us for a spell, but didn't I lure her away from a five-star restaurant in Dublin. Convinced her 'twas only right to return here to hearth and home."

"Pressure in a job like that one'll put a body in an early grave," she admitted. "Anyways, where else would I rather be than here, working for this one?"

"Ah, go one with you." His fondness for the woman evident, he sniffed the air. "Sure, don't I smell something burning in the kitchen?"

Maeve swiped at him with one of her oven mitts and walked away, chuckling softly.

The woman adored him. While Caleb's air of authority commanded the respect of his staff, it took kindness to earn their love.

Arianna buttered a chunk of sweet treacle bread and took a bite, watching him interact with his guests as she chewed. His aristocratic features reflected strength of character. And yet the untidy toss of his jet-black hair charmingly muted the strong lines of his profile.

Though he played well the relaxed role of a gracious host, those searing green eyes of his missed nothing. "Flanagan," he said, giving a discreet nod toward one of the trestle tables. A row was breaking out between two staff members who must have imbibed more than their fair share of the table wine.

As the dishes were cleared, fiddles and pipes, tin whistles and drums, appeared in the hands of some of the diners. An impromptu session began and everyone at the head table moved to sit in chairs grouped together on the floor. For the next hour or so, Arianna laughed and visited with Caleb and his friends until, one at a time, the men said their farewells.

Worn out from all the activity, Arianna sighed. "Jetlag's still doing a number on me I'm afraid," she said. "It's been really nice, but if you'll excuse me, I think I'll call it a night."

"I'll walk you up to your apartment," Caleb said, getting to his feet. "I've to be leaving for Wales tomorrow morning at first light, so I'll be retiring early tonight myself."

"You're leaving tomorrow?" She felt suddenly bereft...abandoned. Absurd, she knew, given that she had only just met the man. "How long will you be gone?"

"A day, two at most. But you're to make yourself at home here whilst I'm away."

At the door to her room, she paused. "Thanks...um, Caleb? Something's been bothering me. Can I...ask you a question?"

His head tipped to the side, eyes wary. "You can, o' course."

She drew in a breath, let it out. "It's the dreaming I told you about. I've tried to explain it away as a result of our having met at Granny's when I was a baby. But that doesn't account for how I recognized you, the way you are now." She licked her lips. "Or how I knew the way your mouth would feel when you kissed me."

"No, it doesn't," he said, surprising her with his candidness. "And it's time we spoke about that." His hand closed around the doorknob and he pushed the door open. "But we'd best do that in here, rather than standing in the hall."

Someone had already set a fire to burning in the hearth in the sitting room. A lamp on the gate-legged table beside the sofa had been left on, and was casting a soft light over the room. Caleb pulled her down onto the sofa beside him.

"I share your memories, Arianna," he said, with no preamble. "I've no understanding of how, or why, we met in the land of dreams. But I remember....*everything*." The look in his eyes told her his recollections weren't limited to their innocent walks in the sand as children.

"Thank you, God," she breathed and closed her eyes. She wasn't crazy after all.

Caleb framed her face with his hands, searched her eyes. "The memories have been driving me fecking demented," he admitted in the merest breath of sound.

She raised her mouth, welcoming his kiss, inviting him to renew his possession. Her stomach took a slow swirl as he accepted what she offered, his hands threading through her hair, his mouth moving carefully over hers, reacquainting both of them with that which could not be explained.

But then he pulled away from her, his lips moist from their kisses. "I'm aching with the need to touch you, taste you, be inside you. To take you in all the ways we both remember. But I regret there are things here, in the physical realm, that make such intimacy between us impossible."

With that, Caleb rose to his feet and left her. Stunned by his admission, trying to make sense of everything he had told her, she sat staring at the door long after it had closed behind him.

Chapter Nineteen

Arianna woke to the cry of sea gulls, to the rhythmic cadence of waves crashing against the rocks below her window. And to a feeling of bliss so powerful it was like Da had risen from the grave, she had won the lotto, gotten married to her one true love and given birth to her first child, all on the very same day. She wasn't crazy. After so many years of wondering what the dreams meant, Caleb had finally confessed to sharing them with her. Admitted that, somehow in the grand scheme of things, theirs was a spiritual connection. He had come to know her, to make love to her, in the sleepy mists of another dimension.

After making quick work of a shower, she headed downstairs in search of her morning caffeine fix. Following the luscious smells of grilling meats and fresh-baked bread, she found the kitchen located beside the Great Hall. As she entered the room, Maeve glanced up from the onion she was dicing. "You're awake, so," she said with a welcoming smile. "Ready for breakfast, are you? How'd you fancy a fry?"

"A fry?"

"A full Irish breakfast. Eggs, rashers, black and white pudding—"

She politely declined the heart-attack-on-a-plate. "Sounds delicious, but that's too much food for me so early in the day. I have to admit I'd offer up my first born child for a cup of that coffee I smell though."

Maeve chuckled. "I just poured out the last of it. Go on and sit yourself over there whilst I make fresh."

Arianna sat at the whitewashed oak table Maeve had indicated and watched her plunk a biscuit-shaped pastry onto a small plate. She stuck it in front of her. "Might as well nibble on one of these fresh-baked scones," she said, placing a crock of butter, a jar of strawberry jam and a bowl of fluffy whipped cream within easy reach.

"Thanks, I believe I will." Arianna slathered butter and jam on her scone and topped it with a big dollop of the whipped cream. She took a bite. "Oh, wow. Now I *know* I'm in Ireland."

"So, did you have a good kip?" Maeve scooped coffee beans into a grinder and let it whir for a few seconds. She dumped the contents into a glass cafetiere and added boiling water from the teakettle.

"Slept like a log, thanks. I swear I can't seem to get caught up though."

Maeve fit the gold metal top on the cylinder and pushed all of the swimming coffee grounds to the bottom of the cafetiere, leaving the freshly brewed coffee on top. She poured Arianna a cup and set it in front of her.

After adding cream and sugar, she took her cup to the window. Pressing her forehead against the windowpane, she checked to see if there was a beach directly below. Apparently, the kitchen had been constructed on a jut of rock about two hundred feet above the crashing surf. "Wow, this view is absolutely to die for."

"Jaysus, Mary and Joseph, now don't be saying that around any of the kitchen staff," Maeve remarked. "Aren't they superstitious enough as 'tis, always whinging about what happened at Dunluce Castle back in the sixteen hundreds."

Arianna frowned. *They're worried about something that happened four hundred years ago?* "What happened?"

"Kitchen there was built out on the verge of a cliff like this one. One day during a storm, it broke off and plunged into the sea."

"That's horrible."

"'Twas. Course, we've no worries about such a thing happening here. Not with faerie magic shoring up the foundation of the keep." Maeve raised the top of a commercial dishwasher and began loading it with cups and saucers left over from breakfast.

Arianna smiled, thinking how refreshingly quaint—how very *Irish*—was this talk of the faeries. It was common knowledge that many of the older folk still believed in the "good people". And even those who claimed they did not were known to hedge their bets by giving the earth spirits a wide berth. Stories abound of farmers who had allowed a faerie rath on their land to be disturbed only to become victims of some magical retribution. To this very day in Ireland, highway construction projects were sometimes delayed, or abandoned altogether, for that very reason.

The woman chattered on about a storm brewing farther up the coast. "'Twould have hit Clare hard had Himself not been holding it back." Maeve clucked her teeth as she stirred the contents of an iron kettle. "Stubborn as a mule is that one, when he's after setting his mind to a thing. And come hell or high water, he was flying that helicopter of his over to Shannon, where he keeps his plane...."

Arianna froze, scone midway between mouth and plate, her gaze fixed unbelievingly on the woman's ample backside. It seemed Maeve's talk of faerie magic hadn't been a reference to the wee people in general, but rather to Caleb in particular. Now hero worship was one thing.... But the woman had to be mad as Alice's long-eared companion, if she honestly believed her employer had magically held a thunderstorm at bay.

Standing at the stove, her back to Arianna, Maeve wasn't aware of the shocked reaction her comment had garnered. Or of the fact that Flanagan had stepped silently into the room behind her.

"Maeve!" His tone was so sharp with censure that the woman jumped, dropping her wooden spoon into the pot she was stirring.

She spun around. "Holy God, Da. If I were a cat you'd have scared eight lives off me."

"I need to see you in the larder...em...about supplies."

"I'm putting a bit of lunch together right now. Suppose we do it in a wee while?"

"*Now*," he insisted, careful to avoid Arianna's eyes.

With a put-upon sigh, Maeve lowered the flame on each burner and followed her father out of the room.

Arianna got up and went over to the counter to top off her coffee cup. It was unnerving, to say the least, to be having a pleasant conversation with someone, only to discover that said person was a full-time resident of La-La Land. Seriously unbalanced. Probably the reason Caleb had talked her into coming home; so that he and her father could keep an eye on her. *Poor Flanagan,* Arianna thought. *So staid and proper. And of a generation when mental illness in the family was considered a shame and a scandal. A deep, dark family secret.*

As Arianna set down the carafe, she realized she could hear the hum of Flanagan's voice through an air-vent in the ceiling.

"Miss Sullivan's an outsider, Maeve. Totally unaware of the family's...em... eccentricities, shall we say."

"Now don't you be giving me a bollocking over that, Da. Not when no one's bothered their arse warning me about it before now."

What were they talking about? Concealing Maeve's mental challenges?

"'Twas a spur of the moment thing, Himself deciding to bring her here. Not that I'd any reason to expect you'd be entertaining a castle guest in the kitchen," he pointed out.

Maeve disregarded the jab. "How long will he be keeping her here?"

"A day, a week, a month? Forever? Sure, I haven't a clue. His instructions were simply that the girl was not to leave the demesne in his absence."

What? "And why is that exactly?" *Yeah, why?*

"Caleb may be like a son to me, Maeve, but ultimately he's our employer. And as such he's not under any obligation to be explaining himself."

"So, we're to be her gaolers then, is it?"

Jailers? Arianna's eyebrows kissed her hairline. Caleb intended to hold her here against her will? All at once, an insidious pinprick punctured her little bubble of joy. Had he just been messing with her head last night, when he'd admitted sharing her dreams? Worse, had he arranged to have her cottage trashed while they were in Galway, giving him a perfectly plausible excuse for luring up here? And if so, why? For what nefarious purpose?

"Just mind yourself around the woman, daughter. I've to go now and alert the servants to keep their mouths shut...and their children away from the front of the property. Himself's after ordering the crocodiles left free in the moat until he returns."

Crocodiles? Holy crap, he was serious. The conversation in the pantry halted abruptly as the mug in Arianna's hand slid through her fingers and shattered into a million pieces on the flagstone floor.

Father and daughter made a hasty reappearance in the kitchen.

Arianna sent them a wan smile. "I'm so sorry. I was heading back to my room and thought I'd take another cup of coffee up with me. The darned thing slipped out of my hand."

"No worries, luveen," Maeve said sweetly. "I'll have it cleaned up straight away." She reached into the cabinet for another mug, filled it and handed it to Arianna. "Here you are now, sweeting, take this and go on. I'll send Molly up to collect you when lunch is served."

Back in her sitting room, Arianna sat staring off into space. Just what the heck had she gotten herself into? Why had Caleb left orders that she was to be held prisoner until his return?

"Yeah. Like that's gonna happen." *Who did he think he was dealing with anyway? Freaking Rapunzel? A woman he could keep locked away in his castle tower, pining for her lover's return.* Arianna huffed. *Fat chance.*

If only her cell worked up here, she would simply call a taxi. But when she had tried to check in with her friends last night, there had been no service.

Pondering her situation, Arianna tapped her nails against the arm of the chair. She was in good shape, so walking the few miles into town certainly wouldn't kill her. The only problem was going to be getting across that crocodile-infested moat. Most people had *dogs* to guard their property. Leave it to Caleb to do the dramatic.

Then she had a light bulb moment, remembering how they had entered the property the day before. If he had a remote control device in the SUV, it only stood to reason that there was a complementary manual switch located nearby, maybe in the gatehouse. All she had to do was find it.

Her master plan devised, Arianna went to brush her teeth and finish getting dressed. As she walked back into the bedroom a few minutes later, she almost tripped over a pile of dirty linen. A girl with long, red curls was bending over the bed, smoothing out the duvet. She glanced up at Arianna with a timid smile.

"You must be Molly." The girl nodded, her cheeks coloring prettily.

"I'm glad you're hear. I've been wanting to thank you, for unpacking for me and everything."

"'Twas nothing, Miss."

"Arianna, please."

"Arianna. Such a lovely name you have there."

"Thanks. Umm…Molly, I'm going to go hiking around the grounds for a while. Caleb…um…Himself, uh…." The girl giggled behind her hand, while Arianna struggled to come up with the proper reference for her employer. "Well, anyway," she said finally, with a grin, "*he* suggested I do some exploring while he's gone. When we arrived, he used some remote control thingy to lower the drawbridge. Would you happen to know where—?"

A brief knock on the door interrupted their conversation. *Darn!* "I've your lunch, luveen." Maeve met her in the sitting room, tray in hand. "Thought you might prefer eating here. You only had a scone for breakfast, so I've brought a fair bit. Molly," she called into the bedroom, "Grandda requires you in the Hall."

As the young girl came through the bedroom door, dirty linen bundled in her arms, Arianna turned to her. "You don't have to change my sheets every day. I only do it once a week at home." With a slight nod, the girl scampered past the two women and fled the room.

Maeve set the tray on a small round table in the corner. Taking a step back, she looked everything over. "Is there anything else you'll be needing before I go?"

Only the location of that stupid switch. "No, thanks," Arianna answered sweetly.

Maeve returned her too-bright smile and ducked out of the room.

"Looks like I've been banished from the public areas for the duration of *Himself's* absence," Arianna observed wryly. Flanagan was taking steps to ensure that no one else blabbed any more forbidden castle secrets.

Since there was no telling how long it would take to escape, Arianna figured she might as well eat, keep up her strength. Sitting down at the table, she dipped a chunk of crusty bread into a hearty bowl of Irish stew. The condemned, enjoying her last meal. Well, at least she wasn't doing her time here, as a prisoner of the castle, wasting away in its dungeon.

Far from it, she thought, allowing the subtle beauty of her surroundings to relax the tight cords knotting the back of her neck. The sturdy Victorian bygones set about on a solid parquet floor scattered with antique rugs spoke longingly of another era. Wooden shutters on the windows held the brisk chill of the North Atlantic winds at bay. A log and turf fire blazed in the twelve-foot hearth, filling the space with a cozy warmth that was completely at odds with her present situation.

How she wished things had turned out differently. That there had been none of the craziness, none of the subterfuge. Arianna jumped at a knock on the door. *What now?*

It was Flanagan. "Himself's on the phone for you, miss."

Caleb? On the telephone? What now, indeed?

Arianna opened the door. "Thanks, Flanagan. I'll get it over there." She gestured toward a black landline phone on an oak table beside one of the armchairs. He gave a short bow and turned to leave.

"Caleb? What a nice surprise." Sarcasm dripped from her words like sap from a sugar maple tree.

"I'd a wee break, so thought I'd check in." *Wow*. Even now, knowing what she knew, the sound of his voice made her spirits soar. She must be insane. "Wanted to be certain you've everything you need."

"Yeah, everything but my freedom," sang the bird in the gilded cage.

"Oh, I'm quite comfortable, thank you. Read a little bit before I went to bed last night. Alice in Wonderland." She had immersed herself in a leather-bound copy she had found on one of the bookshelves here in the sitting room. Her reading choices had spanned the genres from the most technical scientific journal to a copy of a sixteenth century Bible. There had even been a modern-day, faerie tale romance amongst the more literary works.

Left behind by another woman who had been held captive here?

A boyish innocence tempered Caleb's voice as they discussed where and when his family had acquired the first-edition copy. Arianna's heart filled with an almost painful yearning to see him again. God, what was she going to do? Changing the channel on her infatuation, she tuned in to her sixth sense and listened intently to his tone, to the inflection of his voice. And she could detect nothing... *nothing*...furtive or suspect in either one.

Suddenly she was beset with doubts. Could she have misunderstood what she had overheard this morning? Or had Flanagan perhaps mistaken his employer's instructions? If so, this was the time to find out. Before she went sneaking off like an idiot on a miles-long hike down the side of a mountain. "Everyone's been great. I'm glad you called, though. I'm thinking about renting a car. Would it be a huge inconvenience for someone to take me into town?"

He didn't miss a beat. "Not a'tall. I'll have our driver give you a lift whenever you'd like." Her entire body slumped with relief. "In any case, I plan to be home late this evening. Would you care to join me in my apartments tomorrow for breakfast, say six A.M.?"

Accepting his invitation, she got directions to his room and hung up. Thank God, it had all been nothing but a huge misunderstanding.

That night she dreamt of a faerie prince with eyes of green and hair as dark as midnight. As he galloped away on a fiery steed toward the setting of the sun, tears fell from her eyes like molten crystal. A breeze of harp song carried the sound of her cries to his ears, and he reigned in, circling back to return for her. And with one muscled arm, he swept her up in front of him onto a saddle blazing with diamonds and with gold. Together they rode through the moonlit night, through the thunder of shifting time and space, until they came to a land known by the Ancients as Tir na Nóg.

A place where no one grows old...and no one dies.

And there, with a tapered finger raised toward the heavens, Caleb drew a rainbow of precious gems for her across the endless sky.

Chapter Twenty

The next morning she was running late. It was six-fifteen by the time she rapped lightly on Caleb's door. As she walked into the room, he set the Irish Times aside and got up out of his chair. A welcome sight in faded jeans and a blue-and-black-hoody, a slight smile raised one corner of his mouth. With the dark stubble shading his face, he looked like he had just climbed out of bed. As if she had been stranded in a desert of longing, Arianna drank in the sight of him. From the crown of that tousled head to the muscled thighs of an equestrian, the man was raw masculinity. Rampant desire.

Joining her at the door, he bent his head and touched her lips with his. He tasted of peppermint. "Well, good morning," he murmured huskily. "Had you any trouble finding your way here?"

"Kind of, yeah. I tried asking a few people, but everybody was so vague. I was beginning to think the location of this place was a state secret."

Caleb chuckled. Slipping an arm around her shoulders, he escorted her to a small table beneath a mullioned window. "The staff are a wee bit protective of my privacy."

"Yeah. Like the Secret Service are a *wee bit* protective of the President." When the wisecrack earned her a slow, crooked smile, Arianna felt like she had hit a Vegas jackpot.

"I'll have to tell them you're very welcome here in my private chambers, *cailín*." He spoke softly, eyes boring into hers with a meaning as clear as spring water. "Anytime."

A round antique oak table, set for breakfast, waited for them in a cranny beneath a window that boasted yet another spectacular view of the coast. Before taking her seat, Arianna looked out at the voluptuous waves rolling onto a sandy beach below them. *This is it,* she realized. Her heart skipped a beat at the revelation: That just below this section of the castle, Caleb had stood on the infamous day of the lightning strike.

"What a lovely view to wake up to each morning," she breathed. The waking sun peeked over the horizon, scattering a trail of diamonds across the white-capped waves like skipping stones. Already dawn had begun to color the puffy gray clouds in shades of purple, pink and lavender.

"'Tis indeed." He sounded distracted as he poured her a cup of coffee from a silver decanter on the table, then refreshed his own cup from an ivory ceramic teapot. A glance around the room found the masculine space comfortably furnished with Bakshaish carpets, leather wainscoting, and beautifully embossed chests probably imported from the Indies.

Arianna noted the Royal Aubusson tapestry on the far wall. "Is that...?"

Caleb glanced at the wall. "Handed down from my great-grandfather," he said. "Originally a wedding gift for Marie Antoinette's marriage to the Dauphin."

A guilded mirror hung over a huge stone fireplace that took up one end of the capacious room. An elaborate collection of sconces, ornaments, tapestries and other works of art decorated silk-lined walls the color of rich, dark port.

He passed the sugar and cream. "This is my study. The apartment also contains my bedchamber, some smaller bedrooms, dressing rooms, a kitchen, classroom and nursery."

Nursery. The word struck an emotive chord within Arianna, evoking images of the two of them breakfasting here while a tiny dark-haired angel played at their feet.

She swallowed the lump in her throat. "The pipe organ in the corner... You play?"

"Occasionally." An indolent shrug, and a rueful grin. "I find it suits a somber humor."

Serious. Somber. Brooding. All words that described his mood this morning. Although she gave him five stars for his valiant effort to keep things light and easy, she could detect his weariness. What heavy cross was he bearing? What personal trial had left the bruised strain behind those hypnotic sea-green eyes? Did he have an insane wife locked away somewhere in the keep like Mr. Rochester in Jane Eyre? Did he regret inviting Arianna to stay here in his home? Or was his impetuous confirmation of their somnambulant relationship the thing he was regretting?

There was a light knock on the door and Maeve came bustling into the room. A couple of the kitchen girls carrying food trays followed closely on her heels. Stopping by a Chippendale mahogany sideboard to the left of the window nook where Arianna and Caleb were sitting, she began to direct the placement of a buffet of various breakfast foods.

"You've outdone yourself, Maeve. As always."

Caleb's compliment brought a rosy glow to the woman's cheeks as she flapped the serving girls out of the room. "Hope ye enjoy it now. Just give us a shout if I'm after forgetting anything." As Maeve turned to leave, Arianna didn't miss the tight-lipped glance she tossed in their direction. It didn't take a mind reader to know what verdict the woman had reached from the evidence staring her in the face.

She was alone with a man in his private apartments at dawn, and him all sleep-tousled and unshaven. Her eyes were too bright, her cheeks still flushed from the kiss they had shared when she arrived. The tank top and jogging pants she had dragged on because she had been running late make it look like she had just tumbled out of bed. *Caleb's* bed.

"Let's go fill our plates," Caleb said, pushing back from the table.

Joining him at the sideboard, Arianna chose small portions from a selection of eggs, white and black pudding, rashers, sausages, stewed tomatoes, mushrooms and baked beans. A traditional full Irish breakfast. There were also scones, fresh berries, and oatmeal.

As she sat back down, Caleb brought his own filled-to-groaning plates to the table. "Don't let Maeve be winding you up, *cailín*," he told her. *So he had noticed her reaction.* "'Tis all part and parcel of castle life, I'm afraid. Everyone after knowing and involving themselves in everyone else's business. But Maeve forgets herself. And I'll be sorting her out on it, you can be sure."

Arianna shook her head. "No, just let it go, okay? That'll only make me more uncomfortable around her."

Caleb took a deep breath, held it, then let out a heavy sigh. "As you wish." Picking up the frosty crystal pitcher of fresh-squeezed orange juice, he filled Arianna's glass and topped off his own. "So tell me, what mischief have you planned for today?"

Arianna took a sip of coffee. "Think I'll head over to the cottage. Try to put a dent in getting that mess cleared away."

Caleb's brow furrowed, but he held his tongue.

"I wasn't able to get any reception on my cell phone inside the castle. So last night I had the idea to try it outside and was able to get a call through to my friend, Tara." Arianna dabbed her mouth with her napkin. "She wanted to know if I planned to be back in the States by Thanksgiving—which I don't, of course. So she and Michaela have decided to bring Thanksgiving to me over here."

"Your friends are coming to Ireland?"

"That's the plan. I imagine it'll only take a couple of days to get the windows and locks, and a security system installed. Once that's done, I can move back in and take my time getting the rest of the place habitable before they get here."

"You think it's wise, having your friends here?" Impassive green eyes fixed on hers as he took a sip of tea. "After what's happened, I mean."

"I didn't get into a lot of detail with Tara about the break-in. If I had, she'd have been over here like a shot. The cavalry." She shook her head. Cutting off a bite of over-easy egg, she rambled on, ignoring Caleb's deepening frown. "Anyway, I've been thinking of arranging my business back home so I can stay here through the winter." She gave a lopsided grin. "Only thing is, I'm really going to miss the New England snow."

"You've what? Two weeks until your American Thanksgiving? Sure, by then the *gardai* may have the bastard who destroyed your place in custody." Caleb set his cup down, leaned forward. "Until they do, you're not to be going anywhere near that place alone," he ordered, soft words draped in a platform of steel.

"Whoa, just hold on a dog-gone minute."

Caleb gave an exasperated sigh. "Listen to me, Arianna. There's something between us, something long-term that I've not quite gotten my head around as yet. But I care about you, about what happens to you. You're an intelligent woman. You know yourself, going back to that cottage now would be a foolhardy thing to do."

Okay, so give the autocratic Irishman an "E" for effort. At least, he was trying to reason with her, trying to curb the infuriating, chest-thumping male chauvinism that seemed second nature.

"I'll stay here." At his look of relief, she quickly amended, "At *night*. I'm sorry, Caleb, but I simply have to be there during the day to get things done."

He dragged a frustrated hand over the early-morning stubble that darkened his chin. "If I'd my way, you'd be staying away from there altogether, until the bloody nutter that wrecked the place is behind bars." As she drew in a breath to object, he raised a hand. "Clearly, that's not going to happen. So, I suggest a compromise. I'll drop you there in the morning, collect you when you've finished each day."

White-knuckled terrified of heights, it suited her just fine to be chauffeured up and down that treacherous mountain pass leading to the castle. "Works for me."

With an appreciative glance around her, Arianna skillfully changed the subject. "You know, considering the size of the room, it's surprisingly warm and cozy in here. Gotta be the way it's furnished. Lots of wood. Natural fibers. Warm, dark colors."

"Can't take credit for that, I'm afraid. It's been like this for as long as I can remember. Here in the study is where my father worked on castle accounts and such. As a lad growing up, the room was pretty much off-limits to me." A forlorn look darkened his features.

Arianna put her hand over his. "I bet if you had a black-haired, green-eyed little terror getting into all your paperwork you'd be tempted to ban him from your workspace, too."

"Perhaps." A mischievous glint appeared in his eyes. "I've been told I really was full of the devil as a child."

"Do tell." She gave a dry smile. "So, what's the story with Flanagan, anyway?"

"Story? What about him?" Caleb was eating European style as

they chatted, fork turned over in his left hand, knife in his right, which he used as a mini-shovel.

"I get the impression he's more to you than a...what did you call him? A steward?"

Caleb smiled. "You'd be right about that. 'Twas himself who was a father figure to me growing up. After my mother's death, my own father withdrew emotionally. I reckon he was after blaming his newborn son for taking his wife from him. The night of my birth, he handed me over to Granny to raise. 'Twas in her home I remained for the first five years of my life. They were happy, secure, well adjusted years, mind. During that time, the stories Flanagan told of my father during his frequent visits were my only connection to the man."

"You were fortunate. Having a grandmother to give you a loving, stable childhood."

"I was indeed. Until my fifth birthday anyways." Caleb crossed his knife and fork on his plate and picked up his teacup. "My father decided 'twas time for the son and heir to be returned to the castle, to be groomed for the future responsibilities of his station in life."

"What? At the age of five, he took you away from Granny? From the only mother, the only home you'd ever known?"

"Ah, sure, but isn't Granny a force to be reckoned with." His chuckle held wry amusement. "No way on God's green earth was she letting the man get away with that craic."

"But he was your legal guardian. What could she do?"

"Collected her things, along with mine, and moved house, straight up to the castle. 'Twas here she stayed 'til I was twelve or so and content with my lot, before returning to her own place." Caleb paused, his eyes thoughtful, as if he were deciding whether to continue the conversation on such a personal track. Then with an almost imperceptible nod, he carried on. "Even living at the castle I was after seeing very little of my father. Not until my twelfth birthday. That's the age our people...em, our *family* acknowledges a boy's right of passage into manhood."

"Kind of like a Jewish boy's bar mitzvah." Moved by his willingness to share with her something so personal, so clearly painful, Arianna felt something important shift between them. Her heart broke for the lonely little boy he had been. Like her, a motherless child. Only difference was her father had been warm and loving, while Caleb's had rejected him. How very sad that he was made to feel unwanted, unloved. She could almost picture him: A mischievous cherub with sea-green eyes and loads of inky black curls falling riotously around his tiny face. A little boy carrying an unfair burden; saddled with the blame for his mother's death. It was the kind of emotional baggage that stayed with a person.

Knowing intuitively that he would despise any response that resembled pity, it was understanding she offered instead. "Your father must have loved your mother dearly, to have been so affected by her death."

Caleb's expression grew hard, his jaw rigid. "You're wrong about that, *cailín*. Dead wrong. My father loved no one. Sure, 'tisn't in our— 'twasn't in his nature to do so."

"But to have been so devastated—"

"'Twas his honor that suffered, not his heart," he insisted, his face a mask of disdain.

"It's likely he blamed himself for getting her pregnant."

"And well he should have. My mother was...fragile. And the blood of our people...of...the men in our *family*—" Caleb seamlessly corrected, seeming to pick his words with care — "holds certain rare...properties...I suppose you might say. Elements that made it dangerous for my father to mate with a woman whose blood didn't... possess similar properties."

Mate? "You mean, kind of like the RH negative factor?"

"Something of the sort...although more the reverse, actually. Instead of the antibodies in our blood putting the life of the infant at risk, 'tis the mother's life that's endangered. In truth, my father should never have risked taking her to his bed a'tall."

At that precise moment, one of the logs in the grate snapped in half, the resounding crack shattering the intimate exchange. Caleb reached for the coffeepot and warmed her cup.

"You needn't look so distressed, *a ghrá*. Meself and me father were after sorting things out between ourselves in later years. Now, enough about that. For what's the point in opening up old wounds? Dredging up things best left buried in the past?"

Her response was soft, but firm. "First, because an old wound has a tendency to fester if it's not opened, cleaned and allowed to heal. And, second," she said, with a gentle smile. "A burden too heavy for one becomes easily manageable when borne by two."

The sage advice elicited a pensive pause on Caleb's part. "Fair enough. But now that we've opened and cleaned and healed and shared, what else will you be having to eat?"

Arianna pushed her plate away with an exaggerated groan. "Absolutely nothing. I don't usually do breakfast and I'm absolutely stuffed to the gills."

"Grand. Now, I've to be off to the bank in a wee while. If you fancy coming with me into town, we can call over to the cottage afterward. Check to see there've been no further problems."

"Sounds like a plan. Do I have time to dash back to my room for a quick shower?"

"No worries. I still have to shave." Caleb stood and held the back of her chair as she got up. "I'll meet you in the foyer at, say...half-eight. Oh, and I've some contacts with glaziers and handymen. I'll organize someone to meet us there today to bid on the job."

"That would be superb." At the door, she gave him a peck on the cheek.

After she'd gone, Caleb scooped his mobile off the table beside the recliner. When his call was answered, he gave a quick explanation about the break-in. "Just mind you bid low enough so she won't be tempted to ring anyone else. 'Twill be herself paying you for the labor and supplies. But sure I'll be hiring you, as well...for an additional service. Call it body guard duty. I want you minding her, staying with her whenever she's there. Never leave her alone, mate. *Never.* And our arrangement's to remain confidential, just between ourselves."

Caleb ended the conversation with a self-satisfied sigh.

Chapter Twenty-one

They spent the better part of the day at the cottage, sifting through rubble. A contractor showed up to bid on the job and Caleb advised she wouldn't get a better price. As he knew the local market a whole lot better than she did, Arianna hired the man on the spot.

They arrived back at the keep shortly before dinner. Arianna dashed upstairs to shower off the smell of smoke and grime. As planned, she joined Caleb in the courtyard for a pre-dinner walk to the stables and found him standing beside an Irish wolfhound as tall as a Shetland pony.

Leaning down, she gave his ruff a good, hard scratch with both hands. "Aren't you handsome?" The animal lifted a giant paw to shake her hand, his tongue lolling from the side of his mouth like a puppy. *Love at first sight.*

"I can't believe you've no fear of the great, black beast," Caleb commented. "Or the way he's taking to you. Our *Torann* isn't one to suffer fools gladly."

"Hey, wait a minute! Did you just call me a fool?" Grinning up at Caleb, she gave the massive canine a final scrub. "What did you say his name is?"

"*Torann.*" At her quizzical look, he explained, "Gaelic for 'thunder'."

With the dog loping alongside them, they ambled down the curving drive, making small talk as a watery sun played hide-and-seek with purple clouds. The November wind was sharp and brisk and stirred the scent of pine into the salty air. Arianna zipped up her hooded jacket as they veered off the main path not far from the keep. "A short cut," Caleb told her, holding back some willow branches for her to duck beneath. The serpentine trail they were on twisted through a dense thicket of centuries-old trees and evergreens threaded with tender plants, saplings and seedlings.

In great form, Arianna's comedic repertoire first included tripping over the swollen root system of an ancient oak. Then, for an encore, her foot sank to the ankle in some unexpectedly loamy soil, causing her to stumble again—this time right into Caleb's arms.

"Walk much?" he chuckled as he hooked an arm through hers.

"Shut up," she said playfully. "Oh yeah, any word yet on when Granny's coming home? I'd like to drop over to her place to see her."

Arianna watched his jaw twitch. A tell, the muscle contraction so miniscule she would have missed it if she hadn't come to know him so well. "What? Is that a problem?"

"Course it isn't," he protested, then hedged. "It's just that she'll be fretting about your safety if she finds out about the break-in."

"Didn't plan to tell her." Arianna heard a faint neighing, caught a whiff of horseflesh. "Mmm... Stables must be near."

"Just around the bend."

The trail curved, then opened into a clearing at the center of a copse of primordial Scots pines. Large tree rhododendrons were scattered amongst them. The two of them tramped past a vine-covered stable behind a paddock constructed of rough-hewn logs. A boy of about sixteen, mucking out one of the stalls, raised a hand in greeting.

Caleb acknowledged him with a pleasant nod. "The office is over there." He gestured at a small wooden hut. "You'll be meeting my stud master." Eyes alight with mischief, he added, "You know, yer man I was speaking with the night I kidnapped you."

Arianna landed a playful punch on his right biceps. "You're never going to let that go, are you?" He looped an arm around her neck, feigning a chokehold.

A wrinkled little man, about a hundred and fifty years old, appeared in the open door of the office. An amused twinkle lit his eyes at their antics. "Hiya, Caleb. How's things?"

"Grand, grand. Arianna meet Colm."

She smiled. "Hey."

"I'm here to sign those papers you have for me."

"Waiting for you on the desk," the older gentleman replied.

Telling Arianna he'd be right back, Caleb disappeared into the office.

"What a lovely setting," she said, to fill the awkward silence. "Like parkland."

"Aye, some of the trees are centuries old." The man wore a wooly hat, a faded brown denim jacket, dirty beige work pants, and mud-encrusted boots. Resembling some poor unfortunate one might find in a soup line, he scratched his bearded chin. "Microclimate here's congruous to such growth. Now, if ye return to the keep in that direction," he said, indicating toward the west, "you'll find a pair of four-hundred-year-old yews standing guard at the entrance of the walled formal garden." He went on to explain the garden had been planted in the *jardin potager* style, in specially designed rows, as opposed to the informal landscaping everywhere else. *Never judge a book.*

As Caleb re-joined them, she thanked the man for the expert lesson in horticulture. "Colm told me about the ancient yews," she said to Caleb. "Can we go back that way?"

"Absolutely."

As they continued along the scraggly path, Arianna looked to the sky, where pewter-colored clouds sketched the evening to come. "I love the musky smells of a forest." She took a deep breath, enjoying the fresh scents of flowers, leaves and green plants layered amongst the more fecund smells of rich, dark earth and the underlying essence of decay. Through the leafless branches, she could see that the sun hung low in the western sky. "I'd love to watch the sun set. Do we have time to make it to that place overlooking the sea, where I saw you that day?"

Arianna didn't mention the lightning. For some reason, ever since that night at the restaurant, just the thought of it gripped her throat in a chokehold.

Caleb grew quiet. She remembered the strange dream she had had of his mother's funeral. The young boy she had encountered standing alone amongst the brambles, staring forlornly over that same rocky ledge at the sea below. Suddenly she perceived the enormity of her request—that he share with her his private sanctuary. A refuge that had been his alone, since he had been that small neglected child.

"I'm sorry," she said quickly. "I shouldn't have asked. That's been your personal space since you were a boy."

He turned, and considered her. "How is it you know that?"

She looked down for a moment, then just shook her head.

Brows drawn together, he continued to stare at her for several moments. Then, as if he had made a decision, he nodded. "We'll go there now."

An overwhelming rush of compassion filled her heart. Oh, God, how she longed to take him in her arms, hold him, love him, rescue that sad and lonely little boy hiding deep within the man. That one she had watched from a castle window walking along the desolate shore late at night. His inclusion of her, his invitation to join him at his sacred place, felt like she had crossed some great divide. Scaled the lofty heights of a mountain peak.

Caleb threaded his fingers through hers and led her due west, toward the setting sun. Just past the ancient yews and formal walled garden they were passing on the way, her eyes lighted upon an extraordinary Gothic-styled edifice, the size of a small castle. "The mausoleum," she said softly, looking up at him. "The one your father had constructed in your mother's memory."

At his brief nod, a shiver traveled the length of her spine. She began speaking quietly, describing to him every square inch of the small chapel housed within, including how the sun's rays filtered through the stained glass windows and splashed a spray of rainbow colors onto the polished oak of the pews.

He grew silent, reflective. 'Another vision?" She nodded and gave his hand a subtle squeeze, which he returned.

When they reached the western border of the property, where she had seen Caleb from the coast below, he ordered Torann to stay. Though the great beast yipped and whined in protest, he sat obediently beside the crumbling wall. Caleb climbed out onto a wide section of the lichen-patterned outer bawn, then reached out and pulled Arianna over beside him. They sat side-by-side, feet dangling over the edge, a wild and majestic view stretching out for miles in front of them. He scooted back against the curtain wall and urged her to move between his thighs. Then he tugged her against his chest, forearms crossed over her shoulders, and hugged her in a warm embrace.

"Like eagles in a medieval aerie," she said, hardly able to hear her own words for the deafening rush of wind in her ears. It was as if the two of them were perched at the very apex of creation. With her fear of heights, Arianna knew she should have been terrified, sitting balanced precariously on a crumbling stone wall at the edge of a precipice, the strong winds tugging at her insistently, trying to pull her over the ledge. And yet, snuggled against Caleb's strong body, she felt as safe as a child in its mother's arms.

Above them were the vast and changing skies. Below, the barren hillside sloped dramatically toward the sea. The boundless landscape of the distant valley would be glorious in the spring, she mused, when the hills were awash with color, when the rust-colored heather and fuchsia hedges burst into flame. The dappled green of the clover fields would become a lush blanket beneath the leafy canopies of the birch, the white-flowered mountain ash, the large-leafed elm and the yew.

"God, I could sit here like this forever," she sighed.

Caleb rested his chin on the crown of her head and tightened his arms around her. Her heart filled, overflowed with emotion. Gentle as a prayer, it came to her. The quiet knowledge that she loved this man. *This* one. Not the perfect man of dreams and illusion. But this one, with his quiet, brooding ways, his annoying macho tendencies.

In this small tucked-away spot peace was to be found. Serenity in the matchless splendor of the rivers and lakes, the mountains, heath and bogs. The special way the sun set the heavens ablaze with its glory, fiery coppers tempered with molten gold. Arianna understood now why Caleb would hold this place sacrosanct.

She understood other things now, as well. Like why her father had come to her after his death. Caleb was the reason he had sent her home to Ireland. Hadn't he told her it was here that she would meet her destiny? This man...the man of her dreams.

And if Da hadn't passed away, what then? Would she never have known Caleb? Or had their encounter been predestined? The uncanny intertwining of their lives preordained?

Sliding Doors. She had found the movie based on the premise of the road not taken thought provoking. The questions it asked profound. Were the alternate realities of a person's life the result of choices made or simple happenstance?

If she hadn't come here to Ireland, would she have moved on with her life, convinced that her dream lover was only a figment of her imagination? Would she and Damien have been intimate by now? Very likely, given how close they were growing before she had left. And if so, would their relationship have taken a predictable course? Would she have agreed to live with him? Eventually, to marry him?

A shattering thought. What if Da had died a year from now? Five years? And, God forbid, she had returned to Ireland then, another man's wife. Perhaps, having borne another man's child. Arianna hastily banished the thought, refusing to dwell on something that felt too much like grief. A sick, interminable heartache...the tragic notion of not being free to love the man whose arms surrounded her now in a protective circle.

She shivered, and Caleb brushed his lips against the back of neck. "Come, we'll go now, *a ghrá*. Sure, supper's waiting."

After dinner, which was a smaller production tonight without the addition of special guests at the head table, Caleb invited her on a grand tour of the main library. It was a vast room teeming with book-lined shelves. Knowing her love of old tomes, he directed her attention to several glass-encased volumes.

"Incunabula," she exclaimed, correctly identifying the rare texts printed in Europe before the year 1501. "These are museum pieces."

Together they moved along the floor-to-ceiling, wall-to-wall bookshelves, perusing the thousands of titles on display. "Pick something to take upstairs with you," he suggested. He felt strangely contented to see her pluck a leather-bound copy of Romeo and Juliet off the shelf and squint at the original script. By the time they left the room, she had several selections tucked in the crook of her arm.

At the door to her suite, he bent his head and kissed her goodnight. Her lips trembled beneath his, and just that moist, velvety touch set his body on fire.

Closing his eyes, he inhaled deeply, attempting to battle the erotic surge arcing between them. 'Twas a fight the wee woman seemed intent on seeing him lose. She stepped boldly into his arms, all lean, toned muscle and feminine curves. Hers was the body of an athlete, no fat, no unwanted padding, but plush and pliant in all the right places.

"I don't understand what's been between us all these years, Caleb. But I've lo— I've cared about you forever. And I want you to kiss me now, hold me, touch me like before."

He could smell the enchantment of her arousal intermingled with the tangy spice of her fear of the unknown. Fear that would be abject terror if she had any concept of what manner of being she was enticing with her bold words. Sliding his hands through her hair, he held her head in place, forcing her to look up at him. "Have you any idea of the risk you're taking?" he asked quietly.

"I know there's...something...about you that I don't understand. But I don't care. I know all I need to know about you. I want to experience here, now, what we had before."

He might not be *only* a man, Caleb thought, but sure a man he was. And, God forgive him, he would test himself this night, partake of what she was offering. To an extent.

Still holding her face gently between his hands, as if she were one of his priceless museum treasures, he bent to nibble her lips, once, twice. Then he traced the seam of her mouth with the tip of his tongue. She sighed into the kiss and his tongue slid inside her mouth, to explore the moist, warm depths welcoming him home.

"Mmm, you taste just as I remember," he whispered, his hands caressing her shoulders, her back. Cupping the rounded cheeks of her womanly bottom, he bent his knees slightly, then lifted her. She whimpered into his mouth as she wrapped her legs around his waist, pressing herself against the hot, hard length of what she tempted. What she dared.

Among Caleb's kind, sexual desire was a most natural and enjoyable appetite: One meant to be freely explored, freely sated. Quite different, he allowed, from the perception of most mere mortal women, who colored such intimacy with a near-spiritual reverence.

A valid point for them, Caleb allowed, given the natural order of things for them, respective to procreation. For unlike females of his own race, who controlled conception by strength of their will alone, their mere mortal counterparts were at risk of pregnancy with every encounter.

The precise reason—though he'd his tongue in her mouth, his hands freely roaming her warm, yielding flesh—he vowed not to renew, here in the physical realm, the fiery mating the two of them had shared within the Imaginal.

He kissed her forehead, her nose, releasing her slowly to slide down the front of his body. Her cheeks were flushed, lips moist and swollen. "You know, we can't do this," he told her, his voice like tires over gravel. He reached out, pushed open the door to her rooms. "'Twould be a deadly game of Russian Roulette we'd be playing."

"The blood thing." Her voice was a breathless whisper, angel blue eyes blind with wanting. A frown marred the slender arch of her golden brows. "There has to be some way—"

"There is not." His tone was harsher than he'd intended. "Now, go." *Save yourself.*

She forced a deep breath and stepped back. She lowered her eyes, as if she were embarrassed, as if she felt he was rejecting her advances. *Bloody hell.* Didn't the woman know he'd give anything to take her in his arms and finish what they'd started? She turned and walked into her room. The door slowly closed.

Cursing himself for a fool, Caleb made his way to his own apartments. There, he paced the floor of his study until he was sure he'd worn a deep tread in the thick piles of the Persian rug. Aching and hard as the ancient stones at Newgrange, he railed against the untenable position fate had cast him in.

"'Tisn't natural for a man to be denying himself this kind o' way," he muttered to himself, dragging a hand through his hair. What he needed, he decided, was a distraction. A little uncomplicated physical release with one of his regular partners. One of his own kind.

A woman not at risk of dying by virtue of his spilling his fertile seed inside her.

He pulled his mobile from the holster on his belt and dialed. "Brona, it's me, Caleb." He sounded edgy, grim. Just the way she fancied him. "Are you up for company tonight?"

At the soft, feminine purr in the affirmative, he slid the phone shut. Grabbing his jacket off the hall tree by the door, he quickly left the keep.

But, bloody damned *eejit* that he was, he would not be going into town. Why? Because raven-haired Brona wasn't the fair-haired temptress of his dreams, the woman he desired above all others. The one for whom his lust burned and bubbled, bright and hot as molten lead. So he called Brona back and canceled their date.

Bollocks. His short bark of laughter was without humor as he considered the irony: That the little mortal had somehow enchanted *him* with magic of her own.

So, instead of a willing female, he found himself in the stables, mounting his prized black stallion, Aughisky, named after the fabled water horse. The magnificent animal, with a temperament as bloody-minded as his owner's, had refused to be broken. He was as wild and free today as when Caleb had purchased him six long years before.

"Still, we've come to a bit of an arrangement between ourselves, haven't we, lad?" The stallion snorted, raised his massive head and nodded, as Caleb patted his withers.

'Twas true; man and beast had promptly settled the question of who would be master. And yet, Caleb reckoned the horse's submission to his hand had as much to do with the animal's intrinsic respect for the magic in his blood, as it did for his skill as a horseman.

From the paddock, he took the stallion on a slow trot along the leaf-strewn path that twined past the fishpond and, from there, branched off to the north. Soon, the trail intersected the oak grove that household staff referred to in whispers as a faerie rath. And hadn't Caleb assured them time and again that there was nothing mystical about that maze of trees.

Not *that* maze....

Nevertheless, the groundskeepers tended to leave a wide berth around the area whenever their duties forced them to that particular spot on the property.

Now, with the animal properly warmed up, Caleb leaned forward, his muscled thighs tight against the saddle. Heels down, the subtle shift in body weight signaled his desire to change pace. And with a soft-spoken charge, using words not of men but of the Ancients, Caleb tapped his heels into the stallion's powerful flanks and spurred him on to a gallop.

Man and horse broke free of the wild thicket of shrubs and trees, moving like a dart through a splash of silvery moonlight. Flying, as swift and sure as if the splendid beast had sprouted the wings of his magical namesake, they moved as one, soaring over the drumlins, the stony ridges that zigzagged across the open parkland. Over heath and bog, they bounded. Through meadow and vale, they raced through the frigid air as if hellhounds were nipping at the wildly galloping hooves. The echoing crush of frozen earth and the crash of waves against a distant shore eclipsed the eerie stillness of the night.

Slowing only marginally, to round the monolithic boulders marking his ancestor's ancient gravesites and the mausoleum his father had built, he urged his mount further westward, reigning in, at the very last minute, at the verge of the cliff. The animal reared, his front legs pawing at the air in fearful anticipation of the deadly descent before him. And then he began to pick his way carefully down a narrow, gravel path leading to the sea below.

And with the ocean roaring to their left, horse and rider flew through the turbulent wind, through the long, dark hours of the night. Head tossing, eyes rolling, the stallion kicked up sand and foam as he galloped through the mist and moonlight. Strong northwesterly gusts tore at Caleb's hair, the icy blast of arctic air like a knife slicing through the leather of his jacket. But the wintry chill did nothing to cool his ardor, or to dampen the flames of hell licking avariciously at his loins.

As brush strokes of dawn painted the ebony sky in pastel shades of mauve and purple, he gathered in the reins and turned the lathered animal toward home. Back in his room Caleb tore off his clothes and collapsed into his bed, naked and spent.

And still tormented by his desire for the one woman he knew he could never possess.

Chapter Twenty-two

After chucking her cleaning supplies beneath the sink, Arianna stood staring out the kitchen window at the back yard she used to play in as a small child. It was Saturday, the weekend before Thanksgiving. Her friends were due in tomorrow, and she was still chasing down a few last minute details. Thankfully, the work crew would be finishing up later this afternoon, just in time for their arrival.

For almost three weeks now, she had been living an idyllic faerie tale existence; one she would be leaving tomorrow to return to life in the real world. She had been savoring the stolen hours of the last few evenings, her time with Caleb growing increasingly bittersweet.

Not that they wouldn't be seeing each other after she left the castle, she hastened to assure herself. Still, it wouldn't be the same. No more eating breakfast and dinner together. No more quick calls throughout the day just to touch base. No more living together like a married couple.

Married without the sex.

Caleb continued to treat her like a cloistered nun, convinced that his lovemaking would kill her. Unbelievable. He had even nixed her suggestion of using protection. "Wouldn't work," said he. *Wouldn't work? Why?* As usual, no explanation had been forthcoming, which left her swimming in supposition. Was he too big? Was his semen so acidic that it would dissolve the latex? But no, he had said the problem was blood incompatibility, not plumbing.

This, of course, sent her spinning off into a whole new area of speculation. Now, the man sure as heck wasn't a priest. Nor did he claim to be celibate—or, at least, he hadn't been until she came to stay with him at the castle.

"So, what do you do?" she had asked one evening as they snuggled together on a burgundy leather chesterfield, watching a movie.. "Insist every woman you sleep with undergo a "safe-sex" blood test first?" And not to check for an STD, but for 'compatibility'. *Whatever the dickens that was supposed to mean.* "Fine, then. I'm up for a little jab in the arm, if it will prove to you that there's no danger in our being together."

He had spun toward her, gripping her shoulders so abruptly that Torann, curled up and snoring at their feet, growled irritably and slunk away. "Don't be lulled into a false sense of complacency with me, Arianna. Things are not a'tall as they appear. You are in grave danger from me, *a ghrá.*" The softness of his voice was more menacing than if he had shouted and roared. "It's best you remember that and not push me beyond what I'm able to endure."

Which was exactly what Arianna intended for their final evening together.

As she turned from the sink, one of the workers appeared in the kitchen. "Hi, Joe."

He acknowledged her with a nod. "Just fetching a bottle of water out of the fridge."

"Help yourself. So, how's it going up there? Still on target for completion today?"

"Just sorting out the electrical. Another couple of hours, tops." He took a long drink as he left the kitchen.

They were nice guys. And the contractor had done a bang-up job. *Too good*, she reflected. Because, no matter how she crunched the numbers, the company had to have been losing money big-time. A quick tally of the man-hours alone revealed a serious deficit.

Was it possible Caleb had agreed to pay part of the cost? Or was something else going on here? Something that would account for the way those big, burly workmen clucked over her like a pair of old mother hens. Caleb continued to drop her off and pick her up, to save her the treacherous drive down the mountain; however, about a week ago, she had insisted upon renting a car so that she could run local errands during the day. And yet, every time she would tell the crew she was popping into town, she would be flooded with minor emergencies that required her immediate attention.

Always by the time she had attended these *emergencies*, she would have been distracted from whatever errand she had had in mind. Now that she thought about it, she realized she was never left alone. Not for a minute, from the time Caleb dropped her off in the morning until he arrived back at the end of the day to take her home.

Was she totally nuts to think he had hired the work crew to double as personal security?

Maybe. Even so, she had to admit it had been a comfort having them here—especially at first. She would never forget the sick horror she had felt as she crossed the threshold the day after the break-in. And so what if her presumptuous, domineering, mule-headed Irishman had arranged it so she wouldn't be alone? Didn't that just prove he cared for her? That there was more between them than lurid waking dreams and a sexual attraction so intense it was driving them both insane?

Ready to wrap things up, Arianna surveyed the completed work with a sense of relief. The sooty residue that had coated every surface was gone. The walls had been restored to their former eggshell color. And from beneath mountains of rubble and impossible acres of dust and grime, the warm, rich wood of the floors and furniture had reappeared.

She took a deep breath, inhaling the clean, fresh scents of lemon cleaner and wet paint, which had exorcised the dank, musty smell of destruction.

Her cell phone rang. *Caleb.* "Hiya. How's things?"

"Just finishing up now."

"Brilliant. It's about half-two. Will I come collect you?"

Arianna needed to run to *Super Valu* to pick up some groceries and by the green grocer to stock in fresh produce for Michaela, whose latest *ism* related to vegetables. But with Caleb's OTT obsession with her being in mortal danger, she knew he would give her grief about going into town alone.

"Joe said they wouldn't be wrapping things up for at least another couple of hours." *Well, he* did *say that.* "So just pick me up at four, as usual."

"That's grand. I'm around town, so give me a bell if you want me earlier."

"Will do." Arianna disconnected the call and, without alerting her *keepers*, slipped quietly out the front door.

Her errands completed with time to spare, she headed for home. On the way back, she got caught in a gridlock from a traffic accident. No problem, though, because even with the delay she was back at the cottage by three o'clock.

She swung past the hedgerows and into her driveway. She glanced in the rearview mirror and swore vividly. A black Land Rover was pulling in behind her.

"Those *rats*."

For an excruciating minute or two, she and Caleb sat in their respective vehicles, neither of them acknowledging the other. When she finally sneaked a peek at him, her gaze collided with his caustic one and she immediately lowered her eyes. Heart pounding like a tom-tom, she pretended to be searching for something in the glove box. *Coward!*

"The man has no right!" she muttered aloud. Her stomach felt jittery, her knees weak and shaky, like when she was a kid and Da was about to give her a dressing down. "Well, I'm not a child, and I refuse to be treated like one."

Her chin jutted out in defiance, she climbed out of the car. Leaning back in, she grabbed a couple of bags off the passenger seat. She wondered now whether she had endured the embarrassment of one of those purchases for nothing.

Giving a casual wave as if nothing were amiss, she went inside. Would he let it go? Come into the house while she was putting the food away and make nice? *Not a chance.*

As she stomped out of the kitchen, what she really wanted to do was storm upstairs and give "the lads" a good piece of her mind. But Tara and Michaela were arriving tomorrow. She sure as heck didn't need them getting pissy and pulling out on the job.

Good sense overruling temper, she called up from the foot of the stairs. "Hey, Joe, I'm leaving. Just lock up whenever you're finished."

She heard his grunt of acknowledgement as she pulled the door closed behind her.

Avoiding eye contact, she walked around the front of the Land Rover and climbed inside. And ran smack into one of Caleb's cold, forbidding stares. She cleared her throat. "*What?* I had to run into town."

Features hard as flint, he didn't reply. Just looked over his shoulder and proceeded to back out of the driveway.

Arianna heaved a frustrated sigh. Once, twice, she felt his brooding glance touch her. *God, the man knew just which buttons to push.* Shifting in her seat, she drilled him a look. "Enough with the silent treatment, okay?" she bit out. "My friends are flying in tomorrow and I had to get food in the house."

His head turned and he considered her, his green gaze unfathomable, irises nearly swallowed by the angry black of his pupils. Fear twisted her stomach at his unspoken rebuke. She had seen it before. The ancient power that resided in the deep, dark depths of his eyes. A look that warned of magic and monsters, of maniacs howling at the moon. Of demonic entities dancing in the veil of night.

A wild and reckless part of Arianna thrilled to the thought of provoking that dark and unknown peril. What would happen if she poked at the savage creature he fought so hard to contain? What if she taunted it, drew it out? Quenched her obsession with the heady menace that had enticed and intrigued her since the night they had met? And before.

Caleb's foot hit the brakes. Arianna's hand flew out to brace against the dash. His long arm shot toward her. She gasped and flinched at the unexpected movement.

His mouth thinned, eyes froze over at her reaction. Then he followed through with the movement, hooking her seatbelt with his hand and dragging it across her lap. The loud click of the lock engaging reverberated in the strained silence.

As he pressed again on the accelerator, Arianna cursed him under her breath. "That was just a reflexive reaction, Caleb. I did NOT think you were going to hit me."

Maybe if he tried acting more like a prospective lover, and less like an overprotective parent, they would get along better. She was frustrated, both sexually and emotionally. And while he was

Michelangelo's *David* gorgeous, he was undoubtedly the most arrogant man she had ever encountered. Not to mention pig-headed, over-bearing, and temper-prone.

And, oh, yeah, did I mention arrogant?

So, why the heck did she love him like she did?

Simple. Because he could also be sensitive, understanding, and supportive. And while loath to admit it, she had discovered that, more times than not, whenever he was stubborn about a thing, in the end it would turn out he had been right.

Of course, there *was* that seething black temper of his. So violent, so volatile, she shuddered to think of the seismic repercussions if he ever allowed it to fully erupt. But, of course, the almighty Caleb never lost his temper, which he kept locked behind a will of steel...along with his sexual appetites. Personal experience had taught Arianna that the more aroused he was—or alternatively, the more angry and incensed—the more controlled and subdued he became.

Like now. When a good fifteen minutes had passed without him uttering a single solitary word. Arianna swiped a finger idly through the condensation on her window. *Probably a result of the steam that was pouring out of his ears.*

"Caleb, we need to talk."

Silence. Except for the engine's nerve-wracking roar as they began the steep ascent to the castle. "Ah, get over yourself already," she muttered, loud enough for him to hear her.

 By the time they pulled up in front of the keep, she was cruising for a good knock down, drag out. Get it all out there. Clear the air.

He engaged the hand brake, switched off the engine and turned to her. "I've paperwork to catch up on this evening, so I'll not be joining you for dinner."

Without another word, he got out of the Discovery and shut the door with a thud. He climbed the steps to the keep, not giving her so much as a backward glance.

The depths of pain she felt at his callous rejection took her by surprise. She had believed he cared for her, might even be coming to love her. Arianna had planned to seduce him tonight, to give herself to him. Stupid, stupid. Building castles in the clouds, she thought.

The irony wasn't lost on her.

Chapter Twenty-three

There it was again, Arianna thought sleepily. That annoying tap, tap, tapping sound. Pushing up in her bed, she squinted at the luminous dial on her travel clock. "Who the heck hangs pictures at three in the morning?" she grumbled, burying her face in her pillow. When the sound came again, her sleep-fogged brain registered that it was actually someone knocking on her door.

She propped herself up on one elbow. "Just a minute," she called out, her voice raspy.

As she slid out from under the covers, she noticed how much cooler it was than usual. Shivering, she lumbered over to the door and opened it a crack, peeking around the edge.

"Caleb." She kept her voice low so as not to disturb anyone. "Is everything okay?"

"'Tis, yes." The mischievous grin he offered gave her a rare glimpse of the precious little boy who had once roamed these medieval halls. "And you don't have to be whispering. You're the only one in residence on this floor."

"Thanks for sharing," Arianna quipped, stifling a yawn. "So what's up?"

His eyes twinkled, that smile that never failed to take her breath away tugging again at his lips. "Thought I'd call up to see you if you fancied going out to play."

Arianna stared at him. *He was kidding, right?* "Out to play? At three in the morning?"

"Wasn't it you yourself just after mentioning how you'd be missing the snow this season? And aren't we having a virtual blizzard out in the courtyard this very minute."

"No way!" She bounded over to the window with a whoop of

delight. "Wow, I didn't hear anything about snow on the weather forecast."

Buffeted by the strong sea winds, snowflakes twirled above the restless waves in a frantic ballet. A sparkling layer of crystal powder coated the curtain walls and battlements rising off in the distance. Arianna had never seen anything so beautiful...or so strange, she decided, gazing upward. In Maine, the sky would have been low and claustrophobic with snow clouds. But here in Ireland, the glistening flakes of snow seemed to be falling directly from the winking stars above.

Realizing Caleb hadn't joined her at the window, she looked back. His arms crossed, one shoulder holding up the doorjamb, his eyes smiled in enjoyment of her light-hearted reaction.

As she returned to the door, she felt his gaze drift over her in a heated caress. Her night garb consisted of boxers and a thin, cotton tank top, revealing nipples puckered by the cold. "Excuse me," she murmured and dashed over to the foot of the bed to retrieve her white fluffy bathrobe. Looping the belt loosely around her waist, she rejoined him at the door.

Familiar late-night stubble roughened his jaw. And he was still in the same clothes he had been wearing the day before. Their quarrel must have left him unsettled, unable to sleep. *Good.* Though it might not have been particularly nice, Arianna was happy she hadn't been the only one so affected.

She gave an internal sigh. God, he looked good, all rough and rumpled, his black hair disheveled as though he had been plowing his fingers through it. She caught a mild waft of whisky coupled with the scents of sandlewood and Caleb's own unique male fragrance.

She felt such love for this impossible man, "Thanks for waking me up, Caleb. I would have hated to miss this."

As she stretched up to brush her lips across his cheek, he turned his head and captured her mouth in a hot, greedy kiss. But before the erotic spark could explode into something unquenchable, he set her firmly away from him. "What d'ya reckon we build a snowman before it all melts away? Dress warm now and hurry. I'll meet you down below."

"Down in two ticks."

The towering front door opened onto a veritable winter wonderland. A frigid rush of air scattered light powdery snow across the gray marble floor. Caleb held her hand as they climbed down the slippery stone steps into the courtyard. She turned in a slow circle, silent snowflakes falling all around her. "Oh, Caleb. It's enchanting."

Tonight the ancient gray stone of the mighty fortress sparkled a pristine white. The wall walk and battlements along the curtain wall to her right, the round towers and outbuildings in the distance, were all shrouded in a snowy blanket. Naked trees rose above them like behemoth skeletons, snowdrifts bowing their bony arms.

"It's absolutely magical," she sighed.

Caleb lips turned up in a secret smile as he fished a pair of man-sized gloves out of his pocket. "Best put these on. They're too big, but they'll keep your hands toasty."

Needles of intense cold had already been pricking her fingertips. "Thanks."

"And now, we'll go exploring." Wrapping his gloved hand around hers, Caleb dragged her off in the direction of the frozen woodlands.

They sprinted down the path toward the formal gardens like two errant children playing hooky from school. Skirting the paddocks and stables, Arianna could hear the crunch of the ice-hardened ground beneath her booted feet. Vapor puffed from their mouths as they picked their way across a gorse-fringed gully, then circled a fishpond on the other side.

Arianna dropped Caleb's hand and broke away. "Race you to that clump of trees on top of the hill," she challenged. "Last one there's a rotten egg!" As she slipped and slid through the open meadow, her throat began to ache from the laughter and the cold.

"No, *Arianna....*"

His hesitation in calling out to her gave Arianna a head start. Making quick work of the advantage, she dashed toward a frozen maze of trees cresting the brow of the hill. Ducking past a couple of gnarled old Hawthorne bushes that guarded its entrance, she played hide-and-seek amongst the rows of ancient Oak and Ash, Thorn and Rowan trees, her rasping breath loud in the snow-muffled silence.

After a few minutes, she stopped moving. Afraid that she was getting herself hopelessly lost, she turned in a circle, trying to locate the path she had taken on her way in. But her footprints in the snow crossed and re-crossed themselves, and there was nothing distinctive about any of the trees. Trees, she thought with a shiver, that seemed to be closing in on her, bending over her, their great, drooping limbs reaching....

There was a flash of movement to her left. A titter of laughter from behind. Arianna spun around, chills of dread skittering up her spine. She remembered Caleb calling out to her as she began to run. Had he been meaning to warn her off this place? Had she inadvertently stumbled across one of Ireland's fabled faerie groves? According to legend, mortals foolish enough to intrude upon these magical forts risked becoming lost in them forever. For such, as the story goes, was the gravity of the penalty exacted by the faerie folk for daring to disturb their timeless solitude.

"Faeries!" Arianna grunted. "Yeah, right." But a second otherworldly giggle echoed from amongst the trees at her comment.

Her heart pounding, she began to run. But each turn only led her deeper into the wooded labyrinth. "Caleb!"

"Where are you, *a ghrá*?" His muffled voice came from a distance. Did he sound anxious? Fearful for her safety?

"I'm lost in this...this faerie rath." Her words reverberated eerily, as if she had entered another dimension. "Caleb, did you hear me?"

"I'm coming to bring you out of there." His tone was gruff, and, yes, apprehensive. "Stop moving. Just stay where you are."

Seconds later, he was turning the corner on a row of solidly interlaced trees. Arianna darted over to him and leaped into his arms, squealing as he nuzzled her neck with a cold nose. "Sshh, mustn't mention the faeries," he warned in a low whisper.

Was he kidding? If so, then why the surreptitious glance around them? His hand clasped her wrist and he led her up and down the lines of trees until they finally stepped back out into the open meadow.

He shook his head and chuckled, his eyes twinkling with amusement. "You need a keeper."

"You think it's funny? Me getting lost and scared half out of my mind?" Her momentary terror forgotten, she grinned up at him. Scooping up a handful of snow, she patted it into a ball.

"You wouldn't dare—" *Splat*, a snowball hit him smack in the face. With a mock snarl, Caleb brushed himself off, then scraped up a fistful of the fluffy white stuff himself.

With a shriek, Arianna dashed down the slippery path. At the outskirts of a dense section of woodland, she detoured off the trail and ducked behind a tree. She was peeking out to look for him, when he pounced, grabbing her from behind. Her cries resounded shrilly off the frosty hills.

As he was dragging her back onto the trail, his foot connected squarely with the root of a giant oak. They both went sprawling headlong into a shimmering bank of newly fallen snow. Giggling breathlessly, Arianna scrambled to her feet. As she tried to flee, Caleb tackled her to the ground. Rolling her over, he straddled her hips and, while holding her pinned helplessly between his thighs, he scraped up another huge handful of snow.

With a merciless grin on his face, he held the prize-winning snowball threateningly over her head. "Now you pay for your impertinence."

"No! Let me go!" Wriggling and bucking, she shifted her weight, attempting to topple him sideways.

"I think not, you bold brat." With a low, sexy chuckle, he captured her wrists in one hand and dragged them over her head. "You've left me no choice but to punish you." His voice dripped seduction, hot candle wax on moist, cool skin.

As snow flurries pirouetted in a silent ballet, Arianna's smile melted slowly from the intense heat in his gaze. Eyes of endless green snapped and sizzled, evoked a magic that heated the air, set her blood to boiling, her body on fire.

He tossed the snowball away.

His suggestive male heat replaced the wintry freeze and warmed all the cold, empty places inside of her. A reckless passion seemed to overtake her then. All that she had longed for, that she had been craving for weeks, months, years, was suddenly and irrevocably within her reach. Arianna would seize this moment, not let it slip away.

"You're going to punish me?" she whispered, reveling in the masculine weight of that long, hard body pressing her down into the soft-packed snow.

"I am indeed, you naughty girl." His voice was gravelly, his eyes a living green flame.

"How?" Her own voice was so low and sultry she didn't recognize it. "Caleb?"

His eyes never leaving hers, he tugged a glove off with his teeth. "With my hands," he murmured, his deep, resonant voice taking her halfway there.

"Well, if you must." She reached up and dusted the snow from his hair. "Do your worst then." Gloved fingers trailing over the shadow of whiskers darkening his jaw, she lifted her head from the ground and touched the hammering pulse at the base of his throat with her lips, with the warm, moist tip of her tongue.

"*A ghrá.*" *My love.* He breathed the endearment, his voice hoarse with unbridled need.

Releasing her hands, he slipped his hand beneath her head as a barrier against the icy ground. Then his mouth angled downward. His lips claimed hers with a savage intensity that challenged the sanity of her plan to seduce a man so wildly experienced. One so primitively sexual. His mouth was avid, hot and demanding. His tongue darted past her teeth, a ruthless warrior invading every soft and subtle recess with the intensity of a conquering force.

Arianna could hear a clanging in her head. A flashing red alert warning that the shackles on this man's ravenous hunger had finally snapped. A distant memory surfaced now, dragging through a thick, deep fog. It was another instance when he had lost control, when she had witnessed his eyes take on that glittering, otherworldly look. It had been at his friend's restaurant in Clifden. The recollection made her heart lurch in her chest from some unnamed fear.

"I'm so sorry...." Caleb spoke deep and low. But whether he was about to apologize for his surly behavior of earlier, or was asking forgiveness for a sin he had yet to commit, Arianna did not know. Because, his ungloved hand, which was strangely warm, found its way inside her jacket, beneath her shirt. He unclasped the front of her bra.

Her breast swelled into the palm of his hand.

Caleb swallowed her moan with his mouth as he rolled her nipple between his thumb and forefinger. "Not enough," he growled, his desperation fueled by the mounting frustration of having denied himself for so long. "No, not nearly enough."

Breath matching heaving breath, he lifted his hips and shifted sideways. His hand left her breast, to splay across her concave belly; those long, roving fingers angled downward, reaching inside the low-rise waist of her jeans.

"I need your hands on me, Caleb," she panted, her knees bent on either side of his arm. "I'll die if you don't touch me now." Her words slid into a groan as his fingers slipped beneath the silken barrier and found their mark.

He found her wet, aching center, then dipped inside. His tongue thrust into her mouth, setting a rhythm in tandem with the dexterous movement of his finger. Unbearably erotic, a tantalizing harbinger of his body's ultimate invasion to come. His touch drove her higher and higher, had her striving, reaching for the ultimate bliss.

"Mmm, so sweet," he murmured in her ear, nipping her earlobe while keeping up the tormenting rhythm of his fingers. "I can't make love to you fully, but I want to pleasure you, feel you shudder in my arms. I want to hear you scream with the release only I can give you."

She was moaning, trembling, as those clever fingers circled, picked up the pace, brought her almost to peak, then slowed, and began the exquisite torture all over again. "Yes. Oh, yes. Please." Her head thrashed mindlessly to and fro, as she clutched his broad shoulders. Her palms skimmed his ripped abs, then moved lower. She heard him groan deep in his throat as she began to fumble with his belt.

She thought she would scream with frustration when his hand left her, to catch her wrist. "No. This is for you, *a mhuirnín,*" he rasped. "If you touch me, I fear I'll lose control." Then he released her, his hand returning to the land of milk and honey.

Synchronicity. The two of them finding each other in this time, this place. Arianna could feel her heart beating in time with his. She wanted...no *needed*...to have him inside of her. To know the honesty... the truth of that intimate sharing. Not in some dream vision, some paranormal interlude she couldn't comprehend, but now, fully awake. Fully conscious. She longed to climb inside him, as well. To abide there forever, the two of them interwoven into one being. Flesh of his flesh, bone of his bone. Heart to heart.

She whimpered as he broke off the kiss, his fingers went still. No, he wouldn't! If he dared to stop now, she swore she would scream the castle down. Her hips moved insistently against his hand, her fingers curled into his ebony hair, tugging, trying to pull that tormenting mouth back down to hers.

He resisted the pressure and gazed down at her, green eyes on fire.

"Look at me." His voice rough with need, he issued the command. His sibilant gaze forced compliance, holding her in his thrall, as his fingers lay maddeningly dormant upon that part of her that craved his touch. "Like before, *a ghrá*, in our dreams, I want to watch you, to see your eyes go blind, when I take you over the edge." He held her gaze, his eyes dark, mesmerizing, as his thumb pressed down on a knot of nerves at her apex. His fingers curled forward as he softly ordered, "Now."

"Oh, yes, oh, Caleb! Don't stop! Oh!" Shaking violently, Arianna let a scream rip from her throat as she crashed through an invisible barrier. And then she was soaring through time and space, to some mystical place far beyond the moon and the stars. With Caleb her only anchor to here and now, she watched rainbows shatter into sizzling fireballs, spilling glittering shards of color all around her.

Hours, *years* later, as she floated back to earth, she felt Caleb tracing nibbling kisses along the corners of her mouth. "You're so beautiful," he whispered gently, then in a groan of despair said, "Mother of God, whatever am I to do with you?"

As she lay replete beside him, he lowered his head, trailing kisses over her eyes, her nose, her chin. Her breath still shuddering with erotic aftershocks, she watched his eyes close. Jaw locked tight, he rolled fully on top of her. Supporting himself on his forearms, he kissed her mouth and ground their loins together, pleasuring them both.

As if he would take at least this much for himself.

When it was her heart's fondest desire to give him so very much more.

"Take me into the castle, Caleb." Arms curving up his back, over his shoulders, she met each aggressive stroke of his hips with her own, hoping to so inflame him as to rend the last shreds of his self-control. "I want you to make love to me. Now, tonight."

Eyes glittering, crazed with lust, he stared down at her almost accusingly. "I don't want this to end tonight, *a ghrá*," he rasped, taking huge gulps of the frigid air. "Not til I've felt your wet heat wrapped around me, squeezing me dry. Sure, I'd almost wager the fate of the whole world just to be inside you."

As if they were somehow prophetic, his words seemed to bolster his resolve. Caleb pressed his lips to hers, his kiss hard and demanding. Then he rolled off her and stood up. Leaning down, he grasped her hand and pulled her to her feet.

And so, their childish romp in the snow was brought to a precipitous end, eclipsed by the searing passion that flared so ardently between them.

As the star-crossed lovers made their way, hand in hand, back to the ancient keep, the moon shone crisp and bright around them. Warmed by the homespun scent of woodsmoke, the night was alive with the shimmer of magic.

෧෬

After invading the kitchen to share a couple of warming cups of hot mulled wine, Caleb followed Arianna up the winding stone steps to her rooms. At her door, he leaned down to kiss her goodnight.

Oh, no you don't. Not tonight. In the semi-darkness of the hallway, she caught his face between her hands and gazed beseechingly into his eyes. "Don't do this, Caleb." His name fell from her lips as softly as a prayer. "I want you, need you, in my bed tonight." She reached down between them, exalted in his sudden inhale as her fingers trailed boldly over his erection. "I don't want to leave you like this. I want to ease you. Caleb, let me love you tonight."

She triumphed at the torment of indecision in his eyes. "Arianna, *God*, you're making me daft. But you've no idea what you're asking, *a ghrá*. No idea a'tall."

"Oh, but I do." She spoke quietly, resolutely, her affirmation bringing both pain and pleasure to his eyes. "I want to lie naked beneath you, to know your possession. I need to feel you, hot and hard, moving deep inside me. It's what I want... What I've always wanted."

Slowly, relentlessly, he backed her against the wall, caught her chin in his hand. Arianna knew what he was doing. He was trying to appear out of control, threatening. To warn her off. Refusing to be intimidated, however, she locked her rebellious eyes stubbornly with his. "You've asked what I am, *a stór,*" he growled in a voice hoarse with need. "Well, you've no concept. What I am...what I'm capable of. Nor have you the slightest clue what it is you're asking. There are things about me you couldn't possibly fathom. Things I'm not at liberty to tell."

"I know all I need to know. I've lived here with you for over two weeks, remember?" A soft smile touched her lips as she brushed an unruly lock of hair away from his beloved face. "Want to know what I've learned? That you're honest and caring. A man of wisdom and honor, whose friends and associates adore him. And why? Because he looks out for his own. Now tell me, what else could I possibly need to know?"

"That I could hurt you." His voice broke on the word.

"You would never."

Caleb sighed heavily and dropped his hand to his side, clenched it into a fist. "Not on purpose, no." He stopped, seemed to be considering something, making a decision. "What if I told you that my taking you to my bed tonight...that it could cost you your life?"

Arianna picked up his left hand, turned it over, casually uncurled his fingers. "You're worried that what happened to your mother might happen to me." She bent her head and placed a gentle kiss in the center of his palm. Her hair trailed over his hand. Her lips whispered over the sensitive flesh of his inner wrist. "I have a sixth sense about these things, Caleb. And I have a very strong feeling that my blood is completely compatible with yours."

"'Tisn't," he insisted harshly. "Trust me on this, Arianna, it is *not* compatible." There was a flash of something in his eyes, followed by one of his mercurial mood changes. "So, let me understand this. You're willing to risk your life tonight just to get the leg over?"

Arianna hated that crude Irishism for sexual intercourse, and he knew it. Which is exactly why he had done it? To turn her off. Unperturbed by the jibe, she rose onto her tiptoes and brushed her lips lightly against his. "To *make love* with you, sweetheart," she breathed, emboldened by the power of her feelings for him. "There's a world of difference, you know. And we'll use protection. I purchased something when I went into town. I don't think it would suit either of us for me to get pregnant."

His gaze became dismal; he gave a slight shudder. "I told you the rubber sheaths that mortals...em." He cleared his throat. "*Condoms* are ineffective."

"I remember you saying that and assumed you were referring to the latex ones. I did some research and bought polyurethane. They may not be a hundred percent effective, but—"

He swallowed. "They dissolve, Arianna."

"Dissolve?" *Dissolve?* "As in melt?"

Arianna watched him close his eyes. Alarm prickled her skin, as a murky sense of sortilege rose in the air around them. When his eyes opened again, his gaze was uncloaked and aglitter with unveiled magic. A corner of his wickedly sensual lips curved into a lusty, satyr-like smile. "If you truly wish to ease me safely, you could take me in your mouth."

His right hand shot out and tangled roughly in the hair at the nape of her neck. For a heart-stopping moment, she thought he meant to force her to her knees, to pleasure him. But his left arm snaked around her, crushing her against him, trapping her palms against his chest. Bending his head, he licked the shell of her ear, then nipped her earlobe hard enough to cause a sting. She inhaled sharply, trembling in his arms.

"You *think* you know me, *cailín*," he warned, his voice dripping with sensual menace. "But you've no notion. None a'tall. I've never *made love*, you see. When it comes to sex, I like my rides rough and dirty. My women meek and submissive. Preferably cuffed to the headboard of a bed. Or, better yet," he paused for emphasis, then whispered in her ear. "Bent over it."

Arianna forced her eyes to remain level with his. He was trying to make her afraid of him, desperate to dissuade her. But she refused to be moved by his comments, or by the power radiating from that unfathomable gaze. "Handcuffs? Ooh, kinky," she quipped, an amused twinkle in her eyes. Then her head tilted in a reflective slant. "Or trusting. To give another person that kind of power over you, knowing they would never hurt you. The way I feel about you."

She saw him recoil in that moment, her unwavering faith in him stripping him bare. Then he lowered his mouth to hers again. His lips brushing lightly over hers caused her to reach for the gentle pleasure. For a kiss that was beyond soft, beyond tender, almost lyrical.

"God knows I ache to bury myself inside you, *a ghrá*. So deeply nothing can ever separate us again." His heart pounded against her hands, giving truth to his words. But, at the same time, it issued a warning: that his restraint hung by a slim thread. "So I require your help in this, *a stór*. For I've neither the will nor the power to hold myself back from you any longer. If you truly care for me, if you trust me as you say you do, then you'll do as I ask. Without question."

Arianna was touched by the vulnerability of his entreaty, by the severity of a situation she couldn't fully comprehend. "What do you need me to do?" she asked softly.

"No locks are installed on the doors in the keep. So I want you to take a straight-back chair and wedge it beneath here." He indicated the doorknob on the inside of her door.

"You want me to jam a chair in the door?" She was stunned by the request.

"I do. I'll have your promise on that...and another thing. " His voice was gruff.

"Another...? What?" she breathed.

"That you won't open this door to me again tonight." Her eyes opened wide in disbelief. "*Swear to me*, Arianna. You won't open the door. Not if I knock, not if I coax." He grasped her chin, stared chillingly into her eyes. "Not if I threaten. Now, swear."

She repeated the vow in a whisper of sound. "I won't open the door."

He pulled her to him for one last, lingering kiss. "I'll meet you in our dreams tonight, *a ghrá*." Threat or promise, a shiver went through her at the raw sexuality in his tone. He firmly set her away from him. "Now, close the door."

In a sensual haze, she complied with his directive.

His body rigid, Caleb collapsed against the wall. He didn't trust himself to move until he heard the scrape of the chair, confirming that, for once, the headstrong woman had obeyed him. Perhaps she'd realized, at last, that she had barely escaped him unscathed. Or maybe, he mused grimly, she had seen her own death reflected in his eyes. To be sure that she was locked in for the remainder of the night, he gave the doorknob a final twist and shove, before departing for the solar.

Back in his study, Caleb stared out of the window until dawn broke over the horizon. Silver-hued lavenders, splashes of pink and mauve, and luminous streaks of gold kissed the sky in welcome of a new day. What was happening to him? Before Arianna had come into his life, his existence had been comfortable. Stable. Ordered. But then she'd arrived on the scene like a force of nature. Trying his patience, testing his resolve. Making him feel things...a fullness in his heart, a sense of euphoric contentment...things he'd never felt before. Emotions he didn't understand.

His jaw set, he raised his hand. His palm facing the windowpane, he traced an open-handed circle, once, twice, in a counter-clockwise motion, thus reversing the thing that he'd fashioned in the early hours of this morning. The snow had been a gift to herself from him, an attempt at reparation for behaving like a horse's arse earlier in the evening.

As the temperature outside inched slowly upward, reaching for the seasonal average of five degrees Celsius, the blanket of snow he'd caused to spill across the 1,000-acre estate began to melt. By full daybreak, 'twould all be gone.

All, he reflected broodingly, but the poignant memory of it.

Chapter Twenty-four

"I'm so hungry my stomach thinks my throat's been cut," Michaela complained as Arianna led the way to the snug at McColgan's Pub.

As they passed the leering leprechauns at the entrance, Arianna shot them a challenging glance. But the expressions on their faces remained innocent. *Too innocent*, she thought, half-expecting to hear them begin whistling an Irish tune. "Didn't they feed you on the plane?"

"She forgot to order a *vegetarian* meal," Tara explained.

"Yeah, so I just ate that miserable excuse for a salad and the *white* flour roll."

"Poor baby," Arianna commiserated.

With the weekday lunch crowd thronging the place, the three women from America drew admiring glances. Arianna figured the male interest had as much to do with the disparity of their appearances as their decent looks.

Tara was tall and model thin. Her sea green eyes testified to the natural platinum blonde of her hair. Her complexion would have been porcelain if not for the perpetual tan she sported from spending so much time outdoors.

Michaela's hair was washboard-straight, waist-length and black as pitch, compliments of a Native American heritage. All that tawny beauty packed into a petite, five-foot frame contrasted Tara's long-legged, fair and willowy stature.

They chose a table beside a dusty window that looked out onto Main Street. "Doesn't look like you did any better in the sleep department last night than we did," Tara said to Arianna. "Everything okay?"

"Never better." There it was again. That dopey grin she hadn't been able to wipe off her face for more than five seconds. As he had promised when he left her, Caleb had come to her in her dreams. Knowing him as a flesh and blood man, loving him had been different this time... and yet the same. Picking up with their foreplay in the snow, he had lifted her into his arms and carried her into his bedchamber. And there he had made love to her, first fast, frantic, desperate, and then slow, sweet and loving. She had woken up this morning feeling like a bride on her honeymoon. Only the groom was gone.

She caught the direction of Michaela's gaze, which seemed fixated on something—or more likely some*one*—at the bar. Her long dark lashes flirted over slightly almond-shaped eyes as strikingly black as her hair.

"Down girl," Arianna admonished her dryly. "You're only visiting, but I plan to li—, um, to be here for awhile." *Live* here, she had almost said, before the hasty amendment. But that was a bomb she didn't plan to drop until later, in private, when the explosion could be somewhat contained.

"Better watch out you don't bite off more than you can chew one day," Tara added.

"I don't bite," Michaela countered with a saucy wink. A quintessential tease, the girl wielded that dark exotic beauty of hers like a Gaelic claymore. "Well, maybe just a nibble."

"TMI," Arianna laughed as the server she had met before arrived at their table.

"Arianna, is it?" Deirdre said. "You're still in town so."

"Looks like I'll be here for a while. Meet my friends from the States. Michaela, Tara, this is Deirdre."

Greetings exchanged, Deirdre inquired whether Arianna had made it to Inishmore.

"Not yet. All kinds of craziness going on, I'm afraid. I really would like to talk to Conor about setting something up for while my friends are in town, though."

The woman smiled. "He's here, working the bar. I'll send him over in a wee while." She took their order and bustled off to the kitchen.

Michaela gave Arianna an assessing look. "Okay, spill."

"Spill what?"

"Whatever's got you looking like the cat that got the cream." Michaela propped her chin in her hand, eyes narrowed speculatively. Then a grin. "Or was *he* the one who got the cream? Mr. Tall, Dark and Gorgeous. Or should I say, *Lord* Tall, Dark and Gorgeous?"

Arianna glanced over her shoulder. "Could you talk a little louder?" she hissed. "I don't think the people on the other side of the bar heard you."

Tara's mouth thinned. "You didn't. Not your first time with a guy you just met."

"Don't be a buzz kill, Tara," Michaela chided. "Let the girl talk."

"Good grief, what are you two? The freaking sex police?" Her voice lowered to a whisper. "For your information, Caleb and I did *not* have sex." *Does metaphysical sex count?*

Michaela grinned. "You sound like Bill Clinton."

"We didn't... He wouldn't... Look, I'm not getting into this here."

"Ah, just some heavy petting, then. Well, I hope he at least got you off."

Arianna shot her a scandalized look. "Good grief, Mick!"

"Better think carefully before you let things go any further." Tara tapped her fingers quietly against the tabletop as she proffered the sage advice. "Don't forget about Damien. I'd hate for you to have a holiday fling here that you'll come to regret later."

Deirdre arrived with their cokes and sandwiches. "Excuse me, but I ordered chips," Michaela told her.

"Those *are* chips," Arianna explained. "Here in Ireland, potato chips are called *crisps*. But you really gotta check these things out." Arianna took one of her chips, slathered in gooey, melting cheddar, and dipped it into a ramekin of garlic mayo.

Michaela stuffed it into her mouth and groaned her pleasure. Deirdre left to bring some cheese and garlic mayo for *her* chips.

Arianna's cell rang. *Caleb.* "How's things?" he asked, his tone casual and upbeat.

Heat seared through her at the sound of his voice. "Plane was late, so we just got back to town. We're at McColgan's grabbing a bite of lunch."

"I knew you'd not made it home yet or you'd have been ringing me," he said. "Whilst Molly was tidying your rooms, she came across your house keys." Arianna checked the side pocket of her purse where she usually kept them. *Empty.* "I'm heading into town now on an errand. Will I bring them to you there?"

"Thanks. I'd really appreciate it."

"A lover who calls the morning after," Michaela chirped after she had hung up. "No waiting. No head games. Hmm... Wouldn't happen to have a brother, would he?"

"Fraid not, kiddo." She explained about the keys.

About fifteen minutes later, Caleb strode into the room, owning it. Black hair all tousled and windblown, he was wearing his black leather jacket unzipped over a cream-colored sweater. In a pair of faded jeans, worn slightly at the crotch and knees, he attracted appreciative glances from every woman in the room. Arianna waved him over, feeling like some groupie chick, who had caught the attention of a famous rock star.

Michaela turned to Arianna with an incredulous stare. "*Oh. My. God.* You go, girl," she murmured under her breath as he headed for their table.

Arianna ignored her friend as she presented her cheek for the casual brush of his lips. He reached into his jacket pocket and pulled out her keys. "Thanks. It would have been a real bummer to get the cottage without these. I'd like you to meet my friends. Tara, Michaela, this is Caleb." His smile was pleasant, manner amiable. "Do you have time to join us for lunch?"

"*Nil, cailín. Tá brón orm.* No, pet, sorry. Schedule's chock-a-block today."

His interaction with her friends was polite and charming. But the smoldering gaze he turned on her was hot enough to melt concrete. With eyes gone dark as liquid smoke, he sent a private message. An erotic reminder of their romp in the snow. And afterwards. The sensual quirk of his mouth whispered of the intimate secrets they shared.

He turned back to Tara and Michaela and apologized for having to rush off. Then, to Arianna he said, "Walk with me to the door, love?"

With the carved leprechauns snooping annoyingly over their shoulders, he spoke with her at the entrance to the snug. "Are you well?"

She felt her cheeks color. "Did you...? I mean, did we really...?"

"We did." A faint, very satisfied male smile touched his mouth. "And *you* did...several times."

"I don't understand.... Even now, it seems so real." She bit her lip. "It was amazing."

"Indeed." He gave her nose a playful tap. "Now, I'll not be keeping you from your friends any longer. I just want you to know that I'm still concerned for your safety."

Arianna touched his cheek. "I know you are. And I appreciate the way you've tried to look out for me, Caleb. Really I do. But the case is closed. The official police position is that it was a botched burglary attempt. That the thief flew into a drug-crazed rage when he couldn't find anything of value to fence to support his habit."

His jaw went rigid. "A theory I don't agree with." *Well, there's a surprise.* "Just promise me that if you run into trouble of any kind, you'll give me a bell. I've to be out of the country tomorrow, but I'll be available by phone." His voice pitched lower. "When your friends have gone, I want to speak with you. We've things that need sorting out between us."

Now, what was she to make of that ambiguous remark? Was he referring to breaking things off? she wondered. Or taking their relationship to the next level?

Putting it aside for the moment, she stretched up to give him a peck on the lips. Having none of that, however, he cupped the back of her head and sealed his mouth to hers in a kiss of raw possession. A male animal marking its territory. A wild beast claiming its mate. *"Is folamh fuar e teach gan tu,"* he murmured in Irish. Then said softly in English, "The warmth is gone from my home without you."

Arianna floated back to the table.

"Mmm-mmm. Dude is absolutely smokin'." Michaela's eyes narrowed thoughtfully. "It's him, isn't it?"

"Him?"

"You know, your dream guy."

"Oh, for God's sake," Tara groaned. "Would you give that crap a rest?"

"Okay, children, we're overtired and getting cranky." Arianna whisked the check off the table. "Come on, let me get the two of you home and tucked into bed for a nap."

At the register, Conor tucked the colorful euro notes into the cash drawer. His attention seemed to have been captured by Michaela, who was busy lighting up the room with her million-watt smile.

"How's your Mom getting on?" Arianna asked.

"Much better, thanks. Doctor kept her in hospital a while to run some tests, but she's to go home today." He counted out her change. "And who are these lovely ladies?"

"My friends from Maine. Tara, Michaela, this is Mrs. O'Clery's son, Conor."

"Nice to make your acquaintance." He looked back at Arianna. "Sorry I didn't get over to speak with you today. Deirdre says you fancy taking your friends to visit Inishmore."

"They're only here for the week. Can your buddy hook us up on such short notice?"

Conor's eyes narrowed consideringly. Arianna thought he was about to decline, when he gave a brief nod. "You might be in luck if Wednesday would suit. When I brought it up to him a couple of weeks ago, about taking you over there, he mentioned that day specifically."

"Anytime this week would be perfect. Thanks, Conor. I really appreciate it."

"No worries. I'll set it up. Just be at Doolin Pier Wednesday, about nine a.m."

"Conor?" Michaela spoke up coyly. "Will you be going with us?"

Conor stilled, turned his head slowly. Unsmiling gray eyes boldly considered Michaela's mouth. He licked his bottom lip, an overtly suggestive gesture followed with a practiced gaze roving the length of her slender body. "Aye," he answered softly.

Remarkable for the inveterate tease, flags of color sprang to Michaela's tawny cheeks. Tara and Arianna exchanged a knowing glance. Who was to say, but that their wild little friend might finally have met her match.

When they got to the cottage, Tara and Michaela sprawled across the twin beds in the newly remodeled guestroom and took a catnap. When they woke up, Arianna ordered an extra-large pizza and popped the cork on a bottle of Chablis. Like old times, the girls ate in the living room while watching a movie on a new flat screen TV that Arianna had purchased during the renovation. After dinner, Tara stretched out on the sofa and Michaela kicked back in the new leather recliner in front of the hearth. They kept dozing off, so decided to make an early night of it. As Arianna crawled into bed, she recalled the old, savagely shredded mattress and thanked the good Lord that she wasn't spending her first night back here at the cottage by herself.

Chapter Twenty-five

On Tuesday evening, the third week in November, Seamus O'Donnell called to order a special meeting of the Council of Brehons. The ten-member organization had met here at the manor house on the Isle of Skye just three weeks earlier, on the 31st of October. The annual gathering on the Eve of Samhain was a sacred trust, a sworn pledge passed from father to son for nigh onto three thousand years. A second meeting within a month...*within the space of a year*...was unprecedented, however.

Built in the 14th century, the gothic stone fortress in which they met was bordered on one side by a sheer drop to the sea, on the other by a purple sweep of wild heather moorland. The setting had been chosen by their forefathers, not for its staggering beauty, but for its location. A plot of land near enough their Irish homeland for ease of travel, yet far enough away to discourage the spying of otherworldly eyes and ears bound forever to that land.

In the drawing room of the old manse, the musty scents of leather-bound tomes and antique furnishings vied with that of woodsmoke, lemon polish and melting candle wax. The ten men of the Council sat grim-faced around an antique oak table in the center of the room.

At the head of the table, the Chief Brehon acknowledged each member with a solemn nod. Fingers steepled, elbows resting on the curved wooden arms of a cresting rectangular chair, Caleb's pose was deceptively indolent.

And fooled not a single man there.

"As you're all aware, this past Samhain marked the beginning of the end." Caleb spoke in the old language, an ancient tongue not of this earth and known to none except those present in the room. "The countdown to the third millenium anniversary of the *Geis*...to the

Awakening...has begun."

His eyes were cold, dead. No expression accompanied the cryptic reference. Wishing to rinse his mouth of the bitter taste the words had left on his tongue, he let his gaze fix on a frosty pewter pitcher in the center of the table.

He raised an imperious finger.... And the summoned object slid obediently into his outstretched hand.

He swallowed several long, cool sips of water, then set the glass down with a thud—the only evidence of the seething black temper holding him in its grips. Leaning forward, he let his flat stare touch briefly upon everyone at the table. Then his head swiveled on his shoulders, his gaze skewering the man seated to his immediate left.

"So, Liam. I understand 'twas thought *congratulations* might soon to have been in order." Caleb's eyes, two hard chips of glittering green ice, belied the quiescent tone. "Man, have you no willpower to keep your trousers fastened? No understanding of the havoc your indiscretions would have wrought had we been forced to spirit the girl away, to secretly dispose of her body?"

Clad head to toe in chains and black leather, his ash-blonde hair framing his face on both sides, the recipient of Caleb's scathing remarks, Liam O'Neill, possessed the humble good grace at least to lower his eyes.

One or two others, guilty of tempting fate in like manner, shifted uncomfortably.

Caleb returned his attention to the members at large. "As only a year remains before all will be fulfilled, we agreed to come together once monthly, as a minimum. I've called this meeting a week early, so we might attend to the urgent matter at hand. Seamus?"

"As you know," Seamus began, "the question before us tonight is the unexpected arrival in Ireland of an American mere mortal named Arianna Sullivan."

"Irish," Caleb interjected.

"Sorry?"

"She's Irish," Caleb repeated. "Raised in the States, but born here in Ireland."

Seamus nodded and began again. "What we've to settle here

tonight is whether she may be the Chosen One prophesied to fulfill the requirements for dissolution of the *Geis*?"

"I take it, we've all met the woman?" inquired eighty-two-year-old Brian Rafferty.

"I've not bothered me arse." Liam spoke up, ice-blue eyes glowing with disdain. One side of his mouth lifted in a cynical twist. "Ye should all cop the frig on, and live what time ye've left to the fullest. Yer all fooling yourselves, if ye believe some mere mortal woman's liked to show up at the last minute to save the world."

"Very fatalistic attitude, my friend," Seamus murmured.

"Realistic," Liam countered. "And, for argument's sake, let's say she does appear. The Evil will still win out in the end. 'Twill kill this one, sure as it did the others before her."

Though the words stabbed Caleb's heart, he concealed his feelings behind a stone mask. "Has anyone who *did* meet Arianna any impressions to share?"

"Paddy and meself were after meeting her at the pub," offered one of the musicians, young Sean O'Casey. Sean was newly admitted to the Council, assuming his father's seat after the man's recent passing. "Can't say as how I sensed anything extraordinary about the woman. Not as regards to the Enchantment, at any rate." A smirk formed on his face. "I will say, though, that should the mating prohibitions be dissolved, I'll be first in the queue for a taste of that one. Right behind Caleb, o'course."

Sean's bandmate, Paddy, snickered in agreement.

Caleb fixed a murderous scowl on the new inductee.

"Now, Caleb..." Seamus murmured as a hush descended on the others at the table.

Sean began to tug nervously at his neck, as if he were being strangled.

And, in point of fact, he was.

"There is more at issue here, my superfluous friend, than our carnal appetites." Long on sexual frustration, short on temper, Caleb's words were taut. Clipped.

The others heaved a collective sigh of relief. Because, while the turf fire in the grate had flashed with his fit of rage, the floor hadn't begun to ripple beneath their feet. Neither had a wind tunnel torn through the room—a turn of events they'd all been privy to in the past.

Even more to the young fool's benefit was that he wasn't presently crouched on all fours, braying like the jackass he'd just proven himself to be.

"My apologies," Sean croaked, rubbing his throat as the buzz of magic snapped and crackled in the air. Static electricity lifted strands of his brown hair until he looked ridiculously like Pinhead in *Hellraiser.* "I didn't realize...em...I was out of line."

Holding his gaze several beats longer, Caleb rubbed his chin, as if pondering his fate. The beads of sweat breaking out across the younger man's brow communicated most clearly that he had come to realize the full extent of his folly.

Apparently satisfied with the belated show of respect, Caleb folded his hands on the tabletop and turned his attention back to the matter at hand.

Seamus cleared his throat. "I've met Herself, and I've to agree with Caleb. There's something there... Something you can sense lying right beneath the surface. Sure, she's unlike any mortal woman I've ever known."

Father James Conneely gave a slow and thoughtful nod. "I was seated beside the young woman at dinner at the castle, and I'd have to throw my lot in with Caleb and Seamus. There's definitely something sets her apart from the rest."

Caleb went around the table, each man indicating, in one fashion or another, that they shared the same impressions as the scribe and the priest.

Brian turned to Caleb. "You're the one after calling this special meeting, the one who's spent the most time with herself. Why do you suspect she's the Woman of Promise?"

All eyes fixed on Caleb. "A bit of history first. Yer wan was born in Clare, but her father and herself were after moving to the States when she was small. Aside from the fact that her father appeared to her posthumously, telling her to return to Ireland to meet her fate, I've nothing concrete to report. Other than a certainty that she's being stalked by a Minion of the Beast."

"There's evil lurking there, to be sure," Seamus said. "When Caleb attempted to identify yer man using our gift of Innate Knowledge, he couldn't see past the black veil."

Caleb gave a somber nod in assent. "Her home in Ennistymon was broken into the night I brought her to Galway. I'm convinced 'twas the same bastard I sensed spying on her below the castle. As far as being able to report something more specific, however, all I have is a sense—a *very strong* sense, mind—that with Arianna Sullivan, all is not as it seems."

"What d'ya reckon the next step should be?" Thomas O'Dea spoke for the first time.

Caleb paused to collect his thoughts, before answering. "I suggest we go over the old writings. Review the terms for dissolution of the *Geis* as preserved in the sacred scrolls. Perhaps, 'twill help us make sense of whether she meets all the requirements."

He turned to MacDara Darmody, seated on his right. A clinical psychologist, MacDara was adjunct professor of Early Pre-historic Anthropological Studies at NUIG, the National University of Ireland, Galway. "Would you be willing to do the honors, Mac?"

Eyes black as coal, long, brown hair tied back with a leather thong, the man inclined his head. He launched into a brief, but sagacious, monologue that would set the tone for the remainder of the evening. "We're all aware, of course, of the apocalyptic devastation facing humanity should Anathema be released from his hermetical bondage," he began. "Since the beginning of time, the entity has been fettered in a chamber in the depths of the abyss by a divinely inspired sleep."

"Would you start by explaining how this whole thing began?" Paddy asked.

"Of course," MacDara replied. "Close to three millennia ago, the Archdruid of the Formorians, a descendent of the fallen angels spoken of in Genesis, called upon his sire, Anathema, the Prince of Demons, to act as Guardian over a *Geis* he'd cast upon our people. The curse, fueled by a vow of recompense, would ultimately gain the Beast its release. But not before three thousand years had lapsed. And not without the establishment of specific terms for the dissolution of the enchantment," he paused, then spoke solemnly. "The deadline for all to come to fruition is Samhain Eve next."

"Which leaves less than a year before this demonic creature is set free," Seamus said.

"Yes. If the aforementioned terms are not met, the entity will be released from the pit, and begin to possess the minds of man. Just as he did in the time before the Great Flood, prior to his being locked away by the Creator so that mankind might start again, knowing free will. As 'twas in the days of Noah, man's every thought will be evil continually, their frail mortal minds easily subject to the Beast's control. Losing every restraint of conscience, there will remain to them no sense of right or wrong. No self control. Many will be overcome with greed and avarice, hatred, jealousy and murder. Others, who successfully overcome the demonic influence to do harm to others, will be plagued by suicidal ideation."

"If I may say something?" Father Conneely interrupted. At MacDara's nod, he began. "When we think of these things, we imagine violent crime. Rioting in the streets. Murder, mayhem, looting. Man against man. Which is all true enough. But the servant of the Evil One will go even further and begin to whisper enticements of world dominion into the ears of global leaders. Religious intolerance will increase, until Hitler will seem as insignificant as a primary school bully by comparison. As third world countries harboring weapons of mass destruction are persuaded to initiate a conflict, the resulting holocaust will end all life as we know it."

"Armageddon." Seamus spoke in a whisper of sound.

"Very likely 'tis one and the same," Father Conneely agreed, his face solemn. "But dissolution of the *Geis* will avert the ensuing calamity. Settle the unfolding of history back into its pre-ordained pattern." He gave a sad shake of his head. "At least for a season, until mere mortal humankind sees fit to destroy itself on its own."

"Apart from saving the earth, there will be a lesser and yet most tremendous benefit to our own people," MacDara continued. "For the men of our *túath* will be released from the enchantment's prohibition against mating with mere mortal women."

MacDara picked up his crystal goblet and took a sip of water. "In my studies of pre-historic cultures, I've paid particular attention to our own primordial existence prior to the laying of the *Geis*. For several hundred years after arriving in what was to become our homeland, men of our race intermarried freely with mere mortal women. This intermingling of DNA resulted in our experiencing a far greater range of emotion than was before, or is today, relative to our kind. During those centuries, our feelings for our wives, our children and our families differed greatly from that which we experience today. Our personal relationships being defined now more by a sense of honor and responsibility than what mortals know as *love*. Because of the Enchantment's magical prohibition against sexual contact between ourselves and mortal womankind, it was that aspect of our humanity, which has been slowly bred out of us."

He took a deep breath, exhaled through his nose. "Long before the Formorians cast the *Geis*, we men of the *Túatha de Danann* often chose a mortal female as our *anam cara*. Unlike our own women, these were not only more likely to keep faithful to their marriage vows, they were more nurturing of children born of the union. This *maternal* love, which greatly benefited our children, was unconditional. Another aspect of interpersonal relationship for which we as a people have little understanding today. 'Twas a love passed from mother to child—through the blood, naturally. But sure even more so, 'twas a thing learned by the infant at its mother's breast. That basic motherly instinct has been lost to our women after thousands of years of interbreeding amongst our own kind."

MacDara, who knew Caleb's own story about his mortal mother's death, met his eyes briefly. "That, I believe, is what has led many of our race over the millennia to choose immortality over humanity. To transform fully into the *daoine sidhe,* the faerie folk."

"Now, with your permission, I will review the written record of the *Geis*. 'Tis the hasty scribblings of a *de Danann* bard as the Formorian High Priest screamed out the curse from the hull of his sinking ship. Although we've studied the scroll countless times in the past, I ask for your patience. Perhaps, our joint scrutiny will reveal something we've missed. Something that might aid us in deciding the grave matter before us with wisdom."

MacDara carefully emptied a tube-like casing made of bronze and a sheepskin parchment, yellowed with age, slid into his hand. An inscription authenticating the document had been set to the page by the hand of the Grand Chieftain of the Túatha de Danann during the first meeting of the Council, some time circa 1000 BC.

As MacDara began to encapsulate the lengthy formal document Council members settled back in their seats, eyes closed. "The record begins by explaining the immutable terms of the Enchantment, before moving on to quote, as accurately as possible, the incantation intoned by the Formorian Archdruid:

"The *Geis* was to remain in effect and unalterable for a period of three thousand years," MacDara went on. "If at the end of the third millennium the terms of its dissolution have not been met, it is to become immutable for all time. However, as the perfection of all things, since the beginning of time, has come in multiples of three, the destruction of all things by the power of the Evil One requires a waiting period of three thousand years.

"Sorry," Sean interjected hesitantly. "But I'm new to the Council and I've a question about the requirements for removing the curse."

"Of course," MacDara replied. "It's written that, during the final year of each millenium, the Fates will draw a mere mortal woman forth from across the seas. A woman destined to possess great discernment, strength of character, and the impregnable will necessary to fulfill the near impossible terms of dissolution of the *Geis*. Should she succeed, the immediate threat of world annihilation will pass. And all things so affected will return to their state of being prior to the laying of the enchantment."

Tomas O'Dhea, who'd sat quietly throughout most of the meeting, posed a question. "Do we know specifically what occurred with regards to the first two women? Were they recognized by our forefathers? Is their any historical record of how close the women came to meeting the terms of dissolution? Do we know what became of them?"

Caleb answered. "Information about the first woman is sketchy. Not surprising, given she lived around the time of Christ. What we do know is that the Council identified her formally as the Chosen

One for that millenium. Clearly, she failed her mission, as the *Geis* is still in effect. A fact to which I can personally attest."

"May I ask how you know this to be true?" Thomas inquired.

Seamus shot Caleb a troubled look.

"My own mother a mere mortal," Caleb stated. An uncomfortable hush settled over the room. The thought that Caleb's father, a former Council member himself, had sired a child on a mere mortal woman was unfathomable. "My grandmother, with whom many of you are acquainted, has been the midwife for our women for almost forty years. What you may not know is that she is but a mere mortal herself. Her daughter, my mother, died in childbirth, with my grandmother attending. 'Twas a blood poisoning death, compliments of the *Geis*. Slow, tortuous and excruciatingly painful."

Leather squeaked as Liam shifted in the chair beside Caleb. He blew out a breath.

"Sorry, mate," Thomas murmured.

Caleb gave a single nod.

MacDara spoke up. "We're also in possession of a verbal record passed down through the generations, which was eventually transcribed by hand. It reveals that the first woman died horribly, in what appeared to have been a wild animal attack. 'Twas rumored by those witnessing the woman's remains that it appeared as if she'd been torn asunder by demons."

"And the second woman?" Tomas asked quietly.

"The archives are more complete with regards to herself, as 'twas only a thousand years ago. She was after arriving here from an unknown continent to the west of Ireland, which we now know as America. We've no way of identifying how close she might have come to fulfilling the enchantment's terms but we do know that in the process the woman went totally and completely mad. And, in the end, was after destroying herself."

"There are restrictions," remarked Padraig Murphy, who had met Arianna at the castle dinner. "Can you clarify the specifics of those, please, for those new to the Council?"

"Simply put," MacDara replied. "The Woman called by the Fates to this task is at risk of death or madness. And while destined to develop an attachment to one of our leaders—one of us at this table tonight—she is forbidden the knowledge of the existence of our race, and of the *Geis*. Of course, physical consummation of that emotional attachment is deadly to her. The one of us whom she desires is required to be her champion. And that one will be bound by a compulsion to see her safe."

All eyes turned to Caleb, who sat like a pillar of stone, fingers curved around the arms of his chair, his dire expression eliminating any need for words.

Chapter Twenty-six

By the time the three girls pulled into Doolin Pier on Wednesday morning, Conor was already on the dock loading supplies into a 34-foot cabin cruiser. He acknowledged them with a wave.

Michaela called out in a singsong voice. "Hi, there."

He joined them, his eyes taking a leisurely stroll down her friend's body. Her tight white jeans and a navy and red nautical jacket revealed her slim curves to good advantage.

"Sorry, but are you Tara or Michaela?"

Her bottom lip pushed out in a flirty pout. "Michaela."

"Ah, of course. Lovely name for a lovely woman."

Leaning against the back door of the car, Tara mimicked sticking a finger down her throat. An amateur photographer, she went back to snapping shots of the fishing boats bobbing on the feathery whitecaps, a scene framed in the distance by soaring cliffs and a rugged coastline.

Arianna popped the trunk release. Conor followed her to the rear of the car. "I'm afraid my friend, Aiden, won't be making it today. His wife went into labor early this morning," he explained. "Rather than cancel at the last minute, he suggested I take you girls out instead."

Before Arianna could open her mouth, Michaela was gushing. "That's totally awesome. We've been so looking forward to this."

"Pleasure's all mine." Conor's tone made the remark sound vaguely off-color.

Arianna pulled their gear out of the trunk and slammed it shut. "We never discussed how much your buddy charges, so I brought along my Visa. Mick, will you grab the thermos off the floor in the front seat?"

"Aiden said there's no charge. Just throw me a couple of quid for the cost of petrol."

"That's really nice of him. Tell him I said thanks."

Arianna donned her backpack, while Conor dragged the straps of the other two overnight cases over his shoulders. Loaded down like a pack mule, he chuckled. "Moving to Inishmore, are ye?"

Arianna smiled. "Just spending the night. We plan to get a ferry to Galway in the morning."

After herding everyone onboard, Conor pointed out the cabin, where the girls stashed their purses. Topside again, Tara took one of the bench seats at the rear of the boat. Arianna stood beside her, forearms propped on the rail. And Michaela—*surprise, surprise*—commandeered the spot across from the Captain's seat.

The engine sputtered, then roared. As they headed for open waters, thunderclouds reflected the greenish gray of the sea. The sky looked hopeful in parts, with slices of azure blue and shafts of sunlight peeking from between the clustering clouds. As they moved farther away from shore, clinging mists dulled the sharp edges of the coastline. A purple haze shaded the distant mountains, making one peak indistinguishable from the next.

"Weather looks a bit iffy," Arianna shouted to Tara over the loud whine of the motor.

Tara shrugged unconcernedly, green eyes sparkling with enjoyment.

Conor called back over his shoulder. "Inishmore is about thirty miles out. Since we've the whole day, we'll go around the southern end of the island, before heading into Kilronan. You'll get a grand view of the cliffs at Dun Aengus, maybe even cap eyes on a seal or two."

Arianna sent a smile and a thumb's up in his direction.

Tara gave a stretching groan, then stood up. "I need a caffeine injection. Anyone else? Michaela? Conor? Coffee?"

Michaela looked back and winced a major "Oops!"

"Okay, what did you do now?" Tara's voice was a study in exasperated patience

"Forgot to get the thermos out of the car?" Michaela confessed meekly.

"Dammit, Mick—"

"No worries, ladies," Conor called out. "I've a full pot brewed down below. Mugs and plasticware in the cabinets."

"You're a lifesaver," Tara said, then muttered *"Michaela's life"* under her breath. She disappeared down the four stairs to the galley. A second later, her head popped back up. "Arianna, your cell phone's ringing."

Trying to find her sea legs, Arianna lurched down the stairs. She dug her purse out of a pile of luggage on a table in a small booth and retrieved her cell from a side pocket. "Hello?"

"Hiya." *Caleb.*

"Hey," she said, unable to disguise the sigh in her voice. "What's up?"

"Just back from Scotland. I wanted to let you know Granny's taken a bit of a fall—"

"A fall? Is she all right? God, I feel terrible. With all the work at the cottage, and my friends getting here, I haven't been over to see her."

"No worries, she's grand. A bruise or two is all. Despite her threats of physical violence against my person, I've tucked her away up here at the keep for the next few days." His low chuckle warmed Arianna's heart.

"Well, I'm glad she's with you."

"I've to pick up a few things for her in town, so thought I'd call over to your place if you're there."

Arianna made an *oh-oh* face. "Um, when you called me last night, guess I didn't mention we were going to Inishmore today."

His silence was deafening.

"We ran into Conor Sunday at the pub. A friend of his owns a tour company, and he was able to arrange for me to take the girls over to see the Island today."

The silence got even louder.

"You didn't feel the need to report to *me* that you were going to Scotland," Arianna pointed out defensively.

Still nothing.

"Dammit, Caleb. Are you still there?"

"I've one question." Icicles dripped from his words.

"Okay." Arianna gnawed on her lip.

"Were you after *forgetting* to mention your plans, or hiding them from me deliberately?"

It was so tempting to lie, to avoid a confrontation, but Arianna refused to raise a wall of deception between them. Not that he wouldn't see right through any subterfuge anyway. Not with that eerie "mind-reading" talent of his.

"To be honest, I didn't want the drama. And it's no big deal. Really. The owner couldn't make it at the last minute, so it's just the three of us and your uncle. So, you see, I'm perfectly safe. We'll be staying overnight at a B&B on Inishmore, then taking a ferry to Galway first thing in the morning. I'll call you when—"

"I'll be leaving you to your craic, then. *Slán.*" Liquid nitrogen couldn't have been colder.

"Caleb—" Too late; he'd already hung up. "Damn," she grumbled under her breath.

When she turned, Tara was staring at her, a mug of coffee in her hand. "Trouble in paradise, huh?"

"He's upset because I didn't tell him we were coming out here today."

"You neglected to mention your new boyfriend's a control freak." Her tone was flat.

"He's not—*crap*. He's being overprotective is all."

"Already making excuses for the man, are we?" Platinum brows raised over clear green eyes.

"I'm not...not really. I just want you to understand that he's legitimately worried about me." Arianna hesitated, then decided to come clean. "Look, I didn't tell you guys before, because I didn't want you to worry. But there was another incident, besides the break-in at the cottage. Some pervert stalking me at the beach. Caleb believes it was the same guy."

Tara went pale. "Good God, Arianna. You gotta get the hell out of here...go home."

Arianna gave her a bland look. "*Now* who's being over-protective?"

"It's not over-protective when you're really in danger," she shot back. Arianna raised her brows as Tara was forced to admit that Caleb had a reason for concern. "And what's going on with you and Caleb, anyway? Things are moving awfully fast in the romance department, which isn't like you. You can't honestly believe he's the guy from your dreams."

"Look, I know you're a skeptic about that kind of stuff, so I won't waste my time trying to convince you. But I will tell you that it's not just me. Caleb remembers the dreams, too." Tara's face darkened with concern. She started to say something, but Arianna shook her head. "Please...I really don't want to debate this, okay? Can't we just agree to disagree?"

"For now. As long as you don't think this conversation is over."

"As if," Arianna quipped, dropping her cell back into her purse. Then swearing, she dug it out again. "Forgot to shut the darn thing off."

"Shut it off? What if lover boy wants to make up?"

"He won't. Not right away." Arianna shrugged and her lips twisted into a sheepish grin. "I also neglected to mention the man is stubborn as a mule. He'll treat himself to a good brood for a couple of hours, before coming to his senses. Anyway, I forgot to pack my charger and the battery's low. I'll turn it back on later, when he's had time to become properly penitent."

The storm clouds blew away, the weather cooperating beautifully as they headed for the south end of the island. Saltwater whispered against the hull in peaceful harmony with the tranquil murmur of the wind. Skipping in and out of gray cotton clouds, the sun gleamed off the rippling waters, gently warming the brisk sea air. Arianna and Tara lounged on deck chairs sipping coffee, silently soaking up the sun and fresh air.

Giggling at something Conor said, Michaela stood up and leaned over, giving him an innocent peck on the cheek. Arianna glanced at Tara and gave a shrug. Conor seemed to be taking things slow and easy, behaving himself. Maybe they had misjudged him after all.

As he brought the cabin cruiser closer to the panoramic cliffs, Tara grabbed up her camera and managed some amazing shots of the limestone wall. With a rolling gait, Michaela joined them, cup in hand, looking for another refill.

"Coffee's gone," Tara told her.

"Geez, I'm so sleepy I can hardly keep my eyes open and you guys hog all the bean juice," Michaela whined. "Conor didn't drink any, and I only had two cups."

"Don't look at me," Arianna said. "I only had one. Trying to cut back on the caffeine."

"Tara?" Michaela accused.

"The coffee pot's only a four-cupper, Mick," she replied and yawned. "If you hadn't forgotten the thermos—"

"Alright, alright." Michaela plopped onto a deck chair beside Tara.

Conor killed the engine. The sudden silence drew the girls questioning glance. The vessel bobbed up and down as he reached for a backpack stashed beside his seat and joined them in the back of the boat. The three shiny brochures he plucked from the backpack were riffled by the quickening wind. He parked a hip on the rail nearest Michaela. "Compliments of Aiden," he said, offering a flyer to each of them.

Arianna unfolded it to a colorful map. "Didn't realize Inishmore was so small."

"And aren't the most priceless things found in the tiniest packages." He winked at Michaela. "Now I'll describe the heritage sites and ye decide which you fancy visiting first."

Arianna tipped her head back. Black-headed seagulls soared weightlessly on the wind currents, their raucous cries blending with the high-pitched arias of the little terns. Waves drummed against the hull in rhythmic accompaniment to the birdsong, as Conor's melodic voice drew the girls spellbound into the epic tales and sagas of the islanders.

"Inishmore comprises an eight-by-thirteen-mile carboniferous limestone ridge with over 7,000 miles of stone walls." The lilting strokes of Conor's words painted colorful pictures of the island. "They've a garda station, three churches and six pubs, and about as many trees. The people here are Irish speakers, fisher folk with the sea in their blood. Their lives are a testament to a traditional—often ancient—culture."

Conor paused to study each woman's face, before continuing the soliloquy. "Their way of life combines reality with myth. The dry-stone walls, church ruins, round towers, and prehistoric stone forts speak of another time. Dun Aengus is a horseshoe shaped fort stretched on the cliffs three hundred feet above us. At over 2,000 years old, it enjoys the distinction of being one of the greatest ancient monuments in all of Europe."

He paused for another brief survey of Michaela's face, and then Tara's. Both had fallen asleep. His gaze then turned on Arianna, eyes unblinking. A spider watching a fly struggle to free itself from a silken web. *Now where did that come from?*

Arianna blinked rapidly to keep his face in focus as he squatted beside her. Her stomach did a loop-de-loop, and she could feel herself beginning to sink beneath thick, syrupy waves. What was happening to her? She couldn't seem to think...couldn't concentrate.

The sky above them began to dip and roll. Arianna imagined she was melting, her body thick and fluid, folding like cake batter into a deep, black void of eternal sleep. She felt feverish, like she had a bad flu, burning up one minute, chills wracking her body the next. She was nauseated, seasick. And her head felt like someone was going at it with a pickaxe.

Conor's cool hand settled on her brow, his touch soothing... comforting.

"I'm so sick, Conor. Please, take me back...." While her mouth struggled to form the words, they fell incoherently from lips that were Novocaine numb. Eyes like lead weights, she forced them open, hoping he would be able to interpret her beseeching look.

A rictus grin smiled down at her. Arianna shuddered.

Drugged! The warning shrieked from an area of her consciousness now dark and dormant.

"You shouldn't have come here, Yank. Shouldn't have involved yourself in matters not of your concern." The voice wasn't Conor's, but rather a demonic growl that dragged like an old 78-rpm record played on 33. "Now that you have, we've an appointment with destiny, you and me."

With her tenuous grasp on wakefulness slipping through her anesthetized fingers, Arianna began a slow, sinuous slide into the engulfing darkness dragging her under.

❦

Waves were sloshing against the hull, gently rocking the boat, as awareness crept back to her. Blinded by a migraine headache, Arianna's stomach pitched and rolled with every dip of the boat. She heard footsteps approaching on the oaken deck. *Conor.* Pretending to be unconscious still, she peeked at him through lowered lashes. What she saw twisted her upset stomach into a tight knot of dread.

In his left hand, he held two lengths of tan leather, silver buckles dangling off one end. *Hospital restraints.* If he got those things on her, she was finished. But how in God's name could she fight him off, as sick and weak as she was?

As she considered her plight, however, she felt desperate hope bloom in her heart. While she couldn't fight this monster alone, if her friends were to revive as she had done, together they could take him down.

But a surreptitious glance in their direction found them both still sprawled unconscious beside her. How much had he dosed them with, anyway? she wondered. And how had he administered the stuff? *The coffee, of course.* Her next thought sickened her. That her two friends had consumed twice as much of the drug-laced brew as she had. The incessant pounding in her head, the unendurable nausea, was the result of ingesting a single cup of the vile concoction. There was no way Tara and Michaela would be any help to her. She only hoped to God that they hadn't been overdosed. That they would survive this nightmare outing she had taken them on.

Fear for their safety and fury at what this man had done to them fired Arianna's blood. The rush of adrenaline seemed to burn off some of the pharmacological haze. Acknowledging that she might well be her friends' only hope for survival, Arianna lay, body coiled, primed for attack, and awaited Conor's return.

All at once, he was reaching for her, oblivious to the fact that the proverbial tables had been turned. The hunter was now the prey.

Without warning, Arianna bent her knees to her chest and snapped a two-legged kick, pushing her feet into Conor's solar plexus. She felt the give as a rib gave way. She heard him grunt, relished the whoosh of sound as air was forced from his lungs. Eyes wide with disbelief, he bent double, clutching at his abdomen. Taking advantage of his position, she leaped to her feet and followed through with a chop to the temple.

"Like that, you sick fuck?"

He toppled over and curled into an ignominious lump at her feet. Her foot snapped out and connected with his ribs again. She heard another satisfying crack, but he didn't make a sound, didn't move. She toed him over onto his back and watched his head drop to the side, mouth sagging open. "Yeah, that's what I thought."

As she stood over him, another wave of nausea crashed over her and she began to tremble. She spun around, making it to the rail just in time to spew the entire contents of her stomach into the ocean. She gagged and retched, intense, gut-wrenching dry-heaves, until she expected to bring up her intestines. When the vomiting ended, deep shuddering spasms rocked her body. White spots danced in front of her eyes. Dark waves of oblivion threatened to drag her back into their perilous depths.

"Oh, God, help me fight this," she whimpered desperately, as she struggled to restrain Conor with his own leather straps.

But the burst of adrenaline that had ignited the fusillade fizzled like flame on a damp wick. Her knees buckled and she sank into a deck chair. "Get the phone. Call Caleb," she told herself, teeth clacking together. "Get to your feet, dammit. Drag your ass down to the cabin."

But by then, the flurry of white spots in front of her eyes had become a blizzard. Cold, crisp, it took her back in time to her last night at the castle. Suddenly, Caleb's mouth was on her neck, his hands on her heated flesh, his masculine weight pressing her down, down, down into a bed of purest snow....

Chapter Twenty-seven

It hadn't gone unnoticed by Caleb. The way his staff had been steering a wide berth around him and his ill humor since he'd spoken with the infuriating woman earlier in the day. Unable to fake a pleasant demeanor for Granny, he had told her he'd work to do and retreated to his study to brood. Adding insult to injury, he'd accomplished little to naught all day.

Pushing abruptly away from his desk, he stalked over to the fireplace. Bracing a hand against the mantle, he stood there for a long time and stared into the flickering flames. He'd committed a grave error, so he had, having Arianna here, sharing his personal space. This room was usually a comfort to him, a hideaway from the stress and strains of his responsibilites, of concealing the existence of his race from the mere mortal world. When he'd returned from Scotland this morning, a trace of her essence had remained. The warmth of her smile, her teasing laughter, haunted these medieval halls like a ghostly apparition. Her absence left him aching with an emptiness he couldn't explain.

Caleb fell into his chair, dropped his head into his hands. Something was smothering him. 'Twas as if a cold, wet blanket of dread had been dropped over his head, blocking his intake of air, drawing tighter and tighter with every tick of the clock.

"I should phone her again now. Demand she and her friends get their arses back to Clare straight away. When she gets stubborn, as she surely will, I'll fly the chopper over to get them. Render the lot of them unconscious with a fecking thrall, if I must."

He scrubbed a hand down his face, then grabbed up his mobile and punched "9", the shortcut assigned to her number. A short double-ring and his call transferred directly into voice mail.

He swore violently and tossed the phone onto the table beside his chair. She must have powered off her phone in a temper after they'd had words. He glanced at his watch. Ten past ten P.M.

His phone rang and he grabbed it up. "Arianna?"

"No, mate, it's me, Seamus. I wanted to go over a few things with you privately about the meeting. But if you're expecting a call from the little mortal, I'll get with you later on it."

"Her name is Arianna," Caleb corrected, his voice tight enough to strangle him. "I tried to ring her, but the call went into voice mail. I've a sense something's dreadfully wrong."

"If you're feeling that unnerved, why not drive by her place?"

"She and her friends have gone off to Inishmore to stay the night. Conor took them on a charter owned by one of his mates."

"This time of year? That's odd."

"'Tis. And I'd be worried if anyone but the four of them were onboard."

"Herself and her friends are likely checked into their room by now."

"Shite." Caleb plowed a hand through his hair as he mulled the problem over. "Wait, I know what to do.

"What's that?"

"I've only to use the Knowledge to scout out the area. Even if I'm not after sensing her exact location, the absence of any lurking cover of darkness will let me know she's not fallen afoul of any harm. Leastwise, not til I get my own hands around that slender neck of hers in the morning," he growled.

"I've to confess I've an uneasy feeling about this myself," Seamus admitted. "Sure, set your mobile down. I'll hold while you check the area out."

Caleb closed his eyes and cleared his mind, using his gift to project his essence astrally from the mainland to *Inis Mor*. Observing the island, he found the height and breadth of it shining in its clarity. No taint of evil—not even a lingering gray cloud to suggest a pub fight or domestic dispute—had disturbed the sleepy little community that evening.

With a sigh of relief, he picked the phone back up and reported his findings. "She's safe, mate. There's no wickedness, no trouble of any kind on the Island tonight."

"Brilliant. Now, give us a shout if you hear anything...or if you don't."

After banking the hearth-fire, Caleb stripped off and slipped into the loo. Head down, he let the hard, driving pulse of the electric shower beat against his neck and shoulders, drawing out the tension. Then he toweled off and crawled beneath the goose down duvet. He fell asleep, calmed by the knowledge that there'd been no Evil lurking about on Inishmore.

The cabin cruiser was still anchored miles offshore. Tossed about on the rough seas like a matchstick in a maelstrom, the rocking boat encouraged Arianna back to consciousness. Still feeling dopey and confused, it took a few minutes before the harrowing events of the day began to filter through the drug-fogged haze.

Her first conscious thought was for her friends. Where were they? What had Conor done to them? Had they survived what she was sure now had been a drug overdose? Arianna choked back a tearless sob, as she berated herself for having passed out.

For having failed them all.

She was cold, shivering uncontrollably. Gooseflesh pebbled her bare arms and legs. *Bare?* She forced her heavy lids to open, sickened to learn that Conor had undressed her and put her in a white satin peignoir. She felt violated. What the hell had he done to her while she had been out cold?

The restraints she had been trying to get on him were affixed now to her wrists and ankles. Her hands, bound tightly together, were secured to a hook embedded in the bow at the front of the cabin. Her legs positioned spread-eagle, each foot had been secured to another hook on either side of the foot of a queen-sized bunk. On the other side of a drawn curtain at her feet, she could hear Conor clumping about the cabin, grumbling and complaining. Arguing with himself.

She was in agony. Her brain felt swollen, as if it were pushing against her skull in a desperate attempt to escape. Bile rose up her throat and she swallowed repeatedly, trying not to throw up. It was a battle she was destined to lose. She gagged, head twisted sharply to the right as she began to dry heave, terrified she would choke to death.

Afterward, lying in her own vomit, she noted the silence. The only sound was the eremitic creaking of the vessel, the sough of wind and waves. And then...

Oh, God, Oh, God, Oh, God. She lay frozen as she listened to the sound of Conor approaching, his feet shuffling across the wooden floor. She had to remain limp, to appear unconscious, unresponsive. Maybe she could fool him into believing that the vomiting had been a reflexive action. That she hadn't regained consciousness.

The sound of footsteps halted beside the bed. She could hear heavy breathing.

Of course, at that precise moment her nose began to itch. *Maddeningly.*

"I was sure she'd woken up," Conor mumbled. "Must have been mistaken."

The dragging footsteps at her side meant he was lumbering away. Almost whimpering in relief, she felt a large hand slap down over her mouth. Pudgy fingers pinched her nostrils shut, cutting off her supply of oxygen.

Arianna's eyes flew open, and she found herself staring into the cold, cruel gaze of a monster. Lungs starved for air, she began to suck ineffectually against the hand covering her mouth. In a mindless panic, she yanked against the leather straps that bound her.

Her frantic pleas made a muffled whining sound, as she rolled her head back and forth in a vain attempt to dislodge the suffocating handhold.

"Play acting again, is it? Fancy yourself a big man, kicking me the way you did?" He clamped down even harder. Arianna felt her eyes bulge. She wet herself. "Wonder how long it would take a body to die like this," he taunted. "For the lungs to shrivel and collapse in on themselves. For the heart to flutter to its last beat, the brain to die."

Her lungs were on fire! An insidious darkness stole across the edges of her vision. She tried to bare her teeth, to bite his palm, but succeeded only in chewing her own lip. She tasted blood. "Yield to me, you slag!" he bellowed. "Stop fighting and I'll take my hand away."

Oh, God Arianna. You gotta lie still! she ordered herself. *It's a power play. He's demanding your submission. He'll let you suffocate if you don't do as he says.*

But she just couldn't do it. It was impossible. The urge to struggle for air was innate. She began to pray for God's strength and grace. Eyes closed, she began to meditate, locating her center, her faith, a place of calm where nothing could touch her. Her muscles relaxed.

"Look at me." Her eyes snapped open. Her body trembled as she struggled to retain control. "I'll reward you now for your obedience." He lifted the heel of his hand, making a slight tent over her lips. A hoarse, grating mewl came from her lungs as she dragged air in through her mouth. He released her nose then and leaned over her, his face mere inches away. His foul breath turned her stomach. Sour and reeking of alcohol, he smelled like a wino found dead in an alley after several days. He gripped her chin and Arianna flinched, terrified that he planned more torture. "Now you'll apologize for kicking me." he said softly.

"I-I'm sorry," she gasped, choked.

"You cracked a couple of ribs." He massaged the tender area with his hand. "And I couldn't even kick the shite out of you. Any mark or blemish on that perfect flesh of yours and the sacrifice becomes unacceptable."

Sacrifice? Ah, crap.

"Before tonight is over, though, I'll have paid you back in full. I'd planned to leave you drugged, so you'd not feel the sting of the flames. But not now." He smiled in vengeful satisfaction. "No, your flesh will melt off your bones as you scream for mercy. And not even the hand of death will be able to deliver you."

The man's certifiable. Totally freaking insane. Arianna twisted and turned, struggling against the straps binding her.

Conor eyes gleamed in amusement. "You'll not be getting out of those, luveen, not for all your trying. And they're lined in lamb's wool, so's not to bruise or mar your flesh."

"Where...." Her voice creaking like a rusty door hinge, she cleared the phlegm from a throat that was burning and raw. "What have you done with my friends?"

"Trussed up like a couple of Christmas geese, but otherwise unharmed," he replied offhandedly. "They've nothing to do with this."

"And what about me? What do *I* have to do with this, Conor?" Eyes beseeching, tone reasonable, Arianna played a role she hoped would save her life. "I don't even know you."

"Nor do you know yourself, 'twould seem." His head tipped, eyes roving her scantily clad body. It made her skin crawl. "So perfect," he sighed. "Bloody temptation you were in the nip. Easy to see why my nephew was after hiding you away, keeping you for himself."

Keep him talking. "What do you mean, I don't know myself?"

"Something Mam said when she was out of her head in hospital. About your mother, and everyone believing herself dead."

"You're saying my mother's alive?" No, these were the ravings of a lunatic.

Conor yawned and checked his watch. "Half-ten. Time enough to get you to the Island and have everything ready for midnight." He reached for a cup on a table near the bed. "And time for yourself and your mates to have another sip of oblivion."

"Conor, no, please. Don't feed me any more of that stuff—or Tara and Michaela. They're all tied up, and you admitted they have nothing to do with this. I'm already so sick, I think I've received an overdose. If I die, your sacrifice will be—"

"Shut your gob!" he roared. The mattress sagged beneath his weight as he sat beside her. Fingers as inflexible as tempered steel embedded themselves in her jaw as he attempted to pry her lips apart, to administer what would likely be a deadly dose of the noxious concoction. The cup touched her mouth. A bitter, nasty tang coated Arianna's lips. She twisted her head away and spat.

"Bitch!" With a growl of fury, Conor straddled her, a slavering dog hovering above her, jaws locked, lips pulled back over clenched teeth. With the cup balanced in his left hand, he pressed his right forearm across her throat, the pressure slowly crushing her windpipe.

The grotesque face filling her vision began to dim as wavy gray patterns moved before her eyes. She gasped for oxygen, mouth open wide like a dying fish marooned on the sand at low tide. Seizing the opportunity, Conor poured the bitter potion down her throat and lifted his arm. Forced either to swallow or drown, she aspirated the liquid, sputtering and choking until her eyes watered. But he was merciless, single-minded, continuing to tip the cup, spilling more of the stale, spiked water into her mouth to replace that which was running down her neck and into her ears, soaking her hair and pillow.

He left her then. He was going to dose her friends. Helpless despair became numb acceptance of their fate as her muscles liquefied, all conscious thought swept away on a black tide of insentience.

The icy chill of the North Atlantic winds jarred Arianna back to consciousness. She felt the hard ground beneath her. No longer on the boat, but where was she?

And why couldn't she move her arms or legs? Had she been injured? Paralyzed?

Awareness of her surroundings came slowly. She realized she had been rolled to her chin in some sort of woolen carpet like a caterpillar ensconced in a scratchy cocoon.

She struggled to raise her head, which had to weigh at least ten thousand pounds. She had been left in a horseshoe-shaped enclosure constructed of standing stones, the open sides ending at the edge of a cliff. The heavy fog smelled of seaweed and brine. A distant crash of waves sounded below. *Dun Aengus.*

At a muffled thud of footsteps, her eyes located Conor's hunched form moving toward her. In the pallid moonlight, his features looked contorted. The man named Conor had become the embodiment of a devil's spawn.

He was dragging a plank of wood behind him. Inches from the edge of the cliff, he stopped and began to raise it on end. Applying his body weight, straining and cursing, he twisted the wooden post, finally managing to force it between the gaping cracks in the limestone slab.

A survey of the surrounding area revealed that she was reclining on a sort of natural ledge. The square, flat rock formation, measuring some twenty-four feet square, rose about three feet off the ground. A ledge that would have made an excellent pagan altar for ritual human sacrifice.

Sacrifice. The word rang an appalling bell in her head, a reminder of Conor's insane ramblings on the boat. *The sting of fire...* A wooden post.... Surely, he didn't mean to...

Comprehension came with an all-encompassing sense of horror.

Please, God, no, not that. He planned to burn her at the stake. Her only hope, slim as it was, lay in trying to reason with a madman. "So it was you all the time," she began, trying to keep her tone light and conversational. But the drugs had dried up her saliva to the point that her tongue cleaved to the roof of her mouth. "You were the one watching me on the shore."

Conor stilled. "Tailed you from hospital when Caleb went in to see Mam. But the storm blew in, chased you away." A demonic glow lit his eyes. "A slight delay."

Arianna played along. "Yes, only a slight delay."

"'Twas thoughtful you were in leaving your address on Mam's table." He smiled, a taunting curve of lips. "Watched outside your cottage that night in the storm, so I did. I hadn't everything prepared for you yet, so went back a few days later. But you were off somewhere, getting the leg over with my nephew it seems."

"Conor, I know you're still in there somewhere." Fearing to rile him, to push him any further over the edge into the darkness of his soul, Arianna was careful to keep her tone subdued. "Please, *please* don't do this. Think of what it would do to your mother."

She saw it then. A flicker of lucidity at the mention of his mother, at Arianna's personalization of the man he had been. A look of dismayed confusion settled over his features as he took in the ghoulish scene around them as if seeing it for the first time. Afraid to hope, almost afraid to breathe, to upset his delicate mental balance, she watched the bifurcation of Conor's psyche.

It was a rabid challenge, sanity staring boldly into the face of lunacy.

A battle sanity was destined to lose.

As she watched, darkness extinguished the momentary light of reason. She saw it wink out, leaving in its stead a black, empty void. Conor's eyes were flat, dead. Devoid of human emotion. Obsidian, a mirror that reflected no light, as black as the bottomless pit that had given birth to the monster lurking within him. Dark as the remnants of the tarnished soul that had once been Conor O'Clery.

He turned and jumped off the natural platform, moving purposefully toward a small, cave-like recess in the wall created by missing stones. From the alcove, he began to retrieve sticks and pine branches and dried-out brush, items he had to have previously stowed away.

Kindling, Arianna told herself and realized she felt nothing. No fear, no dread. Probably because the horror of it all was too much to fathom. It had left her empty, utterly numb.

She lost count of the number of times the man tramped back and forth, arms piled with twigs and brushwood that he dumped onto the limestone ledge beside her. After a while, he disappeared through a square-shaped opening on the wall's northern end. Five, ten minutes passed. Dared she hope that he had left? That he had been distracted from his diabolical plan? But sometime later, he reappeared, dragging a huge gunnysack overflowing with logs, peat and other tinder.

She let out a squeak as he lunged for her. He grabbed the side hem of the carpet rolled around her and gave it a hard snap. Arianna rolled out of it, coming to a halt breathtaking inches from the edge of the cliff. Sprawled in a tangle of white satin, her first thought was that her limbs were now free, so she could fight for her life. But in the next instant she discovered that her wrists and ankles remained bound by the cruel leather straps. Half-naked in the thirty-degree temperature, the sea winds cut through her like blades of ice. Not that she had to worry about being cold for long, she thought with a sick sense of irony.

Conor's movements had become zombie-like, she realized, feeling suddenly heartened by the fact. Was it possible the dementia had him so debilitated by now that, even restrained as she was, she might be able to land a deadly blow. She watched and waited until he bent to reach for her then, bound hands raised over her head, she struck him. "Don't touch me, you crazy bastard!"

A mercurial rage melted the glazed look off his face. She had heard that insanity could endow a person with super-human strength. The only explanation, she thought, for the way he was able to grab the strap binding her wrists together with one hand and haul her to her toes so violently that her body slammed into his.

"What-did-you-call-me?" he growled in her ear, each menacing word spaced a beat apart. He took a half-step back, and she saw it coming—saw it and couldn't do a thing but brace herself. She cried out as he slapped her so hard in the face that her teeth rattled. Her ears rang. Her knees buckled and he let her drop like a sack of rocks onto the cold, hard limestone slab.

"Now look what you've made me do!" he wailed like a spoiled child. Squatting beside her, he scrubbed madly at the spot on her cheek that was burning like fire. "You're marked, so all is in vain." He collapsed onto his butt, knees bent, head on his arms, and wept in great shuddering sobs.

But the crocodile tears stopped as abruptly as they had begun. His eyes went dead as he crawled to his feet. Movements robotic, he tossed her over his shoulder and picked his way over the uneven slabs to the side of the wooden pole.

Arianna noted what looked like several yards of black fabric wrapped around the splintery wood. *To protect my perfect flesh*, she thought, emotions flat with acceptance of the inevitable. The battle was over. The last flimsy cord mooring the man to sanity had finally snapped. And there would be no going back.

Conor bent and slid her off his shoulder, pressing her back against the post as he forced her fettered hands up over her head. He looped the shackles over an iron hook embedded in the top of the wood. Her feet touched the ground, her toes nearly flush with the edge of the cliff. Terrorized by the dizzying drop to the sea churning below, she pushed her weight against the cushioned wood.

"Conor, please," she whimpered in mounting horror. "For God's sake, don't do this."

Deaf to her pleas, he went on methodically stacking logs and scraps of kindling around her feet. Arianna tried yanking her hands free. But the pole, wedged into a crevice far too shallow to support her body weight, lurched heart-stopping inches forward.

She bit down on her lip, again tasted blood.

Never having been one to lie to herself, she didn't intend to start now. And the truth was that all hope was lost. There would be no last minute reprieve, no heroic rescue. No one even knew she was in trouble—except Tara and Michaela.... *And please, God, let them survive this nightmare.*

Her teeth were chattering, her abused body shaking violently as wisps of vapor frosted the air with each panting breath. She had never even imagined this kind of cold. Salt-scented mists rolled over the rocky ledge beneath her feet. Trickles of moonlight bled through the black tableau of sky and sea spread before her. With a strange detachment, she followed the sound of the frozen sod crunching beneath Conor's feet as he systematically built her funeral pyre.

Spent, she relaxed her weight against her hands. Her breath caught on a startled gasp as the post jerked forward several inches more. Was she destined to be burned alive? Or suffer a bone-crushing dive into a watery grave?

Arianna frowned at the flash of movement to her left. *Conor.* Spinning round and round, he was swiping at the air as if thronged by a horde of bees. Slapping at himself, he turned to Arianna, wild-eyed. "Do you not see them?"

She stared at him blankly.

"Come to rescue you, so they have," he shrieked, still prancing and ducking. "Winged creatures with long sharp teeth, and themselves laughing...mocking...*stinging.*"

Still nothing. No fear, no pain, Arianna felt nothing at all as he fished a lighter out of his pocket and flicked the wick. He fumbled and dropped it to the ground. Frozen fingers, she thought idly, as he swore and snatched it up off the cold, frozen earth.

He flicked it again and a small flame danced in the dark of night....

Chapter Twenty-eight

A shriek pierced the air. Caleb found himself standing naked beside his bed, on his feet before he was even awake. His eyes flew toward the clock. *Midnight.* He shuddered as the sound came again. A piteous keening, like that of a mother lamenting the death of her only child. *Bean sidhe.*

His blood turned to ice as he recalled the only other time he'd heard the banshee's haunting wail. It had been on the night his father died. On that fateful eve, the fairie woman's mournful warning had been for him. It had been personal. Like now...

When it was meant for Arianna.

Caleb went to the window and peered out at the darkened sky. Low, swollen clouds threatened rain. Treacherous winds rattled the windows and made a whistling sound as they forced their way through myriad cracks and crevices in the ancient stonework of the keep. The tempest-torn sea was implacable tonight. A grieving woman spilling torrents of salty tears over the jagged headlands.

Closing his eyes, he pressed his forehead against the leaded windowpane. "Please don't let anything happen to her," he prayed. "Sure, I'll be left a wretched man, lost and desolate, if my fair-haired angel fails to survive the wickedness of this night."

The plaintive cry rolled again across the waters in a wavering echo. "She's dying...*dying...dying*! Go to her now...*now....*"

Caleb balled his fists and cried out in frustration. "Where in the name of God is she?" Sinking into a straight-back chair, he dug the heels of his hands into his eyes. "Think. There has to be a way to find her, to reach her in time."

A minute crept by like an hour. When the answer finally came to him, he hissed a single word. "*Yesss.*"

His mobile rang and he snatched it off the bedside table. "Seamus."

"What's up with you, mate? I was just leaving the restaurant and got a wicked jolt, a warning of danger."

Caleb's jaws locked up, as if to hold back the words. "Arianna's dying."

"'Twasn't danger to the woman I was just after sensing, my friend, but to yourself."

"She's dying," Caleb repeated in a monotone. "And I've to find her. Get to her. *Now.*"

Both men were silent for a long minute. And then Seamus inhaled sharply. "Don't do it, man," he ordered in a stern voice. "It's bloody foolish. Are you hearing me?"

"What perfect irony. In order to find Arianna...to save her...I'll be forced to raze the walls of my own mortality. Sacrifice myself to the very part of my nature that's been responsible for keeping us apart."

Once Caleb had given himself over to the magic, he would no longer be bound by natural laws. No longer limited by time or space. Within a moment, in a twinkling of his will, he would be instantly at her side. Wherever she was, anywhere in the world.

'Twas a matter of choice for his people, the Túatha de Danann, whether to dwell in the mortal realm or transform into one of the *Sidhe*, the fairie folk. And while that boundary could be crossed either way, 'twas common knowledge that once a man tasted immortality, rarely, if ever, did he choose to return to his mortal self.

"You can't do this!" Seamus protested. "Listen to me, man. We'll find another way."

"No time. *Tá brón orm, a chara,*" Caleb apologized softly. As his friend began to shout at him, he disconnected the call.

Caleb could feel Seamus in his mind, trying to dissuade him from his course of action. He threw up a mental barrier to block him. His mobile began to ring, repeatedly. Caleb powered it off.

Then he sank to his knees, his head bowed humbly before his Creator. *For what might be the very last time.*

"Almighty God, Maker of galaxies more numerous than the sands of all the seas, please grant me this boon," he prayed in his native tongue. "Allow me to reach Arianna, before 'tis too late. And in this thing I must now do..." He inhaled deeply, taking one of his final breaths as a mortal man. "I commit my soul into Your keeping and pray You'll instill in me the desire to return from the shadow world, to don the cloak of mortality again once she's safe." He paused. "And *only* then, Lord. For if she fails to survive, I've no desire to return to this empty shell, to the interminable existence that will await me."

Eyes still closed, Caleb rose to his feet. He lifted his hands toward the ceiling, palms curved and facing toward him. The shimmer of magic he called to himself raced up and down his body, raising the hair on his arms and legs much as an electrical current would do. In that single, stuttering heartbeat, he abdicated his humanity.

Abandoned his place in the mortal realm.

When his eyes opened again, he stared into a metaphysical world alight with enchantment. A dizzying rush enveloped him. It was like dying in a world of shades of sepia, only to be resurrected into a universe resplendent with brilliant color. An exhilarating realm snapping with untapped power, the heady glow of immortality fed by an inner fire requiring neither breath nor sustenance for fuel.

His elfin nature flexed its newly unfettered muscles, stretching pleasurably to fill the void left by his humanity. That side of himself, which had always fought him, was now the victor, content at last to be wielding absolute control.

Caleb's sharpened senses were a marvel, sure. Stone and mortar no longer possessed the power to restrict his sight...or restrain his movements. The enhanced olfactory nerve enabled him to detect the lingering fragrance of roses long dead, those that had bloomed in the formal garden in the early fall. He cocked his head and listened to the lonely echo of the humpback whale calling to its mate...from hundreds of miles offshore. All sensations that would once have stirred his soul, however, did so no more.

With a new mental clarity not clouded by man's weak—*pitiful*—sensibilities, Caleb knew in an instant where, in the vast expanse of the world, the woman was to be found.

Dun Aengus.

The knowledge came naturally to him, without foolish anger or pointless angst to hamper his focus. For the first time, he scoffed at how disgustingly *mortal* his own people were, for all their boastings of being half *sidhe*.

"Enough!" Sound waves resonated in a musical baritone visible in the air around him. "'Twould seem I've a rescue mission to perform."

And yet, he knew through preternatural instinct that not so much as a millisecond had passed since his transformation. "Hmm..." he mused airily. "Timelessness, as well."

Something luminous caught at the corner of his eye and he turned, discovering his new form reflected in an oval mirror. His eyes were aglitter, as if lit from within by emerald starlight. A pearlescent glow emanated from his naked flesh.

With a thought, Caleb clothed himself.

The corner of his mouth lifted in a sibylline smile, a sly slant of lips as cold and dark as his soul had become. With a cocky wink, he vanished.

From her obscene perch, three hundred feet above the North Atlantic, Arianna watched Conor struggle with the lighter to get the tinder lit. But the tiny flame was no match for the buffeting sea winds. She made her decision. Death by water, rather than fire. When the pain of her burning flesh became unbearable, she would throw herself forward against her restraints. This would topple the wooden post and catapult her into the welcoming arms of the icy sea.

Whining and muttering at the bad luck he was having, he left the periphery of her view for a moment, then returned with a rectangular can. He began to squirt a stream of fluid onto the wood, the stones... drenching her bare feet. There was a smell of petroleum.

Lighter fluid.

With surprisingly calm acceptance that her time on earth was ending, Arianna bent her head and sought her Lord in prayer. She prayed for Tara and Michaela. For Caleb. For the absolution of her mortal soul. Her final peace with God she made in a familiar prayer, which she modified: "Pray for this sinner now, at this, the hour of my death."

The accelerant ignited with a loud swoosh, but the recent rains and the moist sea air had left the wood wet and sodden. Though the flame only flirted with the timber, Arianna could feel its seductive warmth begin to draw the chill from her body. But then a caustic black cloud began to rise from the smoldering wood, the dense, acrid smoke burning her eyes and sinuses, and making her wheeze and choke.

Arianna watched Conor shoot another stream of liquid onto the tinder, which established a path connecting the weak flames to her fluid-soaked bare feet. Jaw set, her mind rebelled against the appalling reality of what she must soon do.

"No, not soon. *Now*," she told herself as fiery sparks, like a swarm of red ants, began to take stinging bites out of her flesh.

She squeezed her eyes shut against her worst fear, of seeing the ocean rushing toward her as she tumbled to her death from so great a height. She interlaced the fingers of her bound hands into a two-handed fist. This would add strength to the movement as she lunged forward, toppling herself into the swirling, dark abyss awaiting her hundreds of feet below.

"Oh, God, oh, God, give me strength," she whimpered. "I'm so afraid...."

What caused her to open her eyes at that critical moment, Arianna would never know. But the impossibility of the scene that greeted her was such that her beleaguered brain attributed it instantly to a near death experience.

Over the tip of her toes, she could see a slender wraith gliding through the billowing waves. The woman's waist-length hair shone like burnished silver in the pallid moonlight. From family photographs and the vision of her parents on the night she had first arrived at the cottage, Arianna recognized the shimmering presence, the spirit of her long-dead mother.

The woman seemed to command the sea at her feet. The giant waves unfurled and smoothed out, growing calm as if in obeisance. The wind held its breath as a mighty crash of thunder resounded through the heavens, shattering the ethereal silence. Her mother's gaze lifted skyward, a slight smile lighting her angelic features. Her intangible form began to evanesce, to grow lighter and lighter until, within scant moments, she faded completely away.

Another thunderclap shook the foundation of the tiny island. A jagged fork of lightning split the western sky. Arianna looked upward, her gaze fixed in rapturous wonder on the sight that had made her mother smile.

"Caleb," she breathed, his name rasping past a throat that was parched and swollen.

Love filled her heart at the heavenly apparition...*her hero.* Her mystical knight in shining armor sat astride a fiery steed. Its saddle, ablaze with gemstones, paled in comparison to the incandescence of his emerald eyes. His countenance was fierce, like that of an avenging angel, illumined from within by the infinite light of a million stars. Silvery strands of moonglow threaded through his wind-blown hair, as black as the midnight sky that surrounded him.

His glittering gaze captured hers now...*mesmerized.* And the burning blisters erupting on her legs and feet felt as if they had been submerged in cool, spring water.

A haughty flick of his wrist shifted the direction of the winds, directed the noxious fumes and flames away from her body. As if in a tunnel, she heard Conor shriek in frustration, and he began to chuck more kindling frantically onto the fire to compensate.

Calling out his name in a voice that crashed like thunder, Caleb pointed one long finger toward the raving demoniac. Conor's eyes shot to the heavens. As if pinned in place, he stared slack-jawed, only now aware of the unearthly spectacle in the skies above them.

Caleb's lips twitched in wicked amusement at his uncle's unholy terror, as he slowly raised the pointed finger upward. The man levitated off the earth, screaming, arms flailing, legs bicycling in mid-air. A stirring motion with Caleb's finger propelled Arianna's would-be executioner toward the opposite side of the wooden stake.

She felt the post jerk against her back as Conor slammed against the other side, pinioned there by nothing more than Caleb's inhuman gaze. The crazed man screamed in agony, tasting for only seconds the flames Caleb had diverted to the other side of the post, the fiery death Conor had planned for his victim. Then Caleb formed a fist and jerked his hand sideways, which sent Conor flying through the air, his body thudding on the ground close to the cliff.

Scrambling to his feet, the heel of Conor's boot caught on a slippery crevice in the limestone. He twisted, throwing his arms out to catch himself, but he was too near the cliff's edge. Plummeting to his death in a grotesque swan dive, blood-curdling screams trailed after him, growing fainter and fainter until they were extinguished by the sea's tempestuous roar.

How she knew this she couldn't say, but the instant Caleb had appeared in the clouds time had ceased to move forward. All that had transpired since that moment had been in a span of time less than a single breath.

Arm muscles cramped and aching from the weight of her body sagging forward from the leather restraints, Arianna watched her lover's eyes flash green fire. And then he swooped downward, a mighty flood of rain chasing on his heels. The heavens filled and emptied; thunder roared and lightning cracked the western sky. The unleashed rage of the storm was so black...so perverse...the island quaked in fear beneath her feet.

Though the pungent fumes were blowing away from her, she had breathed in too much of the thick, poisonous smoke before her magical rescuer had arrived on the scene. Lungs swelling, she choked up black grit, slowly smothering. Wet and covered with soot, her eyes streaming, she could no longer see Caleb. With her lifeline cut off, she felt the life force draining from her body, sapping her will to survive.

Can't breathe...tired...so very tired.... Can't. Fight. Anymore.

She dragged in one wheezing final breath and, through cracked and swollen lips, whispered, "I love you, Caleb."

Her heart skipped a beat, stuttered once, twice. And then was still. Her head dropped forward, her body limp.

Lifeless.

Chapter Twenty-nine

As his form floated downward toward the earth Caleb felt no warmth of relief at having found Arianna. Neither felt he any sense of cold from the icy winds. Fully submerged within the Otherworld, he rotated the wooden post to face away from the cliff's edge with merely a thought.

As he looked upon the lifeless form of the mere mortal, a frown marred the transcendental perfection of his glowing visage. Not a reaction to grief, but rather an acknowledgement of the lack of retribution the evil Conor had received due to the man's accidental fall. For the *Sidhe* possessed a veritable treasure-trove of damnable faerie magic, the likes of which would have made the man's skin crawl.

Standing in front of the dead woman, Caleb gave a mental push, releasing the leather straps binding her to the post. As she fell free of the restraints, he scooped her indifferently into his arms. Arms hanging limply at her side, her head fell against his chest.

Pain slammed into him like a jackhammer. Apparently, his apprehension over the permanent loss of his humanity had been groundless. For his mortal soul had quickened in an instant, at the first touch of her precious flesh to his. And, with the quickening, the floodgates of heaven had flown open wide, filling him with light and life...and an all-consuming, soul-devouring sense of loss.

"Too late." He choked on the words. The sweet spirit that had been Arianna had departed its earthly tabernacle. Stricken to the depths of his soul, Caleb fell to his knees, her lifeless body cradled against his chest. Positioning her gently on the ground in front of him, he searched frantically for a pulse, the debilitating sense of dread like bands of iron closing around his chest. Rainwater streamed down his face, cascading onto her body, as he brushed a kiss across her soot-smudged brow.

"I'll not let you go." He whispered a vow embraced with all his heart.

Caleb pointed his right index finger skyward, so that his body might absorb the sizzling currents from the electrical storm. Much as he had done to protect Arianna from the minion—from Conor—that day on the coast. Aeromancy, the drawing down of an electrical charge from an existing thundercloud, was an act fraught with the possibility of disastrous repercussions. Using his body as a conductor, a kind of lightning rod, Caleb would direct the thunderbolt to be discharged into Arianna's heart.

The likes of a cosmic defibrillator.

His grave dilemma? The fact that a lightning bolt could reach temperatures of 30,000 degrees centigrade—hot enough to fuse together individual grains of sand. Therefore, the task he faced was to siphon off the appropriate voltage of energy...

Or risk burning the wee thing to a crisp.

His teeth clenched, muscles trembled with the stress of the electromagnetic radiation building inside him. Bitterness was building as well, as he silently railed against the inequities of his existence. Of all the preternatural gifts bestowed upon the *de Danann* people... the gift of healings, of harnessing the weather, the gift of Innate Knowledge, mental telepathy, and mind control among them...that which he needed most desperately at this moment remained sadly out of his reach. For 'twas an inexorable reality that his people held no authority over life and death, a power vested solely in the Creator.

His God, whom he petitioned now as heartily as ever any mere mortal man did. "Please, Lord. Please let her live...."

Electricity crackled over his body, lit his flesh with blue light much as the faerie magic had done earlier that evening. With one hand raised toward the sky, his eyes shot green fire as he placed his other hand over Arianna's heart.

In a voice ringing with the authority of a host of angels, he commanded the lightning. "Into her chest. *Now!*"

The miniscule jolt of electricity he'd siphoned off and directed into the damaged organ caused it to tremble, then begin a sluggish beat beneath his hand. It was faint, laboring. And he knew it would cease in seconds if her lungs didn't work in tandem, feeding her brain with life-giving oxygen.

"Breathe, *a stór*. Breathe," he chanted in his native tongue as he cleared her airways and tipped her head back, his mouth making a seal over hers. Caleb worked feverishly, blowing tiny puffs of air into her seared lungs at measured, rhythmic intervals. Tirelessly he continued, for what seemed like hours, refusing to give up, unwilling to accept that her lungs may have been too damaged to recover.

So much time had passed before he heard a tiny wheeze that, at first, he thought his mind was playing tricks on him. But then she choked, gasped—a horrible, wonderful rasping sound.

Hissing out a long, slow breath, Caleb gathered her crumpled body against his chest. Enveloping her inside his jacket, against his warmth, he rested his cheek against the top of her head and cradled her, rocking her as one might an infant in arms. He whispered desperate promises in her ear, vows of sunshine on a rainy day and snowflakes in July...of her every heart's desire in his power to grant...

If she would only ever just keep on breathing.

Although he had earlier caused the rain to cease, Caleb felt moisture sting his eyes, cloud his vision before a single drop of liquid traced a warm path down the curve of one cheek. Frowning, he caught the solitary drop on the tip of his finger and stared at it. Tasted it with his tongue. *Salty.*

"Tears." He marveled at the anomaly as another teardrop rolled down his face...and then another...until they were flowing freely as a soft spring rain. He was crying. His people had no experience with such a physical manifestation of emotion. Maybe he'd inherited the trait from his mere mortal mother. He considered the timing and thought it odd that the tears hadn't begun to fall while he was grieving her loss, but now, once the crisis had passed.

Caleb rubbed his eyes with the back of his hand. Arianna curled up tighter in his lap, in a fetal position against his chest. Helpless rage tore through him as he realized that she was naked beneath the torn and bloodied gown she wore. Only a remnant of translucent satin covered her nakedness, a garment now blackened with soot, splattered with mud, the hem scorched and tattered. Pain stabbed his chest at the sight of the angry red flesh, all wrinkled and blistered from the soles of her tiny feet to well past her calves.

At last, he thought. *Something in my power to remedy.*

Stretching out his hand, Caleb called upon the healing virtue. Directing its flow to those raw and swollen areas, he accelerated the natural healing process from weeks, or even months, to mere seconds. Though unconscious, she flinched and moaned at the barest caress of his fingertips. His heart squeezed in anguish and he pulled his hand away. "Ah, *mo chroi*, I'm so sorry," he whispered into her hair.

Lips brushing her temple, he leaned down and found her mouth with his. Using that simple point of contact he eased her backward in time, took her to a place where there was no suffering, no pain. "All that I'm free to give, I offer you now," he murmured. And together they revisited the day they'd sat wrapped in each other's arms, watching the sun go down from his secret place above the sea.

His hands radiating with divine heat, he traced his palms lightly over her legs and feet. Skimming her body, he erased every bruise and burn, every injury that marred her tender flesh. He accomplished this, even as the gentle puffs of air he blew into her mouth completed the healing of her lungs, returning the moldering gray organs to a plump and healthy pink.

Only when she was physically restored, did he reluctantly draw her back to the present. To the harsh realities, he knew there could be no avoiding. Her pain relieved, her mind released her to float in and out of consciousness. But each time she surfaced, she clung to him desperately, stark terror in her unseeing eyes. Caleb regretted that he'd no power to heal the injuries to her psyche. Only time and the patient support of those who cared for her would see to that.

The loud drone of an engine drew his eyes skyward. An army helicopter was searching the island, its beacon light slicing a path through the darkness. Caleb had planned to contact Seamus telepathically to send help, but Arianna's friends must have escaped and rung the gardai. The chopper hovered directly overhead now, its spotlight fixed on them.

As she began to thrash about, whimpering at the intrusive noise and the whipping wind, he held her close. "'Tis safe you are, *a ghrá*. No one's going to harm you now...nor ever again," he vowed. *Not if the fate of the whole world hangs in the balance.*

Caleb would see to her protection. Somehow. Quite well, he knew that Conor's death hadn't put an end to the danger she was in. 'Twas written in the sacred scrolls that when one possessed by the murderous spirit of a Minion died, another would rise up to take his place.

"Caleb," Arianna breathed, her voice scratchy and raw.

"*Ciúnaigh, a ghrá.* Sshh, my love, I'm right here." His lips brushed her forehead. "The ruckus you hear is only help arriving."

She settled, nestling against him. "I love you, Caleb," she sighed, and was gone again.

"And I love you," he whispered into her hair, knowing she wouldn't hear.

When Caleb had arrived at the hospital, he parked around back to avoid the journalistic feeding frenzy. The girls' ordeal—a strange tale of three young women drugged and bound, with a bit of torture and even an attempted human sacrifice thrown in for good measure—was the kind of story the tabloids would be feasting on for days.

As Caleb and Arianna were exiting the building, they found a swarm of reporters buzzing around the Land Rover like bees around a honeycomb. With a murderous glint in his eyes, Caleb knocked away several mics that had been shoved into Arianna's face.

"Aren't you the one found her?" a voice called out. Ignoring the question, Caleb bundled his passenger into the vehicle's passenger seat and went around to get in himself.

As he slammed his door shut, Arianna snorted. "Geez. All you need to qualify for your five minutes of fame is to be the main course at a weenie roast." But when a haunted look flashed through Caleb's eyes at her quip, she patted his hand. "I'm sorry, sweetie. But I'm fine now. And it's helped to know that Conor was mentally ill—not evil."

"I knew nothing of the cancer, or that he'd been dying of an inoperable brain tumor, until I told Granny he was gone." Caleb related how she had wept a mother's tears as she confessed how Conor had sworn her to secrecy about his terminal condition. "I grew up aware of his schizophrenia, o'course. And he'd possessed a bit of a mean streak as a lad. You know the type relishes plucking the wings off butterflies. But those tendencies disappeared decades ago along with an adjustment in his medications."

"I feel so sorry for Granny."

"'Tis hard on her, sure. She keeps saying she can't believe her poor boy would do such a terrible thing. And that maybe 'twas the new cancer drug he'd been given interacting badly with the medication for his psychotic episodes."

"That could be the case. Either that, or maybe he dosed himself with whatever high-octane hallucinogen he gave to my friends and me."

Caleb stilled. A muscle twitched just below his temple. "Hallucinogen?"

"Yeah, you wouldn't believe the things I was seeing that night. My mother's ghost rising out of the sea...and other stuff." The man was arrogant enough, Arianna thought. He would be totally impossible were she to admit to seeing him soaring through the clouds like a frigging Faerie Prince.

Before turning onto the road leading to the castle, Caleb checked the rear-view mirror, probably making sure they had successfully ditched the press.

Arianna glanced at him. "Tara and Michaela are waiting for me at the cottage—"

"They're not expecting you straight away. I told them I'd be bringing you home with me for a wee while first." He reached out and captured her hand, brought it to his lips. "We've things to discuss, you and I. And I've something at the keep I want you to have, so we'll speak there." He drew in a long breath. His exhalation was audible. "Whatever happens, *mo chroí*, I want you to know I'd never consciously hurt you."

Nothing good can come out of a conversation that begins like that, Arianna thought.

೪ৎ

Their fingers interlaced, Caleb held his hand behind his back as he led Arianna around the circling stone steps to his apartments. In the family solar, they passed through the study, then went down a short corridor and entered his bedchamber through a thick mahogany door.

"With Granny staying here, do you really think it's appropriate to be showing me your 'etchings' right now?" Arianna teased to lighten the tension she was feeling.

Her inauspicious stab at humor brought a fleeting smile. "She's visiting a friend in town this afternoon, so she'll be none the wiser."

One look at the room and Arianna understood why a master bedroom in a castle was dubbed with the grander title "master chamber". The space was a thousand square feet, if it was an inch. Large, mullioned windows graced the western end of the room, providing a breathtaking view of the sea. A monumentally huge fireplace, constructed from some kind of black granite, took up most of the southern wall. Antique rugs covered the varnished floorboards, adding warmth to the tastefully masculine décor. Heavy drapes encircling the imposing bed—the size of two kings raised on a dais— matched those at the windows and the duvet cover.

From her dreams, Arianna recognized the Celtic knot pattern in shades of brown, black, gray, navy and burgundy. The color combination complemented the highly polished, dark mahogany pieces of furniture, so massive only a room with these dimensions could have accommodated them.

Caleb led her to two over-stuffed armchairs set cozily in front of the blazing hearth. After she sat down, he crossed the room, going to one of the built-in, floor-to-ceiling bookcases flanking the fireplace. He plucked an aluminum slipcase off a top shelf.

Dragging the other chair around so they were facing one another, knee to knee, he slid three books out of the case and handed them to Arianna. "The 1930 Lakeside Press edition of Moby Dick," he said. "'Twas my mother's. A gift from my father on my thirteenth birthday."

"The Moby Dick in a Can series? Do you have any idea how rare this is?" Turning the pages with reverence, she was careful to touch only the top edge of each one.

Caleb smiled at her enthusiasm, the gold flecks in his eyes twinkling in the firelight.

"I was watching you sleep last night in hospital, when I remembered this. Thought how much you'd enjoy it." He paused. "I want you to have it."

She lifted incredulous eyes. "No! I mean...that's really thoughtful, Caleb, and I love you for offering it to me. But you know I can't accept this. It's your mother's, a priceless family heirloom. It just wouldn't be right."

"'Twas mine," he said simply. "And now it's yours."

Arianna hesitated. For some reason, this seemed to mean a lot to him. "If you're sure." She closed the book and gently clasped it to her heart. "I'll treasure it always."

Caleb's demeanor was vague. Distracted. "I've a question to ask."

"Question?" A herd of elephants began a stampede through her chest.

"Have you given much thought to the future?" He floundered, shoving his hand through his hair. "What I'm saying is, are you planning to have a family?"

"Why? You offering to help me with that?" Arianna joked, trying to ease his discomfiture.

His expression slammed shut with a loud bang. "You know I can't do that."

"Caleb, I told you, I have a feeling our blood is perfectly com—"

"'Tisn't compatible! Now would you ever just answer the question."

Arianna rolled her lips together. "Truthfully, I've always dreamed of being a mother." She heard him draw in a ragged breath. "But there are so many unwanted children in the world, Caleb, we can always adopt."

His fingers curved around the arms of the chair. Arianna could see his mind working overtime. His face became a clay mask. "Adopt." He spat the word as if it were spoiled milk curdling on his tongue. "Sorry, luv, but I've no desire to assume responsibility for another man's mistake."

Arianna stiffened. The callous remark had been like ice water thrown in her face. He was purposely *trying* to put her off. But why?

"To be honest, I fancy my life just as it is. Wine, women and song," he went on. "Reckoned 'twas only fair to set things straight between us. You know, so there are no misunderstandings." He looked away, as if unable to tolerate the pain in her eyes another second. But then his eyes locked with hers again, his gaze implacable. "That's not to say I'm not fond of you, *cailín*. We could still be together from time to time. Sure, aren't there safe ways to share our bodies, to bring each other pleasure." A leering grin. "Using only our hands and our mouths."

If he had slapped her face, it would have hurt less. Arianna lifted her chin and rose to her feet. "I don't *think* so." Girders of cold gray steel hardened her heart. "You've been good to me, Caleb. You saved my life. If you hadn't come to the island and rescued me, I'd have died." With a mental fog still shrouding the details of that horrible night, she wasn't clear on how he had accomplished the feat. One thing she did know, however: the man had *not* come soaring through the clouds. "I'm sorry, but I just can't do this anymore. I feel like there's some kind of game being played here, and no one's bothered to tell me the rules." She chewed on her bottom lip. "That being the case, I think it's best if we don't see each other anymore." Her voice cracked on the words. "Now, if you'd be good enough to have your driver take me home."

Caleb stood up. "I'll drive you myself."

He sounded so weary, so wretchedly grim, her heart went out to him. "Thank you, but no." She said it softly, firmly. "I'd really prefer you didn't."

Their gazes locked for the length of several heartbeats. He was the first to break eye contact. "I'll have my driver meet you at the front door."

"Fine." As she stood and pulled the long strap of her purse over her shoulder, she set the Moby Dick edition on a piecrust table beside her chair.

He picked it up and held it out to her. "Please. Keep it as a memento of your stay at the castle." A look crossed his face that she couldn't identify. "Read it to your children one day...and think of me."

Her stoic expression camouflaging her pain, she gave her head a shake. "No, I'm sorry, Caleb. But I don't want to remember...not the castle or you."

He flinched as though she had struck him. In the brief instant that his guard was dropped, she caught a glimpse of the crumbling ruins of his heart. Comprehension came to her then. Rather than withhold from her the magic of motherhood, the experience of new life quickening within her womb, he would sacrifice their love.

He just didn't get it, she reflected sadly.

If she couldn't have *his* child, she would prefer to have no children at all.

But here he was again, the domineering, infuriating man determined to make that decision *for* her.

Arianna rose onto her tiptoes and brushed one final kiss across his cheek. "I don't want to remember, because I love you," she confessed quietly, holding his gaze. "Remembering would hurt too much."

She turned and, somehow, made it across the room. She could feel him watching her every step, letting her walk away from him. At the door, she remembered the lovemaking in their dreams. *God.* She stopped and turned back to him. "Don't come to me in the night...." she breathed, willing him to read the plea she couldn't put into words. "I couldn't bear it."

His expression bleak, he closed his eyes and inhaled meditatively. Then, releasing the breath in a long, steady flow, he met her gaze and inclined his head slowly. "*Saol fada chugat, a ghrá,*" he said softly. "Live long and well, my love. Live long and well."

Chapter Thirty

The week had flown by in a flurry of activity as Arianna got the cottage ready for strangers to move in. She had gone through every nook and cranny, packing pictures and personal items for shipment back to the States and storing some of the more valuable pieces of furniture. With no idea how long it would take to sell her business and Da's home back in Maine, Mr. Kavanagh had suggested some short-term vacation rentals to help offset the costs of upkeep of the property.

Arianna and her friends had gone to the Cliffs of Moher yesterday for a private memorial service for Da and she had finally scattered his ashes. Their bags were packed and waiting at the front door for the cab that was, as usual, running on Irish standard time. *Late.*

Arianna hadn't heard a word from Caleb since she had left him at the castle on Thursday…Thanksgiving Day…a week ago. God, how she missed him, *yearned* for him, until her heart was an open, pulsing wound.

Wanting to say goodbye to Granny, she decided to call the castle landline rather than Caleb's cell. Her pride drawn around her like a cloak, she wouldn't want Caleb to misinterpret the contact as a ploy to get in touch with him. Besides, the mere sound of his voice would destroy her. She dialed. On the third ring, a young woman answered the phone. One whose blood was compatible with his? Arianna felt sick to her stomach. "May I speak with Mrs. O'Clery, please?"

"Sorry, herself and Mr. MacNamara aren't in at the moment." *Mr. MacNamara?*

"Laura?" *The downstairs maid.*

"This is. May I ask who's calling?"

Arianna identified herself and requested to speak with Flanagan.

Flanagan came to the telephone and stuttered his usual greeting. "Miss...Arianna? So nice to hear from you." *Nice? Flanagan? Have I entered an alternate reality?*

"Um, you too. Uh, Caleb mentioned that Gran—um, that Mrs. O'Clery would be staying with him."

"She has been, yes."

"Well, will you give her a message for me, please? Tell her that my friends and I are leaving for the States this morning."

"You're leaving us, Miss?" *Us?* "I'm sorry to hear that." *Yeah, definitely in the Twilight Zone here.* "I'll get the message to Himself right away."

"The message is for *Granny*," Arianna stressed. "But please let her know I won't be here for her to return my call. Our flight leaves at ten and the cab just pulled up outside."

After loading their luggage into the taxi's trunk, Arianna stuck her head back inside the cottage for a final look around. With a heavy heart over all that had been, and all that could never be again, she pulled the door closed behind her.

ꞧ⁓

Caleb was pulling up outside the keep when his mobile rang. "Flanagan?" He frowned. "Leaving? When?" Though he'd known this was coming, sure the news was after leaving him pole-axed.

"Who's leaving?" Granny reached for her bag with one hand, pulled her shawl more snuggly around her shoulders with the other.

Caleb held up a finger while he listened to Flanagan. "Arianna left a message for you, luv. She's on her way to Shannon, returning to the States."

"Humph. And here I'd reckoned the two of ye were keeping company, and yerself the likes of a wounded bear all week long." Granny chuckled. "Had a bit of row, did ye?"

"What's this carryon about herself and meself keeping company? You're beginning to worry me, so you are."

"And just what is it you're finding so worrisome?" She inclined her head and looked over her nose at him...in that way she had of making it clear she'd be putting up with none of his nonsense.

"Oh, nothing. Except 'tisn't possible for me to be 'keeping

company' with a mere mortal." Her brows furrowed in confusion, as he added grimly, "I've no desire to be repeating the sins of my father."

"And exactly what *sin* is it you're speaking of? Are you not aware that yer dear mother hid the fact of her mortality from your Da until only hours before your birth?"

Caleb looked at her, stunned. "What are you saying?"

"I'm saying yer father loved yer mother, sweeting, much as he'd never have admitted to such a *mortal* failing." At Caleb's doubtful expression, Granny explained. "Your mam had met him in town, so handsome and self-possessed was he that she felt an instant attraction. A sweet and gentle soul, her kindness and beauty attracted him in return. Now she was acquainted with one of the castle maids who, after a few jars of stout one evening, told MacNamara family secrets. Speaking of the magic in his blood, she said that Himself would never date a mere mortal. My daughter, unable to bear the thought of being without him, didn't she let him believe there was a wee bit of magic hanging about the branches of our family tree." Granny sighed. "I was newly involved with the *Túatha de Danann* through yer Mam at the time and knew nothing of the Enchantment 'til 'twas too late."

"So you're telling me my father wasn't aware his wife was a mere mortal."

"That's the pure truth of it, luveen," she said. "'Twas only after the signs of birth poisoning became apparent during her labor that yer Da confronted her, and she confessed. Yer Mam, my precious Aoife, was after dying in yer father's arms that night. And I've yet to know a man, mortal or otherwise, to ever take a thing so hard. You being yer mother's son and half mortal, your da was fearing he'd not be able to provide adequately for yer emotional needs. So he sent you home with me. You looked so much like yer sweet Mam, 'twas the reason he stayed away I reckon. But didn't he call Flanagan to him after each visit with you to learn how you were faring?"

Caleb shook his head. "All these years, I've believed that he used my mother, discarded her like so much rubbish, just as he'd discarded me. That said, it still doesn't explain why you'd be thinking I would willingly date a mere mortal, that I'd risk the same fate befalling Arianna as did my mother."

"You said Arianna told you about her mother." Faded blue eyes searched his.

"She did, yes. About her drowning."

Granny's lips drew tight. "Conor didn't tell her, so."

"And what is it he was supposed to have told her then?"

His grandmother's answer left him gobsmacked.

As the plane taxied down the runway, Arianna knew she was leaving Ireland today a different woman than the one who had arrived a month ago. The fiery trials had served to burn away the dross in her character, to forge a more intimate sense of self. And to uncover an ineradicable strength, the extent of which she hadn't known that she possessed.

Gazing out the window as the plane lifted off, she touched her fingers to her lips. "Goodbye, my love...*Slán, a ghrá*," she whispered in the language of the man she would always love.

A couple of minutes later, a strange pinging noise, then a loud clang from the vicinity of the left engine, made her sit bolt upright in her seat. As the plane began to rock and vibrate, she and Tara exchanged worried glances. Michaela gasped from the seat behind her. The pilot's voice came over the P.A. "We are having a slight maintenance problem and will be returning to the terminal. Please remain calm and keep your seatbelts securely fastened until the plane has stopped moving and the fasten seatbelt sign has been extinguished."

The plane landed without further incident. Passengers grabbed up their belongings and spilled into the aisles. As Arianna and her friends passed through the doors leading back into the terminal, Michaela nudged Arianna, with a nod toward the waiting room. "Hey, check it out."

Tara turned her head and muttered, "The mind boggles."

Arianna blinked, but Caleb didn't disappear. Her heart beat a staccato rhythm as her starving senses gobbled up the sight of him. Black hair tousled, he reminded her of a small, naughty boy, leaning against the far wall, legs crossed at the ankles, hands shoved negligently into the pockets of his leather jacket. A crooked grin tugged dangerously at her heartstrings.

Her eyes narrowed. Surely, he hadn't...couldn't have.... No, the idea that he had used some kind of mind control to force the plane to return to the terminal was just plain crazy. Pushing away from the wall, he sauntered over to where they were standing.

"How'd you get past security?" Arianna asked, and then gave her head a shake. "Never mind that. What are you doing here? Is something wrong?"

"'Tis. You're leaving. And I've come to take you home."

"The cottage is rented. The new tenants are arriving tomorrow."

"I'm not speaking of the cottage. I've come to take you home with me."

Arianna's eyes widened in disbelief, the familiar surge of her hot Irish temper comforting. The man was incorrigible. Impossible. Unbelievable. *God*, he knew how she felt about him. Which meant he had to have known that his abandonment of her the last couple of weeks had broken her heart.

"So, that's it?" She stomped up to him, stood toe to toe, hands on her hips, eyes snapping fire. "You have the unmitigated gall to just show up here in front of God and...and everybody? And not to ask me, mind you, but to *tell* me you're taking me home with you? Just like that?" she snapped her fingers in his face. "Did it ever occur to you to call me? To check on how I was doing after that horrible ordeal?" At that, her voice broke and pissed her off even more.

She caught the exchange, the clandestine glance he slid toward Michaela. "He did," she offered sheepishly.

"What?" Arianna asked tersely.

Michaela licked her lips. "He did call to check on you. Every day. But he asked me not to say anything, said that it would only make it harder for you. That you'd already been through enough. And every time I tried to bring his name up, to tell you he'd been calling, you cut me off. Shut me out."

Digesting the disclosure, Arianna felt her traitorous heart take a jubilant leap. She turned back to Caleb. "What are you doing here?" she asked softly. "We said everything we had to say that day at the castle. When I left you standing there, there was no...'please don't go, Arianna. No...'let's talk things through, find a way.' No...'I love you—"

Her words were lost against his lips as his mouth came down on hers, communicating all those things with lips and tongue and teeth. Then he lifted his head, his emerald gaze burning into her with an otherworldly light. "God help me, I do love you, *a mhuirnín mo dílis*, my truest sweetheart. *An bpósfaidh tú mé?*" he asked, his eyes searching hers for an answer.

At the Gaelic, her brows raised quizzically.

"Will you marry me?" he proposed again, nuzzling her ear, his mouth moving over her face with shivery kisses. "Please say you'll be my *anam cara*. My soul mate. My wife."

Was she hearing him correctly? But how? "I'm confused. I thought...I mean, you said we couldn't..." She gulped a breath. "You want me to marry you?"

"I do. *Anois.* Now." He nibbled on her lips. "I've learned things today that change everything for us. Trust me, *a ghrá*, and come home. For I've a faerie tale to tell."

"For heaven's sake, you two. Get a room," Tara said, but the twinkle in her eyes betrayed her tone.

Caleb invited Tara and Michaela to join them at the castle. But the girls had business to tend to at home and decided to board the flight when it was cleared and head back.

"There've been all manner of things I've not been free to discuss until now," Caleb explained as he and Arianna headed toward the car park. "But Granny told me about your mother—".

"Stop." Arianna cut him off. "You've just asked me to marry you, Caleb. The last thing I want to do is sully this perfect moment with talk of my mother's suicide."

"But that's what I'm trying to tell you. She *didn't* kill herself, *a mhuirnín*." And then he dropped the bomb. "Sure, in fact, your mother's not dead a'tall."

Chapter Thirty-one

Stating only that it was complicated, Caleb refused to say any more on the subject until they returned to the castle. When they got there, he took her hand and guided her toward the formal gardens. As they walked along the familiar path, shafts of golden sunlight quivered through the trees' naked branches, spilling warmth over all the cold, empty places in Arianna's heart. Being here with him like this again was a miracle, like having all her dreams come true in a single moment in time.

In the garden, he led her to a carved stone bench in front of a rocky wall smothered in a tangle of woodbine and ivy. As he tugged her down beside him, he touched a silencing finger to his lips, then pointed out a pair of pheasants browsing the fuchsia hedges nearby.

"I know you're anxious to learn of your mother, *mo chroí*," he said, pulling her close. "But for you to have a hope of believing what I've to tell you about her, there are other things you have to understand first."

With his melodic brogue, he wove a tapestry, an epic tale of a people of mystery and magic. When he had finished reciting the story of the *Geis*, he sat quietly and considered her, keeping her hands captured by his as if he feared she might run away.

"Can you understand now, *a ghrá*? The blood condition I told you about is a curse on my people resulting from the Enchantment. 'Twas that which killed my mother as she birthed me. Why I feared touching you. That you would conceive my child and die in agony, suffering the same deadly fate as herself." He reached out and hooked a lock of hair behind her ear as if he could no longer keep from touching her.

Arianna remembered her father's words. *"The Lord has other sheep not of our fold."* "I've always had a feeling that there are other... dimensions...I guess you could say. And it doesn't surprise me that

God would have other creations. What I don't get, though, is all that crazy OCD stuff you were doing about me driving myself into town?"

"My concern stemmed from my belief that you might be the Woman of Promise prophesied to dissolve the *Geis*. And the possibility that the stalker, whom we now know was Conor, was possessed of a Minion sent forth by the spirit of the Beast to stop her."

Arianna stared up at the man she loved, her head spinning. Surely, he wasn't saying that this curse, this...this 'gesh' thing...was anything more than an old Irish legend.

A fluttering in her mind. "That's *exactly* what I'm saying, *cailín*."

She snapped a look at him so fast she almost wrenched her neck. *Holy crap!* So he really could read her mind.

"Okay, so let me see if I've got this straight," she said, her tone measured. "You say it's safe for us to be together now. So, that must mean that someone else is this...'Woman of Promise'. In the last few days, she's somehow managed to locate the ancient artifact and resolve the blood curse thing. So, we can safely be intimate now. Have I got that right?"

Caleb cleared his throat. Rubbed the side of his nose. "Well, not exactly."

Arianna frowned. "Well, then what, *exactly*?"

He took a deep breath. "Before I can explain that, I've a bit more of my people's history to share with you."

"There's more?"

He gave a solemn nod. "The night we met, do you remember mentioning the fifth group of people to settle Ireland?"

"Of course."

"Well, they were my ancestors, Arianna. The *Túatha de Danann*."

Arianna sat in stunned disbelief. "You're claiming to be descended from *the Túatha de Danann*? The *fairies*?"

"In a way, but let me explain. As you're aware, the *Túatha de Danann* are a race of people whose very existence has become an obscure argument between the historian and the mythologist. The former believes we were mere mortals—renowned in the arts, skilled artisans, poets and mighty warriors—now sadly extinct. The latter, as you so eloquently stated the night we met, insist that we transformed into the faerie people."

Arianna swallowed thickly.

"There are yet others who believe we're fallen angels. Cast down to the earth—neither pure enough for heaven, nor wicked enough to be condemned to everlasting torment. Others assert we were born of the gods and arrived in Connaught in, quote, *ships of fire,* unquote—which is more the truth. Not the 'gods' part." He paused here for effect. "But the spacecraft."

Arianna paled at the implications. "So, you're saying you're... you're...." She just couldn't force herself to say it.

"From another world," he confirmed simply, his tone reasonable, considering he was claiming to be descended from space aliens. "You see, an asteroid was on a collision course with our planet, many millions of light-years from the earth. As there were no other sentient life forms in our solar system, in our galaxy, no planets sufficient to support life, our scientists began sending out probes, searching for a new home for our inhabitants. Finally, a signal was received back that such a place existed at the far reaches of the universe. A small planet powered by a sun much like ours, except that our sun shined as blue due to a difference in size and distance. Essentially, earth's atmosphere was the same as ours."

Arianna rubbed her throbbing right temple.

"Lifetimes passed," he continued unabated. "Generations were born, lived and died during the endless journey to earth. The starship finally arrived here about four thousand years ago, landing in a technologically backward world in a time before recorded time."

Arianna could feel her stomach churning.

Caleb carried on. "Through the countless millennia our people traveled through the stars, the solar irradiation began to alter our genetic makeup. Many of our inherent traits were lost—the ability to shape-shift, for example. To teleport over great distances. The ability to pass through solid objects. To fly. And yet other traits became even more enhanced: the power to levitate, to communicate and travel telepathically, to read minds. To bring another under our control through a mesmeric thrall. And to command the elements," he finished, somewhat sheepishly.

"The lightning..." Arianna murmured. "I didn't imagine it."

"'Twas the only way I knew to get you away from the danger," he admitted evenly. "And that awful night on Inishmore, you'd died before I could get to you. Manipulating the lightning was the method I used to restart your heart."

In a crazy, insane, totally bonkers sort of way, everything he was saying was beginning to make sense. There were the waking dreams, of course. And the mind reading. And losing consciousness in the SUV on her way to the cottage that first night. She couldn't deny having experienced the lightning blast, and what she had believed was a near death experience that night on the Island. Not to mention that she had been sensing something...otherworldly...about him from the moment they met.

*Other*worldly indeed, she thought, choking back a hysterical giggle. "So, you're telling me you're not human. You're a space alien from another planet."

Caleb's warm chuckle sounded so normal, so familiar, it began to melt the block of ice that encased her heart. "We're of a different race, my love, but of the same species as the people of earth. Homo sapiens, and ourselves created in the image of the very same God whose mighty Hand shaped the dust on this planet into a living soul. Also, after making our new home here, we began to intermarry. As generations passed, our DNA intermingled with that of the people whose origins are of the earth."

"Until the gesh," Arianna remarked.

"The *Geis*, yes. You see, in our world there'd been no Garden of Eden. No fall from grace, or original sin. No serpent spawning his wickedness. Our magic was pure, innate. Powers invested in us were as those Christ spoke of during his sojourn on earth. A kind of natural faith sufficient to move mountains."

"Or spill snow over a thousand acres," Arianna interjected thoughtfully.

Caleb raised a shoulder. "That, as well. Our magic is divinely inspired, far different from the abomination of diabolic incantations, the malevolent witchery of spell casting employed by those such as the Druids."

"Black magic, you mean."

"Mmm. While there are those who believe our people originated from fallen angels, in actuality, the ancient Druids were the ones descended from those God expelled from heaven. Those who mated with the daughters of man, creating giants. 'Twas the reason for the Great Flood. To cleanse the earth of their progeny. But again, after the Flood, the Evil One caused more soulless beings to be born. Because these Formorians were of their father, the devil, they were eternally damned. Afterwards, God prevented them from ever again mating with the women of earth. Whilst our people, who with sinless hearts arrived here from the stars, were permitted by the Creator to do so. Our magic was pure and powerful. More powerful than the satanic black magic of the Evil One. Therefore, when pronouncing the Enchantment that would ultimately set the Evil One free of the Pit, ending the dominion of man upon the earth, the High Priest of the Druid Formorians included the prohibition that made our intermarrying and producing offspring with the women of earth a deadly act."

"Whoa," was all Arianna could muster.

"The rest you know from Irish folklore," Caleb concluded. "Our people were defeated in battle by an invading force, the Milesians, who were after offering us a treaty of sorts. That we may choose either to share the upper earth with them, or keep for our exclusive holdings the land beneath the hills and seas."

"This is where the faeries come in," Arianna breathed.

"'Tis. Many de Danann warriors, heavy-hearted from the *Geis*-imposed separation from the women they loved, chose to retreat beneath the earth. For some reason we've never fathomed, the change in habitat served to rehabilitate the full scope of traits lost to our people on the journey to earth. Reverting to purely magical beings, these earth spirits constructed a habitation of echoing lakes and golden palaces patterned after our former world. As the years passed, it became apparent that those who had transformed, who remained tucked safely away from the sun's radiation, became nearly immortal. Beings known today as the *daoine sidhe*...or, as you said in English, the faeries."

Faeries. Arianna blinked and stared at him. "So, you're telling me you're a faerie prince."

Caleb paused. "No. Though, for a few minutes, whilst coming to your rescue...."

"So, I wasn't hallucinating that night on Inishmore," she said slowly. "You really did fly through the clouds." *But what about my mother? If she isn't dead, why did I see her ghostly form rising from the waves below Dun Aengus?*

She must have looked as skittish as a wild colt, because Caleb turned to face her then, his hands gently gripping her shoulders. "'Twas a spirit you saw that night, all right," he said matter-of-factly, answering her thoughts about her mother. "A spirit, sure, but not a ghost."

At this point, Arianna pulled away from him and shot him a quelling look. "I don't know how you *do* that. But would you mind staying the frig out of my head?" His mouth twitched, but he hid the smile. Begrudgingly, she asked, "What do you mean, I saw a spirit, but not a ghost?"

Caleb breathed in through his nose. Exhaled. "You're mother's descended from the *Túatha de Danann*, Arianna, just as I am. Only she's from the other branch of the family. She's a water sprite, my love, otherwise known as a merrow."

"But that would make me..."

"Half-mortal, half-fey...like myself."

Okay, I'm going to wake up any minute now.

"The day your mam left you and your father, she was lured by the call of the sea. Not to her death, *a ghrá,* but to her eternal home, the enchanted land from whence she'd come. A place called in the Gaelic *an Tir fo Thoinn*...or the Land Beneath the Waves."

Arianna's heart began to thud dangerously; her breath was coming in short, sharp gasps. The damn man was going to give her a panic attack. Or a coronary. The tale of fairies and an evil enchantment wasn't bad enough. Oh, no. Now he's claiming her mother's a freaking mermaid. A picture formed in her mind: the lovely woman in her visions with a giant fishtail. Crazed laughter bubbled up her throat, but she swallowed it.

"A *merrow*, Arianna," Caleb corrected with only the slightest hint of impatience. "Not a mermaid with the tail of a fish."

She jerked a look at him. "I told you to stay out of my *head*."

"Anyways, a merrow is one of the *sidhe*," he went on as if speaking to an impressionable young child. "Or, in English, the Irish faerie world. She's of the branch of the *Túatha de Danann* that chose immortality, those preferring to dwell beneath the hills and seas in spirit form."

"So, how could she have given birth to a...uh...*mortal?*" She stumbled over the word.

She felt the sun warm her face. All around them, woodland creatures flitted through the underbrush, rustling the dried autumn leaves, squeaking and chattering. Normal, everyday sounds, she thought, in a world gone irretrievably mad.

"It's possible for us to move back and forth from one dimension to the other at will," Caleb explained. "'Twas what I did when you were in trouble on the Island. The only way I knew to find you, to reach you in time."

"I've wondered how you knew to come. How you got there with no boat, no helicopter. But every time I started to contemplate it, it all seemed an irrelevant blur."

"I planted a suggestion that you wouldn't seek out those details."

She could see it in his eyes. His awareness of the dire implications of that admission to a woman who prided herself on her independence. "So you can control me, manipulate my will," she whispered. "Just like that."

"I would never..." She cut him a sharp look. "*Never* would I have done so, had I not believed you a mere mortal in need of my *superior* protection."

"So, you believe you're...your race is superior." She shook her head. "A dangerous supposition, considering a German dictator thought *his* race was superior not too long ago."

"We don't consider ourselves morally superior. But with our preternatural abilities, *we*" —he stressed her inclusion — "are exceptional, both physically and psychically."

She watched the pheasants, the cock strutting proudly before his hen. "I suppose... So, do you...change very often? Back and forth, I mean...from one world to the other?"

"Absolutely *not*." His emphatic reply refocused her attention. "As children, we're taught the dangers involved. I can personally attest to the lure of power in that purely magical state. 'Tis...addictive. Few who taste it ever desire to return to a mundane physical existence, and thereby forfeit their mortal souls. Therefore, those who dabble, who are after crossing back and forth between this world and that, risk losing their humanity."

It finally sank in. What he had risked to save her. His humanity. His very mortal soul. Caleb leaned over and nuzzled her neck. She sighed and settled into his embrace.

"Do you want to hear more of your mother?" he asked softly.

Did she? Was this *The Truth* Da had spoken of? What Granny had been trying to explain to her the day of her heart attack? "Yes," she whispered. "Tell me. Everything."

His arms tightened around her. "A merrow possesses great beauty and great wealth," he began. "Herself differing from a mortal woman only in that her feet are flatter, and there's a very thin webbing near the V of her fingers."

Arianna swallowed, forcing saliva down a very dry throat. "Did Granny mention how my parents met? I mean, with my mother living in the ocean and all." *Did I really say that?*

Caleb covered her knotted hands with one of his. "She did. One evening, whilst out exploring the site of a 19th century lighthouse at Baily, near Dublin, your da spotted herself frolicking in the waters. The merrow's sealskin cloak enables her to travel the ocean currents, but eventually your mother came on shore, abandoning it temporarily, desiring to dance in the light of the moon. A risky business that. Fishermen have been known to force a merrow to marry them simply by hiding her cloak."

It was the most outrageous tale she had ever heard...and yet it seemed cohesive somehow. *The Truth.* Caleb must have misunderstood her shallow gasp, because he hurried to explain. "No worries, love. According to Granny, your mam was after putting her cloak away voluntarily to marry your da. And choosing to give birth to you as well. But sadly, in the end, no matter how deep a merrow's feelings for her mortal family, the enchanted call of the sea will always prevail. 'Tis her nature, you see, that she can never overcome."

"A fish out of water," Arianna quipped and caught her lip between her teeth.

He gave her a squeeze. "'Twas Herself alerted me you were in danger on Inishmore."

Arianna whipped around, stared up at him. "My mother? How?"

"She woke me from a restless sleep. Thought at first 'twas the *bean sidhe* wailing outside my window—you've heard of the screaming banshee?" Arianna nodded. "But after transforming, I knew instantly 'twas your own mother calling to me to save you."

Pieces of a transcendental puzzle began to fit together. The ethereal being rising from the angry waves on that dark and hellish night had been no wraith, no ghostly apparition.

But her very own mother...in faerie form.

Arianna remembered the way the woman's gossamer figure had sunk again into the ocean's depths. But not until she had looked skyward, satisfying herself that Caleb had arrived on the scene, a glittering dark knight swooping from the heavens on a magical steed, riding on the wings of a cloud.

Her father's final words whispered through her mind. *"You must follow your heart, love, and open your eyes of faith."*

My God, she thought, everything Caleb had told her was true. All true. Every bit of it.

Chapter Thirty-two

*D*estiny. Another word Da had spoken to her on his final night. "I understand now why he took me away from here," Arianna said, turning in Caleb's arms. "He must have been terrified he'd lose me the way he had my mother...to the irresistible lure of a magical world."

She also understood why he had kept the cottage. So that, if anything ever happened to him, she wouldn't be lost, without a foundation upon which to resurrect this part of her nature. "He left an inscription for me in a children's Bible I found in the cedar chest in my parent's old room. It was his way of confirming my true heritage, while keeping the revelation vague, in case the Bible were to fall into someone else's hands. What I don't get though is, if I'm m-magic"— she had a problem saying the word—"why am I afraid of heights? Of closed in places? Why the migraines?"

"All likely a result of repressing your own true nature. I reckon you'll find those things won't be troubling you anymore."

"Oh, yeah, and another thing. I've never been able to cry."

A wind gust lifted her hair from her neck and Caleb smoothed it with his hand. "Other than getting an impressive temper on, and possessing a wee tinge of vindictiveness, we of the mortal *sidhe* aren't a highly emotional lot. I've cried only once myself...the night I held your lifeless body in my arms. Because of the *Geis,* it's believed we've lost much of our humanity. That we're incapable of experiencing human love."

Arianna caught her bottom lip between her teeth. "Then you've gotta be wrong about me. About what I am."

"And why is that?" The tone of his voice was a gentle caress.

"Because I love you with every fiber of my being." She wrinkled her nose and added, "Even when you first started talking about all this, and I was sure you were out of your ever-loving mind."

His head dipped, those delicious lips tracing nibbling kisses over her nose, down her cheek, her chin. "Then I must be a fraud as well," he murmured huskily. "For 'twas you yourself who taught me the meaning of the word." He lifted his eyes, his gaze mating with hers. She could feel her body grow soft, malleable, as he unleashed the enchanting power of his sexual thrall. A welcome enticement. "You're my *anam cara,* Arianna, my soul mate. As I am yours. We've been destined to be together, you and I, since time began."

His hand covering hers, he pressed her palm to his chest. Beneath her hand, his heart thrummed wildly, in perfect sync with her own. "Feel what you do to me, *a mhuirnín.* A raging fever you've always been in my blood. Now and in the Imaginal...in our dreams."

Arianna shifted and slid one leg across his lap. Straddling him, she captured his face between her hands. "You just didn't get it before, when you sent me away. Don't you understand that being with you is all...*all*...that matters to me?" She kissed his mouth, nipped his lower lip. "If I couldn't have your child, I would rather have had none at all." She deepened the kiss. His breathing grew ragged. She felt him shudder, the muscles of his shoulders bunched beneath her fingertips. "I love you, Caleb. Only you, *a ghrá.* Now and forever. *Anois agus go deo,*" she whispered in his ear, repeating her vow in the few words of Gaelic she had learned.

Caleb wrapped his arms around her. She could feel his raging arousal as he bent to nuzzle the cleavage between her breasts. Then he lifted his head, eyes glittering with a carnal look that was both promise and demand. "We'd best start back now, *a mhuirnín.* I've waited far too long for this. And I intend to take my time with you."

As he held back a weeping willow branch so that she could duck beneath it, Arianna turned to him. "I just thought of something," she said. "This morning? When the plane started shaking—" A corner of his mouth lifted in an arrogant smile. "You did that, didn't you?"

"You've never heard of our ancient custom then?"

She forced her eyes away from lips that had her thinking naughty thoughts. "What custom?"

"Marriage by capture. 'Tis a practice of great antiquity amongst my...amongst *our* people. The bride being seized and carried off by the groom." Arianna cuffed him playfully on the arm, and he gave an oh-so-wicked chuckle.

"Some of the passengers might have missed connecting flights," she scolded primly.

His teasing expression grew sober. "I couldn't let you leave me, *a ghrá*. Not after learning 'twas safe for us to be together. Learning who you are."

"Who I am." Arianna repeated the words in a daze. "It's odd, you know? Almost as if I've had some kind of selective amnesia all these years. And now, my memory is beginning to return in bits and pieces." She blew out a breath. "How in the world am I suppose to explain all this to Tara and Michaela? I mean, they already think I'm nuts for believing you're the lover in my dreams."

The look on Caleb's face stopped her short. "What? You mean, they know about the waking dreams we've shared."

"Of course. They're my best friends...my family. We tell each other everything. But when they hear this...well, Michaela will eventually get it. But Tara? Not unless she sees it with her own eyes. Wait, that's it. You just do a little magic for them—you know, like that trick with the lightning. Or start a fire or—or something."

"First of all, Arianna, I'm not a trick pony." Oh-oh. The fact that he was using her name, instead of an endearment didn't bode well. "Nor, for that matter, am I a *magician*." He spat the word. "An accusation, which, by the way, is highly offensive to those of our kind." As he walked beside her, his long strides were forcing her almost to run to keep up.

"I-I didn't know..."

"Furthermore, you need to understand that your friends may be privy to none of this. Like the mortal world, our people live by certain laws enacted to protect our society. One of which is that mere mortals may be told of our existence on a need to know basis only. Think of your American CIA. In point of fact, most mortals who are aware of us are like Flanagan, members of old families who've passed the knowledge down through many generations."

"Whoa, just hold on a darn minute here," she protested, a flash of mutiny in her eyes. "What do you mean I can't tell my friends about this? What about freedom of speech?"

His jaw hardened, his expression turned stone cold. "The Council of Brehons, which rules the *Túatha de Danann*, is no democracy, Arianna."

"And if I run my mouth, then what?"

"Depending on the circumstances, revealing our secrets is a crime akin to treason."

She felt herself grow pale. "What are you saying? That I could be executed?"

She read the chilling truth in the pain in his eyes. "Something equivalent. A kind of permanent exile. You would be forced to transform, to leave this mortal existence."

"But you said you're the chairman of the board, or the chief, or whatever," she said, flapping her hand.

"That doesn't mean I could legally intervene on your behalf," he stated sternly, then heaved a breath. "Not that I'd allow you to be cast off alone. I would go with you, stay with you forever." He smiled his crooked smile. "But I'd much prefer ourselves remaining in this dimension, on this side of the vale. So, what d'ya reckon? Will you hold your tongue?"

They were passing the family mausoleum, when Caleb suddenly took her hand and led her through the door of its small chapel. She marveled that the interior was indeed as she had envisioned in her dream. "There are valid reasons for the strict vow of silence, *a ghrá*. As you embark upon the journey to discover all the supernatural facets of your nature, there's a thing you must never forget." He drew her into one of the golden pews and settled down beside her. "Less than a year remains for the *Geis* to be fulfilled. If we violate its terms, the planet will face total annihilation. As there's no way of identifying in advance who the Woman of Promise may be, we've been forced to cloak our existence from the world."

"This...Chosen One. You're sure it can't be me?" Arianna confirmed.

"I am, thanks be to God. The *Geis* requires the Woman be a mere mortal."

A horrifying idea bullied its way into her churning thoughts. "It couldn't be Tara or Michaela, could it? I mean, they're not even Irish."

"The enchantment doesn't designate a nationality," he explained patiently. "It states merely that the woman will come from across the sea."

Dismayed, her mind began to compile a checklist of the life-threatening dangers Caleb had told her the poor woman drawn into this cosmic drama would ultimately face. A woman who would hold the fate of all humanity unwittingly in her hands. And a mere slip of the tongue on Arianna's part might destroy the world's only chance for survival.

Not to mention that, on a much smaller scale, running her mouth could put an entire race of people at risk of becoming the target of lunatics. *Like Conor,* she thought, repressing a shiver of dread. No, she must never allow herself the luxury of forgetting that what Granny had revealed to Conor about Arianna's heritage had been the thing to set him off.

To put the idea in his twisted mind to roast her like a frigging marshmallow.

After sharing a meditative silence, the two of them left the chapel and continued along the leaf-strewn trail. Turning to her, Caleb slid his hand into his jacket pocket, pulled out a black jeweler's box and opened it. An exquisite ring nestled within the folds of antique pink satin. A flawless diamond winked from the center of the setting, at the point where the two halves of a golden heart dipped and joined.

"My mother's *fáinne pósta.*" He hesitated as he searched for the correct word in English—an endearing trait Arianna had noticed only occurred whenever he was nervous. "Her wedding ring," he translated finally. "'Twas my father's mother's before her, and so forth and so on, back many generations. 'Tis a Claddagh made of purest gold, two hands clasped around a heart and the crown above it, for *Cairdeas, Dílseacht, agus Grá*...friendship, loyalty, and love."

He looked down at her, his sea-green gaze melting her insides. "'Tis those three things I pledge to you today, a *chuisle mo chroí*...my heart's dearest treasure." His voice was raw with emotion. "With my friendship, I commit ever to stand for you. Never to judge or condemn you, no matter what trials life may bring our way. With my loyalty, I promise to put you first in all things. Neither anyone, nor anything, will ever take your place in my heart. And finally," he murmured, his lips lightly brushing her knuckles, "I vow to you this day that no man, mortal or otherwise, could ever love you more."

Entranced by his impassioned pledge, mesmerized by his manly beauty, Arianna let her gaze travel over his beloved face, the straight aristocratic nose, the chiseled jaw, the sensual curve of lips. Her eyes traced the dusky trail of hair sprinkled lightly on top of the hands that were holding hers. With a heated shiver, she remembered those truly magic fingers touching her in the snow, a heated prelude to the possession of his body later that night in their dreams. She yearned to belong to him fully in the here and now, to have him teach her the ways of physical love. Not only, what it meant to be a woman, she mused airily, but a woman of the *Tuatha de Danann*.

"An bpósfaidh tú me? Anois?" he asked again. "Will you marry me? Now?"

So swollen was her heart with love for this man, her destiny, that she could hardly breathe. She could scarcely absorb the fact that all her dreams were *literally* coming true. She was going to become the wife of this wild, fiery, mystical, impossibly stubborn Irishman. Could she be dreaming even now?

"I love you, Caleb," she whispered, rubbing her thumb across his full bottom lip. "Of course, I'll marry you. Today, tomorrow. Now this very minute, if it were possible."

He gave a slow, sexy smile as he took her left hand and slid his mother's ring onto her third finger. Then he rose to his feet and swept her into his arms. He kissed her gently, her forehead, eyes, nose. And then his mouth took hers in a scorching kiss that sealed his pledge, promised his possession.

He raised his head. The glitter of magic in his unveiled gaze consumed her. "Our promises have been made and accepted, our vows privately exchanged. As your husband, I offer you the protection of my body, my name, and my home, even as I accept the same from you, *a banchéile mo chroí,* wife of my heart. According to Brehon Law," he intoned quietly, causing the earth to shift madly beneath her feet, "I pronounce ourselves now legally wed."

‿❧‿

When they arrived back at the castle, Arianna discovered that her luggage had been delivered to the family solar. Caleb escorted her down the hall and into a room layered in femininity. Silks and velvets draped the room in shades of gray and mauve, pale pink and deepest burgundy. The furnishings were in the lighter, more graceful Queen Anne style, with *cabriole* legs that curved outward at the knee and inward at the ankle, supported on clawed feet. Several of the pieces, including the highboy against the wall and the matching lowboy beneath one of the windows, had bombe bases. Two accent armchairs, their cream-colored fabric striped in delicate lines of wine and charcoal, sat facing a small hearth, whose wooden mantle was painted an antique white.

"My mother's room," Caleb told her, explaining that, having been constructed in the medieval period, the bedchambers were designed in the adjoining Lord and Lady style. "You'll have privacy for bathing and dressing, or for personal space as required. Though sure I'll wish to have my wife in the bed beside me, sharing the night." That last he added as a gentle reminder to their new marital status.

Caleb had 'tea' ordered up to the study, the Irish equivalent of a late afternoon lunch. While sharing the meal, he patiently answered her questions about the society of which she was now a part. "Despite the fact that we've already exchanged our vows," he assured her, "we'll host a traditional wedding ceremony, so that friends and family can be sharing in our happiness."

Later, Arianna told him she wanted to try out some of her new 'super-powers'

Caleb smiled softly. "I'll teach you our most elemental ability—fire-starting." During their meal, the fire in the hearth had burned down to smoldering embers. "Focus your consciousness," he instructed her. "Find the power that resides deep inside you. Feel it gathering, building, filling you like an evanescent ball of life?" Eyes huge, she gave a quick nod. "Now, throw the arc of that energy from yourself, direct it toward the grate." *Nothing.* Encouraged to try again, she repeated the process. The third time, as they say, was the charm. An anemic, pale yellow flame sprang from what remained of the logs and peat. Though it flickered pathetically, she squealed and clapped her hands with all the bright-eyed excitement of a child on Christmas morning.

After they finished eating, Caleb begged a couple of hours to cancel appointments and put some pressing business matters on hold. "Our marriage was…precipitous." His lips twisted into a wry smile. "I fancy freeing up the next few weeks to devote myself fully to seeing to the needs of my new wife."

To say she was feeling overwhelmed was an understatement. Arianna was grateful, therefore, for the chance to escape to her bedroom for some personal downtime. She climbed up the wooden steps to the plush, queen-size bed and curled up on a duvet of mauve and gray-swirled crushed velvet. She lay staring up at the matching canopy as her brain attempted to assimilate all that had transpired in her life within the space of only a few hours.

Glancing at the fireplace, she noted the flames were dwindling. A thrill of anticipation rushed through her as she practiced the fire-starting divination that Caleb had taught her. A smug smile formed on her face at the resulting flash. She had always been a fast learner, she thought, snuggling into the soft pillow. Within minutes, she was fast asleep.

Moaning low in her throat, she sighed against her dream lover's lips. His mouth brushed over hers. Once, twice. "Wake up, Sleeping Beauty," Caleb whispered in her ear.

She opened her eyes to find him sitting beside her, one arm positioned on the mattress on the other side of her hip. The room was dark, except for the golden firelight from the hearth, and the flickering light of a dozen or so candles scattered about the room. A faerie tale princess awakened by the kiss of her one true love. Not so far from the truth, she mused whimsically, with a contented sigh.

"What did I do?" She groaned, stretching like a lazy cat. "Sleep the afternoon away?"

"Only a couple of hours. 'Tis about half-five now. I've ordered the evening meal served at seven in the solar, if that suits. Our own private celebration. We'll appear in the Great Hall tomorrow night, so you can be officially presented to the staff as their chatelaine. But tonight," he gave a crooked smile. "I fancy keeping you all to myself."

Chapter Thirty-three

All soaked and steamed, creamed and perfumed, Arianna rounded the corner into the study. The ivory silk of her calf-length dress draped over every dip and curve. Mouth dry, palms damp, she found Caleb in front of the fire, reading. He looked up, a slight smile lighted on his lips. He put his book aside and rose to greet her.

She was still reeling from the disclosures of the day, that Caleb—and she—belonged to an otherworldly race. While she had embraced the concept, she had yet to come to terms with all that that really meant. Their eyes met, and she perceived at once the change in him, in their relationship. She felt her heart falter at the touch of his eyes. It was tactile, seeming to burn through the fabric of her dress, spreading a spiral of warmth that coiled deep in her belly. As he moved toward her, it was with that lethal grace that had always fascinated her. The smooth glide of muscle beneath his skin reminded her of a mountain lion, and she a startled doe venturing inadvertently into its den.

"Mine." She felt, more than heard, the possessive pronoun. But rather than ownership, the word conveyed a sense of belonging, of family and security, and many other things too intense to name. He bent his head and brushed her lips with his, testing her, testing himself. The slow, sultry kiss chased away any earlier misgivings. "Sure, aren't you a sight to rival the angels in heaven tonight." His low baritone did funny things to her insides.

"Why, thank you, Sir." She covered her case of nerves with a saucy toss of her head. "You don't clean up too bad yourself."

And he didn't. Arianna had thought him strikingly handsome before...a dark angel in faded blue jeans and cool, black leather. Tonight, however, he looked like he had stepped right out of the pages of GQ. He was wearing a pale beige cashmere sweater in an

Aran knit pattern of black, tan, and navy swirls. The colors perfectly complemented his indigo woolen trousers, the hem of which brushed the tassels of a pair of Italian loafers.

As he took her hand and led her across the room, Arianna was moved beyond words by the ends this strong, silent man had gone to tonight. The setting was a whisper of romance, the lighting soft and muted. The small table in the alcove where they usually took their meals now stood on an Oriental rug in front of the massive hearth, where a rolling log-and-turf fire warmed the room. Dressed in fine white Irish linen, the table was set with Dresden china, crystal goblets and champagne flutes accented by gold flatware. In the middle of the table sat a centerpiece of fresh-cut flowers, a rose in every color imaginable—white, pink, red, yellow and, strangely, blue—with mums, lavender, and sprigs of sweet-smelling honeysuckle added for accent. On either side of the vase, slim tapers flickered from a pair of antique table candlesticks. An alluring Celtic melody played softly in the background, seeming to swirl through the air from every direction.

"Dinner should be arriving soon. Hungry?" Caleb smiled, trailing a finger down the side of one cheek.

"Starved..." She stretched onto her toes and leaned into him. "For you," she whispered against his mouth, then slid playfully away as he reached for her. She settled onto the sofa and crossed her legs in a way that revealed a provocative glimpse of thigh.

Caleb's head tipped, his eyes glinted wickedly as he went to draw a chilled magnum of Dom Pèrignon from a stand beside the table. "Well then," he declared softly, popping the cork with a flourish. "We'll just put off eating dinner, until we're after sating other more relentless appetites."

He filled two flutes with the effervescent liquid. "Champagne, my love?"

She accepted one of the flutes as he sat beside her and raised his in a silent toast. They watched one another over the rims of their glasses as they sipped the sparkling beverage. Arianna's gaze drifted lower, following the constriction of his throat muscles as he swallowed. The light of the hearth fire accentuated the generous curve of his bottom lip, deliciously moistened by the cool, crisp drink. She wanted to taste those lips, drink him in. Their eyes met. His looked like liquid emeralds in the firelight.

It was too warm. Suddenly nervous, she raised her glass to her lips and took a large gulp. Bubbles burst up her nose and burned her sinuses. Eyes watering, she started choking.

Caleb chuckled as he patted her lightly on the back. "You okay?"

Arianna nodded. Caleb—her new husband, she corrected—was watching her closely. The arrogant glint of sexual dominance in his gaze was a reality check. A woman with no prior sexual experience, just what did she think she was doing, attempting to play the Femme Fatale with this virile, seemingly predatory male?

The answer was simple. She was feeling insecure, concerned that she would be awkward and fumbling, that her inexperience would disappoint him. To counteract that, she was putting on an act, attempting to appear confident, coy, and sexually self-assured. Like his other bed partners, those otherworldly faerie women. Like Seamus's girlfriend at the pub.

Yeah, no pressure there.

"We'll have to organize having your things shipped from the States." He trailed his fingers deliciously over the bared flesh above her knees.

"I have to go back." She ran her finger around the rim of the Waterford crystal glass and made it hum. "I have to sell Da's house, our businesses, say goodbye to...friends."

She had almost said Damien. She felt a gentle fluttering in her mind, and then Caleb's expression soured. His hand left her thigh, formed a fist in his lap. "Any *friend* in particular?" he asked pleasantly.

Caleb had obviously already skimmed that information from her mind. "You need to knock that off, that...that mind reading," she admonished him again.

He ignored her. "Saying goodbye to that particular *friend* will be easily accomplished, will it not? You simply ring him from here and tell him you're a *married woman* now."

"I'm not going to break up with somebody over the phone. That's just plain cold."

The temperature in the room plummeted, Arianna estimated a drop of about ten degrees. Her inflexibility on the subject had clearly infuriated him. His irises darkened to an army green, and then he deliberately rose from the sofa. She flinched as he turned and removed the empty flute from her fingers. "More champagne?"

"No, nothing more to drink, thanks." Her reply was breathless. It felt as if all the oxygen had been sucked from the room, leaving them in an airless vacuum.

He refilled his own glass. "You are my wife now, Arianna." His jaw was set in the stubborn lines she was quickly becoming accustomed to. "And I'll not tolerate you seeing that man again. Ever."

Her eyebrows shot up. "Not *tolerate* it? Are you kidding me? After all the time we've spent together, do you even know me at all? Do you think that because we've decided to share our lives, I'm going to suddenly go through some...metamorphosis? Become some meek little mouse without a brain or an opinion of my own?" Arianna stood and paced over to the tea wagon beneath the window. "I love you, Caleb, I really do. With all my heart. But you need to understand here and now that no one—*no one*," she emphasized, meeting his stormy gaze, "is going to presume to dictate who my friends will be."

The room rang with her pronouncement, like the echoing toll of a death knell.

Caleb moved to his armchair in front of the fire and set his glass of champagne on a table beside it. For a long moment, there was silence. And then the corners of his lips curved. It wasn't a pleasant smile, Arianna noted, but chilling, ruthless. A promise of recompense.

She felt like one of those meerkats on Animal Planet watching a circling hawk.

When Caleb finally responded, it was in a voice so soft that she had to strain to hear him. "Oh, but I *do* dare, wife. Do you not know by now, *a ghrá,* that I dare to presume anything I wish?"

Still standing beside the teacart next to the window, Arianna looked out at the roiling sea hundreds of feet below. She picked at a piece of dust on the windowsill. Just what had she gotten herself into? "He's just a friend, Caleb."

There it was again. The flash of a lethal smile. "Fair enough, then.

I've no problem with your *friends*." This time he really did sound pleasant, quite affable in fact.

But when Arianna met his gaze, the stark emptiness staring back at her made her heart ache. She would pick her battles, she told herself. But she refused to hurt him just to make a point. "Look, if it bothers you this much...."

"So, you've never...*bedded*...this friend. Right?"

"No, I...uh." The blunt question caught her off-guard. It brought to mind the way she and Damien had lain spooned together in his bed. There had been some making out, okay, a little petting, too, but—

For a moment, she had completely forgotten his ability to get inside her head. The mental shield she threw up against him was a knee-jerk reaction.

Too late, she realized the implications of her actions. She had only made matters worse. Denying him access to her thoughts at that crucial moment would lead him to believe that things had gone much farther than they actually had.

"This...em...*friend*...Damien, is it?" he asked, having picked the name right out of her head. "This man you're so adamant about seeing again?" The green eyes taking her measure were inscrutable, the gentle intonation of his voice no less deadly for its softness. "So, you've slept with him, *mo chroí*?"

"No. Well, yes, *slept*, but—"

"No, yes.... So, which is it?" He continued with that same easy, congenial tone.

The interrogation frayed her patience around the edges. "Look, nothing happened between us, okay?"

Caleb didn't believe her. He had gotten it into his head that she wanted to continue a liaison with her former boyfriend back in the States. Caleb tipped his head, his impassive gaze regarding her as time passed. Ten seconds. Thirty. Arianna could feel a blush heat her cheeks, even as her blood ran cold as ice. Granted, she knew nothing of the rules governing the new society into which she had been so unceremoniously thrust. Still, something in her...husband's... manner seemed to communicate that she had blown it. That, in their culture, slamming one's mind shut against a spouse was a rude and unforgivable act. A virtual slap in the face.

Considering these outrageous circumstances, she supposed she could understand how such a thing between a committed couple might be misconstrued. How it could create mistrust, leave unanswered questions, create suspicion. And, as a member of a magical race, Caleb would possess a very vivid imagination indeed. Which meant his head was probably swimming right now with forbidden images. Lewd, salacious pictures of his new wife cavorting about naked on another man's bed.

A man, she had just stated her unyielding intention to see again.

Caleb muttered something that sounded like a vile Gaelic curse and closed his eyes. Arianna's gaze shot toward the tall plume of fire that shot up the flu, even as a loud grumble, resembling thunder, rolled across the ceiling. Her eyes grew large at the subtle sway of the carpeted stone beneath her feet. *Scary.* Her husband's anger commanded the power to shake the very foundation of a medieval castle. The word *earthquake* popped into her mind, followed by a frightening picture: The two of them lying trapped beneath tons of ancient stone and rubble.

He continued to sit across from her, his head bowed, eyes squeezed tightly together as if he were in great pain.

"Caleb?" His name spilled almost soundlessly from her lips.

He thrust his hand out, palm up, as he struggled for control. "No." The abrupt tone slapped at her, although he hadn't raised his voice. Agonizing minutes passed, before at last he lifted his head. Everything was calm again, deathly still. The room grew colder. Heart thumping like a jackrabbit, she realized that the penetrating chill emanated from Caleb. A shimmering aura cloaked him now in an enchanted mist that permeated the air with magic.

Arianna felt real fear for the first time. In reality, she knew so little about the man she loved. So little about the potential danger of the powers inherent in his race. *Her* race....

But if they hoped to have any kind of future, she had to put her foot down, set things straight early on. "Caleb, I love you. But I won't be bullied by these...magical temper tantrums of yours. As you might imagine, my head is spinning with all that's happened today. I'm really not very hungry." She stood and rubbed her damp palms down the front of her dress. "I think I'll go back to my room and change into something more comfortable. Call it a day."

"A silk peignoir has been laid out for you in my bedchamber. A gift to you, from your new husband." Caleb spoke softly, his voice a silken invitation as he pushed his long, lean frame out of the armchair. He reached out and took her hand. 'Tis our wedding night, *a ghrá*. Sure, the evening isn't over yet."

"No?" Her voice cracked.

His hypnotic gaze held her helplessly in his thrall. "Oh, not nearly."

A surge of panic shot through her at the imminent threat...the erotic promise...in his words. In the depths of his molten gaze lurked a deadly peril. A sharp thrill of danger reverberated from her head to her tingling toes. His heavy-lidded gaze seduced, lured her into a sensual awareness that warned of no rest, no respite.

Even as it promised the very heights of ecstasy....

Calling upon her own inner strength, she tore her eyes from the heady allure of that transcendental power. "Stop trying to manipulate me with that...that mental thing you do. You say that, according to some arcane law I know nothing about, we're legally married. But I don't *feel* married, Caleb. There was no priest. No ceremony. No witnesses. No marriage license. So, what if I insist on sleeping alone in the adjoining room? Would you use your magical powers to mold me to your will? To force me into your bed before I'm ready?" That last she asked on a whisper.

He dropped her hand and took a step back. "The door's there. Leave if you wish. But do it now. Once our people are wed and the union consummated, we're like the wolf. We mate for life."

Her eyes widened. "There's no divorce?"

His head tilted and he considered her, his gaze pensive. "There's no need. By sharing our bodies, our minds in the marriage bed, we become bound together spiritually as well as physically. Afterward, there's no desire to part from one another. *Ever.*"

Her heart was thundering in her chest, her breath coming in short, hyperventilated gasps. Just how fickle was the institution of marriage, as she had known it? Couples spoke vows promising "until death do us part" once, twice, three times or more in a lifetime. So, the question was: Was she ready to make a truly lifelong commitment to this man? Did she love him that much?

Oh, yes, her heart cried out. *Absolutely.*

She connected with eyes of sibilant green, his gaze flashing with the knowledge of her frenzied thoughts. Her doubts. And then, finally, her acceptance of him as her husband, her mate for life.

But a fear of the unknown lingered. The man she loved, her husband, was a being from another world, another reality. What did that mean? Who was he, really? *What* was he?

He smiled. "I'm a man, *a mhuirnín.* The man who'll protect and provide for you forever. The man who will be taking you to his bed tonight."

The blatant carnality of his words brought a rush of need Arianna had never experienced. She groaned low in her throat. Something inside her had changed, subtly altered. Her inexperience had earlier had her fearing the dangerous edge of this unpredictable man. But no more. It was as if she were connecting now with a part of her feminine nature she had never known. A part that gloried at the thought of his unleashed passion, craved the resounding snap as he lost control.

Through the lust-tinged haze, however, Arianna still had reservations. Her enhanced sense of being notwithstanding, tonight was to be her first time with a man. So no matter how that newly acknowledged part of her yearned to know the fierceness of her husband's desire for her, her little mortal half needed to trust him to exercise restraint.

It was her insistence on seeing Damien again that had set them at loggerheads. In the new relationship they were embarking upon, they were both hiking through uncharted territory. She, having been thrust into a life, a world her rational mind had yet to even comprehend, let alone fully accept.

Caleb, on the other hand, had been sucked into a whirling vortex of human emotion—love, protectiveness, *jealousy*—the rawness of which he had never experienced before.

Arianna smiled to herself. She could fix this. "Don't you know it's always been you for me, Caleb." she whispered. "Always. Only you.

Come look. See." Stripping her mind of all barriers, she invited him into the very essence of her being. She offered herself to him—mind, body, and soul given freely and without reservation.

Chapter Thirty-four

Though she was fully clothed, his wife stood before him naked. She had torn away every shield, every veil, every covering. Caleb's eyes softened. "I'm incredibly humbled by your generosity, *a ghrá*," he murmured. "And surprised by your remarkable bravery. Particularly as I've been behaving myself like a complete horse's arse tonight."

His shuddering breath told her that her guileless invitation, her acceptance of who and what he was, had healed some wounded part of him. By allowing him unconditional access to every corner of her mind, she had demonstrated, without words—in the most intimate way possible—not only her trust in him, but also the irrepressible nature of her love.

Her candor had revealed that, while she cared for this friend, Damien, they had never been lovers. Nor had she shared her body with any other man. She came to him, her husband, tonight a virgin. Her innocence a gift she had reserved for him alone.

He touched his forehead to hers. "How will you ever put up with me, *mo chroí*?"

She leaned back and gave him an impish smile. "Don't worry. I'll manage to get you whipped into shape eventually."

He didn't return her smile, but instead, deliberately held her gaze. "Now, you look, love of my heart. And See." Repeating her own words back to her, he opened his mind to her, teaching her their ways. Drawing her gently inside himself, he knew that one glimpse of his heart and soul would reveal the truth of his staggering love for her.

Love. And he, a man who had believed himself incapable of such *mortal* emotion, he thought with a wry smile.

But there was more to this sharing of souls between husband and wife, an unexpected benefit one might say. Through their mental connection, she also experienced the incredible power of his arousal, his physical need for her intermingling with hers for him. And as her woman's flesh softened, melted, in preparation to receive him, he shared the experience, his own body growing painfully hard in response.

Caleb kissed her breathless, then looked down at her. "I'm going to love you now," he murmured, his voice soft but firm. "I'll try to temper the passion for your first time, *a ghrá*. I'll try to be gentle."

Just as he'd skimmed the fact of her virginity from her subconscious, she'd *seen* his concern that he would be too rough with her. That the weeks of sexual frustration prodding his wild and untamed nature might have shredded his self-control.

"I don't recall asking you for *gentle*," Arianna whispered as she stepped into him, molding her soft curves against the hard musculature of his body. "I want you, just as you are. All of you." She moved her hips in a wanton invitation. "And I want you now."

A throaty, all-male chuckle rumbled from his chest as he bent and lifted her into his arms. "All of me, *a mhuirnín*? Well, we'll just see about that."

His mouth covered hers and, instantly, her consciousness seemed to fracture. Everything blinked out of existence, went totally black as if a fuse had blown. In the next instant, she was swallowed by a blinding burst of white light accompanied by a deafening roar. Like a tornado trapped in a wind tunnel. Or the rushing waters of a killer tsunami.

Then, as abruptly as the strange episode had begun, it was over. Deep down in the still functioning part of Arianna's brain, the small segment not reduced to cinders by Caleb's scorching kisses, came the foggy realization that she was no longer standing, but lying down. *Beneath Caleb.* Groaning, she ground her hips against the part of him she so desperately needed, her hands roaming his body, head thrashing back and forth on the pillow.

Pillow? At once, her burned out brain cells did a double take. They were no longer in the study, but in his bedchamber on a bed the size of a football field.

But how? Teleportation?

She opened her eyes to find the room ablaze with candlelight. Exotic fragrances of frankincense and the applewood crackling in the hearth layered the air. The salt-scented mists rolling through the open window made the flickering flames of dozens of candles appear like ephemeral wisps of fine-spun gold. She felt as if she were floating in the clouds, carried along by the chords of the old Celtic melody playing softly in the background. The setting was ethereal, she thought. *Dreamlike.*

Oh, God, no. That would be too cruel. What if the flight home to the States had not been interrupted and she was actually back in Maine in her own bed fast asleep? What if all that had transpired between them today had been only another waking dream?

Caleb stopped kissing her neck, cradled her face in his hands. "Look at me, my love. 'Tisn't a dream, *a ghrá.*"

"Thank *God.*" She blew out a breath as he kissed her nose. "I was afraid—"

"Sshh…" He interrupted the nervous flow of words by nipping at her lips. He teased her mouth with the tip of his facile tongue, even after she had opened for him. She raised her head, reaching for more, but he pulled back each time, tantalizing her. A low, male chuckle rumbled from his chest as she threaded her fingers through long, raven locks like watered silk and held his head in place. His hand slid inside the bodice of her dress as his tongue met her timid thrusts in an erotic dance as old as time itself.

She whimpered into his mouth as her avid hands got very busy, sliding beneath the hem of his sweater, moving over the warm, hard musculature of his back, then down, skimming the rich, woolen fabric of his trousers, kneading the taut male buttocks, the back of tightly muscled thighs….

She ached to acquaint herself with every inch of this man, who was now her husband. To unwrap the unlikely gift bestowed upon her this day by heaven above.

"What do you want, *mo chroí?*" he asked gently. "Tell me."

"I want you naked," she whispered, surprised at her boldness

"Allow me, then," he said and closed his eyes.

She could feel the intoxicating ripple of unearthly power, an aura that seemed to exude from his every pore. A seductive force that alarmed, even as it thrilled.

It blew across her skin, a wave of energy, an electrically charged breath of air that resurrected the ghost of shadowy reminiscences, of erotic dreams shared. Interludes so fiery, so combustible, that just the memory of them had her body responding like a pile of dried timber struck by lightning.

Propped on his left arm, Caleb opened his eyes and gazed down at her. Her glance swept the length of his body. Totally and completely naked. "How did you...?"

"Lessons for another day. I've other things to teach you tonight, wife." His voice pitched lower, raw and sensual. His hand, which was moving lazily over her hip, up and down her thigh, stopped. His head tipped, brow furrowed. "You're looking a bit peaked."

Arianna bit her lip and sighed. "It's all been a lot to take in."

His eyes softened. "You haven't eaten. We're in no rush, love. We've all night...a lifetime."

"I really don't want anything to eat."

"I've an idea." His eyes took on that sexy, mischievous look she loved. "We've strawberries and hot dipping chocolate to go with the champagne. I'll be right back."

He rose from the bed and crossed the room clad in nothing but frolicking shadows cast by the firelight...and his lusty intentions. Proudly, compellingly nude, he radiated an aura of unfettered sensuality, of raw male power. A whorl of hair dusted his chest, pointing the way downward to the straining rigidity of his erection. She had never seen a naked man in the flesh, much less one at the height of full arousal. *Impressive.*

He was back in an instant, champagne flutes and a bottle of bubbly dangling from the fingers of one hand, in the other a basket of strawberries with a small pot nestled at its center. While they sipped champagne and talked, Caleb fed her strawberries dipped in hot fudge. The feeding grew more amorous as he licked the chocolate from her lips. Finally, setting the basket aside, he took her empty flute and placed it on the bedside table. Then he cleaned the stickiness from their hands with a warm, damp cloth that appeared from out of thin air.

"Come. Let me help you with your buttons," he said, taking her hand and helping her down the wooden bed stairs. Standing splendidly naked in front of her, he tipped his head thoughtfully. And then, so lightly that not a single finger made contact with her dress, he swept his hand down the front of her.

And all the fastenings on the front of the garment slid obligingly out of the buttonholes. Arianna gasped. "Whoa...."

Caleb gave a satisfied chuckle as he parted the fabric, letting it slip off her shoulders and sigh into a shimmering heap on the floor. "Gorgeous." His eyes heated with approval of the whisper of silk she'd been wearing beneath her dress. A study in seduction, the black teddy clung to every womanly curve and angle, yet tantalized with only a glimpse of the intriguing shadows outlined beneath.

"Turn around," he ordered softly.

When she just stood there, gentle hands closed over her shoulders and he turned her to face away from him. He drew her into an embrace then, letting her become familiar with the hard male heat of him. "Close your eyes, *a ghrá*. Let yourself feel."

His hands found her breasts, his mouth the sensitive spot where her neck and shoulder met. She moaned as his fingers tugged on her nipples, tweaking them to hard peaks through the thin black silk. "Mmm.... You feel delicious," he murmured in her ear, as his fingers moved the thin strips of lace off her shoulders. The skimpy scrap of fabric followed her dress into a pool of silk on the floor. "Your skin is like the petals of a rose. So soft. Your fragrance..." he said, breathing in. "Sure, it's been driving me mad for years."

He turned her to face him, nothing between them but a black satin thong and matching bra. "Ah, my love, you've been a torment these past weeks. Sweet, sweet torture." His voice hoarse, his eyes burned a brand of possession on her quivering flesh. "I can scarce believe you're finally mine."

Arianna felt his hands skim her ribcage. He released the clasp of her bra, letting it slip forward, baring her breasts to his hungry gaze. "And you're mine," she whispered, her breath catching on a moan as he palmed her aching flesh, his thumbs drawing seductive circles over her sensitized areolas.

Arianna leaned into him, her body on fire, her soul overflowing with gratitude for the miracle that had been granted them. "I love you so much, Caleb, I feel like my heart is about to burst." Her fingers mapped out the cut of his upper arms, measured the width of his broad shoulders. Then her open hand teased a flat brown nipple, before gliding over washboard abs. When her thumb dipped into his navel, she heard him swallow audibly. She reveled in his low growl as she went lower, forcing him to endure the exquisite torture of her tentative exploration of the wonders of the aroused male body.

He took her mouth, groaned into it as she stroked him clumsily. Growling, he covered her hand with his. Eyes closed, breath catching in short grunts, he taught her the pace of his pleasure.

"Enough now, love. Stop," he rasped finally, peeling her hand away. "I've been insane with wanting you. I plan to make this last tonight, to love you long and hard."

Lifting her, he parted her thighs and slid her legs around his waist, reaching behind him to lock her ankles across the top of his glutes. He moved his pelvis against her, matching the rhythm of his tongue inside her mouth.

Arianna pulled away from the kiss, panting. Her teeth sunk into her bottom lip, hands tangled in his hair, she met his thrusts, rubbing against the part of him she craved like a drug. "Caleb, please," she whimpered. "I can't stand it. I need you...*Now*."

"Patience, *a ghrá*," he admonished her, his voice revealing the strain of holding himself back. "A woman's first time can be uncomfortable. I want you ready for me before I come in out of the cold."

Arianna felt like screaming with frustration. She wanted to provoke the brutal carnality that he kept fettered. To unleash the savage, naked passion he was continuing to withhold from her. She wanted to taunt that sleek, feral beast set to pounce. To mate.

And then he was lifting her away from him. The high mattress pressed against her butt as he nudged her onto her back and followed her down, straddling her body. The rough hair of his inner thighs tickled her hips.

He should have been a musician, she thought airily. Because those talented fingers possessed the dexterity of a virtuoso. Plucking here, strumming there, he had every erogenous zone on her body humming with need. Then he turned her, positioning her on her stomach for his pleasure. She could feel the light prickle of chest hair against her back, the weight of his heavy maleness against her backside, as he leaned over her, stretching both of her arms above her head. She shivered with anticipation as he wrapped her fingers around the wooden slats on the headboard.

"Whatever I do to you, you're not to move your hands," he instructed in a low, husky voice that sent her senses reeling. "If you do, I'll stop. Each time. And we'll start all over again. The personal restraint will serve to enhance the pleasure, *a mhuirnín*. Make it more exquisite, more intense. Will you do that for me?"

"Mmm..." Though she couldn't muster more than a groan of assent, she possessed, at least, the wherewithal to nod.

In her mind's eye Arianna pictured the way she must appear to him, sprawled wantonly on her belly between her lover's thighs. How incredibly *hot* it was. A sensory overload honed to a fever pitch by the knowledge that he was walking a fine line. That he could lose control. Or worse.... Stop what he was doing.

In a limp, lurid daze she obediently kept her hands wrapped around the wood. Not easy as, with lips and tongue and teeth, he nibbled and nipped, soothed and suckled his way down her sensitized spine, over her butt, the back of her thighs, behind her knees, her calves, all the way to her toes. "Caleb... Oh, yes..."

He crawled back up her body and, straddling her, urged her to turn over, so she was facing him again. A distant thought crossed her mind that she should have been embarrassed lying like this, all naked and sweaty, her arms stretched above her head. But the truth was that, by this point, she was so frantic to have him inside her she was way beyond any such virginal reticence.

His eyes mated with hers as he slid his index finger into his mouth and drew it out slowly. Her breath caught as the warm, glistening digit traced the circumference of her nipples and he blew on the sensitized nub. If it were possible to die from sheer ecstasy, she would have surely succumbed the instant his mouth settled over the crested pink tip. He bit lightly on the puckered flesh, his hand cupping her, working his sensual magic. She was ready. "Now, Caleb. Please, I can't take anymore."

But the man was relentless. "Ah, love, but you can," he murmured in her ear.

Kissing his way down her writhing body, his mouth discovered a new center of her universe. She let one hand slide off the headboard, to tangle fingers in his hair. He stopped. She raised her head. "What…?"

He directed a long, pointed look of warning at the headboard. "You're killing me," she muttered, and heard his husky laugh as she grasped the wooden slat again. He rewarded her obedience by adding clever fingers to the ministrations of that skillful mouth.

He drove her higher and higher, again and again, to the shuddering pinnacle of sweet release, where he let her linger, trembling, craving, teetering on the brink of insanity. Still, he refused to send her flying over the edge into life everlasting. "Caleb, oh, God, I need you inside me," she whimpered, her head thrashing mindlessly. "Now, *please*."

"Soon," he growled. "But, for now, I'll give you this." And with a squeeze, with a curving plunge of those artful fingers, he sent her freefalling through spasm after spasm of unimaginable bliss, through an explosion of color and light and sound. In his native tongue, he murmured low, ragged words of encouragement as she flew apart in his arms.

Wow. Was her head still attached? Surely, it had blown off out there somewhere amongst the galaxies. It was all coming back to her, as if the dreams were reality, this reality but a dream. Arianna smiled to herself as she remembered exactly how he liked to be touched, to be held.

She peeled her hands from the headboard and pushed on his shoulders. "Now, your turn," she decreed. "On your back."

Stunned amusement twinkled in his eyes as he complied. She straddled his chest and, stretching over him, forced his hands to curl around the handy wooden slats that she had just abandoned. Arianna kissed his mouth, pulling back each time he tried to take the kiss deeper until finally, in frustration, he tangled his fingers in the hair at nape of her neck and lifted his head, to fix his lips to hers.

"Uh-uh-uh. Turnabout's fair play," she announced, sitting back on her haunches. Leaning over to replace his errant fingers on the slat of wood, she let her bare breast graze his lips. Head raised off the pillow, he tried to take a nip. She moved out of reach. "Remember what you taught me. You know, personal restraint and heightened pleasure and all that."

She smiled inwardly. He wasn't looking so amused anymore.

"Arianna?" He growled her name in a soft-spoken warning that clenched her womb with a thrill of trepidation. "Be sure you know what you're playing at, *a mhuirnín*. And that you're up for paying the forfeit at the end of the game."

"I'll pay." She bent her head and licked a flat male nipple in defiance. She heard his quick intake of breath. "Gladly, if the currency is anything like the first round."

She went for his neck first, inhaling the woodsy scent of him as she moved up to nibble on his earlobe, then she worked her way down the delectable smorgasbord spread out before her. Encouraged by his low rumbling groan, she nipped at his ribcage, dipped her tongue into his navel.

And felt his hands thread through her hair. She raised her head, gave him the tsk-tsking look of a prim headmistress. His face a mask of exasperation, he returned his own hands to the bed slats. "Um, is this where we have to start over?" she asked, all innocence.

His low, feral growl made her heart leap, her senses sizzle.

"Okay, well, you gave me a free pass. Just don't let it happen again," she said, her tongue moistening her lower lip as she considered his erection. It twitched in anticipation.

Caleb's jaw locked and she felt him tremble as her tongue trailed up the soft, satiny skin that covered steel. She licked and explored, finding his scent pleasantly clean and musky. Then, her eyes holding his, she took him slowly into her mouth. "Ah, yes," he rumbled his encouragement, letting her know that she was getting it right.

And then his hands were tangled in her hair. *Again.*

"Three strikes..." she began playfully, raising her head to admonish him. But she stopped short. Sensual fear shivered through her as, breath heaving, muscles taut, his eyes ensnared her. Moss green, they were the dark eyes of a predator.

"Caleb..." Whatever she was about to say was cut off as he flipped her onto her back.

Then he was levering himself above her, his knee pushing her quivering thighs apart. He settled himself between her legs, mouth avid on her flesh, hands skimming her body, as he fanned the glowing embers of her need into another roaring conflagration.

She was swept up in a sexual maelstrom. He was wild, out of control. He had warned her that he would demand a price for the games she had been playing. He had been struggling with his own true nature, wanting to be gentle with her, on this, her first time with a man. But her erotic foreplay had released the beast in him, unlocked the cage imprisoning his otherworldly desires. And now she found herself lying pinned beneath him, legs splayed, her much smaller body trapped by the heavy weight of his hard muscular frame.

She felt too open to him, too vulnerable. She was suddenly afraid that he was too big for her, that there was no way she could take him inside. The heavy weight of all that aroused male flesh would be like a battering ram crashing through the gatehouse guarding her woman's flesh. Instinctively, she tried to close her legs, to protect herself from the assault that awaited her, but the slim male hips settled into the concavity of her pelvis prevented her.

She clenched her teeth, closed her eyes. And waited for the invasion.

Chapter Thirty-five

She was lying there, open, ready for him. The scent of her arousal honed the sharp edge of Caleb's lust, a hunger that had been slicing him to ribbons for weeks. He'd been like a starving wolf chained to a tree, taunted ruthlessly with fresh, raw meat set just beyond his reach. And now that the wee lamb lay spread before him, his carnal nature was urging him to take his fill, to feast and plunder. To ravage her. *There's no need to temper the ferocity in the way men and women of your kind seek their pleasure,* the growling voice of his need insisted, *for she is of your kind. Tuatha de Danann.*

While feeding the ravening hunger inside himself—inside them both—he would teach her well. He would awaken the inherent wildness of her sexual nature lying dormant within.

"Caleb." His wife's timid whisper was a cool wash of rain on the inferno of his desire.

"I'll not hurt you, *a ghrá,*" he vowed, using the spellbinding effect of his voice to help her relax. His weight supported on his forearms, he slowly rubbed himself against her moist heat. "We've our whole lives together, love. You'll let me know when you're ready."

Her lips parted on a soft moan. A glitter of magic revealed itself in the angel blue eyes staring up at him. "Will you stop talking," she breathed, "and make love to me already?"

Brave, bold words, he thought. Like the woman herself. "First I've to recite the Ritual Binding," he explained, nuzzling her neck. Then he looked down at her and warned softly, "'Speak up now, if you've any doubts, Arianna. For this is your last chance to escape me."

Her gaze softened. "I'm not going anywhere. Say what you have to."

Caleb's heart filled, then overflowed with that foreign emotion... love...as he began to invoke the words that would mate them for life. "As we consummate our vows one to the other, as we become one in the physical sense, so shall we be one in spirit, *anam cara,* soul mates for all time. Do you accept me into your body now, *a banchéile mo chroí,* wife of my heart? And in so doing will you bind yourself to me, for now and forevermore?"

"For now and forever," she whispered. "I've always been yours, my love. Just as you've always been mine."

He kissed her, touched her, until she was again writhing beneath him, making pleading sounds of passion. He pushed partially inside her, stopping at the slight resistance of her maidenhead, stretching her, making her ready to receive him. "Look into my eyes, *a mhuirnín.* And I'll share the discomfort."

As she stared deep, deep into his soul, his long fingers curved over the top of her shoulders. He withdrew, then thrust once. Long and hard and deep.

As he tore through the fragile covering, Arianna tensed and squeezed her eyes shut. She muffled a whimper, clamped her thighs against his hips. "Oh, God!"

Caleb held himself rigid, allowing the tight, unused muscles clutching his male flesh to stretch and relax, to adjust to the intrusion. He tipped his forehead against hers. "That's it, *a ghrá,'* he encouraged, his voice strangled. "'Twill be nothing but pleasure from now on."

Caleb felt it wash over him, a strange metamorphosis. Was this unfamiliar warmth of feeling, the overwhelming rush of gratitude at having this woman tucked beneath him, an aftereffect of the Binding? Or was it yet another aspect of mortal love? This feeling of possessiveness. Protectiveness...

Gazing down, he winced at the purpling love-bites he'd left on the delicate skin of her neck, the chafing from his late-night stubble. Whispering hot, sexy things in her ear, both in English and in Gaelic, he began to rock his hips against her. Her eyes closed on a low moan. Her breath caught, held. "Breathe, *a mhuirnín,*" he urged her, with a low chuckle.

She opened one eye. "Yeah. Easy for you to say."

Another rumbling laugh.

"Caleb, is...what we're doing...well, is it different from m-mortal lovemaking?"

"Sorry?"

"I mean, are you...?" She spread her fingers across his chest, stroked a flat male nipple idly with her thumb. He bit back a groan. "Are you using magic? You know, to increase the sexual pleasure?"

His lips twitched. "Now that would be cheating, *a banchéile*," he tut-tutted. Dipping his head, he tasted her lips in small, sensual sips. "The only magic between us tonight are our feelings for one another."

"In that case," she announced, lifting her head to nip at his chin. "I want you to teach me everything you know."

"Everything, is it? All in one night?" His hips began to pick up the pace, starting and stopping, leading her as she learned to match his rhythm. "Sure about that, are you?"

"Yes, I am." Her voice was straining with the building pleasure.

"First lesson: Take control of your own pleasure." Arianna squealed as he rolled onto his back, careful to keep their bodies joined. She ended up on top of him, straddling his hips. Pleased with the freedom of the new position, she smiled, letting her palms skim the corded muscles of his chest. Then she slid one hand behind her, to investigate the heavy maleness invading her body.

Caleb groaned as he gave a long, smooth thrust upward, his hands gripping her hips and pushing down in counterpoint. "Now ride me, woman," he ordered huskily, setting a forceful pace as her eyes closed, head fell back. Her long, golden hair tumbled down her back, spilled over her shoulders. He covered her breasts, fondled her budding nipples, as she moved up and down, athletic thighs gripping his hips, muscles flexing with each deep stroke.

"Learn the magic of your husband's touch," he murmured, pleasuring the small bud of aroused flesh at her center as he increased the tempo of his thrusts. He pumped into her harder and harder, then pushed up into a sitting position, stretching her legs around his waist as he wrapped her in his arms.

"Yes, yes, yes..." Chanting the word breathlessly with every deep thrust, she ground against him, her voice pitching higher, louder with each stroke. Her body was trembling, vibrating, as she reached for the impending climax, but it remained just out of reach. She whimpered in frustration.

Sensing her growing impatience with her own clumsiness at keeping in sync with the unfamiliar rhythm, he moved forward, pushing her onto her back. "*Ciúnaigh anois, a stór.* Sshh now, pet," he murmured, bending her knees and sliding her legs over his shoulders to change the angle of penetration. "Let me take you there, hmmm?"

Arianna's head thrashed back and forth, her nails scoring his back, as he moved inside her, his fingers focused on the tiny feminine nub with the exquisite nerve endings. Applying a pressure that was alternately gentle, then firm, he rotated his hips and thrust, pushing her ruthlessly toward her goal. He could feel her coiling tighter and tighter, the pressure building.

"That's it, my love," he growled. "Let it happen. Come with me now, *a ghrá. Anois. Now.*" Buried deep inside her, his hips delivered short, hard strokes as she bucked against him. Contractions deep in her womb marked the beginning of her shuddering surrender, her body milking his. His wife's screams of release echoed off the ancient stone as, driving into her one last time, he groaned and spent himself inside her.

At long, long last, in the here and now, they shattered together in a blaze of enchantment, the heavens exploding and spilling fiery stardust all around them.

"Are we still alive?" Arianna joked weakly, afloat in the orgasmic afterglow. At one point the two of them seemed to have been levitating high above the earth. She smiled to herself as a verse of her favorite Heart song played through her mind.

He's a magic man, mama. He got magic hands.

Caleb kissed her soundly, then flopped onto his back, taking her with him, her arm flung over his abdomen, head cushioned on his chest, knee inserted between his muscled thighs. "We touched heaven, sure."

Literally? Putting that question aside for later, she stretched up and whispered teasingly in his ear. "I thought the dreams were hot. But I do believe you're even better in person."

Caleb laughed softly and nuzzled her cheek with his whiskery chin.

It was then Arianna felt a strange tingling in her womb...in shades of blue. A flood of joy washed over her, warming her to her very soul.

I've just conceived Caleb's son.

Caleb regarded her silently for a few moments, a strange expression on his face. "A son," he said finally, the awestruck words so softly spoken she could hardly hear him.

He communicated so much in those two words. His wonder at the creation of a precious life. His thankfulness that she was safe and, unlike his mother, would live to cradle her son in her arms. And his worry that their child's future would be cut mercilessly short by the waking evil. Troubles they postponed by silent agreement to deal with another day, as they drifted off to sleep wrapped in one another's arms.

෨ ෬

Arianna awoke to the smell of fire...and brimstone. Before she could settle the question of how she could even know what that smelled like, she was being whisked away, sucked from her bed by some unseen force. She tried to grab for Caleb, to cry out to him, only to discover she was paralyzed, struck mute. No sound, not so much as a whimper escaped her lips as the stone walls of the ancient keep melted around her.

Dragged down, down through a long, gray tunnel at what had to have been the speed of light, her body tumbled head over heels, twisting and turning, bumping and scraping into walls crawling with vermin and unspeakable creatures. A writhing two-headed serpent reached out a talon, clawing at her as she sped past. A large horned insect wearing a man's face filled the reeking tunnel with an ear-splitting hiss.

Landing hard at the bottom of the abyss, within the very bowels of the earth, she stirred up a soot-like gray powder. The molten ash clogged her sinuses and filled her mouth with grit. She forced a small stream of oxygen through the gray mud clogging her lungs and nasal passages, and gagged at the putrid smell. The stench of death and decay, of burning, rotting flesh, mingled with the odor of brimstone.

God help her, had she died in her sleep and gone to hell? The nightmarish terror gripping her heart with an iron hand made the encounter with Conor pale by comparison.

Somehow, she had arrived at the throbbing black heart of the pits of hell. Whispering voices laughed and mocked. Piteous wails rose on waves of torment, then ebbed away into a formidable silence. At once, two Sasquatch-size creatures appeared on either side of her, matted fur crawling with vermin. Thick, crusty nails darkened with human blood locked a steel grip on her arms, biting into her flesh, as they bared yellow teeth as sharp as pikes.

"Come." The unearthly growl raised the hair on her arms as they dragged her into a towering vault of ragged cut stone. The walls bubbled and spit with molten lava. In the midst of the chamber sat a golden box the size of a sarcophagus. Carved into the lid encrusted with precious gems: diamonds, rubies and emeralds, winged monkey creatures faced each other. Two long poles were slid through clawed feet at the bottom four corners of the box.

Arianna felt sickened by the abomination. A satanic counterfeit of the Ark of the Covenant, its design patterned loosely on biblical instructions.

The smell of death grew stronger, more pervading, as the lid began to raise. It wasn't hinged, but levitated flatly above the box. As her demonic escorts fell onto their faces in unholy obeisance, a haunting chant arose all around her.

"Anathema...Anathema...the name which shall not be named."

Suddenly, some unseen force began to draw Arianna forward against her will. Her feet made scuffling noises on the raw stone floor as she fought against it. Terrified to look upon the hideous creature lying in wait for her within the casket, she tried to close her eyes. But her eyelids refused to cooperate.

As her startled gaze took in the form of the sleeping demon, she drew in a sharp breath. And prayed for strength to fight the blasphemous urge to drop to her knees in worship of the ethereal beauty no human eye had ever beheld. An angel of light with a chiseled jaw, a bare muscled chest, and long, golden curls reclined on a bed of white satin. Of her own volition now, Arianna drew closer, her fondest desire to embrace the heart-meltingly luminous being slumbering gently before her.

As she reached his side, his eyes flew suddenly open. The creature's black, bottomless gaze, the very origin of Evil itself, bore into Arianna as if raping her immortal soul. She tried to pull back, but her forward momentum kept her stumbling toward him. Only by gripping the edge of the coffin was she able to prevent herself from tumbling in, to lie with him.

Though his voluptuous lips didn't move, he communicated with her, his foul words soiling her mind. "You," he hissed telepathically, "should never have come back to Ireland. Leave now, while you're still able. For the next time I bring you here...I. Shall. Keep. You."

And with that pronouncement, the gruesome eyes slammed shut.

At once Arianna found herself catapulted back into the bedchamber she shared with Caleb, who still slept like the dead.

What the...? Why would the demonic creature have threatened her? Ordered her to leave? According to Caleb, she was not a mere mortal and, therefore, could not be the Woman of Promise. Could the redemption of humanity still be connected to her return to Ireland? And, if so, how?

A sick sense of dread lodged in her gut as her inner voice whispered a warning. That her return to the Emerald Isle might have been only the fated first step, the connection that will ultimately draw the Chosen One to Ireland.

If that woman should happen to be one of Arianna's lifelong friends.

~~ THE END ~~

Stolen Child

By William Butler Yeats

Where dips the rocky highland Of Sleuth Wood in the lake,
There lies a leafy island where flapping herons wake
The drowsy water-rats; There we've hid our faery vats,
Full of berries, And of the reddest stolen cherries.

Come away, O human child!
To the waters and the wild
With a faery, hand in hand,
For the world's more full of weeping than you can understand.

Where the wave of moonlight glosses the dim grey sands with light,
Far off by furthest Rosses we foot it all the night,
Weaving olden dances, mingling hands and mingling glances,
Till the moon has taken flight; To and fro we leap, and chase the
frothy bubbles,
While the world is full of troubles, and is anxious in its sleep.

Come away, O human child!
To the waters and the wild
With a faery, hand in hand,
For the world's more full of weeping than you can understand.

Where the wandering water gushes from the hills above Glen-Car,
In pools among the rushes that scarce could bathe a star,
We seek for slumbering trout and whispering in their ears
Give them unquiet dreams; Leaning softly out from ferns that drop
their tears
Over the young streams

Come away, O human child!
To the waters and the wild
With a faery, hand in hand,
For the world's more full of weeping than you can understand.

Away with us he's going, the solemn eyed:
He'll hear no more the lowing of the calves on the warm hillside
Or the kettle on the hob
Sing peace into his breast,
Or see the brown mice bob
Round and round the oatmeal-chest.

For he comes, the human child!
To the waters and the wild
With a faery, hand in hand,
From a world more full of weeping than he can understand.

35199080R00191

Made in the USA
Charleston, SC
27 October 2014